Maria Lewis is an author, screenwriter and film curator based in Sydney. Starting her start as a police reporter her writing on pop culture has appeared in publications such as the *New York Post*, *Guardian*, *Penthouse*, *The Daily Mail*, *Empire Magazine*, *Gizmodo*, *Huffington Post*, *The Daily* and *Sunday Telegraph*, *i09*, *Junkee* and many more. A journalist for over 16 years, she transitioned into working in television as a segment producer, writer and guest presenter on live nightly news program *The Feed* on SBS. She has worked as a screen-writer on documentary, film and scripted television projects.

Her best-selling debut novel *Who's Afraid?* was published in 2016, followed by its sequel *Who's Afraid Too?* in 2017, which was nominated for Best Horror Novel at the Aurealis Awards. *Who's Afraid?* is currently being developed for televi-sion. Her Young Adult debut, *It Came From The Deep*, was released globally in 2018, followed by her fourth book, *The Witch Who Courted Death*, which won Best Fantasy Novel at the Aurealis Awards in 2019.

Her fifth novel set within the shared supernatural universe – *The Wailing Woman* – was nominated for Best Fantasy Novel at the Aurealis Awards in 2020, followed by the publi-cation of her sixth novel, *Who's Still Afraid?*, and book seven *The Rose Daughter*. The host, writer and producer of the limited podcast series *Josie & The Podcats* about the 2001 cult film, she's a film curator at Australia's national museum of screen culture.

Visit Maria Lewis online:

Twitter: @moviemazz
Instagram: @maria___lewis
www.marialewis.com.au

Also by Maria Lewis

Who's Afraid?
Who's Afraid Too?
The Witch Who Courted Death
It Came From The Deep
The Wailing Woman
Who's Still Afraid?

The Rose Daughter

Maria Lewis

PIATKUS

PIATKUS

First published in Great Britain in 2021 by Piatkus
This paperback edition published in 2021 by Piatkus

1 3 5 7 9 10 8 6 4 2

Copyright © 2021 by Maria Lewis

The moral right of the author has been asserted.

*All characters and events in this publication, other than those
clearly in the public domain, are fictitious and any resemblance
to real persons, living or dead, is purely coincidental.*

All rights reserved.
No part of this publication may be reproduced, stored in a retrieval system,
or transmitted, in any form or by any means, without the prior permission in
writing of the publisher, nor be otherwise circulated in any form of binding or
cover other than that in which it is published and without a similar condition
including this condition being imposed on the subsequent purchaser.

A CIP catalogue record for this book
is available from the British Library.

ISBN 978-0-349-42723-2

Typeset in Sabon by Hewer Text UK Ltd, Edinburgh
Printed and bound in Great Britain by Clays Ltd, Elcograf S.p.A.

Papers used by Piatkus are from well-managed forests
and other responsible sources.

Piatkus
An imprint of
Little, Brown Book Group
Carmelite House
50 Victoria Embankment
London EC4Y 0DZ

An Hachette UK Company
www.hachette.co.uk

www.littlebrown.co.uk

For Blake and Sam Howard

Chapter 1

Past

You are not a hero.

Those were the first words I ever remembered hearing. It was the first sentence I ever properly comprehended. I was born in a prison, yet it took me years to understand that fact. If you've never known anything but a cell, it's hard to appreciate what you're missing out on.

My father told me, though. My mother had died in childbirth and I still woke from nightmares of her dead eyes staring into mine before she floated to the bottom of the tank. My parents had been captured together, my existence the result of their forbidden union. So, while my mother had only found freedom through death, my father was locked up with me, Dreckly Jones. Indefinitely.

'There are worse things than a cell,' he would say. I knew that to be true. As I lay in bed at night, trying to go to sleep, I could hear them. They were just on the other side of the walls that kept us confined. Walls that also kept *them* out.

The nights of the full moon were the worst. Not that I could see the moon, of course, but I always knew when it was high in the sky. The growling. The screaming. The roaring. The screeching.

'It's not just werewolves who are impacted by the lunar cycle,' my father said, drawing shapes on the wall with a piece of chalk he had managed to coax out of the one, kind guard. 'Goblins are too.'

'They turn into big wolves?' I asked.

'No, but ... they hunger. They're irrational and irritable. Moody, even. You'll understand what that feels like some day.'

'Am I goblin?'

'No, sweetheart. You're something else. Something very special.'

'What does the moon look like?'

'It's beautiful,' he sighed. 'At every stage, whether that's round and full or curved over during the crescent moon. When it's not there in the sky at night, you feel its absence. Like a beautiful woman forced to leave the ball too soon. Like your mother.'

I had never seen the sky. When I closed my eyes at night, my father told me what to imagine: a never-ending sea of what you think is just blackness at first, but the longer you look you see shades of blue and purple and sometimes light pink swirled in. Then there are stars; tiny white specks that exist in numbers you can't even begin to count. They glitter and burn even when you're not looking at them. Even in death.

'Remember that time you jumped from the top bunk and I didn't catch you quick enough?'

I did.

'You bumped your head and all those fuzzy little bits swam into your vision—'

'Those are stars?'

'That's what stars look like. Just on a very different canvas.'

In truth, I couldn't imagine it. I tried very, very hard. Yet it was difficult to manifest a world outside of the three walls I knew and the one translucent one that made up the fourth side of our cell. That was my favourite. The glass wall was unpredictable: you never knew who or what might walk by when you least expected it. The other walls never changed except for what my father drew on them, trying to paint visions of what the world looked like *out there*. I didn't need to have seen any other art to know he was gifted. He had no brushes, just his hands and limited colours, but he was able to create a reality that was better than the one we lived.

Guards would come by and watch as he worked sometimes. The Kind Guard would bring new paints when he had run out. The Mean One would beat us until we washed it away. Yet my father would always paint more.

'What is a little bit of blood in exchange for a little bit of beauty?' he said, attempting to smile and wincing as the cut above his eyebrow opened up again.

We had very few supplies for healing at first. One day, Father cut up a small piece of carpet in the corner of our cell, covering it during the day but working on it late at night when he thought I was asleep. It took months, but he worked his way through to the wooden floor and then the dirt beneath that. It helped him, he told me; just being connected with the earth in even the smallest way made him feel better.

'How come?' I asked.

'It's where I'm from,' he answered, sneaking me over to his special spot when he decided I was ready. 'A long, long time ago that's where I came from: the earth. It's connected to me and I'm connected to it. I can feel it pulsing like a heartbeat, can you?'

I felt nothing at first, the chubby fingers of a child gripping and releasing the dirt granules with curiosity. Then I sensed it: not a heartbeat, like he had said. It was a presence, really. Like a warm blanket being thrown over my shoulders when I was cold, except this blanket knew me, it welcomed me, it greeted me like an old friend.

'Is this where Mamm came from too?'

He smiled in that sad way he did whenever my mother was brought up.

'No, my rose. She came from the East China Sea, which is very far away from where we are now.'

I had more questions, I always did, but they drifted away with a gasp of surprise as something began to burrow out of the tiny patch of dirt. It was green at first, and long, climbing into the sky until it was at eye level. It uncurled right in front of me, slowly and then faster as the green bulb gave way to white then pink and eventually a deep, blood red. I reached out to touch it, ever so gently. The petals were softer than anything I had ever felt. And the smell! It was intoxicating, almost too sweet.

'What is it?' I breathed.

'A rose.' He smiled. 'For my rose.'

I didn't know it at the time, but it was also the key to my freedom.

Chapter 2

Present

'I'm not a hero,' Dreckly murmured, not bothering to look up from the passport she was doctoring. 'So put those heart eyes back in your head.'

'You are,' the man purred. 'You're my hero for this, truly.'

This time, she did glance up if only to scowl at Simon Tianne as he sat there before her, smirking. Dreckly's eyes ran over the tattoos that snaked up one arm and spread across his chest. She couldn't see those, but they peeked out of the top of his singlet like a teaser of what was below. He didn't know about the tattoos on her body. He didn't know about the people who'd given them to her, about the peace it had brought her in a time when she didn't think she'd ever know peace again. He didn't know any of that and she didn't tell him. It would have meant they had something in common. Dreckly didn't want to give Simon Tianne the 'in' she knew he'd been looking for.

'Your family have been my best paying customers for years now,' she said instead, choosing her words carefully. 'I forged documents for your mother, your auntie, and your uncle back when he was still alive.'

'And I appreciate it, all of it. These ones though—' he tapped her desk for emphasis '—these ones will really count.'

'Access to anywhere within the European Union isn't that difficult,' she muttered, holding up a hand as she anticipated that he was about to speak. 'I don't want to know, Simon. And if you don't tell me, I *can't* know.'

'I'm looking for my cousin.'

'Everyone's looking for someone.'

'And I think I've finally found her.'

'What is it that makes you so chatty, huh? The women in your family just let me work. They tell me what I need to know, I make what they need, then they leave.'

'They're not trying to hit on you.'

A woman's voice spoke up and Dreckly smiled, recognising the cadence of his auntie Tiaki Ihi. Her best customer. *Good*, she thought. Her presence would do more to verbally pat off his advances than she could. She needed to concentrate, as manufacturing a German passport in under four hours was stretching even her very impressive skill set.

'Auntie.'

'Nephew. You letting the wāhine work?'

'Of course, just making small talk.'

'Mmmm hmmm.'

Dreckly could hear the woman's amusement in her tone and she smirked as she blew gently on the drying ink. She'd seen someone use a manicurist fan to dry documents once, it providing exactly the right amount of air and the right amount of pressure so there was no bubbling on the paper. Dreckly didn't need such a tool. She'd only needed to watch it in action once before she was able to gauge the pressure and distance required to recreate that exact same effect with her mouth.

It was her gift, after all. Her mother had been of the water, her father of the earth, and together they had created her: *air.* Little could they have known how useful a sprite's control and manipulation of the element could be to her chosen profession of forgery. Leaning back with satisfaction, she held the passport up to the light to make sure it passed the eyeball test. It did. They always did.

'That's my last RFID chip,' she said, handing the document over. 'You need that biometric certificate, but with the tight deadline it's going to cost you extra.'

'Choice.' He nodded, taking it from her.

'And here, a national identity card, gym card, library card, and customer loyalty card for Oslo Kaffebar in Berlin.'

'Always going the extra mile.'

She *always* did. Having passable identity documentation was one thing – it would get you into a country – but if you were stopped and properly inspected, an empty wallet would be as much of a giveaway as a dodgy stick-on moustache and fake nose.

'Money, please.' She held out her hand with a tight smile.

'*Tēnā koe*,' he replied, handing over a thick wad of cash. She didn't count it. She knew it would add up to twelve thousand. In truth, it was a bargain: most fake passports as good as the work she did could cost anywhere upwards of fifteen thousand, let alone the complimentary documents. Yet Dreckly had meant what she said. Simon Tianne was a prominent member of the Ihi werewolf pack and – if word on the street was anything to go by – the heir apparent now that the previous pack leader Jonah Ihi was dead.

7

She had worked with him too, albeit briefly. The past generation of Ihi werewolves were not as mobile as the present ones, which was perhaps a good thing given that many of their key men were dead. The women and their children endured. Collectively, the Ihi pack were her best and longest customers. Because of that, she always gave them a small discount for their loyalty. And their secret keeping.

Sure, Simon had been hitting on her and he was needlessly chatty every time he visited. Yet Dreckly intimately understood why: she was a safe space. Her life, her business, everything about *her*: all of it was safe. She was probably the only outlet he had outside of his blood relatives where he could actually talk about real shit, the nitty-gritty, and know nothing was leaving her boat. There was no one Dreckly would tell his secrets to because she had just as much to lose. More.

She also had no one to tell.

Simon got to his feet, thanking her again as he followed his auntie out on to the jetty. Dreckly trailed after them, pausing at the edge of the stern to watch them leave. Her associate Wyck was sitting in his usual spot, fishing rod propped up for all to see and line trailing aimlessly in the water. Rifle at his feet. He and Simon exchanged a smooth handshake, Dreckly rolling her eyes with frustration. Tiaki caught her in the act and smirked, mouthing the word 'boys' at her.

'Good luck with Berlin,' she told him. 'And your cousin.'

'I'll see you soon,' he promised.

She watched them leave, not bothering to speak until the metal gate that blocked the entrance to the jetty had clicked shut behind them. Werewolf hearing was significant and she didn't want to be overheard. Dreckly whacked Wyck on the shoulder, hard enough so he would feel it but soft enough so he wouldn't actually be hurt.

'Don't encourage him,' she hissed.

'What?' He smiled, offering her his best shit-eating grin. 'You know I always like it when Simon comes around.'

'You date him then.'

'Uh, don't think I'm his type in case you haven't noticed. Given how slappy you always get, though, I'd guess you've noticed.'

'Never mix business with pleasure,' she muttered, heading back inside.

'I'd say that's why you haven't had any pleasure in a while.'

'I heard that!'

'You were meant to!'

Dreckly exhaled, running her hands over her face and gently massaging the headache she could feel building at her temple. *Pleasure.* She wanted to laugh at the very notion of it. Her mind flashed involuntarily, like it always did, jerking her back to that place with *him*. Hands touching, mouths meeting, laughs mixing together like two dancers seamlessly moving across the floor. She jumped slightly at the electric jolt she felt run through her just like she had back then as he came indoors, dripping from the freezing rain because it was *always* raining in England that time of year.

He'd returned from his post a week earlier than expected, surprising Dreckly with a bouquet of the ugliest roses she'd ever seen. If it was possible for flowers to look soggy, they did, but the fact he'd even managed to find them during wartime was remarkable. She'd snatched them as he'd snatched her up off the ground, Dreckly not caring as the wetness from his clothes soaked into hers, and she kissed him like a scene off a soppy postcard.

The churn of an outboard motor kicking into gear hurled her back into the present, unceremoniously dumping Dreckly into the tiny kitchen of her tiny boat. Her knuckles were white as she gripped the counter, cuticles visible as her acrylic manicure continued to grow out. Her heartbeat thudded beneath her chest and she had to take a few seconds to adjust emotionally to the whiplash of her memories. She had a lot of baggage and she knew it, but her recall was always the heaviest to shoulder.

So she did what she always did when she felt a little bit shit about herself. Checking her schedule for the rest of the day, she punched a code into a small safe and retrieved what totalled some fifty thousand dollars in cash. She stuffed it into a bag that resembled a fluffy, plush unicorn soft toy. Adding the money from Simon, she zipped it up and tossed it on to Wyck's lap. He crinkled his nose with disgust as he looked at the creature, which was sitting at an odd angle due to its internal organs being wads of cash.

'Deposit time?' he asked.

'Deposit time.'

Dreckly made sure there was never more than sixty thousand in her safe, just in case. That may have seemed like an outrageously unsafe amount as it was, but anything less than that and Wyck would be rolling to the bank every damn day to make deposits. And that would be noticed. She took electronic payment and credit card as well; however, most of her supernatural clients liked to pay cash.

'All right, I'm on my way,' he said, pulling his legs off the railing of the boat where they had been resting. Wyck had been paralysed from the waist down ten years earlier after he got jumped by members of a rival motorcycle gang. He should have been protected at the time, should have never been vulnerable, and he'd remained a cut-carrying member of the club largely thanks to their guilt.

He'd been working as the club's accountant out of sheer necessity more than anything else when Dreckly first docked at the Sydney Fish Markets. He'd been their sergeant at arms previously and although he couldn't ride anymore, he could still shoot *anyone* with *anything*. Most useful, though, was a borderline supernatural ability to read people: it was something that couldn't be learned or lived. You either had it or you didn't it. Wyck had it.

'You need anything else while I'm out?' he asked.

'Yes, I made a list. Mainly electronics.'

He inspected the piece of paper she passed to him. 'I can get this from the goblins.'

'They're expecting you. This envelope has what I'll owe them. And this envelope is for you.'

He took them both with a wink. 'Bless your organisational skills.'

'Bless my OCD. That will take you a minute, so have the rest of the night off.'

'You sure?'

She nodded, jerking her head towards the massive blue structure that made up the Sydney Fish Markets. It was usually bustling with people as they bought, bartered, and consumed seafood from the myriad of vendors that were packed into the place. But it was late on a Tuesday afternoon. Serious restaurateurs came early and tourists came mid-morning to stay through lunch. Everything was winding down now and it was mostly quiet. There were a cluster of folks from the Ravens Motorcycle Club lounging on one of the dozens of benches that sat on a deck overlooking the water where her boat was docked alongside many others. They were picking at fish and chips cradled inside a wad of butcher's paper and swigging beers. Their vice president was among them and caught Wyck's gaze. The man gave him a nod, which he returned, before retrieving the specially built ramp that bridged the gap between the boat and the jetty.

'They'll keep an eye on things,' he said, wheeling away from her. 'I'll leave Betty with you, but I've got Sandra.'

He patted an area on his thick, barrelled chest where Dreckly knew he kept his favourite pistol under the busy print of his shirt. Her name was Sandra and the rifle left behind hidden under the designated holder for a fishing rod was Betty. Each of his weapons were named after women that had been important to him in one way or another. Dreckly never questioned why.

'See you in the a.m., Dreckly.'

She gave him a mock salute, before returning the small wave his club members offered her from a distance. If the stereotype of bikers was black leather, tattoos and crew cuts, none of the Ravens M.C. fit that mould. Most had attire like Wyck: board shorts and singlets and thongs and patterned shirts. They all looked like washed up surfers who dressed appropriately to survive the Australian heat in a Sydney summer. But it was more than that: they looked just like anyone else at the fish markets, tourist or otherwise. They were smart and they knew how to blend. Just like her.

She grabbed her purse, which fitted little more in it than keys for the jetty, some cash, two different types of knives and her water bottle. Dreckly knew that putting physical space between herself and her memories didn't make any sense – they went wherever she did – but that didn't decrease her pace one bit. The sun was hiding behind clouds as she treaded the pavement for nearly twenty minutes, enjoying the huff of her breath as she marched up the steep hill to her destination.

If choral music played as the neon-pink sign that said 'Klaws By Katya' came into view, thick letters dripping as if they were made from puff paint, Dreckly was certain she was the only one who heard it. It was right on lunchtime, but the usually quiet hour for other businesses didn't impact this place. As she pushed through the glass door and into the salon, she was unsurprised to see all but two of the fifteen stations occupied with customers. The owner, Katya, parted a pink and purple beaded curtain as she emerged from the rear of the store, as if detecting Dreckly's presence. She was a goblin and they had a keen sense of smell, so for all she knew it was likely her perfume had tipped her off.

'Hi there, do you have—'

'I've got it, Melody,' the woman said, cutting off the counter girl who nodded politely at the order from her boss. 'This way.'

Dreckly followed her to one of the remaining stations, with something jingling at each step Katya took. Whether it was the Hello Kitty baubles in her pigtails or the small bells that sat inside her giant, love heart earrings, it was like a sultry Christmas ornament come to life as she sashayed to her seat and gestured for Dreckly to sit down.

'These aren't that bad, babe,' she said, the two never wasting time on pleasantries. 'It has only been . . .'

'A few weeks,' Dreckly answered. 'I just need—'

'Self-care.' Katya beamed.

'Surrrrre.' *Your words, not mine,* her answer said without saying.

'Refills or new set? I can do something fancy over this matte lilac if ya want it? It will make it feel fresh and give you a few more weeks wearage.'

'Not Playboy bunnies.'

Katya feigned offence, slapping her own perfectly manicured hand to her chest as her plump lips formed the perfect 'o'. Dreckly didn't miss the detail there either, with diamanté versions of the iconic bunny symbol twinkling back at her from Katya's nails.

'What about a sweet Animal Crossing set?'

'I don't cross animals.'

The goblin snorted, a smile making the small crescent moon decoration under her eye crinkle as dimples appeared. 'No, it's—'

'Something blue,' she offered, before they back-and-forthed any further about one of the designs Katya always tried to talk her into. 'Something . . . aquatic, like the ocean.'

'But pretty!'

'*One* crystal, Kat.'

'Three. And a feature nail.'

'*One.*'

'Two.'

'One. No feature nail.'

Katya grumbled under her breath, getting started as she dived into her little toolkit that was the same shade of turquoise as her dyed hair. She was the cousin of the same goblin who manufactured the biometric chip readers for Dreckly that she planted in passports. Unlike Ruken, however, Katya kept her business strictly above board: she ran a nail salon that had both human and supernatural clientele, but mostly the former. She was also the most skilled nail technician in the country, in Dreckly's opinion, and she'd been going to her ever since she moved to Sydney seven years ago.

'Speaking of selfcare . . .' the goblin murmured.

'Mmm?'

'I may or may not have heard of someone who wants to take care of *your* self.'

It took Dreckly a moment to sort through the jumble of words before she understood Katya's meaning.

'Unlikely,' she replied.

'Hey, just because you never come off that boat doesn't mean people don't wanna jump on it, ya know?'

'I do not enjoy that metaphor,' she grumbled, before adding, 'I came here, didn't I?'

Katya stuck out her tongue in defiance. 'Who gets ya groceries?'

'Wyck.'

'Who picks up your *supplies*?'

'Wyck.'

'If I gave in and came to you like you've been begging me all these years, you'd never step foot in this salon.'

It was true, Dreckly admitted to herself. If she wasn't on the boat, close to water and where she felt safest, then she wasn't far from it. She knew all the supernatural hotspots in the city, all the human ones too, but she rarely visited them. She'd made herself a one-woman island on purpose.

'I rest my case,' Katya said, taking Dreckly's silence as an answer. 'And don't you wanna know?'

'Know?'

'Who has got a raging stiffy for you?'

'Strongly, no.'

'Gah! Can you just pretend to be fun for one moment?'

Dreckly blinked. Taking a deep breath, she raised the pitch of her voice just a fraction.

'*Like omigod I'm totally dying and I really need to know before I positively perish in this chair, bebe.*'

Katya laughed, nodding with approval. 'That wasn't bad, that wasn't bad.'

Dreckly gave an attempt at a bow, or as much of one as you could give when your hand was being held firmly in the grip of another.

'So, he's Indian,' she started. 'And you're Chinese, so you'd make beautiful babies.'

She'd never told Katya she was Chinese, but the goblin had heard her speak Mandarin once and assumed ever since.

'His interests include long walks on the beach under the full moon.'

Dreckly caught the goblin's true meaning: he was a werewolf. It had to be someone from the Kapoor pack, which was Sydney's dominant one, and she thought of the tall, lean leader she had often seen hanging at the fish markets with the motorcycle club.

'Ben Kapoor,' Katya said, as if plucking the man's name right from her mind. 'His sister-in-law comes here actually and *might* have mentioned he was into some chick who works at the fish markets.'

'How'd you know it was me?'

'Said he only sees her off the boat when she's working the oyster cart. Never at The Wisdom or—'

'No thank you.'

'You don't think he's a total hoddie with a boddie?'

She didn't bother denying either of those things.

'Cos I wouldn't say no to a double date if you two wanted to join—'

Damp roses. Wet lips. His hand gripping tightly at her hips.

'*No*,' Dreckly repeated, more firmly as she tried to maintain her hold on the present. 'No thank you, Kat.'

The goblin got the message, dropping the subject altogether. Besides making a comment about 'loving this new Jojo track', they didn't converse much for the rest of the appointment that Dreckly hadn't booked.

When she left a little over an hour later, she paid more than the amount that was due – she always did – but it was worth it. Katya did incredible work and as she walked back to the fish market, she felt bad about the way she had shut down the goblin's attempts at matchmaking. There had been several over the years and she secretly wondered if her and Wyck were in cahoots. Then the moment was gone, with her guilt washed away with the knowledge that this was what was best. Staying safe. Staying isolated. Staying free.

Returning to her boat, she resolved to stay on board the *Titanic II* for the remainder of the afternoon as it turned into night. She had two big jobs she needed to finish by morning, so it was going to be a late one. That didn't mean she couldn't find pleasure in another way, however. Gently, she retrieved a sheet mask from the stash she kept in her room. She had them sorted by their various uses – anti-aging, revitalisation, hydration – but today she was feeling particularly bougie.

Watching her reflection, she carefully unfolded one of the most expensive masks she had until she looked like Hannibal Lecter-lite. She patted the excess serum into her neck and chest as Katya's teasing words came back to her: *self-care*. Moving into the kitchen, she chopped cucumber, strawberries, dumped a touch of mint into a glass with ice, Pimm's, and ginger beer. Lemonade was usually the mixer of choice, but ginger beer had changed the game for Dreckly a few years ago when she finally cracked the secret to the perfect Pimm's cocktail. Stirring her beverage as she walked, she paused by a record player on the way. There were close to two hundred vinyl records stacked on the shelves next to it: these were just the essentials to Dreckly, the ones that would get the most play. She had another six crates of treasures down below, each full of memories pressed into the chords of every musical number.

She unsleeved a rare Patrice Holloway pressing, the powerful vocals soon crisp as they echoed through the boat and she sung about stolen hours with a forbidden lover. Dreckly nearly changed the record, her memories too sharp today to risk the reminder. She thought better of it, swaying gently on the spot as the song transitioned into a duet sung with Brenda Holloway, Patrice's mother and Motown legend. She didn't like many pieces of modern technology, just what she needed to get by, but her record player was one of those vintage recreation designs often favoured by hipsters and those rediscovering the medium. It was an indulgence and she allowed herself that one.

Heading through the interior of the boat, Dreckly peeled the sheet mask off her face and blended the residual fluid into her skin. Flopping down in the big, comfortable chair behind her desk, she put her feet up and took a slow sip of her Pimm's. Little things were important, little pleasures, especially when she denied herself so many of the big ones. This boat was her entire life and her entire business. It was one of the few places she felt safe, largely because she could be mobile in a matter of minutes if she needed to be.

Dreckly had established rules for herself years ago, rules she lived by. Without them, she knew it was unlikely she would have survived this long. One of the most important was to never stay in one place longer than ten years. She was coming up on seven in Sydney and she liked it there: she loved it, in fact. Yet sooner than she would like, she would have to move on. It was inevitable. She had been on the other side of the world when a werewolf rebellion in the Asia Pacific region in the nineties had drawn her attention: the Outskirt Wars.

It was unsuccessful ultimately, but she knew rebellions never really died. The supernatural government, the Treize, had put it out like a spot fire thanks to their combination of immortal soldiers – the Praetorian Guard – and those she referred to as 'little rat fucks' – the Askari. They had no real power except for that which they were able to collate through gathering information, collecting documents and spying. She hated them the most. Then there were the Custodians, who she considered mostly useless hippies. They were the ones who looked after beings who had no other pack of pondant grouping. It sounded warm and fuzzy, but she doubted any well-intentioned body that worked under the Treize.

The rebellion had been good for business, as she'd skirted the major conflicts and stayed under the Treize's radar. It wasn't hard, especially when there were bigger and uglier creatures to focus on. Another rule she had was to stay near – preferably on – water and there was *a lot* of it in this part of the world. This area suited her lifestyle. And she suited it.

Straightening up, Dreckly pulled open one of the drawers in the massive oak desk that took up most of the space in the main room. When she'd first acquired this boat from a salesman in Samoa, this had been the master bedroom. She'd converted it for her purposes, taking the second, smaller bedroom as her own. In its current form, it had everything one could possibly need to create a fake identity. In the various cabinets that lined the room, she had wigs and disguises and hair dye and jewellery. Both little and big things that could tweak someone's existing appearance enough so she could take a new passport photo, a new driver's licence photo, a new identity card photo, a new *whatever* the client needed. She hadn't been joking about the OCD and in drawers marked with various country flags, she had dozens of pre-existing passports and documents of real people.

Some of these folks had unfortunately died, with Dreckly acquiring their materials through various means. The ones that were alive were simply for reference purposes, so she could make sure her handiwork was accurate to the era: whether that was an Italian passport from 2017 or an Australian one from 2013. Others were blanks, ones that she pre-made and were sitting there waiting for a new owner. All she would have to do is add the cover page and a few stamps from nations visited then it was good to go.

She preferred working with existing passports though, just repurposing them for her own needs. The wear and tear was more authentic. It was meticulous, detailed work that required real artistry. Dreckly had tried a lot of different professions over the years, but forgery was by far her favourite. Plucking a passport from her 'work in progress' drawer, she wondered what her father would think about how she was applying the artistic skills he had passed on to her a lifetime ago.

There were so many moving parts to this job. Collecting passports and identity documents from countries and territories and states all over the world had become somewhat of a hobby for her. Then there was the collecting of stamps used to mark one's entry and exit from various nations. Not easy to get, but not impossible with the right placed bribe here or the occasional break-in there. It was the technology that was hardest to keep up with: various chips, holographic codes and biometric data hidden in the covers of most modern passports. Some – like the one she was carefully extracting with a pair of tweezers from the current document – were able to be lifted and transplanted if you were careful. Others, like Simon Tianne's and the last lot she had made for his auntie, had to be manufactured to the exact specifications.

That's where the goblins came in, as there were few supernatural species more gifted with hacking, coding or minute engineering than they were. *Even nails*, she thought, Katya's technical skill displayed perfectly on her fingers. They started as a dark midnight colour at the base of her now-covered cuticle, before bleeding into a turquoise shade. Three tiny crystals in the same colour glinted at the tip of each nail, Katya getting her way with that element. They reminded her of the sea, like they were supposed to, specifically the waters she had once dived into searching for her mother's people. It would have been impossible to depict anything further than that on such a small surface area, but then again Dreckly wouldn't put it past the goblin to paint entire frescoes across her ten digits if she asked.

But that would have meant revealing more about herself, about what she was, about where she'd come from, and she wasn't prepared to do that. Secrecy was an elemental part of any sprite's existence and she preferred it that way.

Father would be proud of this life, she thought, using one of her long, acrylic nails to secure a sticking agent between the chip and paper. *He would be proud because I have a life that I have made my own. And that I'm alive.*

Those things could be enough. They'd been enough for her in the forty-four years she'd spent on this earth according to her human identification documents. She'd made enough sacrifices to make sure it stayed enough. From negotiating with the Ravens M.C. for a permanently protected spot on the jetty in exchange for a cut of her earnings and whatever documents they needed, to making sure no one got too close ever again to expose her or her history, Dreckly understood that gains didn't come without losses.

'Zuleika Morozova,' she said, sliding the passport under a magnified lens that lit up when she touched her fingertip on a spot at the base. 'Welcome to Russia, *printsessa.*'

She funnelled the air around her fingertips just enough to run over the coarse edges of the passport, drying anything that she couldn't visually perceive. *Perfect*, she thought, taking another celebratory sip of Pimm's. Slipping it into an envelope with the name marked on the front, she placed it in her desk's top drawer. This was dedicated to completed jobs. The ones in progress had the drawer down below. Those yet to be started had the one below that. And the very bottom drawer was reserved for urgent tasks, which was empty.

When the sun set, Dreckly would wander over to the lockers at the front of the Sydney Fish Markets where tourists placed their belongings in locked sanctuary for the cost of one dollar. There were three completed jobs she would deposit into different lockers, picking different security codes for each that she would text to the client. She didn't own a cell phone, but she had a handy piece of software on her laptop that allowed her to send messages from an unknown number whenever she desired. The client would then come and pick up what they had paid for and be on their way. Most of them she never saw again.

As the boat gently rocked with the wash of a passing vessel, Dreckly looked around the interior of her cabin as the light outside began to dim. She was alone, yet she was surrounded by people. Thousands of them, some alive, some dead, some fake, all of them existing purely on paper. That was the safest way.

Chapter 3

Past

The rose was just the beginning. From Father's tiny patch of dirt, he was able to grow anything. He had to be careful, of course. The cell was searched once a week like clockwork. But he concealed it cautiously and it went undiscovered. The rose would disappear back into the earth where it had come from and he would grow something else in its place, something we needed.

I tasted my first ever strawberry during that time, which I loved, and my first ever brussels sprouts, which I didn't. The slop we were served three times a day inside the prison was secretly being substituted with any and *everything* Father could grow.

'This is designed to keep us alive,' he said, running a spoon through the poor excuse of a stew that had been slid through the portal in their glass wall. 'Just alive. Nothing more. Not strong, not sustained: just subservient and alive.'

Our diet, on the other hand, was nutritious. There was a massive demon in the cell across from us, a creature so big he looked like a sneeze might see him burst through the walls

10:03:27   28/05/2024

Receipt for Borrow

Patron details:

Name --------------- S*********Y
ID --------------- 2***********
  *3

Outstanding fees ------------ £0.00

The rose daughter
Item ID: 30129086182970
Due back: 18/06/2024

Item count: 1

Successfully borrowed: 1

attempting to confine him. He had horns growing from every surface of his scalp, which looked like tight curls until he moved into the light. From the outside, he was everything you would say a monster was. On the inside, however, I could tell he was sweet. I'm not sure how, I could just *tell*.

He played peekaboo with me one day, that's when I was certain. Then the next time Father was painting, he sat as close to the glass as he could and watched from his cell. He would disappear for long stretches, the guards coming to take him away, kicking and screaming. When he returned, he was always unconscious. It would be days before he would make a sound again.

'What do demons eat?' I asked, watching as slop dripped down the glass of the demon's cell. He had thrown it there with a roar.

'It depends,' Father said, cautiously. 'Sometimes little girls.'

I had been sitting cross-legged at the very edge of our cell, observing with interest, but I spun around with a jerk. I had expected to see a knowing smirk on Father's face. Instead, he was deadly serious.

'It's okay, blossom, he can't get out.'

'None of us can,' I huffed. There was a long beat before he spoke again.

'Meat, most demons eat meat. They usually have a specific type they like.'

'Not just "little girl"?'

He laughed. 'No. Not *just* little girl. It can be anything: lamb, beef, venison.'

'From a sheep. From a cow. From a deer.'

'Good job, that's right.'

I had been learning. That's all my days were filled with, mostly: learning. Those days bled into years, but my father was always teaching me as much as he could, as quickly as he could. Sometimes he would disguise the lessons in games, but not always. I didn't understand the rush.

'You should be able to feel it,' he'd told me. 'Reach out and *feel* every particle of air.'

I had always assumed everyone could do that, that the tingling across my skin as the air puffed and heaved with movement was normal. Yet it was Father who taught me how to understand what that meant, even though he didn't really understand himself.

'Real air, fresh air, will feel different,' he said.

'Different how?'

'It won't feel . . . stale. Close, like this. You'll know it when you feel it.'

I wasn't sure about that.

'And if you follow it to the source, Dreckly, that's where our freedom is.'

He rarely spoke about such things, but the implication was clear: learning and understanding what I could do was part of learning *who* I was, *what* I was. More importantly, however, to both him and I, it was likely the key to leaving this place. That's why he made me do it, practise moving the air to rustle the leaves of the latest plant he had grown. Then float a leaf, manipulate the almost non-existent air current so that it hovered like haunted greenery. Then two leaves, three, a paintbrush, and eventually knocking things over inside our tiny cell.

It was difficult, with little to no airflow in the tiny space we were forced to call 'home'. That would only make me better at it, Father said. Stronger.

At night, when I wished I'd been able to fall asleep so my old nightmares could wake me, I'd listen to his breath as he slept. You couldn't see air, only feel it, so with my eyes closed I would feel the particles as they were pulled through his nostrils, ran through his lungs like the water in a stream, then exhaled through his mouth.

It was comforting, that rhythm and routine lulling me into a state of rest if slumber wouldn't come. He caught me doing it once, while he was painting, and I was trying to concentrate on anything but the sounds coming from a cell that wasn't ours as an inspection was carried out. Father asked me directly what I was up to and I made a mistake in telling him. It was one I couldn't take back as he asked me a follow up, something horrible.

'Pull it away,' he said, my hands twisting nervously as I sat on his knee.

'W-what? Da—'

'The air, I know you can. Follow it just like you've been doing. Then pull it away.'

'But . . . you won't be able to breathe?'

'Just for a moment. Then you'll release your hold and I'll be able to. It won't hurt me.'

He was lying. It mightn't be as painful as an encounter with the Mean One when he was on duty, but just because it wasn't a punch or slap didn't mean it wouldn't hurt him. Yet he pushed me, goaded me into doing it, begging as he dropped down on his knees. He was still taller than me in that position and my hands shook as I prepared to do what he asked.

'Please don't make me,' I whispered, tears springing up.

'I have to, my rose. You need to learn how to use your thorns.'

My tears turned into small sobs as Father continued his urging, tone turning sharp as he demanded that I 'do it, *do it*, DO IT!'

His eyes went wide as I did, simply reversing the motion of the air into his lungs as I slowly sucked it back out like a receding tide. His lips moved, a horrible dry sound escaping them as he attempted to speak. He was supposed to offer a hand gesture when he wanted me to release him, but I didn't wait as I let go of the strain on my mind with a shuddered sob. He lunged forward, gulping air on all fours as I watched.

'Good,' he gasped, the words close to the last thing I would have expected him to say. 'Next ... time ... we'll try ... longer.'

I didn't answer. All I wanted was to never do that again, ever, to anyone I cared about. Yet I knew what he would say. I didn't have his gifts. I didn't have my mother's. I needed to work out how to weaponise the ones that I did have.

I didn't want to look at Father any longer. So I chose to sit with my knees pressed to the glass and my back to him as I watched our demon friend instead.

'What about vegetables?' I asked, after the hours of silence became too much. 'Do you think he would like some of those?'

There was a heavy pause and I knew what that meant: *no*.

'Sweetheart, we've talked about this. We have to keep our little garden a secret: not just from the guards, but from everyone. Each creature in here is desperate to be somewhere else and they will do anything they can to achieve that goal. Say we grow him something, he could dob on us to a guard – do you understand? He could use information against us and we have no way to trust him. We don't know this demon; how do we know that he's nice?'

He'd barely finished asking the question when I pointed, watching as a thick, calloused finger drew two dots and then a half circle into that day's thrown slop as it dried against the glass. It was a smiley face. I beamed, blowing on the glass of our own cell until I saw condensation. Quickly I drew a smiley face back.

'You're not a hero,' he sighed, clearly watching from over my shoulder. 'We can't help others; we need to only help ourselves.'

'Is growing him a potato really that hard? It's just one potato, *Tas*, please.'

He sighed again, before shuffling to the corner of the cell. I hoped he felt guilt for what he'd made me do. Maybe that would grant me a favour.

'Are there any guards?'

'No, Da.'

'Are you sure?'

I closed my eyes, feeling around us, sensing the breath of the creatures in each of their cells, and measuring the particles of movement as the guards pushed through the air. The nearest one was on patrol two cell blocks over, the last cell inspection now complete. My eyes snapped open.

'I'm sure.'

I watched as he reached his hand into the dirt, finding one of the few spaces that wasn't occupied by the aloe vera he had grown to heal a cut on my arm. His face was impassive, almost completely blank as he looked up at the wall in front of him and waited. It was an undramatic display, but I knew what was happening: he was reaching out through the earth, chasing its pulses and rhythms to the demon's cell. He could see this whole prison through his patch of soil, map out the entirety of Vankila with just a touch. He was making me memorise it.

There was a grunt and I turned around, watching with excitement as the figure of the demon moved in his cell. It was difficult to see exactly what was going on as his discarded meal was blocking most of the view.

'Did it work?' Father asked, both of us watching for some sign.

Suddenly the slop was wiped clean in one corner, the glowing eyes of the demon even brighter than usual as he bit into a potato like it was an apple. He laughed, the demon's chest rising up and down with the movement as he continued to devour the unexpected treat that had forcefully pushed its way through a crack in his floor.

'There's more than one potato!' I exclaimed, surprised to see the cluster of a dozen.

'He's a big boy,' Father answered. 'He'd need more than one since he hasn't got any meat.'

I was careful to hide the smirk creeping on to my face. It was a kindness and a risk, but it was a small heroic act to right the less heroic one. He lay down, seemingly tired from the exertion of using his powers. At least that's what I told myself.

'I'm going to take a little rest now,' he murmured, flopping on to the bottom bunk.

I turned back to the demon, who I'd decided was going to be my new friend. Heck, he was going to be my *first* friend: Father didn't count. I held a finger to my lips, making a shushing gesture without the sound. The demon nodded, making the same signal back.

He would keep our secret. And we would keep the potatoes coming.

Chapter 4

Present

Dreckly was working at the oyster counter when her next job presented itself. When things were quiet, which they occasionally were, she would don a horrendous blue plastic apron and grab her favourite set of knives. It gave her a purpose at the fish markets and that was important to present publicly at times. It also gave her peace of mind. Shucking oysters could be dangerous work if you didn't know what you were doing: the shells were sharp and the knives even sharper.

Dreckly was more than proficient with a blade, however. She could fillet a fish as quickly as anyone at the Sydney Fish Markets, except for Zhang Yong, the chef who had taught her in the first place. It was easy for her to fall into a meditative state as she rinsed, shucked, repeated over and over again. As an added bonus, it was cheaper than therapy.

When a young couple approached the oyster cart she was manning, she didn't bother to look up. She worked at a display just in front of the vendor Zhang owned and it was designed to draw in the tourists. After all, who could resist an oyster straight from the ocean as it was handed to you by someone wielding a knife?

'Tray of half a dozen oysters, please,' the man said.

'How do you want 'em?' Dreckly replied, her eyes focused on the task at hand as she ran her blade through the hinge on each oyster shell and waited for that satisfying release of pressure that meant she'd done it right.

'Natural. Dreckly as you like.'

She paused, not missing the way the girl had elbowed her male associate to prompt him into the second part of the sentence. It was code. If someone wanted to acquire her services, and she didn't know them, they needed to say *exactly* the right thing in *exactly* the right way. You needed to order a tray of half a dozen oysters from the counter. Natural. Dreckly as you like. You only knew what needed to be asked if you had been given those exact instructions from someone who had dealt with her before, someone who had something to lose, but also someone who could be trusted because they needed her business. It was a layer of protection and also the only way she would agree to meet new clients.

If she wasn't working at the counter, Zhang and his people knew what the dialogue meant and the customers would be escorted to the jetty, where Wyck would assess them and sometimes they'd be allowed on the boat. Sometimes they wouldn't. The Ravens M.C. weren't populated with supernatural beings, but they knew supernaturals existed. They worked with them, around them, profited from them, all without asking too many questions (which was key). Wyck had never once questioned what she was, but he knew it wasn't quite like him.

All of this was running through her mind as she scrutinised the pair, who looked barely out of their teens. She knew a look of desperation in one's eyes when she saw it. They had it. Along with something else: *love*. The love between the two of them was palpable, even though they were working very hard not to show it. She wondered if they knew it yet themselves. The thought made her sad and she had to shake it loose to focus on other concerns. She was curious about who had helped them find her. And suspicious. So she asked the security question, the final test for when she was unsure.

'Want a quarter of lime with that?'

The man looked uncertain, but the woman didn't hesitate as her hands moved through the air to tell him a message Dreckly couldn't read.

'We prefer lemon,' he said, clearly translating her sign language. They'd passed the last test.

'Righto,' Dreckly said, pausing in the middle of her task as she spun around and looked for Zhang's son.

'You need to take over for me,' she told him in Mandarin. 'I've got customers.'

'They're children,' he replied as she lifted the apron over her head and placed it on him instead.

'Even children pay.'

She patted him on the shoulder, sheathing her knife as she directed them to come with her. Dreckly's blades stayed with her at all times.

It turned out they had been referred by Tiaki Ihi. The minute the man told her his female associate's name – Sadie Burke – Dreckly flashed to another client, one she'd had years ago. A banshee, a Burke, a woman who had been desperate to escape the country and willing to break the Treize's law that was supposed to control all banshees: The Covenant. The penalty was death at the most and a lifetime in Vankila at the least, but the reward was freedom.

Banshee kind had been expelled from their homeland centuries ago and brought to Australia back when it was being treated by the colonists as a prison island. Time hadn't been kind to their species, which – like the witches – saw only women gifted or cursed with the power, depending on how you looked at it. Also like the witches, and the werewolves, banshees had been persecuted by the supernatural government. They were supposed to be trapped in Australia until the Treize – probably optimistically – thought they would die out. Dreckly knew that not to be the case, with the cattle they'd attempted to herd being much more resilient than the Treize cared to imagine.

So when the girl signed to have her companion ask about her sister, cleverly assuming that if she needed Dreckly's help to get out of the country then Sorcha Burke had likely needed it too, Dreckly told her what she knew . . . which wasn't much. She'd set out for the United Kingdom, hoping she could blend among the larger supernatural population there. As the story went, Sorcha had drowned at sea on a boat that had been operated by Tasmanian devil shifters and smuggled all kinds of beings off the continent. Her body had never been recovered and neither had dozens of others. She suspected the latter had become fish food or trapped in the confines of the ship that was supposed to be their sanctuary, but she wasn't so sure about the sharp-tongued woman she'd met.

Banshees tended to fare well at sea, especially if there were any selkies around. When she'd properly taken their order and gotten all the necessary details, she did something she rarely did. Dreckly walked them up the jetty, holding the steel gate open as they left and doing her best to duck a handshake or any other form of physical contact with them. Someone would be on their tail. She wanted to make sure her scent wasn't amongst it. Wyck was grinning at her from his usual position – Betty at his feet, legs on the railing, fishing rod in the water – as she strolled back to the boat.

'What?' she barked.

'You're going soft.'

'Am not.'

'Are too. You felt sorry for them. *And* you gave them a discount.'

She opened her mouth to reply before pausing. She did feel sorry for them. She even felt a little bad for taking their money, but Dreckly never did anything for free.

'They're doomed lovers, that's all. I feel sorry for their doom.'

'They might be all right, you don't know.'

Dreckly didn't have the predictive abilities of a banshee, but, regardless, she felt death looming around both of them.

'Maybe,' she muttered, her thoughts dark as she wandered into the kitchen. She hadn't made it this far without help from others, lots of it, and the course of her life had been shaped by the small kindnesses offered by strangers. The not-so-small cruelties too, but she was trying to focus on one and not the other. There was a bouquet of Australian native flowers that she had carefully selected on the counter and she quickly swept up the fallen bristles of a red bottlebrush that had sprinkled below.

'You making lunch in there?' he called.

'Maybe.'

'You know what I like.'

Presumptuous bastard, she thought, making rice paper rolls from the ingredients she had prepared earlier. She followed the instructions taught to her by Meili Han, the woman who had been the closest thing she'd ever had to a mother. Dreckly's hands became Meili's as they took over in front of her eyes, assembling the bean sprouts, lettuce, cucumber, carrot and adding some chunks of tofu to tangle with the noodles.

'You want the *crunch* in there with the soft,' Meili had instructed, Dreckly able to see her face scrunched up as she emphasised how the food was supposed to feel as much as how it was supposed to taste.

Dreckly added prawns to Wyck's, mixing up Meili's special peanut dipping sauce before she returned to the back deck with a tray for the both of them. He kept a small esky at his side full with cold water and cans of Solo. He'd told her once that he'd battled with alcoholism in his youth before going clean, but the soft drink gave him the sugar hit he needed. Wyck handed her a beverage as she exchanged the food.

They munched quietly, looking out over the water and the people bustling in and around the fish markets. In truth, there wasn't much of a view. Dreckly always kept the *Titanic II* docked the same way: bow pointed out towards Blackwattle Bay and the Anzac Bridge. It faced the exit so if she needed to, she could make one a few minutes quicker than she could if the boat was facing the other way. It probably didn't seem like much, but she understood a few minutes could be the difference between freedom and captivity.

The view from the stern was towards land, with the vessel parked in the aquatic equivalent of a cul de sac. It was a dead end, with Sydney city beginning just a few hundred metres away from where the water ended. Cars zoomed by on Bridge Road, which was in sight and busy at all hours much like the footpaths that ran alongside it.

A seagull squawked overhead, Dreckly following the path of its flight with her eyes as it circled past the high-rise buildings she could see off in the distance. It was a noisy fucker, swooping down to join its noisy fucker associates as they hovered near a family of twelve that were devouring a seafood feast on one of the benches. It was a constant turf war between the bin chickens – ibis – the noisy fuckers – seagulls – and the sky rats – pigeons. Magpies were the occasional outside contender, like Coco Chanel with their classy black and white aesthetic. Yet the power balance between the different types of native birds waiting to scavenge people's leftovers was always changing.

'These are good,' Wyck said, swallowing the remnants of his fourth rice paper roll.

'As good as the duck ones?'

'*Nothing* is as good as the duck ones. Or your dumplings.'

The duck ones had been Meili's favourites.

'Noted,' Dreckly replied, hiding a smirk at what the woman would have thought about her tofu take on the classic recipe – she had hated tofu.

'You haven't done kangaroo in a while. They were good too.'

'What am I, your personal chef now?'

He grinned, taking a massive bite of the one he had in his hand and disappearing half of the roll in one go. There was never a lack of seafood available to her, let alone meat of any kind with an array of wholesalers who had stores at the car park entrance to the fish markets. There, you got *any* kind of meat you wanted: kangaroo, emu, you name it. Australians were proud of the fact they ate the animals on their coat of arms. Dreckly didn't partake, but she liked to experiment on Wyck. The man would eat almost anything she gave him and he was a willing recipient of whatever new dish she was trying that month. In truth, cooking was one of her biggest joys, in part because of the memories it brought back.

'I know something you don't,' Wyck said, interrupting her thoughts.

She tilted her head, wiping a drop of peanut sauce from her lips. 'Okay, I'll bite.'

'Someone has the hots for you.'

It had taken Dreckly months to understand what 'the hots' meant the first time Wyck had flagged other people's romantic interest in her. Enough years had passed for it to be processed as a compliment.

'That's nice,' she murmured, ignoring the initial ping of excitement as she thought about Katya's comments on the same subject.

He huffed, clearly annoyed at her lack of engagement. 'You don't wanna know who?'

'Ben Kapoor,' she said, grinning at the absolutely *crushed* look on his face as she swept the reveal out from under him. He huffed with frustration and fell silent. Knowing Wyck would crack eventually, she watched a seagull land on the edge of the jetty near them and optimistically evaluate their lunch consumption.

'Go on a date—'

'No.'

'—with him.'

His exasperation was delightful.

'Why not?' Wyck whined.

She took a big swig of water, letting her friend wait a few painful seconds for her explanation.

'I'm not going on a date with the leader of the local were-wolf pack just because he's tight with your bikie mates. That's not a glowing endorsement.'

'Yes, it is! It means you have shared interests: crime.'

She laughed. 'Dick me dead, bury me pregnant. Did you scheme this with Katya?'

'Of course not! She scares me. But you have come up in conversation more than once, Dreckly. He's into you.'

'What kind of man gets someone else to do his dirty work? And how many bloody people is he talking to about me?'

'How else is he to get you alone?'

'I don't want to be *alone* with him, Wyck. That's what I'm saying.'

'Fine, how about a dinner date? All classy and shit.'

'You had me at "all classy and shit".'

'You don't have a phone or anything normal like that, so I can set it up. What about a double date?'

He was so invested in this narrative, Wyck didn't notice as the seagull was blown off the jetty and into the water with a very specific gust of air. It squawked, head popping up with ruffled, wet feathers array as it squawked again in shock. There was a noisy splashing as it flew from the water and far, far away from the *Titanic II*.

'I'd rather die than go on a double date,' she muttered. 'And Katya already suggested it.'

'Dinner date, then? Let me set it up. If it goes terribly, at least you will have gotten laid and you have my full endorsement to continue building your own moat for the rest of eternity.'

'I'll wheel you into the sea, Wyck, I swear it.'

'Do your worst.'

'I hate you.'

He made a smooching sound, phone already out and thumbs flying over the screen as he texted who Dreckly could only assume was Ben.

'I need to go,' she said, frowning as she grabbed their plates and headed inside. Distracting herself with work was a better idea than thinking about her pending date and what she'd just agreed to. Panicking about it. Overthinking it. These were all things she knew she would do if she didn't occupy herself immediately. Besides, she had a rush order on the banshee's documents and they would not forge themselves. She left the dishes for Wyck, the matchmaker, and retreated to her desk.

As she clicked her computer mouse and directed herself to the reference documents she needed to check before finishing their passports, she forced herself to stay in the present. *Don't think back*, she urged. *Don't think back*. There was only pain there. Hitting the volume dial on the record player so music drowned out her thoughts, she was mostly successful for the next few hours as she worked into the late afternoon.

Dreckly was sealing the clear, plastic strip on a New Zealand driver's licence for Sadie Burke when she heard Wyck roll to the edge of her office. There were a series of steps that prevented him from going any further and she'd purposefully never installed a ramp there so he couldn't come and bother her when he was bored. The amount of dates she would have had to duck then would be astronomical.

'He's picking you up at eight,' Wyck said.

'When?' she replied, looking up.

'Tonight.'

'*Tonight?*'

'I know what I'm working with. The only time I've ever gotten you off this boat on set-ups has been when I move quickly. The longer you have to think about it, the more likely you'll back out.'

He was right, but she didn't need to acknowledge that. 'Fine. Where are we going? Nowhere supernatural, remember?'

He held a hand over his heart like she wounded him. 'Please. I know your preferences. He suggested Rockpool Bar & Grill.'

Dreckly smirked. Okay, that was an accomplishment. It was somewhere that Ben Kapoor didn't easily blend. He looked more like someone who played drums in a punk band than someone who could get a table at short notice in one of Sydney's most sought-after dining spots. In fact, she thought he might actually be in a band exactly like that as her mind tripped over a memory of Wyck discussing having seen them live once. Both feats were impressive. He was trying to impress her.

'That's fine.'

She could tell Wyck took that as a victory, but he was careful not to be too outward in his celebration.

'Righto, well, I checked your schedule. You've got no one for the rest of the day so I'll be up on the main deck with the boys.'

'Tell them I said hi,' she muttered.

'Will do.'

She waited until she heard the metallic clung of the jetty gate slamming shut before she sprung to action. It was nearly six now, she didn't need that long to get ready, but Wyck wasn't exactly lying when he said it had been a while since she'd been out and about. Her hair was slicked up into a high ponytail and on day six of her seven-day wash cycle. She hated hairdryers, so if she wanted it to dry naturally in time for her date then she needed to jump in the shower now. In the end, Dreckly kept putting off getting ready long enough that by the time it got to seven thirty, she was *just* pulling herself away from her desk.

This was better, she tried to tell herself.

This way she wouldn't overthink things as she scrubbed herself clean with a rushed shower, spritzed perfume, and applied her make-up as quickly as she could. She never wore much foundation, just a light smattering of mineral powder and highlighter on her cheekbones. It was the eyeshadow and brows she cared about the most, glancing at the clock in a panic as she ran a brush under her bottom eyelid to smudge the liner she had placed there. Standing back, she nodded with satisfaction. That would do. Effortless chic, ironically, required quite a bit of effort.

Stepping off the boat in low, strappy heels, the night air was cool along her back, which was mostly exposed in the dress she had chosen. It was black satin and skimmed her figure rather than clinging to it. Completely plain and modest from the front, it swooped at the rear so the thin straps were the only thing covering her exposed skin until mid-back. She'd re-done the ponytail she'd been wearing all day, with delicate silver jewellery to complement and a small purse in the same shade as her shoes and dress.

Ben Kapoor was already waiting for her, even though Dreckly guessed she wasn't more than a few minutes late. He had been leaning on the bonnet of a muscle car, looking up at the sky as it began to shift with the setting sun. It was right in the middle of daylight savings, so evening didn't start in earnest until much later. He looked cool in that position, wearing all black just like her and with the sleeves of his dress shirt folded up to expose his forearms. He had a crop of dyed green hair, with his own natural black emerging from the unnatural colour as sideburns merged with a light five-o'clock shadow.

With his superior werewolf senses, she knew he would have heard and smelled her coming from the second she left the *Titanic II*. He feigned surprise anyway, straightening up as she approached. His smile was dazzling. Wyck might have given her shit for so rarely accepting the dates he set up for her, but honestly? If more of them looked like Ben Kapoor she'd consider it.

'Hi,' he said, voice like a low growl.

'Hi.' Her reply was short, giving no ground. He'd wanted this date, so she was going to take some small satisfaction in making him work for it.

'Uh, I was going to shake your hand but that seems kind of strange. Like I'm a car salesman or something?'

'I only date boat salesmen, so it wouldn't have worked anyway.'

There was a twinkle in his eyes as he processed her joke. 'You look . . . I don't know the salesman word for it, so I'll settle with beautiful.'

'Thank you, you too.'

His snakebite piercings wiggled as he smiled. 'Shall we?'

'Sure.'

She slid into the passenger side, noting that if he was driving, he wasn't planning on drinking much during the evening. Could responsibility be sexy? She decided it could. The engine growled like a tamed lion, the seat rumbling beneath her as they rolled out of the fish market's car park.

'So . . . you're into Australian muscle cars?' she asked.

He grinned, only taking his eyes off the road for a minute. 'The dream was a sixty-seven Mustang, but it's hard enough finding one over here let alone getting used to the switched driver's side.'

She opened her mouth to reply that she'd owned a '67 Mustang once, but stopped herself. That had been in the *actual* sixties.

'A 1970 HG GTS Monaro is a pretty good compromise,' he continued.

'Sounds like a V8,' she murmured, only half engaged in the conversation as she scolded herself internally for the almost stuff-up.

'Good ear.' Ben smirked, his hands running lovingly over the steering wheel. They passed under a streetlight, which highlighted the deep blue of the car's exterior. The ocean swam to the front of her mind. It was a short drive, no more than ten minutes in reality, but taking closer to twenty with the Sydney CBD traffic.

'I'm sorry,' he said, glancing at her for a moment. 'I know this whole set up is kind of . . . old school. You're not online, though, so it's a little hard to swipe right on you.'

'I think that's a compliment?'

'It is. I would have slid into your DMs a long time ago if that was a possibility.'

Dreckly smiled, looking out the window as the city zoomed by so she didn't have to admit that she didn't know what a 'DM' was. Between that and the car, their age gap suddenly felt very apparent and she started to regret agreeing to this date.

'I didn't know how else to get you out though,' he continued. 'I never see you at the usual places. Just the fish markets.'

'I've only ever seen you at the fish markets too, if that's anything to note.'

'Yeah, but you live there so . . .'

He was able to get a parking spot less than a block from the restaurant, which was a supernatural feat in and of itself. As she walked next to him, she had to guess he was around six foot four and even with her father's height, her five-foot ten stature next to him made her feel small. The restaurant was inside the City Mutual Building, one of the few art deco structures in Sydney, and Ben held open the door for her as they climbed the few steps to the foyer inside.

'After you.'

'Chivalrous,' she responded.

If he heard the sarcasm in her tone, he didn't react. Dreckly watched his reflection in the dark glass ahead of them as he admired her from behind, not aware that she was watching him watch her. *The outfit worked, then*, she thought.

A waiter led them through the main dining area to an intimate table for two, which was somewhat tucked away from the other duos and larger groups scattered around the space.

The interior was stunning, with high ceilings and huge marble pillars that reached towards the sky. Candlelight flickered from a small lantern that sat on the table between them, Ben chatting idly about what on the menu was good before a waiter came and took their orders. He was nervous, she realised, which made her feel a little bit better. And a little more powerful in the situation. She had done this dance before, there was little to be nervous about anymore. He ordered a red wine, which surprised her. She got her usual Pimm's cocktail and relaxed in the chair, stirring it idly as she waited for him to start the conversation.

'Your tattoos are stunning,' he said, which was not what she was expecting at all. He noticed. 'What, you wanted me to start by comparing our astrological signs first or something? I'm a Scorpio, if you were wondering.'

'Taurus,' she lied. She didn't know her exact birth date, never would, so astrology seemed rather pointless to her.

'Really? That's . . . not what I would have picked.'

'You don't know much about me to pick, honestly.'

'That's true. I know your name though: Dreckly Jones. It's unusual.'

'It was my father's,' she said, glancing down at her drink so he wouldn't see the slight smile she felt twitching on her lips as he said *her* name with *his* Australian accent. *Dreckly*. Maybe Wyck was right? If all it took was a toy boy to say her name, maybe it had been too long since she'd been out.

'Your father was named Dreckly?'

'Huh? Oh, no,' she replied, shaking her head as she tried to concentrate on the conversation. 'My father was Cornish. He chose the name.'

'What does it mean?'

'Soon. Pending.'

'You have a Cornish name when you're . . .'

'Asian?' she offered, filling in the blanks.

'Yeah.' He shrugged, looking awkward.

'Your name's Ben. You're Indian. We're from the same continent. And yet you have a first name of Latin origin, most famously taken by a sixth-century Italian saint who went on to found his own order of monks.'

He beamed at her. 'Point taken.'

The waiter arrived with their food, the conversation falling quiet as he set down their plates. Ben had ordered a steak, rare. *Such a lycanthrope cliché*, she thought. She had ordered the garlic herb mushroom spaghetti.

'Do you want a bite of my steak?' he asked, hands hovering over his cutlery.

She smiled, twirling the pasta around her fork. It was a cute gesture.

'No, thanks, I'm vegetarian.'

He choked on a sip of his wine, clearly shocked. *Such a lycanthrope reaction.*

'Why on earth would you choose to be vegetarian?'

'Because I don't turn into a man-eating monster on nights of the full moon and exist solely on the flesh of helpless innocents.'

'Shot and chaser,' he replied with a chuckled. 'I only ate someone helpless that *one* time. And they weren't so innocent.'

They were quiet as they ate, Dreckly sneaking glimpses at Ben. He consumed his food like a wolf, but about halfway through he slowed down. He started taking smaller, human-sized bites, until he was the first to restart their conversation.

'Your mother was okay with you being named after a measure of time?'

'She—' Dreckly stopped herself. She was about to tell the truth. *Again.* She was about to reveal something deeply personal about herself. She hadn't done that in a long time. She didn't like how easily that inclination rose to the surface around this werewolf.

'She what?'

'Let's talk about your family, shall we? For a change of pace.'

'If you think the pace needs to be changed.'

'I do.'

'Then I can keep up.' He grinned, leaning back and lacing his hands behind his head. 'What do you want to know? My family? My mum and dad split up when I was little. Mum stayed in the pack; Dad went rogue. I have two siblings, older brother and older sister. He died in the Outskirt Wars. She was imprisoned after them. I've got three nephews through a widowed sister-in-law and I took over the pack when I was nineteen.'

'So last week then.' The second the words left her mouth, she regretted them. She was about to apologise for saying *the worst* possible thing at *the worst* possible moment, but she didn't get a chance. Ben was cackling at her instead. It quickly turned into full-on laughter, so much so it attracted the attention of diners at the tables next to them.

'Bleak,' he said, taking a breath after a long moment. 'Your sense of humour is bleak.'

'That's not the first time I've been told that.' It wasn't.

'The age thing bother you? Because it doesn't bother me.'

'It never bothers the man,' she said quietly, sipping her Pimm's.

'What do you mean?'

'The man *wants* to bag the older woman. It's a badge of honour. They want to be taken under their wing, learn from them.'

He smirked, his dark eyes watching her carefully.

'Younger men are just looking for someone else to call Mummy.'

'I would never call you Mummy.' He smirked. 'Unless you asked me to.'

She barked a laugh, knowing she was blushing.

'You look barely a day older than me.'

'And how old are you, Ben Kapoor?'

'You've never made an ID for me, so you don't know,' he answered, cutting another piece of his steak. 'I'm thirty-one.'

'I'm forty-four. That's thirteen years older than you.'

'But who's counting?'

If they were counting, *really* counting all the days and years and decades, she wondered if he'd be so blasé about it. Technically it wasn't a lie. She guessed – because that's all she could do – that she had been born some time between 1888 and 1890, which if you divided her roughly one hundred and thirty-eight years by three . . . forty-four was about as accurate as it got.

'Let's change the subject then,' he suggested. 'Since the age thing makes you uncomfortable.'

Dreckly laughed, more amused than he would understand. 'It doesn't.'

'Your tattoos, who did them?'

'That's personal.'

'You don't wear a dress like that if you don't want them to be seen.'

'I never said I don't want them to be seen, but I don't necessarily need to give you the artist's blood type now, do I?'

He held her stare, a challenge in his eyes that had dipped past flirting a few courses ago. She felt her skin flush with the way he was looking at her, and Dreckly couldn't help but imagine his hands running over the very tattoos he seemed fascinated by. They started on her right buttock, but he didn't know that, and weaved up her spine like the vine her father had once grown from the dirt in their cell. It ended just below the baby hairs on her neck, with every type of flower she'd ever seen her father paint committed permanently to her flesh in black and white ink. Roses, tulips, blossoms, hydrangeas, daisies, it all blended together in a beautiful explosion of growth. Wyck had glimpsed it partially once when she had emerged from the water in a bikini after cleaning the exterior of the *Titanic II*.

'The Girl with the Rose Bush Tattoo,' he'd joked, the hilarity of the pun falling flat after she'd asked him to explain it to her.

'Why did you agree to come out with me?' Ben was saying, refocusing her attention.

'Something to do,' she teased, with a small shrug of her shoulders. Playing it cool was easier. Safer. The truth was that she was lonely. Yet Dreckly knew if she said that to a man, it would send him running – werewolf or not. She was lonely and had been for a long time, plain and simple. And she needed to make new memories so she wouldn't be so haunted by the ones from her past.

'I think we should get out of here,' he growled. 'I know a place.'

A place. It was a charged phrase and she downed the last sip of her cocktail. Dreckly wanted to go there, to a place.

'All right,' she replied, setting down her glass, 'what are we waiting for?'

Chapter 5

Past

'No one has ever escaped from Vankila,' my father said, chin propped on the edge of the bunk bed as he tucked me in one night.

'No one?'

'No one. If you did it, you would be the first.'

'We'd be the first.' He smiled as I corrected him.

'We. You're right. But remember, we can't go together. You have to go first—'

'And deeper into block T, before breaking into the arachnia's cell and climbing into the vent.'

'Good girl. I'll be going the opposite way, so you have nothing to worry about. I'll meet you outside. What's next?'

'I follow the air.'

'Uh huh. You crawl in the direction of the fresh air flow, okay? That will take you precisely where you need to go. It will be small in there, a tight fit, so only you will be able to make it through. Don't listen to the voices outside of the vent, don't be frightened by what you might hear, you just have to ignore everything else and keep going. Don't peek, don't stop for anyone. And Dreckly?'

'Mmm?'

'Most importantly—'

'Don't be a hero,' I answered, knowing what was coming. 'Just get myself out. And if you're not at the waiting point when you said you would be, go. You'll find me.'

He leaned forward, placing a kiss on my forehead that lingered. 'So long as you're on this earth, I'll always be able to find you, my rose.'

'Will you read to me?' I whispered. I wanted him to read to me. I wanted him to treat me like the child I was. I wanted him to be my father and I his daughter for a moment, just a moment, rather than his accomplice.

Over the years, the Kind Guard had brought books a few times, when I was old enough to read. Only four books, but it was better than three. Better than two. Better than none. The rest of the time Father had tried to tell me his favourite stories from memory, including the one he told me now about how he and my mother had met.

'The sea was very rough,' he started, maybe sensing how vulnerable I felt. He pulled me into his bunk and we cuddled up together. His scent was thick with lavender, almost dizzyingly so, as he'd grown it to place under my pillow to help me sleep. It hadn't worked, but being next to him would. I felt safe that way. The safest I did anywhere.

'We weren't meant to be out there; we were meant to have turned back a day earlier. Yet the trip had gone well, better than expected, and our captain had gotten greedy. He wanted more, so when the storm hit, we shouldn't have been anywhere near where we were, let alone out at sea. It sunk. The ship went down, most of the crew with it, except for myself and four others. We managed to cling to the wreckage, shouting out to each other in the night until our voices couldn't be heard over the waves anymore. I was so terrified, so sure that was how I was going to die. I thought about my older brother, Galin, and how he had drowned just like I was about to. I never cared much for God, so I prayed to my brother instead. I sung his favourite song, "Come, All Ye Jolly Tinner Boys".'

'Will you sing it, Tas?' He had a beautiful singing voice, higher than you would expect, but beautiful.

'*Come, all ye jolly Tinner boys, and listen to me,*' he started. '*I'll tell ee of a storie shall make ye for to see. Consarning Boney Peartie, the schaames which he had maade. To stop our tin and copper mines, and all our pilchard traade.*'

I understood why it had lured my mother to him. He was enchanting when he sang and she was a selkie who had been enchanted.

'I thought I was dead, Dreckly. I thought I had died and she was the angel who had come to deliver me. Except she didn't look like an angel. When she smiled, her teeth were sharp like a shark's. Her eyes, your eyes, were the bluest I had ever seen. Her skin was grey and when I touched it, I could feel shapes there: swirls and curves and patterns. She said it told her who she was and who she belonged to. I don't know what made me say it, but I said she should belong to me.'

'And what did she say?'

'She laughed. She said she would never belong to a man. And she never did. I belonged to her from the very second she decided to save my life.'

'It's just like "The Little Mermaid",' I whispered excitedly. It was my favourite of the stories I had read in a book that was a collection of Hans Christian Andersen fairy tales. It was the saddest of them all, which was maybe why I liked it. Father must have been thinking the same thing, because he frowned.

'Not quite, petal. I fell in love with the mermaid, I didn't run off and marry a princess. And then the mermaid and I both fell in love with you.'

He rubbed his thumbs over my eyelids, forcing me to close my peepers as he began humming the same tune that had ensnared my mother. I fell asleep like that, his smiling face sitting in my mind's eye as, not for the first time, I noted how old he looked. I didn't have his blond hair that had now turned white or his eyes that were lined with deep wrinkles. I was all my mother, he said. From her fat top lip and thin bottom one, to the bright-blue eyes that haunted my dreams as she sunk away from me while I floated upwards.

When the candles were dimmed in the hallway and the prison was plunged into darkness, forcing everyone to go to sleep on their pre-set schedule, I could sometimes catch a glimpse of my reflection in the glass of the cell wall. It was never clear, just a blurred outline of features. I had never seen what I looked like, properly, and I knew it was a vanity but it was one that I wanted. An indulgence in a life that had precisely zero.

'Repeat,' Father said to me the next night, as we continued our evening routine. First, I spoke the plan to him in English. Then Cornish, the language of his people. Then Mandarin, that of my mother's. I had started incorporating demon too, as encouraged by my friend Yixin across the way. He had been teaching me the universal language of his kind, something that was encouraged by Father, surprisingly. He had become friends with the demon now, enough that I sometimes woke to hear them chatting without me.

That's how I learned he wasn't the only one Father was helping. He was growing vegetables, fruits, herbs, and any plant of choice for the entire cell block. He had even managed to drive moles towards the cells that were desperate for meat, those of the werewolves and goblins and demons. He was making them strong, all of them. And he was waiting for his moment.

'You can't sustain this,' I'd heard Yixin say when I was pretending to be asleep. 'It's draining you. You're doing too much.'

'I'm doing enough. It's what needs to be done, so she has the chance her mother and I never had.'

'At what cost?'

'Any.'

Any. I fell asleep to those words, specifically the tone in which he said them. *Any.* When I woke, the Kind Guard was lighting candles outside our cell. The sole electric bulb above was flickering on, and I squinted, adjusting to the sudden brightness. The guard smiled at me, opening the portal for our food. It was too early for breakfast, I knew. He placed more paints there instead.

'Good morning, Dreckly,' he said.

'Morning,' I answered, hopping down happily to inspect what new colours we had. He moved on to the next cell, never lingering too long. My father was already awake, sitting in the bunk below as he watched the man.

'What did I say about speaking to him?' he said, quietly enough that only I could hear him.

'I know, but Pa – look!' I collected up all of the paints he had left and carried them over to the bunk, spreading them out on the thin blanket so he could see. There was turquoise and periwinkle and fuchsia and a beautiful, burnt orange that reminded me of a fruit I had eaten for the first time just weeks earlier.

'Look at all the paints he brought us! He's the nice one.'

I held up a rich purple for him to see. He carefully prised it from my hand without examining the colour.

'None of them are nice, Dreckly. Do you understand?'

I frowned, uncertain about what he meant.

'He's the one who caught us, petal. He's the one who caught me and when your mother tried to save me, he caught her too. He brings the paints out of a sense of guilt. Not because he's kind.'

'Guilty over what? Keeping you here?'

'No. Your mother and I would be where we belong in his eyes. It's guilt over you: he did not know she was pregnant when he brought us here. Being born in this place . . . it's a terrible thing.'

'It's not so terrible. I'm here with you.'

He smiled, but the gesture never left his lips. 'We wait until the Mean One is on duty.'

'Why?' I asked, resting my head on his knees as I looked up at him. 'I hate him.'

'Because the Kind Guard is efficient: he's too good at his job. He caught us, after all. The Mean One is lazy. Violent. He misses things. When the Mean One is back, then we move. Now . . . let's practise.'

*　　*　　*

Time was a difficult thing to track in the bowels of Vankila. Father said that it showed differently on me. Three human years counted as just one and by the time we escaped this place, I would look little older than the child I was. This was a good thing, he said. Out there in the real world, it would make me harder to track. It would buy me more time. Because inside Vankila, time was running out. When the Mean One was finally back on duty, Da could barely walk.

'Oy, what's wrong with 'im?' the guard demanded, banging on the glass.

'He's sick,' I recited, just like I had been told.

'Well, get him up. Cell inspection in fifteen minutes.'

They inspected the cells one by one, with a guard inside and another waiting on the outside with an alchemist, who would redraw the symbols that kept the glass unbreakable and the prisoners trapped inside. The Kind Guard would search through their things, while the Mean One waited with us in the corridor. I dreaded cell inspection days. They usually always came with a beating and, as I helped Father limp to the glass, I wasn't sure how much more he could take. Or how much he was faking. He had liked magic as a child, he'd told me. There were a few witches clustered in and around his town in coastal Cornwall, enough that he became fascinated by magic and illusions. It was what would keep me alive out there, he'd said: presenting an illusion. It was what would keep us both alive out there, I had corrected.

The Mean One could not help but kick things when they were down and, as we limped out of the cell and into the corridor, he whacked the back of my father's legs. He went down, landing painfully on his knees.

'Stop it,' the Kind Guard snapped. 'He's an old man, that's unnecessary.'

'I'll decide what is and isn't unnecessary, Lorcan. I'm stationed here permanently. You only do six monthly stints.'

'Exactly,' he replied, drawing himself up to his full height so that he towered over his shorter, stockier colleague. 'So remember where you rank and remember our policy: *no* names.'

If they hadn't been so caught up in a measurement of each other's power, they would have noticed how quiet the cell block was. Eerily quiet, as all the other creatures watched and waited. By the time the Kind Guard noticed, it was too late. The alchemist was standing by, candle in one hand and vat of bubbling liquid in the other as they hid beneath their cloak. The Mean One was agitated at being shown who was boss, meaning that he was paying even less attention than usual.

I watched as the Kind Guard searched our cell, pausing as he came to the corner of space we usually spent so much time carefully disguising. We had left it exposed on this occasion and he frowned as he crouched down, inspecting it. He looked back at us, Father and I, standing as far from the Mean One as we could.

'What?' the guard barked, looking in at Lorcan.

'The silence . . .'

'What of it? The monsters are finally fucking quiet for once.'

The guard was frowning as he stood up, holding a rose between his fingertips.

'They shouldn't be,' he murmured, eyes narrowing. It was the last thing he said for a while as the soft, small thorns on the rose shot forward and pierced his fingertips. He cried out, but the plant didn't relent as it wrapped its way around his hands, cutting and slicing them as it attempted to curl up his arms towards his neck. He yelled with surprise. So too did the Mean One as I released my father and rushed forwards.

I threw all of my weight against the glass, pushing the fourth wall back into place until I heard it click shut. Lorcan realised what I was doing too late, throwing his own body against the only vulnerable section of the space. It was of little use. The biggest threat to us was now trapped inside that cell, just as we had been for far too long.

Feigning to be weaker than he actually was, Father had been carefully carrying an entire pod of rosary peas in his hands. Straightening up, he lunged at the Mean One while he was distracted by the imprisoning of his colleague. They were a harmless plant if found intact, but I was still warned to stay away while he carefully grew it over the course of a year. Yet if the seed pods were broken, the amount of poison contained in just one was enough to kill a grown adult.

Da wasn't taking any chances as he crushed more than a dozen seeds against the exposed skin of the Mean One. He even managed to slip a pod into his open mouth while capitalising on the man's shock. The guard yelled, quietly at first, then louder and louder. He tried rubbing at his skin and spitting on the ground to get the seeds out of his mouth.

'One broken seed pod can see organ failure within a matter of days,' Father told him. 'I wonder how long you have?'

Alchemists were not designed for combat: they were scholarly beings, obsessed with the line between magic and science. This one seemed just as fascinated by the effect of the rosary peas as I was, leaning forward as the Mean One dropped to his knees and began foaming at the mouth. Meeting Father's stare, he nodded at me.

'Excuse me,' I said, having to tug on the alchemist's robes to get her attention. 'Excuse me, but I will light you on fire.'

The hood fell free, exposing a woman's face as she stared down at a little girl making threats. The flame of the candle in her hand shot up, rising metres in the air as I illustrated the point. The alchemist jumped back in fright, but held on tight to the burning implement.

'I can, but I won't if you help us quickly,' I pressed.

'H-help you do what?' the alchemist stammered.

'Clear the symbols from this cell,' Father ordered, pointing towards Yixin, who was waiting patiently at the glass. Da didn't even look towards them; he was focused on Lorcan instead as the guard continued to fight and then free himself from the morphing rose over and over again. He couldn't relent his manipulation of the plant until the demon was free.

'Again, Dreckly.'

I did as ordered, funnelling extra air around the candle towards the flame so that it jetted skywards once more. In truth, I couldn't set the woman on fire. At least I didn't think so. The trick was to make the alchemist think it was a possibility.

'Aye, all right, I'm clearing the symbols,' the woman said, rushing over to the glass of Yixin's cell. Quickly, she used the liquid contained in the vat to wipe the markings free.

'They told me you were dying,' the alchemist said. At first I was confused, as I thought the woman was speaking to me for a moment. 'They told me you were weak, sickly. It was the old age.'

Stepping back, the alchemist and I both jumped as the demon smashed the glass with his body as soon as he could. She let out a yelp as Yixin snatched her from where she was standing, his enormous hand wrapping around her like she was nothing more than a doll made out of straw.

'He's an earth elemental, you twat,' the demon said, in his native tongue. I could understand him and it was clear the alchemist could too as her eyes widened with fear. 'This prison is buried deep underground. You just moved him closer to his power source.'

'Not now,' Father grunted, finally relinquishing his control on the rose in our cell as Lorcan still had to cut himself free. Sweat was pouring from his temple, my father's skin positively drenched.

'Tas—'

I went to help him and he surprised me with a deep, crushing hug. 'My petal,' he whispered, 'when I release you, it's time to go.'

I nodded, head moving up and down against his chest. I couldn't help the small shred of relief I felt at knowing I wouldn't have to suck someone's air from their lungs. That was plan B.

'My clever girl. I love you. Your mother loved you. Don't be a hero, just stay alive: that's the future we wanted for you. A life.'

'I'll see you up top, Tas.'

'Of course.' He smiled as he released me. 'Now go.'

I took off at a sprint, marvelling at the sheer amount of space I had in front of me as I streaked down the corridor. Almost every cell in their block was open, all manner of creatures pouring out as Yixin dragged the alchemist from one to the other.

'Wait!' the woman cried as I ran past her. 'You said you wouldn't kill me!'

'If you did what the girl said,' the demon answered for her. 'Which you did. I, however, didn't make any such promise.'

Mashing down my hands, I tried to cover my ears and block the cries as I darted around the corner and into the cell of an arachnia, who was crouched up in the corner of the ceiling. They looked wary, eyes darting backwards and forwards between the enclosure and the open space that stretched between them. It was just a second of understanding, but I knew how they felt.

'You should go,' I told them. 'It's not a trick.'

That was all the encouragement they needed, with the limbs of the giant, spiderlike creature stretching out as the being scuttled from the cell. I felt my heart deflate slightly as I looked at the square shape overhead. It was high up, much higher than I was. There was no bunk bed in this room, no furniture of any kind. I couldn't get up there.

'Need a lift?'

With a yelp, I spun around to see Yixin blocking the only entry and exit. He was covered in blood, alchemist's blood, and it was dripping from his lips. He inched towards me and I couldn't help but take a step back. Understanding crossed his features as he crouched down, offering his extended arms.

'I'm not here to hurt you, child, not after all these years.'

I looked at him cautiously, trying to focus on the words and not the monstrous vision I was presented with. Appearances could be deceiving, I tried to tell myself.

'Everyone your father has helped release, we will try to help escape. I know that it's likely I will not, as do many of the others.'

'Why help us then?'

'We will probably die down here. Probably today. The opportunity to wreak a little havoc . . . it is not one I thought I would have before my end. I have you to thank for that.'

I bit my bottom lip, hesitating just a beat before dashing into the demon's arms.

'Oh, little sprite. There, there, do not cry. It's just the beginning for you.'

'But I could stay? We could all stay here, together.'

'It's no place for any creature, monster or otherwise,' Yixin said, as he lifted me into the air. 'Besides, you need to meet your father up top.'

Setting me on his shoulder, I watched as he punched a hole free in the ceiling and exposed the vent that distributed air to each and every cell. I closed my eyes, letting just the faintest breeze sweep across my nose. It was the sweetest sensation I'd ever felt.

'Do you know which way to go?'

There were six small tunnels that stretched out in front of me, all dark and only illuminated from the little light that was coming from inside the cells below. The third one had the cleanest air, cool air, that carried upwards. I climbed forwards, wedging myself into the tight space. I really was the only one who could fit in here. Turning back to Yixin, I paused for a moment. Bending forward, I planted a kiss on his forehead just like my father had done each night as I went to sleep.

He smiled up at me. 'In this life or the next.'

'Bye, Yixin,' I replied in perfect demon speak.

He shoved me gently, pushing me forward through the dust. There was a roar – a proper roar – from behind me and I began crawling as quickly as I could. Terror felt like it was clogging my limbs, making them move slowly, and even though I couldn't see anything, I could hear everything. The electricity in the prison went out and I was plunged into even darker conditions, which I didn't think was possible. I knew when I crawled over other creatures' cells and they knew as well. Some could smell me, some could sense me, but all begged and pleaded for me to stop. *Free me. Help me. Let me up there. Hey, how did you get out? Please, I'll do anything.*

Don't be a hero, I repeated. *Don't.* I needed to get out, get free, and meet my father. *Don't stop for anything.*

So I followed the air, followed it all the way up to the top where a steel grate blocked the exit. My fingers were just small enough to fit through the cracks and I held them there, feeling freezing cold air on my skin for the first time. I pushed and pushed, trying to see if my body weight could do it. At first, I thought it had. The tunnel around me rumbled slightly, dirt shaking loose from old fixtures. There was a metallic pop and the grate clicked free. I pushed as I climbed upwards and on to the wet grass of a cow paddock. It was night, but even the bare sky was brighter than where I'd been. Looking around, my ears pricked at the sound of rustling. Vines that hadn't been there before were unwrapping themselves from the grate and slipping back into the exposed soil below, like green worms.

'TAS!' I called, excited at the sign of my father and searching for him in the darkness. 'Da, where are you?'

I couldn't see him, but he'd helped. He'd got me free of that place at last. Wherever that place was. Vankila, I'd been told, a supernatural prison buried deep underground in St Andrews, Scotland. There was a town not far away and I would walk to it, find food and shelter. I could even see the small, glowing lights in the distance, and I focused on them as I repeated the plan in my head. It was never warm in the prison, but never overly cold either. It was tepid, in between. Up here though, out there, I was icy cold. My lungs hurt from the endless gulps of fresh air I was taking and just how artic they were.

I'll count to three thousand, I told myself. *When I've reached that, just like Da said, I'll go.*

As I huddled there in the wind, waiting longer than I should have, I counted to four thousand. Then five. When it started to rain gently, I still didn't move. I was waiting in the night for a man that would never come.

Chapter 6

Present

The 'place' Ben took her to was different to what she had imagined. Interlacing his fingers in hers, he pulled her gently through the city after him, navigating the streets like someone who had lived there his entire life and knew them intimately. Dreckly didn't, finding the numerous twists and turns disorienting as skyscrapers loomed above.

This modern city spliced with images of others, older cities, as her own laughter had echoed off those buildings and her heels had clacked along the wet cobblestones of Bethnal Green. It was a London partially in ruins, but it had always thrown her how life managed to go on in wartime and people adapted to their new reality regardless of how grim it was.

She'd been told a dirty joke, his hand tightening around hers and squeezing gently as the volume of her own joy surprised the both of them. Kids were playing marbles at the edges of a mountain of rubble, Dreckly wondering how they could discern who was winning in such low light. All the while, her hand was safely clasped in his as his thumb constantly ran over her skin in a soothing gesture. He maintained a steady thrum of chatter as he talked, talked, talked to her like the words had been bottled up inside of him all these months as he waited until he saw her again.

The past was shattered by the present as Ben led her through what looked like the dingy doorway of an old office building and up just a few stairs to where an elevator was waiting.

'Is this where you live?' Dreckly asked, not making the connection between who he presented on the outside and this place on the inside. 'And will this lift likely send us plummeting to our deaths?'

She was uncertain as she stepped into the small, metal box.

'It won't,' he answered, stepping in after her. 'I promise.'

It was a dangerously tiny space, even with just the two of them. She had her back to the wall and Ben had followed her face first so the doors closed behind him. He never took his eyes off of her as he hit the button for where they needed to go, Dreckly feeling the heat between them like her hand was hovering over a stove top.

'I get it,' she whispered.

'Get what?' Ben replied, voice low as he inched closer towards her.

'Why you like this shitty lift.'

He wanted to be up against her, no longer making eye contact as he stared down hungrily at her lips. But he was hesitating, waiting for her to initiate the contact she was desperate for. It was never that easy for Dreckly, though. If she was any other woman, any other person coming back from a date of verbal sparring, any other being who could feel the tension between them the way she could, there would have been no hesitation.

She would have tugged him towards her by the waistband of his pants, his hand reaching up and tracing her collarbone before settling at the base of her throat in a way that drove her crazy. Dreckly Jones would have kissed him in a reckless, passionate way that might mean something tomorrow or it might not. She did none of those things. Instead, she watched him watch her and couldn't help but wonder if Ben was thinking the exact same thing.

The elevator doors pinged open and of all the things she was expecting to shatter the moment, a butch older woman looking unimpressed with her arms crossed was not one of them. Hell, it wasn't even in the top three.

Ben stepped back, following Dreckly's gaze to where the woman leaned, although his senses would have told him she was there from the moment they reached the floor.

'Well,' the lady said, eyes illuminated with amusement as she glanced between the two of them, 'that's certainly one way to get her here.'

The elevator doors went to shut automatically, but the woman stuck out her arm to block them. She was strong, with thick muscles in her upper arms that flexed with the gesture. She looked somewhat like a retired bodybuilder, Dreckly noted, as she stepped into the hallway and towards the open doorway that had been propped ajar with a brick.

It was the only exit from this awkward situation and as she did exactly that, she froze. Ben and the woman were right behind her, bickering back and forth as the door slammed shut. The surprises, they just kept coming.

It looked like Dreckly had strolled right into the middle of Christmas itself. The entire place was illuminated with the tacky festive lights that alternated between one of three colours at a stroke-inducing frequency. The ceiling was covered in that same artificial greenery Christmas trees were made of, with whatever surface there was underneath it unable to be seen: that's how thick the layers were. Baubles in red, white and gold dangled at intervals alongside ornaments that depicted a shirtless Santa in festive boardshorts and thongs.

'Deepest apologies for looking like a Mariah Carey video,' the woman said. 'The Wisdom is usually more, well, aesthetically carny. 'Tis the season, however.'

Dreckly didn't celebrate Christmas; she didn't even recognise what day it was most years. She just had a rough idea of *when* based on the climate of wherever she was that particular year and the music that would sink into her brain by osmosis. Her spine stiffened as she realised what was playing: Bing Crosby crooning about how *Mele Kalikimaka* was Hawaii's way to say 'Merry Christmas to you'. The voice was like a time machine, sending her back to a place that invoked happiness and sadness in equal measure. She needed to focus on the present, the threat in front of her, but she found it difficult to swallow as her throat tightened. Only when the song ended was she able to regain her composure, the shift in tone like a slap to the face as the opening chords of 'Mr Sandman' transformed into a heavy bounce beat.

'Lower the volume on Big Freedia, will you?' the woman called to one of her associates. 'Can barely hear myself think.'

'The Wisdom,' Dreckly repeated, her mind feeling groggy as she fought to catch up. 'The night spot run by wombat shifters.'

She wasn't able to look Ben in the eye just yet, but she focused on the woman who was clearly in charge.

'Run by you.' She pointed.

'Sharon Petersham at your service, but folks call me Shazza.' She nodded. Dreckly realised with horror that she was even wearing seasonal earrings: they were wombats with little, fluffy Santa hats. She hated them immediately. 'I'm surprised you know this place, given you've never come here.'

'I don't frequent supernatural establishments,' she muttered, tracking Ben as he moved in front of her to join the group of people assembled. No, not people. Three demons. Two shifters. A witch. One arachnia. Ruken, Katya's cousin and the goblin she frequently did business with, and an alpha werewolf.

'Curious, that is,' Shazza continued. 'Intentional, I think. Ben does too.'

'Shaz,' he practically growled.

She didn't interrupt. She wanted them to keep talking while she felt the air around them, moved through every square of The Wisdom to make sure everyone she had to worry about was in front of her and not lurking out of sight. She could assess the number present or hiding by how the air particles moved around them. Or didn't.

Dreckly didn't think she could take them all on and survive. There were too many variables, too many different spectrums of power. She wasn't sure why she was there, but she'd have to do her best to talk her way out this situation rather than flee.

'It looks like she's casting a spell,' the witch remarked. It wasn't said in a threatening way, but she cocked her head with curiosity. Her comment interrupted the bickering between Shazza and Ben, which the arachnia was trying to mediate. Everyone fell silent and watched her. Subconsciously, Dreckly guessed she might have been moving her fingers. It happened sometimes, when she was using her powers: it could look like she was playing a very subtle air piano.

'The air's changed,' Ben whispered, frowning as he looked at her. 'Or there's a breeze coming from somewhere.'

'I don't feel anything,' a demon with an afro that looked like a halo commented.

'There was something.' Ben frowned. 'I didn't imagine it. I thought you said she wasn't a witch, Kala?'

'She's not,' the actual witch snapped. 'But she's something.'

Shazza scoffed. 'Or course she's *something*. We're all something. She wouldn't have been able to handle this city's collective criminal business for as long as she has if she wasn't *something*.'

'I don't know,' the arachnia mused. 'I don't see anything special about her.'

'Watch your mouth,' Ben muttered.

'Don't defend me,' Dreckly snapped, feeling truly angry for the first time. The heat from the elevator had been redirected to a new outlet: her rage. 'You brought me here, dickhead. You lied to me, pretended you wanted to go on some bullshit date. Worse, you had Wyck *and* Kat do your dirty work for you. At least you paid for the overpriced dinner, but that's the only good you did.'

She knew it was dangerous to turn her back on a room full of so many monsters, yet that was exactly what she did as she went to storm from the place.

'Wait!' he called after her. 'Please, don't you want to know why I brought you here? Why we're *all* here? The Wisdom is shut tonight so we could make this work.'

'Boo-fucking-hoo to their bottom dollar, Ben. I couldn't give a shit. I don't want anything to do with . . . whatever this is.'

'What do you think this is?'

'A bunch of supernaturals clustered together in a bar? In secret? I don't know what "it" is, but it's trouble. And I don't want any part of it. It's what leads to the Treize tossing people in Vankila and throwing away the key.'

'Don't joke about that,' Ben warned. 'You know my sister Sushmita has been in there since the Outskirt Wars. It's not a laughing matter, Dreckly.'

She blinked. 'Does it look like I'm rolling around on the ground laughing? I wasn't joking. I was stating facts.'

'Please, just five minutes,' the witch pressed. 'Ignore him, just . . . listen to us quickly. Then you can go. This concerns all of us. And your business.'

She'd said the golden 'b' word. Dreckly sighed. For better or worse, she needed to hear this. It would determine whether or not she needed to start the *Titanic II*'s engine the second she got home or whether she could stay.

'Fine. But I'm not taking a seat. And when this is done, I walk out that door alone regardless.'

'Okay.' The witch nodded.

'And I never want to see Ben Kapoor at the fish markets again.'

'I can understand that.'

Dreckly met the woman's gaze and resisted the urge to feel a little bit of solidarity there. These creatures were not her friends. The demons were talking amongst themselves, speaking in their native tongue and asking whether the risk of bringing Dreckly here had been worth it. She listened with half her mind, not giving away that she could understand what they were saying.

'Kala Tully,' the woman in front of her said, offering a hand to shake. 'I'm a witch, I'm an Aboriginal woman, and I'm an inadvertent mother. I'm here as all of those things because we need your help. Supernaturals are going missing. In fact, they've been disappearing for a while. Only now we have facts to start assembling some kind of truth.'

'What does this have to do with me?' Dreckly asked.

'Nothing,' the haloed demon said, stepping forward so that she was alongside Kala. 'I'm Fairuza. We know you helped the banshee and Tex Contos escape the country.'

So they made it out, she thought. *Good for them.* Her positivity was replaced with worry almost immediately. Sadie Burke had become the first banshee in history to successfully break The Covenant. It's likely the Treize didn't know she had left the country yet, but regardless: they would be tearing the city apart looking for her. It was the kind of heat none of them needed.

'I accepted the business of paying clients,' Dreckly replied.

'Not quite true,' Kala corrected. 'You helped point her in the direction of her sister.'

'Sorcha's alive?'

'We don't know. But you supplied them with more than you should have for the fee.'

'They were Tiaki Ihi referrals,' Dreckly countered, not afraid to say the woman's name. She knew the Ihi and Kapoor packs were tight. It's likely they already knew this information. Her hiding it would have said more than if she didn't. 'The Ihi family are my best customers. You look after your best customers.'

The witch shrugged. 'So look after us. The Treize have been abducting these supernaturals but we don't know the purpose . . . yet. What we do know is where they're being held.'

'Whoever is still alive,' Fairuza said, 'we're going to break them out and get them to safety, us too probably. This is going to throw the whole country's supernatural dynamic on its head and those on the run will need to leave Australia, get as far away as fast as we can. We'll need documents. We'll need advice. We'll need you.'

Dreckly's gaze flicked between the two of them, these two women who were standing side by side and partially blocking her view of Ben and the others. It was smart to have them try to appeal to her: they were both women of colour, like her, and trying to make their case on compassionate grounds rather than making her feel cornered like Shazza and her *date*.

'When is this happening?' she asked. There was a snort from the goblin, Ruken.

'Come on now, Dreckly, you're intelligent enough to know we're not going to divulge information as crucial as that. What's to stop you running from here right to the Treize to tell them what you know?'

'Sheer numbers,' she replied, gesturing to those around them. 'Between the lot of you, you have eyes everywhere.'

'We wish,' Shazza murmured.

'You'd be able to stop me before I even got close to St James Station.'

The Treize's base of operations was located in the labyrinth of empty tunnels under one of the city's most historic and underused train stations. Except those tunnels – once intended for an exclusive, upper-class travel facility – weren't so empty now and hadn't been since the Second World War when they were utilised as underground bunkers.

It was little more than a ten-minute sprint on foot from where she was currently, but Dreckly knew she would never make it out of this bar alive let alone out of the building if that's what she intended. She would also *never* report *anyone* or *anything* to the Treize, yet they didn't know that either.

'I stay alive and unbothered because the secrets I know stay with me,' she said carefully. 'For all my clients. For all those who could be a threat to my safety.'

'We're not threatening you,' Ruken huffed. 'Look, I have the tech ready: I've been building an excess of passport chips and biometric certificates since this became a possibility. What we'd need you to do is build a number of blanks that could be quickly doctored to send these beings wherever they needed to go as quickly as possible. You have connections to the criminal underworld we can't cultivate.'

They must have seen the look on her face, because Ruken quickly course corrected.

'Yeah, they know Ben. They know the werewolves. But that's a relationship of convenience and proximity to power. They actually like you, trust you, work with you. If you asked them to smuggle someone out of the country, they'd do it. And not in a Tasmanian devil way. They'd actually survive to arrive at their destination safely.'

Dreckly pondered Ruken's words, in fact, all the words that had been spoken since she arrived. Her life was a constant weighing and assessing of threats: choosing one location over another, skipping one job and taking the next, leaving on this date rather than that one. It was the only way she had stayed alive but, most importantly to her, *free.* All of those things were running through her mind as she did the math and they patiently waited for her answer.

'No,' she said, finally.

There was a groan from the arachnia and the slump of shoulders travelled through the room like a Mexican wave. They were disappointed.

'We have to kill her, then,' one of the demons was saying to Fairuza.

'You don't, actually,' Dreckly replied in perfect demon speak, catching the glimpse of surprise on their faces before she switched to English. 'Nothing you've said to me tonight will leave this room; you have my word. Yet I will not partake in this. It sounds like you're all prepping to do some heroic shit and it's admirable, but I'm no hero. I have not endured by throwing myself into conflicts that don't involve me.'

'You're supernatural,' Kala pleaded. 'I can sense it.'

Dreckly sighed, long and deep. 'So . . . what? Then I must be involved with you all? This is not my fight.'

'It will be,' Fairuza muttered. 'If not today, then tomorrow, next week, next month, or next year. This impacts all of us.'

'You have my answer: it's no. Am I free to leave?'

'Of course,' Shazza said, moving forward to lead her towards the door.

'No, let me,' Ben urged, stepping past her with a hand on the wombat shifter's shoulder. He held open the door for her and Dreckly marched through it, spinning around to say one last thing before she left but he anticipated it.

'Listen, Wyck didn't know,' the words spilling from Ben's mouth quickly. 'Don't think he's a part of this, because he's not. I tricked him as much as I did you.'

'Well, aren't we a pair of fools then,' she said, noting how he didn't mention Katya. Her cousin being there was confirmation enough. Dreckly frowned at the mistletoe that was dangling above their heads. She slapped it out of the way so hard it flew from its hanger, landing with a *thwack* on the ground. 'You're an asshole, Ben Kapoor, with your all-black-Johnny-Cash-by-candlelight schtick. I don't care what your cause is and it might be petty of me to say, but I hope it fails because of you.'

'Don't.'

'I hope it *fails*.'

And your car's dumb, she thought, but couldn't say it out loud with any kind of conviction. Dreckly turned and flew down the stairs, skipping the elevator altogether. She didn't want to wait for it with him in that tiny corridor. Even worse, she didn't want the reminder of what she'd wanted to happen inside it.

As she stepped on to the street, she looked around for a sign until she saw one marked Clarence Street. It was for times like these that it was practical to have a phone so she could utilise the map function. Yet she didn't like the device's tracking capabilities, so it was better to go without. Instead, she followed the beacon of Sydney Tower far above the other buildings because she knew it would take her towards a train station. Any train station. A light rain started as she marched, her dress clinging to her body and her feet straining against the straps of her heels as they slipped.

'And *this* is why I don't go out on dates,' she said to herself, wiping a water droplet from her eyebrow.

Chapter 7

Past

It took hours for me to understand that Father never intended to escape. He must have known he wouldn't make it, that there was no way out for him. Yet he had trained me regardless, taught me everything he possibly could, so I would have the best viable chance out there in the world. Without him.

I felt his death somehow. Not the specific cause or even when – it could have been minutes after fresh air caressed my face or hours – but at some point it rocked through me like an earthquake you could only feel in your heart. If someone was watching me, it would have been invisible from the outside even as I dropped down to my knees in the mud. Yet on the inside, it was as if the foundations of who I was had cracked open and revealed a void that he had once filled.

I was angry at first, walking towards the glowing lights of the nearest town, St Andrews. He'd made me memorise the plan and I would make sure his sacrifice wasn't in vain, but that didn't mean I couldn't stay furious. And utterly heartbroken. I cried the whole way to the town, which sat on the edge of a massive river that was black and sparkled in the night.

The water looked calm and inviting, even, but it was the River Tay and I'd been warned not to go in. There were several boats docked at a nearby port and I was freezing. My skin was damp from the rain and there was mud on my knees. I shivered as I walked through the quiet streets, feeling the cobblestones beneath my bare feet. It was late at night, perhaps closer to morning, and it was a morsel of luck that had gone my way. It meant there was no one to ask why a dirty child in tattered clothes was strolling around unaccompanied.

'There will likely be Askari in that town,' Father had said. 'Those who monitor any unusual folks who pass through and keep tabs on the townsfolk's perception of any unusual goings-on, so Vankila stays secret, just like our whole existence.'

If I'd made it to the surface during daylight hours, I was to wait. Thankfully it was dark and I was free to wander, counting the houses on the left side of the street until I got to number twenty-five. The residence had a huge rose bush out the front and an enormous, oversized garden as I pushed open the gate and crept up the dirt path.

'Walk around the back of the cottage,' I whispered to myself, hearing Father's words. 'The back door will be unlocked.'

The more steps I recited, the more a few other things started to click into place. No wonder he had aged so poorly, no wonder he looked so drained. Stretching his powers this far had exerted him well beyond what he could and should do. This house had more greenery than any of the others, so he could direct me to it more clearly.

It was also empty, which was clear as I lifted one of the stones at the rear and plucked the chain of keys hidden there. The family who lived here only visited intermittently, according to Da. There was a caretaker who checked on the property every morning and did the required maintenance.

By then, I would be long gone. My eyes were good in the dark, I was used to it, and I sniffed away my last stream of tears as I concentrated on the task at hand.

'No light,' Father had warned. 'There shouldn't be light of any kind coming from that house when the family isn't there. It will draw undue attention.'

So I moved quietly, carefully, through the house. It had hot and cold water taps, a luxury for the area, and after burning myself by accident and letting out a quiet yelp, I established which was which. I filled an enormous basin with warm, soapy water before stripping naked and edging into the depths.

It was sensational. I'd never experienced anything like it as I sat there, crammed into the strange shape and scrubbing my skin. In Vankila, our only options for bathing were wet rags and a small bowl of water. It wasn't ideal, but it was what I was used to. In comparison, this seemed opulent. The feeling in my fingers and toes had even started to come back and I wiggled them accordingly.

I knew I had stayed too long when the light outside the cottage started to lighten. The water had cooled long ago, but I had been unable to remove myself once I had rubbed soap all through my scalp and hair, getting some in my eyes and not realising until afterwards that was a huge, stinging mistake. Now I was running out of time.

I didn't know the difference between a towel and a blanket: one was fluffy and one was not, but I wrapped a huge square of material around my body as I disposed of the evidence of my bath. Father had manufactured mud and grass beneath my feet in our cell so I would know what it felt like, but I'd never felt carpet before and I gasped as my toes made contact with it on my way up the stairs.

It was like pillows under my feet, I couldn't believe it. I dropped down on to my stomach, letting my whole body experience the sensation as I rolled around. Somewhere a rooster could be heard announcing the arrival of morning. I sprung up, panicked. Sprinting from room to room, I came to a stop when I found the one that was shared by the children. There was a boy close to my age, Father had explained. It was his clothes I dressed in, not only because they came closer to fitting me but because it was easier to travel as a boy. Or so they said.

I stuffed a change of clothes and shoes inside, before taking a pair of gloves and heading out into the yard. I locked the back door and returned the key to its hiding spot. The longer it took for anyone to discover the house had been disturbed, the better. The longer it took for them to retrace my steps, the longer of a head start I had.

There was a cluster of people already awake and working at the dock, unloading and reloading boats, with children my age working alongside the men so it was easy to slip by unnoticed. I was to get on one of these boats and get as far *away* from Scotland as possible, but that was where Father's instructions ended. And now there would be no further help, no further guidance or instruction.

I had to bite my lip to stop it trembling as the realisation that I was utterly on my own dawned. Shoving it down, shoving it *all* down, I listened instead. Mandarin, English, Cornish, demon and Spanish were the five languages I had a grasp of. I heard the last one and marked that ship as my target. It was easy to get on board, just picking up one of the many crates being carried to the ship and depositing it in the storage hold . . . where I stayed.

Bunkering down, I wedged myself into one of the crates, emptying its contents into another before climbing inside. I'd picked one at the very top, so it was difficult to get into but it meant that at least I wouldn't be trapped as more materials were placed above. I was small enough to make it work, my satchel somewhat of a pillow as I curled up and listened to the sound of the ship around me. It was the first time I'd felt safe since leaving Vankila, which was ironic in and of itself. Just the memory of that place made me want to cry as I thought of my now dead father and of Yixin left behind. I would not be discovered and my freedom jeopardised over tears, however. So I shoved my fist in my mouth and made sure the only person who had to endure the muffled cries was me.

I lost track of the days once we were at sea, even though I tried to track them by carving markings into the side of the crate. Once it got past thirty, I gave up and just maintained my routine: sneaking out only when most of the ship was asleep and taking small enough chunks of food and water from the kitchen so it wouldn't be noticed. Once I ran out every few days, I would repeat the cycle. It took me longer to realise something was wrong – seriously wrong – than it should have.

There were fewer people about every time I ventured upwards, the smell growing putrid as I measured the air around them to avoid running into sailors. Men died and were thrown overboard as the others tried to triage the growing sickness as it spread. I stopped going up, wondering if my immune system could take it. I guessed the answer was yes, given I had two non-human parents. It wasn't worth the risk regardless; I had enough water and enough extra portions to last a full week.

When those seven days had expired, I waited another day. But things were quiet. Their quarters were packed full of people, too many people even if they weren't deathly ill and probably contagious. They weren't a threat to me in their weakened state and as I tiptoed around them, I couldn't help my curiosity. I poured over their things, examining the sketched portraits of family members and reading the letters of loved ones they carried with them.

I played with their treasures, marvelling at a golden locket and nearly cutting myself on a man's switchblade. When I discovered a pocket watch ticking in the pocket of a dead man, I took it. I felt bad for barely a second, remembering what Father had said:

'Stealing might be the only way you survive out there, Dreckly. Do what you need to.'

I didn't need this to survive, but I wanted it. The sounds it made, the way the hands ticked and ticked past numbers my father had taught me. He had never explained how to read time, however, so whatever the watch was telling me was a mystery. I liked it all the same.

I began climbing to the top deck when a hand reached out and clasped my ankle. The grip was cold and clammy, the skin moist from sweat and Lord knew what else. It was a man, one of the last survivors. Vomit had dried into his beard and it looked as if death was not far from making a visit.

'Are you . . . an angel?' he croaked in Spanish.

I was paralysed with fear, my heart pounding as his grip tightened further. I gulped, shaking my head slowly.

'Please,' he continued. 'Please help me.'

I heard my father's voice in my head as if he was right there on that very boat with us.

You are not a hero.

Slowly, I reached into my satchel and took one of two sacks of water I was carrying. I untwisted the lid, hooking my elbow around the wooden ladder so I wouldn't slip as I poured several sips worth into his mouth and over his face, to clear the filth.

He had crawled from wherever he had been lying, his legs clearly too weak to stand. His eyes fluttered shut with relief as he licked his lips, basking in the hydration for a moment. My hands were shaking as I placed the sack on his chest, patting it to make sure he knew it was there. His hand was still around my ankle and, with a yank, I pulled it free.

'I can't help you,' I whispered, the words coming out unsteady as my voice broke.

When I emerged on to the ship's main deck, I couldn't see at first. It was only sunset, but even so the light was bright enough that my eyes couldn't adjust and I fell to my knees. Wiping away the tears, I only took fleeting peeks at the sky until I could stand it.

Father was an incredible artist, yet even his talent couldn't capture what I was looking at as the red and orange sky began to get swallowed by the purple, then the blue, and eventually the black, which I knew was coming. I was breathless, my lips gasping for air as I stared at the sight I had only dreamed of seeing.

Stumbling to my feet, I steadied myself on a railing and looked overboard. The horizon was the only thing I could perceive, with endless ocean stretching out to meet it. Keeping one hand on the ship to guide my unsteady legs, I followed around the perimeter until the view started to change.

Hills, huge ones. And mountains. Maybe they were the same thing? I had never really understood the difference. Either way, there were thousands of tiny lights set into them and even more beyond that. I wasn't far off the coast. I had walked further. Using the man's knife from down below, I cut hastily at the ropes that held a small lifeboat in place. It landed in the water with a splash and I watched as it floated gently away from the ship.

I steadied myself on the edge of the boat, counting down in my head. Throwing myself forward, I sailed through the air for a few glorious seconds before plunging into the water. My cries were muffled as I sunk below the surface, the ocean far colder than I had been expecting. I'd never learned how to swim, never had any opportunity to, but I seemed to know what to do as I kicked my way to the surface and shrugged out of the heavy clothes in the process.

The initial shock of the cold quickly subsided and the ocean instead wrapped around me like a warm hug. It was welcoming me, as if remembering who I was in the same way I was remembering it. It felt like home here, like I could stay, but I knew that I couldn't. It seemed as if my own disappointment rippled through the water as I gasped, taking a massive gulp of air as my head popped up. The lifeboat was nearby and I moved towards it, pushing the water with my hands while my legs moved in an opposite motion. Getting in was a struggle and I exhausted myself with half a dozen attempts before I was successful, landing in a wet heap inside the boat.

I jumped with the sound of a blaring horn, my head sticking up to see the light of another boat off in the distance. This was a real boat, a huge boat, and it was chugging towards the ship I had been on with purpose. I wouldn't be there when it arrived. Taking an oar in each hand, it took a few attempts before I figured out precisely the best method to row towards the coastline.

I warmed up quicker than expected, the current seemingly helping me with a forward path as I made my way towards the brightest lights. There were more boats, seven that I counted and all big. I followed where they were going, but far enough away that I wouldn't be spotted or crushed beneath their girth. It looked like they were bound for another dock, this one much larger than St Andrews. It had a name though, with a massive sign definitely not made out of stone illuminated by several lights on the ground that shone upwards.

'Port of Los Angeles,' I read out loud, squinting to make out the final words. 'Established nineteen zero seven.'

With a tired smirk, I kept rowing. I made land in San Pedro, a suburb of Los Angeles, which was inside the state of California and part of the United States of America. This was a damn good thing, I realised. Here, I soon discovered, they spoke English. There were also plenty of people who spoke Spanish and, as I wandered further, I found a whole part of the town that spoke Mandarin and Cantonese. That was the place easiest for me to blend, as the people here looked like me. I could linger in alleyways and walk around aimlessly without anyone wondering who I belonged to or where I was going. This was important. Blending was important.

So too was shelter, but that last one had been a lot harder to come by. The air was warmer here though, so for my first few lights in Los Angeles I didn't mind sleeping outside. It was possible, but I was filthy. And I couldn't do it forever.

'Please, I'm just looking for a place to stay,' I begged a man at the reception for his run-down hotel.

'That's what your parents are for! I'm not your parent!'

He had chased me away and back on to the street with a broom. *A broom!* It had been fortuitous though, as a night market was taking place and I paused in front of a stall selling flowers. I smiled, ignoring the tears that began involuntarily welling up as I bent down to smell a pink bouquet. They reminded me of my father. He wouldn't have the opportunity to grow anything this beautiful ever again.

'Stay away from the orchids, street urchin,' a boy hissed in Mandarin, a rolled-up magazine in his hands. He looked fifteen or so, and I glared at him, fully done with one more moment of meanness from anyone.

'They're not orchids,' I snapped. 'They're *cabbage* roses.'

A woman who I assumed was the boy's mother had been watching from inside the stall and she stood up with a laugh, whacking him on the shoulder with a fan in her hands.

'Cabbage roses?' she said, grinning with smudged pink lipstick. Nodding at the bucket of flowers at her feet, she asked: 'What are those?'

'*Those* are orchids,' I answered, looking pointedly at the boy. 'Moth orchids.'

'And those?'

She pointed her fan at another bouquet.

'Peruvian lilies.'

And so it went, the lady pointing at different species of flower while I named them. I didn't get a single one wrong. I could have played this game all night, because that's what it felt like: a game. When there were no more lilies or orchids or roses or daisies left, the woman waved at me to step behind the makeshift counter of the market stall.

'What's your name?' she asked.

I was about to be honest, I was about to tell the truth, but I hesitated. It was not smart, in this place. It was not smart so soon.

'Tulip,' I answered. It had been my mother's favourite flower, apparently.

'Tulip, well, now that makes sense. No wonder you're the flower expert.'

'She's a street urchin!'

'Quiet,' the lady snapped, silencing the boy. 'My son, I'm sorry. He's too tough, sometimes. Too tough. But that's okay, because I'm the softer one. Is he right, are you on the street?'

I nodded. This was the first person who had shown any form of kindness towards me since I'd escaped. It was so shocking; I was kind of hypnotised as she asked her questions and I answered them.

'Where are your parents?'

I shook my head from side to side.

'Brothers and sisters?'

I repeated the gesture.

'No one? Huh, just like my parents when they first came to this country. Would you like somewhere to sleep?'

I froze, unsure if the offer was sincere or not.

'Something to eat, somewhere to wash?'

'I . . . yes, yes please.'

'My name is Meili.' She smiled. 'I'd be honoured if you'd come and stay with us. Just until you find your way.'

I was stunned by how easy it was to integrate into the Han family, like a barnacle attaching itself to the hull of a ship. The boy's name was Delun Han and his father Li Jun Han, the whole family living in an apartment above a florist they operated in Chinatown. I had the first shower of my life in that apartment. I slept in my first *real* bed in that apartment. I ate my first real meal in that apartment, surrounded by a family that wasn't my own but treated me like I belonged anyway.

They'd had a daughter, I learned, Jiu. It was her room that I slept in. They didn't talk about what happened, just that she'd gotten sick and passed away. Their grief was like the fifth person at the table as they ate steamed vermicelli rolls, fried shrimp with cashews, and a type of cabbage salad that blew my mind.

I'd never had shrimp before, nor the beef that was inside the rolls. I'd never experienced that texture or the taste on my tongue. Rice was a whole other challenge. Delun made fun of me for not being able to use chopsticks. He teased me about it relentlessly, so much so that I became determined to master them as quickly as I could. I practised at night, when everyone else thought I was asleep, and surprised him by picking a single grain of rice off his plate with a triumphant *ha*.

The questions about my family never came up again after that first night. I seamlessly just became part of theirs, working in the shop every day. I was the extra set of hands they had desperately needed, with my father's knowledge of plants making me extremely valuable to Meili along with my understanding of basic artistic principles.

'Line and balance and colour harmony,' Meili explained, showing me how to assemble a basic bouquet. 'It's not hard if you've had any kind of art training, which it's clear you have.'

'Some,' I had muttered, keen to avoid the question and the memories of my father it evoked.

'Good, that's a start then. You assemble shorts and talls, find a transitional plant like baby's breath, and build around that.'

I might know what various plants and florals were, where they came from, and what they could be used for, but floristry was a different application of that information. Sunflowers weren't just sunflowers: they were a round flower, like roses. A line flower could be a snap dragon or even a moth orchid, and I needed to carefully make sure I had the perfect amount of each per bouquet.

Yet this was something I could do, something I could contribute not only to this family but out there in the *real* world. Looking back at everything he'd taught me and all the lessons, I realised my father's greatest fear was that I wouldn't be able to make it out here, that I wouldn't be able to survive on my own. Yet here I was, doing it. And he'd never get to see.

There was so much I didn't know, however, like how to wield a florist's blades without stabbing myself. Multiple times. Dethorning roses, I learned, basically required a blood sacrifice.

'We do it like the Europeans,' Li Jun said, walking me through how to use the surprisingly thin and bendy blades. 'They use knives like these too, not rose strippers. That's lazy and it should be a part of proper flower conditioning, if it can. Gloves are a must, even for weathered professionals like me.'

My mind leapt back without permission, taking me to the memory of the Kind Guard stabbing his way through the endless vine of thorns my father had grown to buy me enough time to escape. No gloves for him.

It was hard, physical work in a way I didn't expect: early starts and early nights. It was hard on your hands, which were always cut or pricked in some way. It was hard on your shoulders and your back. Yet we made a great team, the shop's business already significant when I started. It felt like things only got even busier from there.

'It's the war,' Meili said, one day when we were unpacking Li Jun's purchases from the wholesaler.

'The war?' I asked, sorting the roses into a pile of shorts and talls. The flowerheads came wrapped carefully in cardboard to preserve them; wearing my own pair of gloves, I liberated them one by one.

'Nobody wanted flowers during the war, but now? Enough time has passed that it doesn't feel like such a luxury to people anymore. They want nice things. They want roses.'

I didn't attend school with Delun, asking if I could just work in the shop instead. They agreed; after all, it cost to attend and that was an extra fee we couldn't afford. *Especially* when I could be helping in the shop instead . . . and avoiding questions about my background that would inevitably be asked in a proper institution. I read Delun's textbooks though, every night. I read his homework too: and corrected it. I was trying to learn as much as I could about the world.

It was revising Delun's history homework that I first learned what Meili meant by 'the war': The Great War, from nineteen fourteen to nineteen eighteen. It had been over for four years now, but the impact was felt everywhere, according to Li Jun. I knew nothing of human wars. Yixin had given me a detailed history of the supernatural ones though: from the persecution of witches and werewolves during the hunts of the early Middle Ages, to the deportation of banshees. War was everywhere, it seemed.

It was easy to pass the years like that, with them. I started every morning the same way, up at 4 a.m. and going with Li Jun to the wholesale market to help him select the best plants on offer. I told him which flowers to buy, which ones were the best quality, and which were hiding secret viruses or bugs. It was one of the few residual gifts from my father's side and the only earth elemental trait I truly carried. Li Jun bartered with the seller, haggling the price down even if it was a bargain on that particular day.

'It's the principle of it,' he told me. 'You can't let people think you're a pushover, especially in this country.'

I watched with fascination at his skill for that, with the man respected and feared in equal measure every time he stepped into the marketplace. On the way back, he would take a detour and pull the truck over at a beach where I would sprint straight from the vehicle and right into the water. It was like a magnetic pulse was pulling me towards the ocean without my control.

I needed to be in it, submerged in it, wading into the deep and diving beneath the waves. It was a euphoric sensation; the way the water ran through my hair, over my skin, it was like being embraced by a loved one.

In a way, it was. It didn't matter what time of year it was, winter or summer, Li Jun would always stop and I would always swim. It was never as long as I would have liked, but I had to be quick so no one would see me: female bathers were frowned upon, especially without a male escort.

Wringing the salty water from my hair, I would jog back to the car with a smile on my face and wrap the towel around my body that was always sitting in the passenger side. Then it was straight to the shop, Meili scolding her husband for indulging my seaside ritual while he just nodded obediently then did the exact same thing the next morning.

The shop opened at 8 a.m. each day and they needed that extra time to prep as much as they could, even though their peak trading hours were usually from lunchtime onwards. They had regulars who came by early, often with seasonal orders that I would set aside for them.

'Assistants,' Meili had whispered like a conspirator. 'Fixers. They pick up bouquets for famous clients who can't be seen this side of town.'

'What's "this" side of town?'

'Chinatown,' the woman said, as if it was obvious. 'But they know we're the best in the city and people want the best. So they send assistants instead, early, before anyone can make the connection between who they are and what they're getting.'

They stocked the store from the outside in, making sure the

exterior looked beautiful and packed with blooms, while the rest of the day was spent filling the interior and moving items with a longer vase life towards the back. Meili's shop was on the outskirts, towards the Los Angeles State Historic Park, and it was easily the nicest store in the area.

Not that the building was newer or fancier than any of the others: it too was old and run-down, just like most of the structures in the district. But she was part of a handful of other business owners who worked hard to keep their stores clean and tidy. They all leased their properties, with very few outright owning thanks to a combination of local corruption and the ever-present threat that the whole area was going to get demolished so they could build a train station there like they kept threatening.

Delun went to college, a historic first in the family, and studied to become a teacher. When he turned twenty-one, I was conscious of the fact that the six years I'd spent with the family weren't showing like they should have. I'd had to make up a birthday for myself as Tulip, because birthdays were something they treasured. And when they asked how old I was all those years ago, I had just nodded when Meili suggested eleven or twelve. I went with eleven in the end, because I thought it would buy me more time.

Time was a funny thing and, sooner than I thought, it started to become tricky to conceal my age. I looked little more than fourteen, yet I did things to disguise that fact. I stuffed my bra just enough so my chest looked more suited for girls my age rather than those yet to hit puberty. I learned how to do my make-up so I appeared older. I cut my hair short, making it fashionable and finger-waved like women in their twenties.

These were all incremental things, but they helped. They

dragged out what I knew was inevitable: I would have to leave this family sooner rather than later. It was one thing for Meili to attribute my appearance to 'good genes'. It was another altogether if it got to a decade and I had barely changed. Delun would be a married teacher and the woman he referred to as his 'cousin Tulip' would be frozen in time. The weird things about me that the family brushed over would be unavoidable by then.

Chapter 8

Present

If felt like everything went to shit after that. Not that she one hundred per cent blamed the date, but she seventy per cent blamed the date. And Wyck at first, even though it wasn't his fault.

'What happened?' he'd asked the following day when he'd rolled up for work at the usual hour.

'I'm not talking about it,' Dreckly snapped. 'He's an asshole, you're an asshole for setting me up with him, I'm an asshole for trying to find a Band-Aid solution.'

'Did he hur—'

'No! He didn't hurt me. He wouldn't be walking if that was the case, just . . .'

She simmered down slightly, her own words coming back to her for a moment as she felt bad for what she'd said to her friend. Yes, he was her employee. Wyck was also her mate. Both deserved to be treated with kindness.

'*Je suis désolé*,' she murmured, sighing.

'Say what now?'

'I'm sorry, Wyck. There was no need to go full bitch-a-rama on you. It's not your fault. It just went badly and I don't want to see Ben Kapoor again. I don't want to see anyone, actually. No more dates for a while. I want to lay low.'

That turned out to be quite the timely decision, with news slowly filtering through even to her corner of Sydney that shit was going down. Sadie Burke had made it out of the country, breaking The Covenant not just once, but twice, by predicting and diverting the death of the man who had been with her: Askari Texas Contos.

Dreckly wasn't an idiot; she knew what she had agreed to do at the time by helping them. The Treize had caused a significant stir when Sadie's sister Sorcha Burke had first bounced two years ago, but everyone involved had been careful then. There was no way that would have led back to her and, in the grand scheme of things, the incident made only a small ripple. This, in contrast, was a motherfucking tsunami.

Praetorian Guard soldiers and Askari were ripping the city apart, searching for not just the young couple, but *all* the Burke sisters now and their family members: their kids, their aunties, their cousins, their husbands, their girlfriends, their boyfriends, their wives. Any 'Burke' was under threat and, wildest of all, none of them were where they were supposed to be. It was unheard of, an entire banshee family going on the run. They were a fairly obedient species after years of oppression: the opposite of the werewolves and the witches.

Yet Sadie's actions had sparked something. The Burkes had sparked something. Word started to trickle in that other banshees had disappeared too. The Covenant was being broken en masse, with entire families up and leaving overnight. It was unprecedented, an entire species attempting to flee. The key word was *attempting*. Many were being caught, but it was a scenario the Treize had been completely unprepared for and even more were successfully escaping. Where they were going? Dreckly didn't know, but they weren't coming through her.

With as much heat as there was, the smart thing to do was close down shop for a while and wait until things blew over. If the banshees could, she guessed most of them would try and get offshore by any means necessary. She suspected many more had remained in Australia, heading inland to the middle of the country where the Treize had the weakest footing. Considering the statistics alone – the sheer number of banshees that had vanished successfully compared to those who had been unsuccessful – it was obvious they were receiving help.

At night, she tossed and turned in bed, unable to stop thinking about the ragtag group of people who had been assembled alongside Ben and the Petersham family of wombat shifters. They were willing to help species outside of their own, help beings they hadn't even met escape from whatever kind of operation the Treize had been running on the low. There must be others. They must not be the only ones willing to put their own safety on the line to help the banshees elude capture.

Survival wasn't the most important thing to these beings though, clearly. Word had gotten back to the Ravens Motorcycle Club at some point, as their usual supernatural points of contact had begun acting differently. Everyone was bunkering down, tightening up, playing it safe. Dreckly explained that she needed to do the same, at least for a brief period until things returned to normal. It was safer for them too, she told them. She had worked with the M.C. for a long time, so they trusted her. And they listened.

They maintained their presence at the fish markets, but they scaled back their operations too, so that it was just illegal activities pertaining to the human world: gun running, debt collecting, muscle when necessary. Wyck checked in twice a day, but it was more for social reasons than practical ones. And to be fed. With her business on ice, she didn't need the added layer of protection that he provided. His daily tasks went back to being delegated by his bikie mates, yet she still sensed he was looking out for her.

All the Ravens were, in fact. The commission she paid them for that added layer of protection and to dock at the markets wasn't insignificant, but she was still surprised. They considered her one of them, in whatever way, even though she had made very few attempts to integrate herself into their lives. Time could do that, however. Dreckly had been around and part of their world for long enough now that she crossed the invisible threshold of someone they would protect. It was a nice thought.

She still needed something to keep herself busy and give her a reason for being at the fish markets in the first place. Zhang Yong provided that for her, with Dreckly working every day at the oyster counter, grateful for the physical distraction *and* the mental one. Worrying continuously was pointless, but that didn't mean she was overlooking red flags. She'd lived through rebellions before and knew that even when the battle was won, the war was over, it was hard to distinguish the big victories from the devastating personal losses.

The Treize and their operatives were *everywhere*. She started to see Askari patrolling the fish markets, trying to pass as tourists or locals just there to get a bargain. They were pretty shit at it, namely because the tattoo at their wrists, which marked them as the foundation of the supernatural organisation, was unique. If you didn't know, you didn't know.

Dreckly knew. She started seeing it more than she would like, the stiff lines and circles that represented the alchemist symbol for wood peeking out of long-sleeved shirts. Just wearing a garment like that was cause for suspicion alone, because Christmas had come and gone in a swelling mass of people during what was not just the busiest time of the year but the hottest. Long sleeves were suss. Those that didn't bother to cover that tattoo were more common and they were a visible threat. That concerned her less than what she feared was around them every day: the threats she couldn't see or sense.

It was New Year's Eve when the opposite of both of those rolled up to her oyster cart. She had her eyes down, keeping her gaze focused as she worked her way through the latest shipment of oysters that had come in fresh off the boat that morning. Most had been for customers smart enough to pre-order in bulk before their New Year's Eve soirées. It felt like the whole city became one big party on December thirty-first. Just behind Auckland, New Zealand, Sydney was one of the first in the world to usher in the new year and by its very definition that meant a ruckus.

'What's the difference between Sydney Rock Oysters and Pacific Oysters?' a voice asked, reading the small sign that was positioned at the front of the glass to tell customers what was on offer.

Dreckly paused for only a moment, the blade of her knife wedged inside the muscle of the oyster after she had cut in from the hinge. She glanced up to meet the gaze of Ben Kapoor, who looked sheepish as he stood there with his hands in the pockets of the black denim overalls he was wearing. They were ripped and torn in places, with a big chain hanging off the side of one pocket, and a black and white striped singlet underneath. She had never seen anyone make dungarees look rock 'n' roll.

'Have you had oysters before?' she asked, voice neutral. It would have been easy enough for him to get the correct codes to engage with her, but he hadn't. He wasn't here on business.

'No. Always seemed a bit gross to me.'

She arched a single eyebrow, letting him know how lame she thought that answer was. He chuckled and shrugged.

'Not much of a seafood guy.'

'Sydney Rock Oysters are local,' she said. 'Obviously. Pacific Oysters come from all over Australia. I'd recommend those if you're new to the game. They're saltier, taste more like the sea.'

'Which . . . I assume you want to throw me into?'

She smiled, rinsing off another oyster she was just about to slice into. 'Wouldn't mind.'

'How'd you become so good with a blade?' he asked, leaning against the cart as he watched her work.

'Floristry.'

He laughed at her answer, like it was a joke. She let him, switching a Pacific Oyster from the Sydney Rock Oyster pile where it had gotten mixed up: one had a slight bend in it; the others were symmetrical, which is how you could tell them apart.

'All right then, florist. I'll take half a dozen Pacific Oysters. Pop my cherry.'

'You'll take two,' she answered, placing them in front of him with a quarter of lemon. 'You'll never make it through six. Then you can fuck off. I believe I made it quite clear I never wanted to see you again.'

'I know, Dreckly, but I felt the need to explain.'

'To apologise?'

'No, I mean – yes. I'm sorry, I can't imagine how it made you feel—'

'Being tricked? Having someone *pretend* to like you just so they could get you where they wanted you? To be used?'

'I – hey. You felt what I felt in that elevator, okay? I wasn't pretending.'

'That doesn't change the fact you used me.'

'I did. And that's what I want to apologise for. I'm not sorry I did what I did: I had to. I'd do it again if it meant we'd get you there. Doesn't mean I don't feel bad about it.'

Dreckly put down her blade and leaned against the counter, scrutinising Ben Kapoor's face as he waited for her response. He was the kind of guy a mother would fear their daughter coming home with: dyed green hair with black roots, piercings, punk energy, and distinct fuck-ability. He couldn't have looked more different on the outside from the first person she had truly fallen in love with, but what scared her was that underneath they had the same spirit. She wondered if that was part of her attraction to him, before she'd even known he was a key figure in a supernatural rebellion . . . maybe she'd sensed it? If that was true, Dreckly hated that about herself. Being drawn to righteous trouble was a hazard, no matter what package it came in. It only led to heartbreak.

Ben picked up the first of the two oysters, squirting a generous amount of lemon, then threw it back. The werewolf made a slurping noise in the process, his lips moving as he half-chewed, half-swallowed it. He looked confused momentarily, as if he might spit it out. Then the expression changed to one Dreckly recognised: he was a lifer now.

'I regret not buying six,' he murmured, quickly devouring the second one and looking thoughtful as he ate it.

'Technically you didn't buy two,' she answered, holding out her hand for payment when she froze.

A man was moving through the crowd, just the back of his head and top half of his physique visible, but it was enough to shake loose the memory. For years, that walk had been one of the few highlights of her world as he'd moved through the halls of Vankila bringing treats. He turned his head just slightly to the left, giving her enough of a glimpse at his side profile to confirm it was him: the Kind Guard.

Every inch of her body was stiff with fear as she watched him wander from vendor to vendor in the distance. She was positioned right at the end, near the fruit and vegetable market, and eventually he would make his way to her. Would he recognise her? Would he see through the woman she had become to distinguish the young girl in a cell from more than a century ago? She couldn't wait to find out. She had to leave. Now.

'What are—'

Ben went to turn, following her horrified gaze when she grabbed his arm. She dug her fingernails deep into the skin, forcing him to keep looking at her.

'Don't turn around,' she said, quietly. 'Don't react. Please.'

His eyes were wide as he read what was on her face, what was on her body. He repositioned his posture slightly and she realised he must have a weapon on him. He was a werewolf, so *of course* he did. Dreckly tracked the man she knew only as Lorcan with her eyes, waiting until he passed behind a wall and into the store of a rival. The second he was out of sight, so was she.

Dragging Ben with her, she tossed her apron at Zhang as they cut through the back and out on to the decks.

'I have an emergency,' she told him in Mandarin. 'If anyone asks after me, tell them nothing.'

He looked alarmed by her alarm and she tried to get herself together.

'What about tonight?' he called.

'It's still on. I'll see you at ten as planned.'

They emerged on to the decks, which was always the busiest part of the fish markets as people lobbied to find a smooth surface and a seat to eat their purchases. She would usually skim along the top walkway, where it was slightly less busy, but Dreckly took the longer path. It required Ben and her to weave through families and flapping birds, yet it offered them protection as well. They were less likely to be seen from inside the market. Even if you were looking for them, you would only be able to get a glimpse before she had the key in the lock to the jetty gate and the two of them racing towards her boat.

'Who was that? Dreckly, hey! Talk to me, what did you see? Who has you so terrified?'

'Why did you have to bring an olive branch today, Ben? Of all days!'

'What do—'

'People know you, especially *Treize* people. If they see you talking with me, they start to pay attention and – fuck! I'm not wearing contacts.'

Dreckly yanked him on to the boat after her, pushing him deep inside and closing the door behind her.

'Why would you wear contacts? You have the most beautiful blue eyes I've ever seen.'

She ignored him as she stared out the windows, searching the mass of hundreds – maybe thousands – of people for that face she was sure she recognised. The windows were tinted, so there was no chance of anyone catching her watching, but she didn't see the Kind Guard pop up again.

'Ah, that's it – isn't it? Your eyes don't disguise you.'

'No,' she muttered, gaze still roaming the market crowd. 'They don't. They're one of the few parts of me that is actually memorable.'

'That's not true.'

She spun around. 'This person would only need to recognise a few things about me to be suspicious. My eyes would probably confirm those suspicions.'

'I've never seen you wear contacts.'

'No, I've always just had my natural eye colour since I came to Sydney. I . . . I got lazy.'

'You'd switch it up in other places?'

'Always.'

'And this person would notice if you hadn't?'

'They haven't seen me since I was a child, but they'd probably notice me the same way I noticed them: physicality.'

'You . . . you're not sure if it's them?'

She turned back to the windows and kept watching, arms crossed over her chest. 'I'm certain it's them. It moved like them. It looked like them. Slightly different hair and the beard was new but . . .'

Dreckly saw Ben in the reflection slip a phone back into the pocket of his overalls – no doubt ready to call the pack – as his shoulders relaxed slightly.

'The only person who could recognise you from physicality alone is a Praetorian Guard soldier. Are they a threat just to you or to all of us?'

'Just to me,' she answered, before rebutting him. 'And that's not true: I recognised physicality and I'm not Guard.'

He shrugged. 'You could be for all I know. And you *think* you recognised them. You're not certain.'

Dreckly let out a deep breath, her hands running through the long strands of her ponytail as she combed out several knots with her fingertips. The banshee situation had her on edge. Shit, it had everyone on edge. Did she see what she thought she saw? Or was it her paranoia? Praetorian Guard soldiers were immortal, so if he hadn't been killed in the line of duty there was no reason to assume he wouldn't still be alive.

She'd thought he was Irish, with the slightest twang in his accent all those years ago. It could make him a perfect candidate to hunt down errant banshees, given his familiarity with their kind. If she was unlucky enough for Lorcan to be in the same city as her, she was lucky enough that he wasn't there for her. If he was there at all.

She felt a hand on her shoulder, Ben seemingly cautious about touching her as he slowly turned Dreckly around to face him. He was much closer than she had expected, Dreckly unable to stop her eyes from being drawn to the scars that marked his chest. His fingertips traced the concave around her eyes, the act so soothing and calming to her she was unable to move as her scalp tingled. He was hypnotising her, was that possible?

'You're in trouble, aren't you?' he whispered.

The werewolf was taller than her and she arched her neck upwards to meet the yellowish brown of his eyes.

'All my life.'

His hands were on her neck now, just like she'd imagined they had been, but in reality and not her fantasy it was like he was making sure she stayed planted on the spot.

'Let me help you. Let us help you.'

She shook her head. 'That comes at a cost, Ben.'

The life she had made for herself in Sydney was as close as she'd come to other supernaturals in a long time and even then she was still a few steps removed. But Dreckly had learned it was important to her. It was healthy: much healthier than complete isolation. Sometimes the things that were good for us were a little bit dangerous as well. Accepting help from Ben and the others was *too* dangerous. She'd be indebted to them and Dreckly knew they'd collect.

'Not everything's a trap.' He smirked, his teeth a flash of white against his dark skin.

'No, just you,' she replied.

She pulled him towards her by the strap of his overalls, the readiness of his kiss telling her that he wanted this as much as she did. They had all the time in the world now, an exuberant amount compared to the elevator ride, but they were rushed as she unclipped his clothes and he tore at hers. The adrenaline of fear was still coursing through her veins and she'd learned there were few better outlets for it than sex.

'Where?' he asked and she pointed off to the bedroom, Ben fumbling behind him for the doorknob as she pushed him backwards.

He fell down on to the bed, Dreckly on top of him as they rolled around and interlocked their bodies in the new space. There was a condom thrown at him and he caught it in the air, tearing the foil so quickly it was a marvel. She was rough with him, throwing his hands where she wanted them to be and he reciprocated in kind. Sex was not a solution, but it could be a numbing balm to the both of them and she felt the throb of loneliness begging to be filled as he kissed her. For once, she was able to focus on the present instead of the past.

'Is this okay?' he asked, the curve of his hand pressing gently against her throat. She nodded, letting out a soft moan as he pushed himself inside of her and she relished the feeling of being *full*.

'*Yes*,' she replied, willing him to tighten his grip. '*Yes*, yes, YES.'

Dreckly wasn't able to say much more for a while. Frankly, that was just how she wanted it.

She had learned to read the stars when she was in Hawaii, the art of wayfaring passed down from generation to generation among the people she knew there. They didn't sail the oceans with the purpose of exploring new lands anymore, but they could still take you on a journey by navigating with the stars. Ben's body was like a constellation in that way, with the stars replaced by scars. She couldn't read them yet, but she was learning as her fingers traced a shape from a long one on his hip to a jagged hole on his torso.

'This one?'

He tilted his head to look at which she meant. 'Same guy, actually. He was a usurper; that mea—'

'I know what it means.'

'Heh, okay. He wanted to be alpha of the pack. Thought he could do a better job, so he challenged me for it.'

'How old were you?'

'Twenty-one. Too young but I'd taken over as soon as Sushmita was jailed so I had a few years under my belt.'

She stiffened just at the mention of Vankila, trying to pick another subject quickly so he wouldn't notice. 'Because of the Outskirt Wars, because the Kapoor pack was involved in all that?'

'Yeah. Shit, she has been there so long now ... I can't imagine what it's like; not to see the outside world for over a decade.'

'It would be hard for her, I imagine. She knows what's out there.'

Dreckly was off in her own thoughts, her acrylic nails running through the hair that seemed to cover every inch of Ben's defined torso. They were naked, a sheet wrapped around the mounds of their bodies as they lay there on her bed.

'Have you been to prison?'

His question surprised her and she lifted her head off his chest, looking to see how serious he was. He brushed a strand of her hair back behind her ear, the length finally out of her ponytail and laying across the pillow liked a black, silky snake.

'That's it, isn't it? That's why you're so careful with everything. You don't want to go back.'

'Don't try and read me like one of your other flings. It won't work, wolf.'

'I'm right though, aren't I? That's why you wouldn't help us break other supes out. We're all coming together, you know. You could too.'

Dreckly scoffed. 'Seven misfits teaming up for good? This isn't an Akira Kurosawa movie, Ben.'

'Akira who?'

'*Seven Sam*—ah, forget it.'

'Don't make this an age thing.'

'Age is no excuse for not having seen a Kurosawa classic.'

'Fine, have you ever seen a Gurinder Chadha movie?'

'You're damn right I have. *Bend It Like Beckham* is a perfect film.'

'Crap.'

She laughed, delighting in the frustration on his face. 'Keep testing me all night long. I guarantee whatever movie you name, I've seen it.'

'That much of a film buff, ay?'

'I love cinema.'

'*Cinema*,' he repeated. 'Shit, even the way you say that makes me believe you.'

There were a series of enormous bangs and Dreckly leapt up, reaching for the knife she kept under her mattress when Ben stopped her. He had jumped too, hands shifting to werewolf claws and back again in a matter of seconds.

'Fireworks,' he told her. 'Listen.'

He was right. Her heart was still pounding in her chest, but her grip loosened around the handle of the blade as she listened to the rhythmic explosions happening off in the distance. Ben checked his phone, the light illuminating his face.

'It's the nine o'clock ones.'

'For the kids,' she replied, getting out of bed properly for the first time. With the exception of a few brief bathroom visits, they hadn't left her room *in hours*. They'd completely run through her supply of condoms and she wasn't the slightest bit mad about it.

'Where are you going?' Ben asked, as she wrapped a silk dressing gown around herself. The need in his voice made her smirk.

'You can see the fireworks from up top.'

Dreckly expected him to follow her out and he did, joining her just a few minutes later with a blanket as she leaned against the glass that would usually be used to scout the direction she'd be sailing in. She'd said 'up top' but it was barely an extra level on the *Titanic II*: just four stairs to the vessel's central navigating system, engine controls, and steering wheel. There wasn't even somewhere to sit up there, Dreckly having little use for it. If you skirted around the side very carefully, the best vantage point would see you sitting at the bow as fireworks on the Anzac Bridge continued to explode like colourful pompoms.

'Here,' Ben said, offering her some of the blanket.

'Too warm.' She shook her head, but she handed him one of the two ciders she had grabbed instead. He smirked, using the railing to pop the top.

'Too right.'

They sat there for a long while, sipping their drinks and watching the grand finale as colours spiralled up into the clear sky then exploded into a thousand glittering pieces. The reflection against the black water made it look like they were getting twice the show for half the price, the fireworks igniting endlessly.

'They're doing experiments on them,' he said, the lightness she'd come to know in Ben's voice over the past few hours entirely gone.

She cast him a sideways look, but he didn't meet her gaze.

'They didn't want to tell you, didn't want to give you any more information than was necessary.'

'Information that could hurt them.'

He nodded. 'That's what they didn't say: the reason they've been abducting *us*, all of us for years, was to cut us open and look at our insides.'

'How many years?'

'What?' Ben looked surprised at her question. 'I tell you the Treize are performing live lobotomies on innocent people and you want a timeline?'

'Yes,' Dreckly affirmed. 'That's important, not to the justice of the thing but the why.'

He let out a long, unsteady sigh as he thought about replying. 'Two years, far as we can tell. Something happened, *something* changed. It was just a few at first, a few outliers so it would be difficult to notice they were missing.'

'Ghouls,' she said. 'Vamps. Demons. Elementals. Rogue werewolves. Witches.'

'Sprites,' Ben added. Just his tone told Dreckly that he didn't have any inkling about what she really was. 'Any type of supernatural that would be on their own and unmissed for as long as possible, that's who vanished. They've gotten more desperate in the past six months, sloppy to the point that suspicions have become confirmations.'

'To what end?' she pushed. Ben opened his mouth to tell her, but hesitated. She could see that he worried he'd already revealed too much, the line blurring between who was using who. They fell silent again, their respective troubles the invisible third companion as they sipped their drinks and watched the fireworks.

'Your dressing gown is the same colour as your eyes,' Ben remarked. She caught him looking at her with the same hunger he'd displayed below deck, then glanced down at the gaping split in her robe that meant most of its contents were exposed to him. She readjusted, tightening it around herself.

'Nah, don't do that,' he muttered, his own torso bare as he slipped a free arm from the blanket and reached over to her. He traced the shapes of her body that were outlined under the silk, her nipples stiffening through the fabric at his touch. He smirked at her reaction, lazily undoing the ties and reaching inside her robe as he kissed her. Dreckly's own kiss slowed as she heard the metallic clank of the jetty gate slamming shut, one type of panic being replaced by another as she pulled back.

'Shit!'

'What?'

'Sssshh, quiet. Stay up here.'

'What? Why?'

'Because I don't want Wyck to know you're here,' she whispered, hastily wrapping herself up again as she climbed over Ben's eager lap. 'He's coming down the jetty as we speak.'

'Where are you going?'

'I have a meeting.'

'With who?'

'None of your business,' Dreckly snapped. 'Wait thirty minutes after I've gone, then leave.'

'I – uh . . .'

She left him stammering where he was, sliding down the railing to the main level just as Wyck rolled on board.

'You ready?' he asked, taking a look at her. 'Oh, you're not. Did you forget?'

'No. Kind of.'

'You called this meeting.'

'I know, I know – fuck, just give me two secs.'

It really only took her a few minutes to throw her hair up into a bun, spritz herself with perfume, apply deodorant, throw on a thong, before she was pulling on the straps of a loose cotton jumpsuit and dashing up the stairs. The longer she spent on the boat, the more likely it was Wyck might spot Ben's errant shirt across the other side of the kitchen or notice the number of bottle caps on the counter. Time was of the essence and she knew that with Ben's superior werewolf hearing, he'd know when they were gone and it was safe to move. There were a pair of white tennis shoes near the door and she quickly jammed her feet into them. As she marched up the jetty after Wyck, she realised she'd forgotten a bra but there was little point in turning back. She owned four versions of this exact jumpsuit in varying shades of black and navy, so that would provide her with enough cover.

'You're walking funny,' Wyck noted, casting her a sideways glance as he wheeled towards one of the fish market's side entrances.

'Huh?'

'And you look frazzled.'

'It's a new vibe I'm trying.'

He laughed. 'Is it because Ben Kapoor came by today?'

Dreckly threw him a look and he shrugged.

'I was offsite. Zhang told me. If you want—'

'It was fine,' she interrupted, swiping her fob in front of an electronic reader that gave them access to the building after hours. 'He apologised profusely, actually meant it, I told him to fuck off, there you have it.'

'Hmmm.'

The markets always seemed creepy to her at night, not so much because of the darkness but rather the emptiness. If they weren't crammed full of people, it just didn't feel right. They took an enormous, industrial lift up to the second floor where Zhang's mother ran a very popular Chinese restaurant. It had closed early tonight, however, with Dreckly holding open the doors for Wyck and revealing a select clientele. It was most of the members of the Ravens Motorcycle Club, along with Zhang, some key staff, his mother Jia, and about a dozen other business owners from the markets. Most of them ran legal operations, a few dabbled in hybrid structures like her, some were outright fronts. All were people she had established some kind of business relationship with over the seven years since she'd been there. And all were aware there were things out there other than 'human'.

'Thank you for coming tonight,' she said, sitting down at the spot that had been clearly left for her at the enormous round table.

Wyck rolled around to join his colleagues, who were at the back and wearing their cuts for once. It had been the M.C.'s idea to have the discussion she proposed on New Year's Eve, when there was so much else going on the focus would be elsewhere.

'As I'm sure you've noticed, there has been a lot of unusual activity happening on the outskirts of your businesses. Given I'm the one with the most knowledge about all of that, I suggested this be a fitting way to address some of those concerns.'

'What happened?' Zhang asked. 'And are we under threat?'

'Not right now,' she said, answering the second question first. 'But there are extra eyes looking where there weren't before, which is why I've shut down my business in the short term.'

'Looking for our illegal operations?'

'No, looking for anything *other*. But that doesn't exclude you from the threat: they're desperate and causing a ruckus, so I wouldn't underestimate them following any thread they could back to its source. Hence the caution.'

'What does that mean for us?' asked Chino, President of Ravens M.C.

'If you have any big shipments coming in, *any* kind of valuable operation, pause it. Delay it by at least a month. The people that have caused this issue will either be caught by then or the search to find them will have moved offshore.'

There was muttering around the room as the parties gathered began talking amongst themselves, theorising what they could do to make this possible.

'There's more,' Dreckly said, taking a napkin from in front of her and using a pen at the table to draw the Askari symbol. 'If you see anyone walking around with this tattoo on their wrist, just here, take note. You'll be seeing more of them, so too those wearing an Egyptian ankh symbol around their neck in silver.'

That identified the immortal Custodians: they were less of a threat and less likely, but the more she could tell these people the better.

'What age are we talkin'?' Chino asked. 'What do they look like?'

'Any age, any gender, any race, it doesn't matter. They could and should look like anyone and those are just the people you will notice. The good ones, the ones you need to worry about, will slip by undetected.'

'That's why you're saying caution at all times,' Wyck mused.

'Exactly.'

Dreckly stayed there for more than a full hour, Jia restocking the table several times with fresh dumplings and small plates to keep everyone fed. She may have been hospitable and small in stature, but Dreckly knew – just like everyone did – that Jia ran the show. Wyck had even told her once that it was the old woman who coordinated with the M.C. directly, not Zhang. She did her best to answer as many questions as she could, providing them with as much information as possible. When she stepped back out into the fresh air just before midnight, Wyck and Chino by her side, she felt somewhat better about the whole situation.

'That was necessary,' she said, as she walked slowly with them towards the car park. 'Right?'

'We need to know as much as we can,' Chino agreed. 'Keep us out of the shit.'

'We've been seeing a lot of new faces around,' Wyck noted. 'Being able to put that into context helps.'

She paused at the jetty gate, where they'd go their way and she'd go hers. 'You all off to some loose party, I assume?'

'Off to break one up,' Wyck snorted. 'Chino's daughter has thrown a rager that's gotten out of hand.'

'If we don't make it there by midnight, I'm worried someone's gonna get stabbed,' the man agreed.

She laughed, waving them off as she unlocked the gate and made her way down to the boat. Dreckly had told Ben to leave and she would have assumed that he did, her abrupt ending of their romantic dalliance enough to force anyone's exit. The lights were off on the *Titanic II*, but there was enough external light for Dreckly to navigate her way into the kitchen where she grabbed another cider. She hesitated at taking one for him, admitting to herself that she actually wanted him to still be there. Not that she was overly into the werewolf, but there was something to be said for coming home and not being alone. It had been so long since she'd done that. She thought she heard movement in her office and she grabbed the other bottle, smiling as she felt the air particles.

'Ben?' she called, stepping inside just as the needle dropped and a record began playing. It was the Andrews Sisters. Dreckly felt the cool glass of both cider bottles slip from her hands at the sound. They didn't smash, just landed with an unceremonious *thud* on the ground with the beverages bubbling over her toes and into the carpet. The lamp at her desk clicked on, revealing the Kind Guard sitting in *her* chair with his feet propped up on *her* desk. He stared at her for what felt like hours, Dreckly saying nothing as she returned his stare. Hers, in actual fact, was more like a glare.

'I wasn't sure it was you at first,' he said, leaning back as he watched her. 'It had been so long for both of us, you know? And it has been a weird year, so I thought, "No, Lorcan, you're imagining it".'

'Turn this off,' she growled, hating that out of all the records he'd chosen to play, it was this one. The Andrews Sisters was not meant for him.

'But then I started to do the math,' he mused, taking his feet off her desk and planting them down on the ground. 'You don't age like regular people do, neither do I, mind you. Sprites don't even age like werewolves or demons: you age like goblins, about one year for every three human ones.'

'Turn. This. *Off.*'

'Your parents went inside on February fourteen, eighteen eighty-eight. You were born six months later. That would make you about forty-four by my calculations.'

She gave nothing away. Dreckly had searched for years for answers to seemingly simple questions other people had the privilege to grow up with, like, when was her birthday? How old was she? What was her star sign? Now she had two things she didn't have before: a year and a month.

'Don't you want to ask about your father?' the Kind Guard questioned.

'No. I know he's dead.'

He tilted his head, curious at that answer. 'How?'

'Because the flowers don't grow the same.'

'Ah, well, you would notice that difference. I barely noticed you, you've done such a good job of surviving and blending.'

'Evidently not good enough.'

'You've eluded the Treize for over a century. Not many people can say that.'

She closed her eyes, sensing a presence at her back. He hadn't come alone, because of course he hadn't. Lorcan had underestimated her father once. This was someone who learned from their mistakes. As the lamp clicked off and she felt hands come down upon her, Dreckly knew it was stupid. Yet she couldn't help herself as she concentrated her power on blowing over the record player so that it smashed and the Andrews Sisters were cut short mid-'Ferryboat Serenade'. That was more important to her than anything else.

After all, Dreckly never stood a chance.

Chapter 9

The opportunity to maintain my cover, maintain my life, and stay under the radar by avoiding suspicion presented itself in the most unlikely of vessels. An actress began visiting the florist regularly, neither Meili or I knowing who she was but Li Jun recognising her from posters that were plastered outside a nearby theatre.

'That's "*Rough House Rosie*",' he said in Mandarin, so she and her chaperone wouldn't know we were talking about them.

'What does that mean?' his wife snapped.

'She's a screen star, from the pictures!'

That was unusual. The actual stars rarely visited the shop themselves, but there was something about the way the woman carried herself. I observed her over the bouquet I was assembling in an old vase that I'd picked up at a second-hand store.

She strolled over, watching me as I carefully placed the flowers and bridging greenery one at a time. Los Angeles was full of two types of people: those who didn't want to be observed and those who liked to loudly proclaim they didn't want to be observed. I suspected this woman was the former rather than the latter, so I kept my eyes on the task at hand.

'What's that you're doing there?' she asked, voice raspy.

I looked up as the woman removed her sunglasses, deep eyes and dramatic brows meeting my gaze.

'I'm making a bouquet.'

'And how! You do it like that? So slowly? You don't just—'

She mimed throwing something in my general direction, with a descending whistle for added impact.

'Placement is important,' I chuckled. 'Round or domed makes a difference and it takes a lot of work to put things in one by one, but you have to think of the design people will be viewing from the top.'

She leaned over the bouquet, inspecting my handiwork as I kept my eyes trained on the vase.

'*Oh*, I see. How do you know what to choose?'

'Depends on the person's budget.'

'Ah ha! Who's got the berries,' the woman said with a wink.

'And what they want; sometimes they give specific instructions like colour or only natives. Otherwise it's a pattern like anything else: five, three, then five again.'

'You're a very chatty dame. What's your name?'

'Tulip.'

'Tulip! Zowie, what a beautiful name! Lionel, did you hear that? Her name is *Tulip*! Wouldn't that make a great stage name?'

'I know Tulip,' the man said, nodding politely at her. He was one of our early clients, coming right at 8 a.m. and picking up several bouquets for different starlets he looked after. I'd never actually seen him with one, though. This was new. 'How are you doing today?'

'Very well, Mr Gardin. Meili has your daily order at the counter for you, whenever you're ready.'

'Wonderful, thank you.'

He made his way towards the register, exchanging pleasantries as he paid. He had a clipped British accent that made him stand out and I wondered exactly how he'd ended up in Hollywood.

'He's not exactly Wheeler and Woolsey, is he?' the lady said, watching me work. 'I was bored, you see. I wanted to come out on his daily errands, see what a day in the life of Lionel Gardin looked like: Hollywood fixer to the stars! He thinks I'm a sap.'

She said it so dramatically, her expression bringing the words to life as she held up her gloved hands and moved them through the air like they were splashed on a billboard only she could see. I giggled, the woman delighted by my reaction.

'He really trips his muscle, keeping us all in line. Even heard a rumour he was a British *spy* in the war. Might have even done a jolt in prison!'

Of the five people in the store, I was quite certain I was the only person who had done a jolt.

'He comes by every day,' I remarked, keeping the conversation moving. 'Collecting at least half a dozen bouquets. He's our best customer.'

'One of those bouquets is always for me. I just *adore* fresh flowers, every day if I can spare the kale. Actually, I made my manager work it into my Paramount contract, a floral budget! Can you believe it? The things they'll do to keep you on a leash.'

'The hydrangeas?'

She looked surprised. 'Excuse me?'

'Are the hydrangeas yours?'

'Oh! Yes, yes they are.' The lady looked puzzled. 'How did you know?'

'It just seemed right for you,' I murmured, smiling.

'Golly, how perceptive. How old are you, Tulip?'

'Eighteen,' I answered, the lie coming off my tongue so easily.

'Eighteen! I remember what it was like to be eighteen. I hated it. Desperate to get away from my parents, desperate to get away from New York, desperate to be a woman. Tell me, do you do private work for clients?'

'I'm sorry, ma'am, what do you mean?'

'Say, could I hire you? To fit out my home every day with fresh flowers, whatever you think I would like? It would save Lionel the trip.'

'What would?' the man asked, joining us.

'Tulip here is going to be my *private* florist!' she proclaimed. 'Make sure that Silver Lake swamp is my own personal heaven, aren't you, darlin'?'

My gaze flicked to Meili, who was nodding enthusiastically and throwing her thumbs up. Li Jun seemed more reserved.

'Of course, we often do house calls,' I lied.

'Nonsense, house calls! You can come live in my guest house. Wouldn't that be swell, Lionel?'

'You can't have an undesirable living in your house just so it's adequately stocked with flowers, Clara.'

'Undesirable' was a word only *ever* used in that context by men who looked like Lionel: white, blond, all-American . . .

until he opened his mouth. It meant foreigner and it wasn't as derogatory as some of the other slurs I'd heard, but it didn't help me like him much either.

'Why can't I? Who says I can't? I'm not Evelyn Brent. I'm *Clara Bow*, silent screen star! I will do what I very well please for as long as I have the mazumas.'

With a huff, she stormed out of the shop. Lionel followed behind her, muttering an apology. I thought that would be the last we heard of that, but Clara returned the next day asking whether I had thought about her offer. I had, actually. The whole family had discussed it that night at dinner and afterwards Li Jun had taken us all to the pictures. It was the first film I had ever seen: *Rough House Rosie*. Clara Bow was the star and hilarious as a scrappy young woman infiltrating society.

'If she comes back, you say yes,' Meili told me. 'Those Hollywood types are loose with their morals, but they're also loose with their money.'

'This could be a great opportunity for you,' Li Jun agreed. An opportunity to leave is what he didn't say, but it was implied. An opportunity for a fresh scene with a fresh start and fresh faces who hadn't had the chance to wonder why I didn't age quite like they did.

When the silent movie star asked for my answer, the woman I was pretending to be said she would be 'delighted'. And I was, at first.

Clara lived in a fairly modest two-level home in Silver Lake, which was an area I had made a point to avoid since I first arrived in Los Angeles. It was rife with supernatural beings and I had theorised it was probably safest to stay away from my own kind. Wherever there were arachnia or demons or shifters or goblins, there were the Treize. There were the Askari. There were the Custodians. There were the people who had caught my parents in the first place: the Praetorian Guard.

That was the sacrifice I made to stay safe and unnoticed. In my mind, it was worth it, and I knew my father would have agreed with the decision. And as Clara Bow's live-in florist, there were few questions asked of me. The proximity to Clara's star power brought access to a world I had never seen before: Hollywood. The *real* Hollywood.

Silver Lake was just far enough from the Paramount lot so Clara felt like she wasn't still at work when she left, but close enough they could get her there quickly when she was late, according to Lionel. Which was often.

I stayed in Chinatown for the first week of my employment, Clara sending a car each day to pick me up and bring whatever floral arrangements I had selected. It came late by my standards, not until 9 a.m. each morning, so I continued doing my usual tasks with Li Jun and Meili.

Clara would be finishing her breakfast when I arrived, perusing the choices I had made for that day with interest. Then she would leave for the studio, Lionel often dragging her there while the resident housekeeper Rosa would clean up breakfast and begin her chores.

I would clear out the flowers from the day before, bundling them up for Rosa and her family. Clara never asked where they went and didn't seem to care how I disposed of them, so it didn't make sense to waste them. Once the canvas was blank, I would rebuild dozens of new arrangements for her.

'I'm feeling fancy free, Tulip,' Clara would say. 'Make that happen.'

I had to interpret that as best I could.

'I'm moody! I'm sad, I'm forlorn and broken-hearted! Make it work.'

So I did. Lionel gave me other jobs, such as clearing the house of booze and pills when I found them.

'She has scared Rosa into doing her bidding,' he told me. 'We can't let that happen to you too. If the studio find nose candy, hooch, or both, she'll be fired. Tobacco is fine. Diet pills are fine. But no hard narcotics.'

I had to ask Delun what that meant and was shocked by the answer. My shock dimmed the longer I worked for Clara, eventually taking up the guest room she had offered and squirreling away every additional cent. I still woke early, having breakfast with Meili and Li Jun every day as I picked up the order of flowers. I missed them, though. Even though they were just a short ride away, I preferred the closeness of their family home. I missed the apartment, the smells, the laughter, the music, the people I recognised in the neighbourhood every day.

'Children can't stay with their parents forever,' Delun had told me. He was married now, to an American girl named Ethel who I didn't think much of. They lived in Burbank, and Meili and Li Jun were looking at moving there too. The talk about the whole of Chinatown getting demolished to build 'Union Station' was becoming more than talk. Shops were getting vandalised and crime was getting rougher. He was pushing for them to close the business and move next door to him.

Delun was right about me moving out and moving on. It didn't stop it being any less hard, however. A lot of times, it was as if Clara forgot I was there. Others, I had to weather her mood swings like a small boat in the middle of a stormy sea. Both things had their challenges, yet I got to meet lots of interesting people. There were parties, *so many parties*. Clara was always throwing them and attending them, often with me at her side. I was somewhat of a novelty, often hearing myself referred to as Clara's 'little oriental girl sidekick'.

'Fuck 'em,' Clara had said, slurring her words in the back of a cab on our way home from the premiere of her latest film, *Wings*. We'd gone hunting for a dizzy-water parlour afterwards, Clara proclaiming how badly she needed to get greased. 'They didn't like me when I first moved here, still don't. I'm too crass, too rough, too unpolite for fine society. It's all bullshit, Tulip. They're all bullshit.'

Her breath might have been perfumed with whiskey, but there was more than just kindness to her words; there was truth.

'You go to school?' Clara asked.

'No.'

'Good! You don't need it. I went to school; where did that get me? In fights and trouble. Life is your teacher, Tulip.'

I laughed. 'Then I'm passing with flying colours.'

'You're damn right! Tomorrow, tomorrow you're coming with me to the studio.'

'I am?'

'You are! Zowie, this is Hollywood, baby!'

Weirdly, the first proper supernatural I crossed paths with in Hollywood happened to be on the Paramount lot, where I would deliver a fresh bouquet to Clara's trailer every day. It was the kind of place where there was a melting of other languages and accents, some real, some fake. The security guards at the gate all spoke Spanish and my conversations with them helped improve my vocabulary *and* allowed me to learn all the dirty slang my father would never teach me.

It was useful. And if I could stay useful, I could stay employed. That was important now that Meili and Li Jun had officially shut down their business and moved to Burbank, just like Delun had wanted. He said it was good for them, to retire. What he didn't know was they maintained their very exclusive list of clientele, keeping them busy and me amused as they ran a smaller, condensed version of their shop out of their back-yard. It also meant they kept making their own money, which Meili and Li Jun were insistent they do after I had Lionel help me sort out the paperwork to buy the Burbank house in their name with the nest egg I had been growing.

It was handy for me too, as I purchased all of Clara's floral needs through them. My standing order grew, with other cast members and Paramount executives wanting 'the flower girl to work her magic' in their offices and trailers too. It was there that I first met Dorothy, who had been working her way through various departments: from script and costuming, to props and set design. She'd drawn my eye because she dressed like a man, wearing impeccably tailored suits and wide-legged pants that made a *whooshing* noise as she marched with purpose across the lot.

'How'd you learn to do this, kid?' Dorothy said one day, leaning against the wall of a soundstage as she took a cigarette break.

'My father had . . . a green thumb, is that what you call it here?'

The woman nodded, a cloud of cigarette smoke blowing out through her barely parted lips.

'And he was an artist, so it uses essentially the same principles,' I answered, unpacking three bouquets from a small trailer I had attached to the rear of my bicycle. It was the easiest way to get around the lot, especially if you needed to be at an opposite sound stage as quickly as possible. The ever-ringing bells of bicycles as crew pedalled from one end of Paramount to the other was something I associated as just part of the studio's soundtrack now.

'Was it hard to learn?'

'The principles, no. The physical stuff, yeah.'

'Physical?'

'There's this thing called spiralling – do you have cigarettes?'

Dorothy offered me the supply, which were all held in a beautiful hand-painted holder. I demonstrated by tucking the long cylinders between the fingers on my left hand.

'It looks simple enough: you hold a stem between your thumb and your forefingers. Like this.'

'I get it.'

'Right, but you have to keep adding to it, you keep adding to the spiral. You find the narrowest point and that's the end that sits in the vase and makes the flowers sit the right way. Well, the right way to display nicely. The woman who taught me said it's best to think of it like a witch's broom.'

I packaged the cigarettes back up again, returning the case to Dorothy.

'Those paintings in Clara's trailer, they're yours too, aren't they?'

I nodded; it was a hobby of mine and something that made me feel connected to the memory of my father. Using his techniques, painting the world as he'd seen it, it made me feel close to him.

'You ever thought about set decoration, Tulip?'

'Uh . . .' I stalled; it still took a beat to respond to my fake name – Tulip Han – rather than the one I was born with, even after all these years. 'No, I don't really know what that is.'

'Come on, let's ankle,' she said, stamping out her cigarette with the tip of her polished brogue. 'This will only take a second.'

I followed Dorothy around the side of the sound stage, pausing in front of a door that had a huge light affixed above it. It was red, which meant they were filming right at that moment. A few seconds later, it switched to green – someone had called cut – and Dorothy twisted the door handle and led me into the darkness inside.

'Reset!' a voice shouted. 'Reset and let's go again!'

Dorothy pulled me out of the way of a rolling rack of clothes that was rocketing forwards, pushed blindly by a woman with a cigarette dangling out of her mouth and thick, cat-eye glasses. It was hot inside the sound stage and I fanned myself as I bent down under an enormous lighting rig. I was brought to a stop in front of what looked like an enormous, two-storey house . . . except that it was cut in half.

There were three small wooden steps that led up into the interior and various people were moving around inside. Turning around, I looked out from the house to where all of the cameras were positioned in the expansive, dark warehouse.

'These are for the interiors,' Dorothy explained. 'This is what the internal parts of the house look like. They'll shoot exteriors somewhere else, in Beverly Hills, I think.'

Seeing my blank expression, she added: 'The outside of the house.'

'Oh.'

'It's all hooey, Tulip. Bullshit. The trick is to make the audience believe it's not. Now look, that's Mildred over there. See what she's doing?'

The individual she pointed out was an African-American woman I had seen around the lot countless times, yet what had me transfixed in the moment was something else entirely: she was quietly, softly, speaking demon to another woman who appeared to be her assistant. What's more was that her colleague spoke flawless demon back.

'Dusting?' I replied, realising I'd paused for just a fraction too long.

'She and Georgette are reapplying a portion of the wallpaper, which has come off between takes. They work with the production designer – Michel, in the corner – and they bring this place to life. This was built inside here outta nothing. They need to make it reflect the story, the characters, you name it.'

'So they build stuff?'

'Or buy it. Or make it. Or paint it. That combining of artistic principles you talked about? That's what this job is. You'd be good it.'

I looked over her shoulder, where a man was yelling at two of his colleagues and waving a rolled-up script wildly in the air.

'The director's the boss, right?'

'One of them.' Dorothy nodded, following my gaze. 'There are producers and studio heads above that. The boss depends on where the Hoover dollars are coming from.'

'I don't want him to be my boss,' I said, looking pointedly around the set. There were only four women present who weren't actresses: Dorothy, Mildred, Georgette and myself. And everyone else was white. 'Clara's my boss and she's not exactly easy, but I sure as hell like her a lot better than him.'

'What if I was your boss?'

'You? You're a woman. I don't know any women directors.'

'They're out there, not working for the studios, but they're out there. Tell ya what, I'll make you a deal: if I get my way and end up directing a movie one day, you come and work for me.'

I laughed. It was a fairy tale, but Dorothy and her demon-speaking associates had me intrigued.

'You've got a deal,' I said with a grin as I shook her hand, quite confident it would never happen.

Chapter 10

Present

The thought 'oh good, I'm not in a cell' shouldn't be something that brings joy to most people. It brought joy to Dreckly, however, as she began to regain consciousness and take stock of her surroundings. Glass, *fucking* glass, all around her as she pressed her hands against the surface of the long cylinder she was being held inside. It was like a giant test tube she realised, initially thinking it was whatever she had been drugged with creating some kind of hallucination in her mind. The longer she was conscious the longer she realised what she was seeing was actually reality.

It was narrow enough so she could only sit down when curled up in a vertical foetal position, which needless to say was incredibly uncomfortable. She was meant to stand upright for as long as possible and Dreckly did her best not to descend into a claustrophobic panic. After all, she wasn't the only one.

The room itself was dark, but directly above her was a low light that illuminated not just her but dozens of other beings encased exactly like she was. She understood the purpose of the XXL test tubes then: it was so they could control the environment. There was a selkie next to her and they obviously needed to be submerged in water, whereas the fire being of some kind – whether they were an elemental or demon, she couldn't be sure – was constantly inflaming themselves head-to-toe in an attempt to escape. They'd been there way longer than she had, clearly, and had continually been trying to break out. Unsuccessfully. That was one of the reasons she cooled it initially.

There was no point physically reacting and panicking when it was likely they were all being watched anyway. She didn't want to give the Treize or anyone the satisfaction of seeing her panic. The other reason was because she wanted to conserve her energy. There was clearly air being filtered in from somewhere, but with that exception the tube was tight. There was no give, no weakness that she could exploit, no point in trying *anything* until they took her out of there and . . . did what?

The Treize have been abducting these supernaturals. The words of the witch, Kala Tully, came swimming back to her as she pivoted on the spot, counting the number of other creatures she could see and guessing the ones she couldn't by the space left to the wall. Thirty-eight, she figured, or thereabouts, as not every case was full. She'd joked about the *Seven Samurai*-assembly of do-gooders, refusing to help them because of the risk to her own safety. Now here she was: abducted, drugged, and imprisoned. The irony wasn't lost on her.

Live lobotomies. That's what Ben had said, his voice and their time together on her boat already seeming like a lifetime ago. It could have been hours in the past or days, she had no idea, since they had been wrapped up together. And that's when – despite her best intentions – Dreckly felt the panic begin to curdle up inside of herself. *Live lobotomies.*

That's what they were doing here. That's what they were going to do to *her.*

'No no no no no,' she murmured, the words all a stream of fear as she realised she was in the exact place she'd spent her whole life trying to avoid. 'No no no no no no.'

'Hey, it's okay.'

She jumped, just the presence of another voice enough to do that to her. It was the selkie.

'You're staying much calmer than the others,' he said.

'I'm panicking,' she snapped, not afraid to admit that's exactly what was happening no matter how hard she'd tried to fight it.

'You're not panicking as much as I was.'

'Uh huh,' she muttered, the chorus of 'no no no no' still echoing in her head.

'It's okay,' he continued, kindness rich in his tone. 'It's okay to panic.'

She was about to retort that she *knew it was okay to panic, damn it!* but Dreckly stopped herself. That wasn't her. Even in this horrible situation, that wasn't who she was.

'There's lots of us here with you, though, just know that. It's always scariest when you first wake up.'

She assessed him in the tube he was floating inside of, water covering every inch of him until just above his head where he bobbed there.

'As opposed to . . .' Dreckly murmured, having regained enough of her composure to attempt a proper sentence.

'I'm Amos,' he said, pressing his slightly webbed hand to the glass. She smiled, returning the gesture as she placed her own fingers against the glass.

'Nice to meet you. How long have you been here, Amos?' Her eyes ran over the marks she could see covering his arms and torso. These weren't like Ben's. These were fresh.

'A year, I think.'

She blanched. '*A year?!*'

'I think,' he corrected. 'It's hard to tell.'

'In this . . . tube?'

'I was in a larger pool at first, with others.'

'Where are they?'

He fell silent for a moment, looking down towards the end of his long, muscular tail. It was telling.

'They would take us out, one by one, return us, and then . . . the others stopped coming back. One by one.'

He said it calmly, all matter of fact. Maybe that's what made it all the more horrific to Dreckly, who could feel the fear working its way through her veins.

'Maybe they're okay though,' Amos said, brightening up. 'There's lot of different places they could have gone to. I was transferred here from somewhere else, you know.'

'Oh yeah, where?'

'Up north. We're in Sydney, I heard one of the doctors say it. I was caught in North Queensland.'

'Who caught you?'

'Who caught me *first*, you mean. My friend Atlanta told me there were multiple parties in pursuit of us, shifters and trees.'

'Treize,' Dreckly corrected. 'We're being held here by the Treize.'

She had to guess the shifters after them had been Tasmanian devils, as they were notorious for their trafficking of whatever had value: sometimes that would be drugs, sometimes that would be produce, sometimes that would be people. Dreckly thought about the ship of devils that had sunk off the coast of North Queensland a while back, the one Sadie Burke's sister Sorcha was said to be on. She knew the case well, anything happening in the waters off Australia of interest to her as she sought to stay in touch with her mother's heritage. They'd said there hadn't been enough bodies, not found in the wreckage or washed up on shore. Those that had been lost at sea had been eaten by sharks, they theorised.

If there was a captured selkie on board – or more than one – that might explain it. They had a penchant for being helpful when they wanted to be. Dreckly examined the one next to her, Amos. If he wasn't still a teenager, he was barely in his twenties from the look of him. He had the beginnings of a beard and a body that told her she was right, but he spoke like a child. There was a naivety there. He didn't have a full understanding of their world, it was clear. There was something about him that reminded Dreckly of herself when she had just escaped Vankila and was still trying to find her way. Everything she knew had been learned rather than experienced. Amos seemed like an echo of that to her.

'Your friends are dead,' she said, watching as he flinched at her words. He'd been kind to her, sweet even. It hurt her to be so direct, but coddling him wasn't going to help anyone.

'How do—'

'They have to be, otherwise you'll never escape this place. They haven't come back in months, right? Yet you're still here.

There's another selkie six tubes to your left that I'm assuming you don't know.'

Amos glanced where she had pointed and shook his head. 'No, I don't know them.'

'That's what I thought. So if they're bringing in new samples of your kind . . .'

'They're dead.'

'That's right. Mourn them and move on. Take them with you in your memory and cherish them later. There's no other way to get out of here.'

'You can't escape, believe me. I've tried. I've watched others try.'

'I'm not others.'

They were quiet then, a door opening far to the right and several figures moving into the space. Dreckly only watched them briefly, using the additional light instead to inspect the size and shape of where they were being held properly. They were taking the very selkie they had been talking about from the tube, the creature floating unconscious and slumped as the water was drained.

'When you're taken, how does it happen?' she whispered.

Amos shrugged. 'I just wake up there.'

The water, she thought. *They infuse something into the water when they want the subjects compliant and unconscious.* Her eyes ran around the circumference of her own tube and she reinspected the small holes that were providing her with fresh air. That's how they would drug her. Again.

Footsteps told her they had company, with the echo of heel against concrete heralding the arrival of someone she knew would come and visit her eventually. They had too much shared history; he wouldn't be able to help himself. Sure enough, the Kind Guard came to a stop in front of her personal, glass prison. He was flanked by two women who Dreckly had to guess were the same ones he'd been with on the boat: the ones she had sensed just out of sight, quiet, waiting for orders. They were identical in appearance, with blank expressions and shaved heads. Not small in stature but not large either, Dreckly paid them little attention. There might have been only one of him, but he was the bigger threat.

'Lorcan,' she said, addressing him.

'Dreckly. How are—mhm.'

'How am I feeling?' She chuckled, sensing the words he had cut himself off from saying, likely because of the scorn she was now offering. 'You're a fake fuck, enquiring after my well-being. I was attacked. Kidnapped. Drugged. How do you think I'm feeling, Mister Kind Guard?'

His face twitched at the use of that last title, as if her words had resurrected the memory from so long ago when she – just a kid – had designated that to him.

'My father always said you were the more dangerous of the two because you were smarter, had compassion, could think like us. I didn't really get it at the time, but I guess that's growing up, isn't it? You start to understand the things your parents were trying to teach you.'

'I don't want to be here any more than you do, Dreckly.'

She snorted. 'Easy for the wolf to say to the lamb'

'But this is bigger than you, bigger than me.'

Right.

'I'm not saying the ends justifies the means, but your presence here is important. So is everyone's.'

'Important to what?'

'The future of our world. The safety of it. The security.'

'What scares me is you really believe that: I can see it in your pretty, green eyes. Every villain thinks they're the hero of their own story.'

'The Three are *dying*,' he said, the words low but urgent. 'There is no one else like them, no power greater in terms of helping the Treize navigate a world full of threats—'

'Threats to their rule,' Dreckly pushed, filing away the information he had revealed about the Three for later. It may be true, it may not, but as the rumoured origin of the phrase 'hear no evil, see no evil, speak no evil', the Three were said to be a trio of prophetic beings who guided the governing supernatural organisation in matters past, present, and future. They had been the Treize's greatest asset for centuries and if they really were dying, sick, diseased, all of the above, then this attempt at Frankenstein-ing a cure out of the gifts of other supernaturals made a lot more sense. It was a desperate and destructive move, the kind of move you made when you were left with no other option.

'I'm not a villain,' Lorcan was saying. 'Neither are you. I'm just . . . trying to do the right thing for the continued existence of our world.'

'Look around,' Dreckly said, moving so close to the glass her breath created steam. 'Supernaturals in cages, beings you probably perceive as being "lesser" harmed for a collective "greater". It's been over a century and you're still doing exactly the same thing for exactly the same people as you were back when I was born. Spare me the introspection; it's hollow.'

He stared at her, really stared hard through the glass so that Dreckly might as well have been as naked as she felt. She didn't give a shit. When she was free, she might have toed the line: stayed meek and kept her head down. Yet she wasn't free anymore; she was caught. They were going to do to her what they had done and were doing to every other creature in here, whether that fixed the problem they were trying to solve or not. They wouldn't let you go if you were nice to them, so she may as well say what she really thought. Hold nothing back.

He broke the stare first, crossing his arms as he leaned against the tank in front of her, back to the glass.

'You won't see me again.'

'R.I.P.,' she snarled sarcastically. His lips twitched with the smallest of smiles.

'I'm not Praetorian Guard anymore, haven't been for a while. And I wasn't supposed to be here in that capacity when I found you so . . . I'm back to trying to help someone now, as a Custodian. Save their life before it wastes away.'

Dreckly longed to be outside of her tiny glass cell. She wouldn't be distracted by her emotions or her painful memories this time, wasting her one opportunity by severing a connection to the past and destroying a record player. This time, she would suck all the air from his lungs until he was blue-faced and on his knees, fingers clutching at the ground as he begged for air. She had done it before, to men not dissimilar to him in ideals. She would do it again.

'They'll come for you soon,' he said, as if sensing the murder in her eyes. 'You're the first real sprite they've had in . . . well, maybe ever.'

She didn't reply. Instead, Dreckly just tracked his exit with her eyes as he eventually accepted their conversation would not proceed any further and left. The doors were shut. They were plunged back into relative darkness, Amos quiet as he floated in the tube next to her. Dreckly related now to the fire creature she had observed when she first regained consciousness. She felt aflame.

'You're a sprite,' Amos remarked.

'Mmm.'

'This world, I came to it late and everything's . . . new to me. I'm still not sure if I understand it all. But a sprite is something I've never heard of.'

'It means I had one parent like you,' she said, 'and another that was an earth elemental. Their offspring makes a sprite in theory, but most of what supernaturals call a "sprite" is not what I am.'

'What does that mean?'

'It means somewhere down the line, there was probably a sprite like me: the first manifestation of that union between a selkie and an earth elemental. Their powers are a reverberation of that, but that's all: just a reverberation. Now listen, he said they'll come for me soon and he might be a brainwashed idiot, but he hasn't proven himself to be a liar yet. So they will. And we don't have much time.'

'Time for what?'

'For you to tell me everything you know.'

She got him talking, the selkie recounting everything he could remember about the room he would wake up in. It was always the same room and Dreckly had him detail everything he could see. Then everything they would do to him. She wouldn't let them get to that part on her; she'd be in too much pain as they extracted and experimented that she wouldn't be able to use her powers. The purpose didn't matter much, she didn't care about who the Kind Guard alleged they would be saving. The Three had never been proven to be real, only an urban legend shared between monsters. She had to think about herself. And the longer the selkie talked, the more she started thinking about him.

There were too many creatures in that holding bay; there was no way she could save them all. In fact, Dreckly had no intention of doing that. Her priority was *her* escape and, if she could manage it, Amos as well. More than thirty supernaturals would never make it, but two definitely could.

With a pang in her heart, Dreckly thought of *him*. He would never leave anyone behind; it wasn't in his nature. Yet she wasn't him. When the opportunity came, she would abandon as many creatures as she had to if it meant her freedom. Even Amos, although the more he spoke the sadder he made her. He'd been raised in a lake, he told her, after becoming entangled in a net as a child and discovered by an old scientist. That man had been a father figure for him, up until he was murdered, and he'd been left alone. Until he wasn't.

'Have you ever been in love?' he asked, a dumb look on his face that told Dreckly his own answer without him needing to say it.

'Yes.'

'I'm in love with Kaia, although it's kind of a sad story.'

'All love stories are sad stories,' she murmured from her crouched position at the bottom of the glass tube.

His was more tragic than sad, in truth: no one had died, which was always Dreckly's barometer for things. *Did you die though?* If the answer was no, keep it moving. Amos and this Kaia girl had a true love: she'd found him in the lake and they'd found each other. In her quest to get him to his people, freedom, and a life inevitably without her, she'd been injected with a tracking agent of some kind that circulated in her blood. He didn't know who had been in pursuit of them at the time, but in hindsight he guessed it was the Praetorian Guard on behalf of the Treize.

'Askari,' she said, correcting him.

'Oh?'

'This all sounds too sloppy for the Praetorian Guard, too human. Askari are just as ambitious as any of them, so they'll kill if they have to.'

And they had, it seemed, in the pursuit of Amos. He'd gotten away but his proximity to Kaia had been restricted forever because of the tracking agent: they couldn't risk meeting up too often, because, wherever she was, their interested parties might assume he would be.

'We still find ways though.' He smiled. 'She's an ironwoman, so races in the ocean a lot and trains there too. That gives me an excuse to say hello every now and then.'

'That's nice,' Dreckly said absent-mindedly. 'How long have you been, uh, doing that?'

'Almost two years I think, maybe longer.'

She smiled, not saying what she was thinking. One lover that lives on land and another that lives in the ocean, the two things keeping them apart. Her favourite fairy tale went exactly that way, right up until the point one character fell in love with someone else and the other died of sorrow. She was skipping some parts, but that was the meat and potatoes of it.

It was also eerily like her parents. Amos must know it was unsustainable. She guessed the family he'd reconnected with at sea had told him as much. The girl's family on land had probably said the same, but the heart wants what it wants.

'Can you shift?' she asked him. 'Most selkies can shift shape, transform in part to exist wherever they need to.'

'Oh,' he replied, looking deflated. This was clearly not the first time the subject had been broached with him. 'I've tried to, I keep trying, but they think because I had no one to teach me in that key developmental phase I can't do it. At least not yet, I'm just catching up to a lot of things I didn't know.'

She frowned. 'I don't know if it's something you can teach rather than, well, instinct.'

'That's what Atlanta said.'

'She sounds smart.'

'Why do you ask?'

'Would have been handy, that's all.'

'You have an escape plan.'

It wasn't a question; it was a statement of fact. He was naïve in many ways, but he was smart. This sheltered selkie had realised what she was doing as she questioned him extensively, knowing that he was giving all the answers to someone who had no reason to take him with her, *especially* if he was frustratingly immobile on land. Dreckly glanced around, not liking all the eyes she saw looking back at her. Most weren't close enough to hear, but some were.

Yes, she thought. *I have a plan.* She wasn't keen to verbalise it. Doing so wouldn't have been clever, especially if any of the creatures they'd be leaving behind heard. Information was leverage and they could use it against her. Dreckly chose to ignore his question instead. She shut her eyes, stayed curled up in the uncomfortable position she was in, looked vulnerable, and waited.

They would come for her soon. She'd get one chance. Dreckly would be ready.

Chapter 11

Past

I lost the bet. Rather epically, too. Less than two years later, I was working for Dorothy Arzner on her *fifth* feature film. Clara was working on it as well, but it wasn't as exciting for her as it was me. *The Wild Party* was her first 'talkie' and she wasn't making the transition from silent film star willingly; she was being dragged.

'I have to, that's what they said, Tulip! My agent told me I *have* to do this or my career's as good as over. I hate it! Hate it! You know, on my first take the microphone exploded? Exploded! It's not safe, it's an absolute nightmare.'

She was pacing up and down the length of Mildred's workshop, where I now worked as an assistant set decorator. I wasn't the only woman: the whole department was women. Supernaturals too, more than I was used to being around. I'd never discussed this with Dorothy, who didn't know what *I* was but probably knew what *some* of her beloved colleagues and friends were. She didn't care regardless.

Maybe she did, maybe it just mattered to her less than the other things about us. Maybe we all flocked to her because we sensed a kind of kinship there, a solidarity in our otherness. Regardless, she'd given me my first opportunity to meet Mildred and after a month of working in and around her, I finally felt safe enough to speak up. We'd been working on painting a type of tile, just the two of us back late on the lot as we rushed to make the shooting deadline for the next day.

'I need to ask you something,' I said to Mildred, but not in English. I asked her in clear, crisp and concise demon speak. Her immaculately manicured hand froze on the paintbrush she was wielding, a sharp gaze piercing me through the lens of her horn-rimmed glasses.

'Talk, child,' she answered, voice steady but low.

I could see the confusion on her face, see her tracking back through her senses to see if she had missed the tell-tale signs that I was one of her kind – a demon. But I wasn't.

'It's a risk asking you, but it has been years and I have no other choice.'

'Speak on it.'

'I need to get a message to one of your kind, a demon named Yixin.'

'Why can't you ask him yourself, since you know my language so well?'

'He's imprisoned in—' I nearly couldn't say it; I hadn't said that word *Vankila* since I was a kid and I hated the fear it struck within me. She could see my physical discomfort and I took a shaky breath. 'Vankila. He was there, in a cell across from an earth elemental.'

'How do you know this?' she asked.

'It's not important.'

'It—'

'I'm telling you everything I can, *please*.'

She set down the paintbrush. 'Fine. How long ago was this?'

I shook my head. 'Years.'

'Then what's the message?'

'Tell him . . . tell him the rose bloomed.'

It sounded stupid out loud, but I couldn't think of any other coded language that would communicate to him I was okay. He had risked everything for my father's scheme. He had risked everything for *me*. I had thought about it in my empty moments, the ones where my thoughts wandered and I dwelled on the past. If he was still alive, I wanted him to know his sacrifice hadn't been in vain. I was free and it was partially because of him.

'Yixin is well known to our kind,' Mildred said, choosing her words carefully. 'He was taken due to perceived crimes against the Treize and no one has heard from him in many years. We did not know if he was—'

'He is. Or was alive. I believe he still is.'

'And what is this earth elemental's name?'

'I've given you everything I can, but I will not give that.'

Interesting, Mildred's tilted head gesture said without saying.

'I can get a message to him, now that my people know where to look . . . thanks to you, not-quite-demon girl.'

'If necessary, I can pay—'

She clicked her tongue, seemingly annoyed. 'Please. The information is payment enough. When I have something, I will tell you.'

I had liked working with Mildred before, her atten- tion-to-detail making her one of the best production designers in Hollywood. Like Dorothy, she had to work five times as hard as anyone else, be five times better, just so her gender and her race wouldn't be held against her. After I showed my hand and played my cards the only way I knew how, I liked her even more. At first, I kept my guard up, my senses working overtime just in case I was foolish enough to think trusting another supernatural was the same as having an ally.

Yet it was. From that moment on, I couldn't help but feel like Mildred was keeping an eye out for me. Not *on* me, but watching my back. I started to see more and more supernaturals in her workshop, as if they were sniffing me out, checking to see whether the new girl was worthy of the approval I had invisibly won from the older demon. When I occasionally got invited to parties that had nothing to do with Clara, it was a subtle shake of the head from Mildred that told me whether it was safe to go or not. Some parties you didn't want to be caught at. All the while, I waited. I knew demons had ways of communicating with each other that were species specific and I had to guess proximity was an element, so all I could do was have patience. And wait.

When news eventually came, I knew it was bad when Mildred asked me to 'come for a drive to the coast'. Proximity to water *always* made me feel better, even if it was the heavily populated chaos of Santa Monica Pier with families running about and fairy floss wielded as an airborne pathogen. I dodged a sticky cloud of it that had been caught in the breeze, coming to rest against the railing with Mildred as we looked at the view of the coastline and the people dotted across it.

The Rose Daughter

'Yixin is alive,' she said and I let out a breathy gasp of relief.

'Oh, thank God.' I beamed. 'I thought when you signed us off early . . .'

The smile faded on my face as I watched her more carefully, Mildred's eyes hidden behind sunglasses and her complexion cast in shadow by a wide-brimmed hat.

'The earth elemental is dead, Tulip.'

I knew this. I had known it for years without definitive proof, but hearing someone say it out loud for the first time ever . . . I felt the weight of my body give out as I slumped against the railing, needing every bit of structure it had as it offered me support. Mildred tightly but firmly kept me standing when it seemed like I might collapse, the gesture insignificant to anyone passing by as she grasped my waist. Yet she was holding me up entirely with her strength alone, such was the gift of some demons.

'Yixin said that he died not long after the last time you saw him.'

'How?' I finally managed to ask. 'I mean, I knew he was gone but . . . how?'

'He wouldn't say, except to note that it was quick. Not painless, but quick.'

An audible sob escaped my lips then and I hung my head to hide the tears as they started to form.

'The demon also said to say thank you for your message and he knows what you risked to send it. He said although he's still there, he thinks of you often and the kindness you showed. It's a kindness we're to continue showing you for as long as you need it. And . . . do not come for him. It's not your job. Our kind will see to it. The best thing you can do for him and the memory of that earth elemental is continue living and loving freely. To bloom, as you put it.'

It was a long while before I looked up, glancing around at the carefree faces of those on the pier as they licked at dripping ice creams and giggled at a clown making balloon animals.

'They're not better off,' Mildred said, as if reading my thoughts. 'They know pain – yes, not like us; never like us – but they're not better off living in darkness, not knowing they're ruled by monsters who pretend to have the best interests of all at heart.'

I stared at the wisps of her sharp, orderly bob that were visible under her hat as they tickled the neckline of her formal blouse.

'I never realised a revolutionary could look so sophisticated,' I whispered.

'My dear,' she replied, looking at me over the brim of her sunglasses, 'the revolution comes in many forms. No one said you can't look good while doing it. No one said living and loving freely when there are those determined to see that you don't *isn't* a revolutionary act. Your survival is a revolution.'

The silk of her gloves made contact with my hands as she gripped them.

'And you are not alone. Whether it's the witch in the costuming department or the driver who needs to take three nights off a month when it's full moon, there are more of us around you and here for you if you need. And if you don't, we're still here regardless.'

I was lost for words, my tears and snot having mixed together at some point as Mildred handed me a beautifully monogrammed handkerchief.

'Why are you so nice to me?' I asked, dabbing.

'If we're not nice to our own kind, who else will be?'

'I'm not a demon.'

'I know. Yet the species lines never mattered much to me. They matter even less the older you get.'

As we walked from the pier and back towards Mildred's car, the demon told me to take a week off work, but that she'd expect me back to business as usual within seven days. She couldn't know what the 'earth elemental' meant to me, yet I'm sure she guessed they were family in some capacity. I couldn't help but smile at that; a week was such a *massive* consolation for Mildred knowing how under the pump she would be without an assistant. Yet she'd been willing for me to take that time off anyway. Thankfully for her, I refused.

'Please,' I begged, 'I need the distraction. I need something to keep my mind and hands busy.'

She looked doubtful. 'If you're sure—'

'I am. I'll see you same time tomorrow, black coffee with three sugars as always.'

Driving through the streets of Los Angeles, the heat was dispersed somewhat by the breeze that attempted to whip my hair back from where it was clasped tightly under a scarf that was knotted at my chin. Mildred kept the top down on her convertible, and, as we cruised, it struck me for the first time that I was alone. *Truly* alone. I shook my head slightly, reminding myself that's exactly the opposite of what Mildred had just reminded me.

Yet these were new friends and I was still cautious. They weren't family yet in the same way Meili and Li Jun and even Delun felt like family to me, humans who had also shown kindness to me when they had no reason to. I'd moved out of Clara's guest house some time ago, craving the comfort and sanctuary that had first been offered by the Hans. They had two spare rooms and Meili teased me that since I'd bought the house, I was entitled to both of them. Despite us no longer living on opposite ends of her swimming pool, I was still one of Clara's favoured confidantes.

'They say it's the future of cinema!' she exclaimed, continuing on one of her many anti-talkie tirades that usually saw me as an audience of one in Mildred's workshop. Conveniently, the demon always managed to find herself somewhere else whenever Clara showed up.

'Soon it will be talkies and *nothing* else, that's what they say! But I can't move, I can't physically perform, it's debilitating.'

It had been a struggle for Clara and indeed everyone working with her on set. She was the star of the film and, if that aspect didn't work, it was unlikely people would see the other details. Fan brush between my teeth, I looked up from painting one of the matte landscape scenes that would hang behind windows on set to give the illusion of wilderness outside.

'Speak to Dorothy,' I urged, tucking the utensil behind my ear. 'She'll listen to you, Clara.'

'Gah, Dorothy! She's not the messiah you think she is, Tulip, not one bit!'

She stormed from the workshop, heels clacking along the cement like a dramatic heartbeat.

'Is she gone?' asked Mildred's familiar drawl, materialising once Clara had left.

'Like the wind.'

She sighed with deep relief. 'She's cuckoo, I don't know how you managed to work for her for so long.'

I was immediately defensive, as Clara definitely had her flaws, but she had done a lot for me. Yet I also understood she wasn't everyone's cup of tea, with Dorothy inventive and able to think on her feet around her. I'd watched on set one day as she got a gaffer to affix a microphone to a fishing rod and lower it over Clara's head so they could get the sound quality they needed without restricting her movements.

The twenties became the thirties and Clara's fearful prophecies proved accurate: silent films all but disappeared. Eventually so too did Clara: she found a husband, she settled down, she left the business.

I stayed in it, working with Mildred and the rest of the female supernatural posse on Dorothy's next ten feature films. They were all hits to varying degrees, but she was *still* the only female film-maker active in Hollywood's golden age and she copped a lot of shit. I was just grateful to be there for the ride, because I had nowhere else to be and this definitely wasn't going to last forever. In fact, I was certain it wouldn't.

Chapter 12

Present

It was called the Texas Switch and she'd learnt it on the set of a movie where Dorothy had been shooting uncredited additional photography. Two performers would play the one character: the first usually being the stuntie required to perform a tricky manoeuvre and the second being the actor who needed to be front-facing towards the camera. At some point, they would switch in a move that would ideally be disguised by a large prop or a cut if necessary. The end result would look seamless in most cases. Or at least it did back then.

Dreckly remembered watching it being performed on location as Dorothy explained it to her. There was no way she thought it could feasibly look as good as the filmmaker said it would. When she watched an assembly cut in the editing suite, she was surprised to be proved wrong.

'And that, kid, is the Texas Switch.'

Dorothy's drawl came back to her, fresh and sharp in her mind. That's precisely what Dreckly was intending to pull off. All of those Treize workers who poked and prodded them wore white caps and masks, largely cloaking their identity. Amos told her he thought there were two women among the assembled scientists or whatever the hell they were. In their uniforms, they were largely indistinguishable: it's all she had to go on.

When Dreckly felt the air pressure subtly change in her tube, just a particle at first, then more, she was ready. Using what little air there was inside, she redirected it to block the fumes that were intended to make her unconscious. This was a task she could do with her eyes closed, which was good because they were required to be as she slumped over and pretended to be as impacted by whatever they were pumping in there as they thought she was.

'Dreckly!' she heard Amos cry, his hands slapping against the glass. He repeated it a few more times, the sweet kid even begging with the folks in the lab coats when they arrived to take him instead. He was a kind-hearted idiot who would have died on the first day of Operation Overlord, never making it much further than the first jump. The faces of a hundred boys she had met *just like that* flashed through her mind in an instant and she resolved to save this one. Somehow. He made enough of a ruckus that they pumped his tank full of the same drug, his protests eventually settling down as he slipped into unconsciousness too.

Good, she thought. That would make it all the easier for her. She couldn't risk a peek, so she had to listen to their movements instead to give her a clue about what was happening next. A swipe card was used to unlock her prison, which was important. It was better than a code she likely wouldn't get. A swipe card she could steal. She lurched over in her slumped position, those who had come to grab her using that momentum to pull her on to a wheeled stretcher. *Also good*.

She'd known this was coming, Dreckly still as she was positioned on the trolley and rolled to her eventual destination. Amos had detailed this part to her, not from his own recollections but from watching others be taken. She hadn't told him at the time, but it was vital information to have: a wheeled stretcher was exactly the kind of device she would need to roll an immobile selkie out of the building.

'Do we need to strap her down?' one of them was asking.

'Of course, Rudolph.'

'No names!'

'What does it matter? No one here is going anywhere.'

'Yes, strap her down,' another was saying. 'When did we just stop following protocol?'

'Well, it says she's a sprite!'

'So?'

'They don't give us much trouble usually.'

'Wait, she's a sprite?' a third was asking. 'I thought they were little pixie things. This is a grown woman.'

'You're thinking of actual pixies.'

'Pixies aren't real.'

'Whatever, but sprites are a foot tall with spiky little faces and wings.'

'No, they're from Greek mythology.'

'You're getting water sprites and selkies all mixed up. Look, let me Google it.'

'Google Images please – see! Spiky little faces and wings!'

'Stop it!' the one in charge snapped. 'You, strap her down: follow protocol. You, no more Google searches for sprites – Jesus Christ. Look where you work? The answers are at your fingertips, not on some mythology subreddit.'

'Yes, ma'am.'

'Yes, Sandra.'

'*No. Names.*'

They both mumbled an apology, with Dreckly having listened carefully to their bickering. Rudolph was to her left and didn't want to follow protocol. He did as his boss asked, but barely: it was a slight act of defiance, the way he strapped her down. It would have probably looked fine if someone was staring at it, yet it was too loose. She wouldn't have to wiggle her way out; she could just lift her arms free. The unnamed one invested in searching sprites was a male and to her right, Sandra, their boss, was at her feet and controlling where the stretcher was wheeled. Three of them.

She memorised the route in her head: weaving through the tubes containing supernaturals, swipe card used to exit the room and proceed down a long hallway, right at a set of swinging doors, pause, then up two floors in an elevator, another short trip down a hallway, left through swinging doors again, swipe card entry to their final destination. Dreckly repeated it to herself several times until she was certain she had the path committed to memory. She had a brain for this kind of detail, but she kept going over it again and again just in case. This room was sealed, she could feel it. There was no natural airflow. In fact, this whole building was stale: air was being pumped in from somewhere just like their tubes but it wasn't naturally occurring.

It didn't feel that different to Vankila, actually. She pushed the bubble of panic that burst inside of her at that thought deep down into her gut. This wasn't Vankila. They were still in Australia, still in Sydney somewhere, but they were likely underground. Treize headquarters under St James Station made the most sense, yet it was also risky running this kind of operation so transparently official. She'd gotten the impression from the wombat shifters and Ben that this was off the books, secret. Understandably, given most supernaturals would object to being experimented on by a roster of aspiring Doctor Dooms.

She had to listen for a moment, which was the hardest part: trying to keep her cool while they prepared to do Lord knows what to her. Yet Dreckly needed to be certain by assessing the air particles around them that there were just the three workers, no one else in the room or observing from the other side of a window. There wasn't. They were alone. Sucked to be them.

There was a camera in the top right-hand corner of the room, which she used the air to push down and slightly to the right so it was facing the wall. If someone was watching it, a case could be made that it had just been bumped out of place. If she disabled it all together, its lack of operation would likely alert a technician somewhere. And then others. All three staff had to go down at the same time and slowly, so they wouldn't realise what was happening to them. Dreckly gradually began sucking the air out of the room, redirecting it anywhere but where they were. In just a matter of moments, each of the scientists started to display symptoms of hypoxia: it's what happened when your body was deprived of oxygen. Shortness of breath, wheezing, a nasty cough from Sandra, but most importantly, confusion.

They didn't have the clarity of mind to alert whoever they would need to alert in case of emergency. One by one, she listened to their bodies slumping to the ground. As a precaution, Dreckly waited just a little bit longer before she pulled her hands free of the straps and undid the binding at her waist. Sitting up, she scanned their three unconscious bodies with a glance: the man named Rudolph was closest to her size. She undid the straps at her thighs and calf, sliding down to the ground and slipping him out of his lab coat, pants, shirt, and shoes. She – like all of the human-formed supernaturals – was dressed in plain, beige binding that made her look like some kind of haute couture mummy.

Shoving her hair under the white surgical cap, she added the mask and took Sandra's key card. She was the boss. She would have the best access. Taking a breath, she let her heartbeat calm down just a touch. Dreckly needed the moment to make her mind steady. *Calmness and clarity*, she told herself. His words. She took stock of the room. She immediately hated it: it looked like somewhere you came to die. There was an operating table, lamps, and a tray of utensils that made her want to vomit just looking at them. She pushed past the feelings and neared a bench that had – among other things – two computers logged on and ready to go.

They were going to perform a biopsy on her, it said. She clicked through other documents, reading them as fast as she could and committing names to memory. Her file was there and she deleted it. She took the printed version they had with her as well, attached to the clipboard so it would look like she had a purpose if she was stopped. She continued searching through the computer, looking for some kind of key as to how she could get the hell out of there. Nothing. Dreckly would have to figure it out on the fly, which she hated. She wasn't a natural improvisor but there were no other options. Just before she left, she hesitated.

'Fuck it,' Dreckly murmured, typing 'sprites' into Google and hitting the images tab. She wrinkled her nose at the dozens of *extremely* inaccurate renderings of her kind.

'Not even close,' she snorted, wiping the computer before shutting the whole thing down.

Grabbing the stretcher, she was wheeling it out of the room when she noticed up on the wall, laminated, an emergency exit plan in case of fire.

'Brilliant,' she breathed, ripping it down and placing it in front of her as she walked. Swiping out of the room, Dreckly didn't need to look where she was going to know how to end up back at the elevators. There was no one around, so she kept her gaze focused downwards: away from the cameras and reading the emergency plan attached to the clipboard instead. She hit the elevator button, moving into the metallic cube and swiping her pass again as she hit floor five. She was on floor three, with the numbers descending rather than ascending. This confirmed her theory about them being underground.

Calmness and clarity.

When she hit the floor she needed, Dreckly whacked the button for the first floor before dashing out and using Sandra's pass to swipe herself into the room full of tubes. She hustled and, like a kid in a supermarket with a shopping trolley, she whizzed across the concrete by running and gliding at intervals. She'd counted how far her tube was from the edge of the room and that's how she found her way back to Amos.

He was still unconscious as she swiped the card once more, the usual process clearly being to drain the water from the

tube first. There was no time for that and she had to purge the
system. Letting herself get soaked, she held the stretcher as
close to where Amos fell as possible. His tail landed well, but
the rest of him rolled sideways and he was about to connect
with the ground head first when Dreckly caught him. It took
some work to reposition the selkie on the stretcher, with those
tails essentially just one long, thick, scaled muscle. And they
were *heavy*. You had to guess that when they came to take
Amos, they needed more than three people to wheel him away.
As she strapped him in, it was hard to ignore the banging of
the other creatures who were conscious and seeing what
Dreckly was doing.

'HEY!' the fire elemental closest to her yelled, Dreckly fighting the urge to swing around and tell them to shut up. Because
others were yelling now too, asking her to 'free me', 'help us',
'let me out', 'I've been here so long'. Just like the creatures
who'd begged her in Vankila.

Her hands were shaking as she taped the small digital screen
that had her name displayed on it, negotiating her way through
until that file was deleted too. There were backups somewhere
she guessed, so it was more of a symbolic gesture. In her experience, symbols could be powerful too.

'Don't leave us here, *please*. We can help you!'

They couldn't; they could only hinder her and the safe exit
she was so desperate for with Amos. And yet, she froze, fighting against her better judgement. *I can't leave them behind,*
she thought to herself. *I can't.*

But where would she take them? What would she do with
them? Who would be responsible for this many injured creatures? She could barely negotiate her way out with Amos, let

alone *dozens* of others. Dreckly had to move, knowing that at any moment this whole facility was going to be flooded with the exact kind of activity she didn't want.

Spinning the stretcher around, she took off at a slow jog and pushed Amos in the opposite direction of everyone crying for her to help them. There was a maintenance elevator this way, one she had to pray the Treize weren't using already because there were enough other active routes behind her.

'YOU FUCKING BITCH! DON'T YOU LEAVE ME DOWN HERE!'

'I'm sorry,' Dreckly sobbed. 'I'm sorry I'm sorry I'm sorry.'

She came to a stop, pulling the lever that activated her chosen form of transport. This wasn't like the other elevators: this was loud and jangly and mechanical. In summary, a cheese grater with gears. She shoved Amos into the elevator, hoping the damn thing would take his and her weight. She hesitated again, her heart pounding as the seconds ticked by and she agonised over what to do as she looked out at the tubes and the creatures writhing inside them.

You're not a hero, she told herself, yanking the caged doors shut and throwing the lever down to take them upwards. It wasn't promising at first, but they eventually shuddered towards the top level. The movements were violent enough that they stirred Amos, the selkie groggy as he strained against his confinement.

'Hey, it's okay,' she said, leaning over so he could see her face. 'It's me. I've got you. We're getting out of here.'

Chapter 13

Past – 1934 . . .

The Hays Code fucking sucked. It was brought in around nineteen thirty, but things didn't start to get bad until a few years later. Interracial relationships were banned from being shown on screen, so too queerness in any form, debauchery, abortion, proximity. Heck, even female characters with any kind of agency were slowly but surely being shoved from motion pictures thanks to the production code. And it wasn't just in fiction.

Chinatown was gone completely, demolished like they had threatened it would be. The businesses were gone and those who ran them. Meili played a weekly mah-jong game with her friends from the old neighbourhood and she kept me updated. They were trying to rebuild further across town and set up once again, but things were tough. Los Angeles corruption was always bad, yet the growing racism and anti-Asian sentiment was worse.

'You don't have papers,' Li Jun said one night, while we sat quietly at the dinner table making dumplings. 'I've heard things, rumours about camps and rounding up anyone who looks vaguely Japanese. You can't prove that you're not and you know those idiots can't tell the difference. And they won't care to.'

'You don't need to worry about this,' I said, squeezing his hand. The flour that was left on my own from handling the dough rubbed off on his skin. 'Sorry.'

I patted him clean, passing over the small circle of dough that I had just rolled as he began spooning a pork mixture into it, sealing it shut.

'I do worry; Meili does too. We're a lot better off than some families, but you should think about it, Tulip.'

'And where would I go?' I asked. It had been building, but suddenly the bubble of peace I'd managed to create for myself had finally burst. It felt like everywhere was on the brink of war, with the human world I had worked so carefully to integrate myself into not providing as much sanctuary as I'd thought.

'Go where?' Meili asked, swooping into the dining room to pick up the tray we had just finished.

'Nowhere,' Li Jun replied, throwing me a look. I stayed quiet, but his words stayed on my mind.

'He's right,' Mildred said, as I recounted the conversation to her at a house party thrown by Dorothy's girlfriend one night. The conversations I'd had with Dorothy scared me even more.

'I don't know how much longer I can keep doing this, keep making movies in a business where you can't be a woman *or* a lesbian. It's the double sin.'

The thought of her quitting made my soul ache. She made *wonderful* movies: they were smart, funny, subversive, and beautiful to look at. If they lost her, they lost more than just another Hollywood film-maker; they'd lose a unique voice.

Censors became a regular addition on set, with those working to enforce the Hays Code often watching quietly from the sidelines during a shoot. They'd already seen the scripts and given their notes, but they made more, and the production schedules were constantly being readjusted.

There was a new guy I didn't mind too much though, mainly because he didn't have anything to do with the Hays Code. I'd gotten the goss on him from Mildred, who of course had sources everywhere and knew that Harvey Schwartz had served in World War I. He had retired from the army once it ended and they had little use for soldiers anymore. Now, he worked in Hollywood with his brother-in-law who ran some part of the studio, she wasn't sure which.

'He a Valentino?' I asked. That was the kind of thing I needed to know: this business was populated with semi-handsome, semi-charming men who had got into it solely to prey on young girls. You could spot most of them on sight and it was easier to navigate around them once you knew who to avoid.

'No, he's one of the good ones,' Mildred said, which immediately sparked my interest. That wasn't the kind of comment she made about humans often, with the roster of 'good ones' in her book usually limited to Dorothy's people and Lionel. 'He's married but . . .'

'But what?'

She looked hesitant to say at first, staring at her reflection in the workshop mirror and readjusting the silk turban on her head before offering a small shrug. He wasn't one of us. We didn't need to keep his secrets.

'His wife left him, apparently; took the two kids and moved to Minneapolis.'

'Yikes.'

'He still wears the ring for show and the marriage is intact far as anyone knows.'

'To save face or protect her reputation?'

Being a divorced woman was bad enough. Being a divorced woman with kids? Our society was not designed for women to survive, let alone thrive.

'Don't know,' she replied, the light reflecting beautifully off the pale gold shade of her chosen headwear. 'So long as he's not a threat to any of us, I couldn't care where he sends his pay cheque each month.'

I first crossed paths with him on a war picture we were shooting where he was serving as a consultant. The movie wasn't really my bag in terms of enjoyment, yet it meant I got to do lots of meticulous, delicate work. That I *did* enjoy.

'These are very good,' he said, examining my recreations of legitimate army documents he had supplied for reference. The real names had been removed, with several characters details replacing them instead. 'Did you make these yourself?'

'That's my job. Today, anyway.'

'How did you do this so well? If I didn't know better, I'd think these were as authentic as the ones I brought to set.' He rubbed his fingers together, inspecting the material. 'Even the paper feels right.'

'That won't come across on camera, so it's a bit of wasted detail. I like to think that it will help the actors *believe* it's real when they pick it up during a take,' I answered, adding the finishing touches to the final piece I was working on. 'It's something Mildred taught me, something small but it makes a difference. I looked up what kind of paper they used for those documents and with war rations, and it was mostly recycled. Once the Depression hit, it was still cost effective and they kept making it so it wasn't as hard to get a hold of as you might think.'

'And the logos? The seals? Even the photographs—'

'Oh, those aren't photographs. I painted those with water colours. They cut the budget right back so we lost the money and time allotted to hire a photographer.'

'They look perfect. I wouldn't be able to tell the difference.'

'You can keep one if you like.'

'Don't you need it?'

'No, I always try and make a few extras so I have backups. Just in case.'

'Very resourceful.' He threw me a considering glance. 'Tulip, was it? Tulip what?'

'Tulip Han,' I responded, trying not to bask in his praise. Film sets moved at a thousand miles an hour with a million moving parts. The times when anyone had a moment to pause and acknowledge your work, let alone acknowledge that it was *good*, were rare and something to be treasured.

'Tulip Han,' the former soldier repeated, smiling deep. 'Thanks very much for this. It's quite the racket you've got here.'

Harvey was still examining my handiwork as he left and there was something about his manner that told me he would be back. That afternoon, he was, and I tried to ignore the warmth in my chest that bloomed when he reappeared. In fact, he became frequent company as I worked over the next several months. He felt like a fixture in the workshop before too long, with a stool always next to mine that I dubbed 'Harvey's' as we maintained a constant chatter about everything from the news and politics, to gossip and the film business. Sets bored him, he said. There was so much sitting around and inaction between all the 'action'. He thought it was a tremendous waste of money most of the time, but it paid well and that's what mattered for his family.

'I got welded too young,' he said, wedding ring twinkling in the sunlight. 'Want a cup of You and Me?'

'Sorry?'

'Tea,' he offered, making a second cup for me and one for Mildred as we lingered near the catering tent. 'She wasn't much a fan of army life, especially when I came back like this.'

He gestured to a scar that ran down his cheek and over his chin.

'I think it's quite fetching,' Mildred remarked, not revealing in even the slightest way that we already knew his nuclear family had imploded.

'Fetching?' Harvey smirked. 'I was maybe fetching in my twenties, but I'm halfway through my thirties and no one has called me fetching in a long time, Mildred dear.'

'Well, I think it makes you look fetching *and* handsome.'

'All the best characters have scars,' I murmured, 'not just the villains.'

I felt his gaze fix on me at the comment, his chuckle covering the sound of Mildred's 'hmm' as I glanced away. He had the kind of smile that would make you stupid, so it was best not to look directly at it. Like the sun.

I was someone who was purposefully careful about men, only bothering with a few boyfriends over the years that I'd kept mostly secret. I had passions and urges like everyone else, but I was careful not to have Lionel find me one of the doctors who took care of the other girls' indiscretions. Contraception *now* was better than it *had been*, but it was risky. And I tried to take as few risks as possible.

Harvey made me want to take risks. His scar and his smile and the whole package made me want to take dangerous risks. I knew he was still married on paper. I knew he was working for my bosses. I knew I couldn't entertain him as anything more than my secret crush. That didn't stop my eyes searching for him every day when I first arrived on set, his tanned skin, gentle muscles and light-brown hair making him look like any one of the stuntmen they had filling in for the stars when needed.

He and Lionel had served together, I learned, with the Paramount Pictures fixer having quit Hollywood to go back into the army. I was surprised to hear this and when I asked exactly what he was doing there, Harvey evaded my answer with a small shrug and the word 'intelligence'.

Whenever a shoot was completed, wrap parties were a ritual. They were always loose, loud, and lit with the kind of debauchery censors were desperate to stamp out in Hollywood. They were also extremely fun.

This one, however, felt muted. It felt like the end of something, I thought, as I grabbed a gin and tonic and made my way to the balcony of Mildred's mansion in the Hollywood hills. The city blinked below; the lone howl of a coyote heard off in the distance as whoever was banging away on the agony box continued to play inside. I leaned over the railing, looking down at the dirt below.

'What are you looking for down there?'

I jumped, having not seen Harvey smoking quietly in the shadows. The whole place stunk of tobacco smoke, so that wasn't surprising. But I felt the air move differently around him. I should have sensed his presence. I was getting sloppy. Or I was quite drunk.

'Uh,' I stalled, looking back down at what had caught my attention. 'I was looking for flowers.'

'Find any?'

'No.' I knew my voice sounded sad as I said that. I was thinking of my father.

'That's what you used to do, wasn't it? Floristry?'

'Mmmm.'

I took a sip of my drink as he joined me on the balcony, his bare forearm brushing up against mine. It was hot that night, right in the middle of summer. Even though the sun had set, the heat was still exhausting. All of the men at the party were wearing short-sleeved shirts, capri shorts, and – in some cases – no shirt at all.

'Blue really is your colour,' he said.

His words surprised me and I cast a sideways glance at him to see if he was serious. His face told me that he was.

'Are you putting the eye on me?'

'Maybe.'

'Then you've done more elbow-bending than I thought.'

He laughed, bending his elbow theatrically to take a swig of his own drink and illustrate my point.

'Thank you,' I whispered. 'Georgette in the costume department made it for me.'

'Why do you do that?'

'Do what?'

He reached a hand towards my face, fingers gently skimming my skin as I stayed frozen in place.

'You blush all the time; it's amazing to watch. It's like paint spreading in water as the colour moves across your cheeks.'

I felt like I couldn't breathe as he touched me, our faces so close to each other as he spoke.

'I don't blush all the time,' I said, emboldened. 'Just around you.'

He moved towards me, chin touching mine as he inched forward to meet my kiss. There was a yell behind us, followed by an enormous splash and we jumped apart. Water sloshed up and over the ruching at the front of my dress, and Harvey stepped in front of me as another man dived into the pool, creating an even bigger splash. His cigarette went out with a depressing *flit*.

'Oh shit, sorry, Harvey! Sorry, Tulip! Didn't realise you kids were out here. I'm positively fiddled!'

'That I can see,' he said, wiping his face. 'You drenched?'

'No,' I replied, regaining my composure as I patted myself down. 'You took the brunt of it.'

My dress had loose sleeves but a plunging neckline, with all of the drama contained at the centre of the waist as the fabric wrapped together and draped down my middle. Harvey looked like he was drinking in every detail and I felt embarrassed by what had almost happened.

'Stop ogling me like that,' I snapped.

'It's Georgette's fault.' He paused, before continuing. 'She's like you, isn't she? Undocumented?'

I was surprised by the question, because Georgette *was* like me – a supernatural – but Harvey had made a more likely assumption, a more human one.

'Don't be mad,' he said hurriedly. 'I've just been trying to figure you out.'

'Well, stop it.'

'Lionel!' one of the splashers from the pooled yelled. 'Mr Fix-It is back and slumming it with the hooligans!'

'Only temporarily,' Lionel answered, scanning the balcony until his eyes settled on Harvey and me. He waved at us, gesturing to follow him.

'Let's breeze,' the former soldier said, taking my hand and me letting him as we slipped into a side room. Mildred was already waiting.

'Did you speak to her?' she asked, as Harvey shut the door.

'Not yet. I was waiting for Lionel.'

'She doesn't like to be cornered. You were supposed to do that before he got here.'

'Nobody likes to be cornered.'

'Please stop talking about me like I'm the Invisible Man,' I said, looking between the three of them. 'Speak to me about what?'

'We've got a job offer for you,' Lionel said. 'I wish this could be more formal, but discretion is key.'

'I have a job.'

'For how much longer?' Mildred asked. 'Dorothy's days are numbered and she knows it. I'm one of the last "coloured girls" working on any major studio set. This town might be more liberal than most, but this country won't be safe for you much longer, Tulip.'

'What are you saying?'

'Get out,' Harvey said, voice quiet but serious. 'Get out now and come work for us.'

'Us? You work on sets. All of you do.'

'Not anymore,' Harvey answered. 'I'm going back.'

'Back . . . into the army,' I whispered, finally making the connection. 'Back into intelligence, with Lionel.'

'We could use the skills of someone like you,' the fixer remarked.

I scoffed, a full-blown laugh on the tip of my lips before I hesitated. Everyone was staring at me with serious focus.

'Someone like me,' I repeated. Glancing at Mildred, she gave me a small shake of her head. She hadn't given me up. She never would. They didn't know I wasn't human like them. Lionel lit a cigar, taking slow, measured steps as he moved around the room.

'Someone with no background,' he puffed. 'No trackable records, no real name.'

He said that last part pointedly and I wondered how long he had known my 'real name' was not Tulip Han. A while, probably. Yet he'd never let me suspect a thing. Lionel continued.

'How many languages can you speak, Tulip?'

'Three,' I said, as he shook his head.

'Huey. Don't lie. Spanish, English and Mandarin we know. What else?'

I paused, staring at Harvey. He gave me a slow, reassuring smile, urging me to be honest. *God damn it*, I thought. *I trust him.*

'French, Cantonese and Cornish,' I added, notably leaving 'demon' off the list and registering Mildred's smirk. Harvey and Lionel exchanged a look like they had just hit the jackpot.

'I told you,' the former smiled. 'Do you think you can learn German?'

'I guess so. I tried a few years ago.'

'Why?'

'I got bored,' I admitted.

Harvey grinned. 'Her mind, I'm telling you—'

'I agree,' Lionel said, cutting him off. 'A war's coming, Tulip. If you pay attention to the world outside of this circus then I guess you already suspect that. Harvey and I here are working for a very special, very secret racket within British intelligence and we could use a forger like you. You'd be coming with us to England and then maybe France and wherever else we're needed. You'd be protected under the British and US governments and when we're done, we can give you a new name, a new life, a new identity, whatever you want.'

'I'm not a forger, I wouldn't even know what to do.'

'Yes, you do,' Harvey said, taking my hands in his. His skin was rough from the battles he'd fought seen and unseen. My skin was scarred too; whether it was from my escape or a florist's blade, my history was etched on it. Yet he didn't seem to care, protecting my flesh with his own as our fingers wrapped together. When he looked at me, it was like everyone else was furniture.

'I showed Lionel your work from the set,' he continued. 'It's a hundred times better than the guys we have working for us now and you didn't even have their resources. We could give you all of that, whatever you need, and you'd be making a real difference. You'd be getting our lads into Europe and innocent people out. You'd be helping deep cover agents like Mildred gather intelligence and maybe, just maybe, we can avert another war.'

'*Vive la révolution,*' Mildred remarked, drily.

'You could save lives, Tulip,' Harvey urged. 'You could be a hero.'

I should have yanked my fingers free from his, folded from the room and out into the night. Stupidly, as I looked into the soft greyish-blue of Harvey Schwartz's eyes, I ignored the first thing my father had ever taught me.

'I'm in,' I said, squeezing his hands back. 'When do we start?'

Chapter 14

Present

Nobody said wheeling an unconscious merman out of an underground supernatural lab would be easy. In fact, if they could make shirts with that exact slogan on it Dreckly would buy several. Amos had only managed to slur a few words, maybe a full sentence, before he passed out again. By the time they reached level one, Dreckly felt her hope crumple. He was a dead weight, literally, and she'd likely be more successful if she left him behind. *That's the fear talking*, she said. *It's the fear.*

She let out a panicked cry, allowing herself just one, before she dragged them both out into what looked like a loading dock not that different to the fish market. She'd left them behind. She'd abandoned all those others like a coward. Yet Dreckly Jones knew what she was: she was a survivor first, everything else second. She couldn't doubt those instincts now, despite how wrong it felt.

This area was completely empty, not a soul in sight, although there were clear signs it had been occupied by life, probably just moments earlier. A coffee cup still steaming, a truck idling, music playing from a radio. Maybe the drama she'd created downstairs had drawn everyone away. Maybe. She looked for an idea, scanning the space before her eyes settled back on the truck. She had no clue where they were or how far away the water was, so she would need transport.

The rear of the vehicle was much too large and stocked with all sorts of cables. A ramp had already been extended as the stock was offloaded, so Dreckly took it at a run as she rolled Amos up it. This was going to be bad. There was no way she could secure him properly or safely, let alone spare the time for it. He was going to end up bloody and bruised.

Yanking the door down and securing the latch, she kicked away the ramp as she climbed into the front cab. It was an automatic and she threw the vehicle into reverse, fanging it out the way it must have come in and towards the only path she could see.

A side lane opened up, showing her the exit route and she braked, moving into drive and following the arrows towards what she prayed was freedom. Swiping Sandra's card one last time, the security gate folded upwards and she put her foot on the accelerator. She took the exit ramp way too fast, but she didn't care by that point. She had glimpsed the night sky and that was enough.

Swerving out on to a surprisingly new albeit empty street, Dreckly straightened up the truck after hearing a loud bang from the back. That was probably Amos's stretcher, knocked over with him still attached to it. *If we both survive, he'll forgive me*, she thought. *A broken flipper won't mean shit.*

Her eyes swept the area for a landmark, anything that she could recognise or would tell her where she was. She drove past the Barangaroo Dental Clinic and let out a laughy breath. She was less than fifteen minutes away from the Sydney Fish Markets. Hell, they could've taken her unconscious body to the Treize labs via boat if they'd wanted to. *That's* how close they were.

So that's where she went. How long would it take them to figure out that she and Amos were missing? That three of their own were down? All she needed was enough time to get where she needed to go: out of Sydney. When she screeched into the fish market's car park, her eyes widened with shock as she drank in the sight of the entire Ravens M.C. assembled at the entrance to the jetty. There were dozens of bikes and everyone was dressed in their leather cuts, their backs to her at first.

The arrival of the truck drew their attention though and more than a few guns were quickly drawn before she had the idea to stick one hand out the window as a sign of surrender. She saw Chino point, shouting something to the others. It must have been her name, because several of the men lowered their weapons as she screeched to a stop as close to the water as possible.

'Dreckly!' Wyck shouted, wheeling his way through the group as she jumped out of the cabin. 'Where have you been?! We thought you'd been abducted! We were just about to start looking for you.'

She sprinted to him, planting a kiss on both his cheeks. 'Was abducted, now escaped, never been happier to see you.'

Standing back, she spun around to observe all of these men gathered in front of her, about to embark on a mission to find and save her even though they had *no idea* where to start and what she was facing. Ronaldo and Barto, two men she'd been on failed set-ups with courtesy of Wyck, were among them as well. Touched wasn't exactly the word for it; she was moved.

'WHAT IN THE EVER-LOVING FUCK?!'

There was a cluster of four lads at the back of the truck, staring inside with horror.

'Shit!' Dreckly cursed, sprinting over. She was relieved to see their reaction was because, well, there was a massive merman and not because Amos had been smooshed to sardines with her dodgy driving.

'HOLY H20: JUST ADD WATER!' Ronaldo exclaimed.

Another shouted, she thought his name was Pino. The story went that he had been hospitalised trying to get high off Pine O Cleen washing liquid or something like that.

'Oh, that's Amos,' she sighed. 'Help me with the stretcher, will you?'

'IS THAT A FUCKING MAMMOTH FISH IN A WOOLIES TROLLEY?!? WHAT THE FUCK, DRECKLY!'

'Amos,' she repeated, Pino and the others helping get him down. She checked his pulse. He was fine and she exhaled deeply.

'Can he be out of the water?' Ronaldo questioned. 'Is he dead?'

'No, he's not dead,' she said. 'And they can survive outside of the water for . . . a long time, actually. Longer than you'd think if they're adaptable, but Amos is a special case. I need to get him wet soon. Help me, will ya?'

It was the weirdest thing, an entire motorcycle gang carrying the stretcher towards the *Titanic II* as the wheels had been knocked off in transit. Someone had the jetty gate open, someone else had the lights in front of her boat illuminated, while Wyck was getting out the ramp he usually used for himself.

'You gotta get rid of the truck,' she told Chino, her shaking hands finally letting her hair free of the medical cap.

'I know a thousand ways to do that.'

'There's stuff in the back you might want to strip first, sell on or whatever. But I came from Barangaroo so my path here is gonna be caught on traffic cameras, maybe even the odd witness. It will be a few days or even a week, but people are going to show up here looking for it. And me.'

'And thicc fish boys?'

She barked a laugh. 'Answer D for all of the above.'

'Let me guess, you won't be here then?'

'I can't be, not for a while. Hey – wait!'

She stopped the bikies as they got to the boat, Dreckly helping unstrap Amos before she propped him up on the edge of the jetty. She dangled his tail into the water, waiting for the connection with the ocean to help him regain consciousness. He stirred again and she lowered herself into the depths, which were cold and dark at that time of night. It didn't matter though; this was more important.

'Dreckly—'

'I know what I'm doing,' she told Wyck, who looked concerned as she treaded water. 'Can y'all pass him to me? Slowly?'

'Won't he drown?'

'No, his natural instincts will take over soon as they get the chance.'

'How do you know that?'

She didn't answer, but the boys did as she asked, gripping under his armpits as they dipped him like a giant tea bag. She told them to let go and he splashed under the surface for a moment, Dreckly using her legs to prop him up as she balanced his head on her shoulders. It was difficult and her body strained to keep them both afloat as she used the same position lifesavers used to swim an unconscious patient to shore. Amos wasn't that anymore, his eyelids fluttering as the water surrounded them both. She cupped small amounts of it in her hand, running it through his hair and his chest so that as much of him was getting covered as possible.

'Ka . . . Kaia?'

'Afraid not,' she replied. 'It's Dreckly.'

He startled, his natural instincts doing what she'd said they would.

'It's okay, we're not there anymore; feel the water. Let it tell you where you are.'

With each passing second, he grew more alert. It was less than a minute before he didn't need her help anymore, Dreckly gripping on to the jetty with one arm as he swum away from her, dipping beneath the surface and reappearing again. She knew the look on his face, knew how just the sheer physical contact with the water could reinvigorate your very core. That's how he looked as he blinked away the water droplets. She kicked herself upwards, straining as she climbed out of the water and rolling on to her back as she panted on the surface of the jetty. She was exhausted, physically and emotionally.

'I don't . . . I can't thank you all enough,' Dreckly said, her eyes closed as she lay there. 'You all looking to come after me. I don't deserve that.'

'Yeah nah,' Wyck whispered. 'You do. We all know it.'

She sat up, smiling at her friend as she gripped his fingers. She looked over his shoulder at her boat, which appeared perfect from a cursory glance.

'Did you tidy up?'

'No,' Wyck replied, shaking his head.

'Everything looks exactly the same as it was. No sign of a struggle. How'd you know I'd been taken?'

'Besides your obvious absence?' he snorted. 'The whole place didn't feel right. It was off. And the record player was gone.'

With a heave, she pulled herself to standing. 'Damn, you're the best.'

'And you have to go.'

She met his gaze, both knowing what was next. 'I don't know when I can come back.'

Dreckly was addressing all of them, making sure they understood.

'We get it.' Wyck nodded. 'You know how to reach me and Chino. Just get out of here now, while you're still safe and you still can. We'll take care of the rest.'

'I'll pay you back,' she said, unwinding the rope that tethered the boat and making the preparations she needed to as quickly as she could. 'I don't know how, but I'll find a way.'

'Just go,' Chino called as she started the engine and switched the button to pull up the anchor. She swept down, giving both the president and his right-hand man one final hug.

'Wait, Wyck – I need you to get a message to Ben. I'm not sure how long I was gone for, but he'll come looking for me.'

'Already has,' her friend replied, a question for another day in his eyes. 'Said there were unfamiliar scents on the boat, which I argued could be any one of your customers but he felt differently. And you were gone two days.'

'Two . . . shit, okay. Listen very carefully to what I'm about to tell you. It won't make sense.'

'Your crap rarely does.'

She laughed. 'Tell him he's right, they're all right, and those that are being taken are being held in a five-floor subterranean facility in Barangaroo. Maybe fifty are there, maybe less, I counted just over thirty that I could see. With staff probably half that.'

He nodded, listening intently.

'You got all that?'

He repeated her message as Amos resurfaced and watched the proceedings carefully, just his eyes and the top of his head visible above the water. Wyck waved her off and she kissed his cheek once more, before calling out to the merman.

'Feel better?' she asked him.

'Yes, but not—'

'One hundred per cent. It's gonna be a while. Can you get up into the back of the boat? You need to rest and recover your strength while you can. The *Titanic II* is faster than you can swim right now.'

He did as she ordered, Dreckly not bothering to wave to the motorcycle club as she pulled out of the dock. They weren't looking back at her; they were already rushing and moving around with purpose as they sought to destroy the truck. She followed their lead, spinning around and keeping her eyes on the bow as she maintained the exact amount of knots she needed to stay right on the threshold of the speed limit.

As she steered out towards the harbour, she knew the Water Police patrolled twenty-four hours a day and it was just as likely she could get stopped now as she could at lunchtime. Focusing on the dark skyline ahead and the illuminated Sydney Harbour Bridge as she passed underneath it, all Dreckly could do was keep moving. Never look back.

Chapter 15

Past

'You have everything you need?' Lionel asked me, leaning back in his chair with a deep sigh. He was observing me over a stack of documents that – no matter how hard we worked – never seemed to get any smaller. There were dozens of desks that had been crammed into the dining room of the residence we had taken over in the English countryside, each one occupied by those working for the Allies in some form. Phones were always ringing, typewriter keys were always being smashed, and high-ranking military personnel were always swooping in and out.

Lionel was important enough to have a separate office, which was basically just a repurposed smoking parlour, and I maintained real estate on one third of his desk. The specifics of his job were top secret, but the nuts and bolts of it was that he was responsible for managing a number of 'military assets'. Mildred, basically: spies of all ages and nationalities and backgrounds and reliabilities.

'I do,' I replied, double-checking the six names on my list and the individual packages I had for each of them. My role was to provide them with whatever they needed in terms of fake papers, passports, forged family photographs, birth certificates, housing records, even fraudulent letters from key officials depending on what the aim was. I had already been employed by the Allied forces for a year when World War II began in earnest.

Strangely, working on film sets had prepared me well for this job. Perhaps that's why Mildred had thought I'd be good at it. I excelled under pressure, except in Hollywood if I fucked up they might not make their days. Here if I fucked up, someone died. In fact, someone could die anyway due to absolutely no fault of mine: the documents could be perfect and it might be some other small, seemingly insignificant thing that tripped them up. It might just be bad luck.

'Better get going then. You can make the early train.'

'I thought you didn't want me to motor until the afternoon?'

'Catch the early train, soldier. Send him my regards.'

It was a loaded order, but I agreed and began packing up my things in a way that I hoped didn't come off as too excited. This was where I had been situated for the past six months, with my geographic location changing depending on where Lionel was needed, but it was the closest I had been to the city for a while. I was halfway out the door when he called after me.

'Heed the sirens, Tulip. Intelligence is telling us to expect nightly bombings in the city.'

I nodded, a mix of emotions swirling through my stomach. There was fear, but it was so constant and consistent I was growing used to it now. And excitement, which I felt sick about but couldn't help. It had been two months since I'd seen *him* and I was prepared to sprint all the way to London if I had to.

I had an escort into the city, always did. After all, most people didn't know I existed and those that did weren't clear on what 'Officer Daniels' did. That didn't stop the threat to me being very real. My side would kill to get their hands on someone who knew the aliases and last known locations of dozens of spies, so it was understandable their side would as well.

My security was a different plain-clothes officer every time, often a man but frequently women as well. It was their job to accompany me into London, then hang back at a distance while I did my business. It was usually at least one or two meetings with other military officials, a liaison with a source or several, then the best part of my job: Harvey Schwartz.

The train was never full on the way into London and out the window I watched the English countryside zip by. The way back was always packed: standing room only. But since the Luftwaffe had taken to bombing the city so frequently, people were trying to get out and get elsewhere as quickly as they could.

The train journey in was always a strange experience for me, because this land I was travelling across was the same one in which my father had his roots. Hundreds of kilometres away, sure. Yet these rolling hills and green plains looked just like Scotland – just like St Andrews – and just like the territory I had been so desperate to escape. Deep within this same soil were hundreds, maybe thousands, of supernatural prisoners exactly like my father had been. Exactly like I had been. Exactly like Yixin was.

I had a jolt for a moment, catching a glimpse of my own reflection as we passed through a tunnel and the cabin darkened. My hair was still short, still styled as best I could with the limited time I had, but it was blonde now: platinum blonde. I also had on a thick pair of specs, yet plain glass sat in the frames instead of a prescription from an optometrist.

It was one of the things I had learned from Mildred's 'deceit team' when I was getting my military training. They taught me to change little things, like the shape of someone's face or the style of their hair, as those tiny tweaks could do enough to subvert the image of the person someone was looking for. Anything unique had to be filed down: my eye colour had been used as an example.

'Too memorable,' one of them had said. 'You want to blend, but not too obviously.'

Oh, I was good at blending. They had no clue, but the reason I was so good at picking up their lessons was because I'd been blending my whole life. Only now there was slightly better technology: hair dye, contact lenses, lipstick, tanning lotion, any variety of cosmetics and, of course, clothing. Sometimes just changing the silhouette would be enough.

When I was on any kind of military black site, I dressed like the other women there: if not pants, then a skirt of modest length and a buttoned blouse. Today I was a civilian. I wore a floral dress that laced up at the front with fussy, lavender straps. There was a ribbon in the same shade that wrapped around the base of my black fedora, which was tilted slightly at an angle so that a portion of my face was covered.

Grabbing my suitcase, I slipped into my black overcoat and wiggled my fingers into a pair of leather gloves as I stepped off at King's Cross station. The aim was to look like a proper, English rose: but not rosy enough that I would be an easy mark. Hence why my shoes were a little scuffed and my suitcase tattered at the edges. These were details a potential thief would notice and hopefully think I was posturing.

The platform was packed, but I was more than used to pushing my way through the throng of bodies now. You had to have a little rascal in you, I realised. And a little bit of magic. I pushed people out of my path with air rather than elbows half the time and, because things were so hectic, it was rare that anybody noticed. In fact, I was using my powers more than ever.

I'd had to stop trying to sense changes in the air at night, searching for signs that a bombing was imminent. There was too much activity up there from the Royal Air Force and everyone else; I couldn't pinpoint anything useful. I was able to work faster than any other forger, thanks to my enhanced drying techniques. And when it got too cold in the winter, a particular black site or home base for nearby troops too draughty, I would redirect warm air flow their way as well.

I knew I wasn't the only one. There was Mildred, of course, yet she was so deep behind enemy lines in Europe that I rarely saw her. But I had been spotting all kinds of supernaturals popping up in places I didn't expect, like a coven of witches working in a military hospital in Manchester. To the casual eye, they behaved just like any other nurse. Yet they were casting spells constantly, slipping healing charms under patients pillows, and making their own home remedies.

After everything the human world and the supernatural one had done to their species, I had been floored to discover them there. There were countless reports of pilots washing up on the shores of Britain, Scotland and Ireland relatively unscathed and hundreds of miles from where their aircrafts had reportedly gone down. They couldn't explain it, while others spoke of 'angels' that had emerged from the sea and saved them. Those accounts were written off as PTSD-related ramblings.

Selkies, I had thought.

In fairness, I had seen just as many supernaturals ducking out of the way of the war as I had those who were involved in it. Werewolves were human from the outside, so they had often been drafted without their superiors knowing what kind of asset they had acquired. For the most part, I got the impression the mass consensus was leave the humans to it. This had happened before and it would happen again: the supernatural world would evolve and grow around whatever was left. For me, there was never any question. I wasn't siding with the humans; I was siding with *good*. Even if I had no special abilities and had a normal, mortal life, I had no doubt that I would have ended up in exactly the same spot: involved in this war and using the skills I had for what I believed was the right cause.

Stopping at a pub en route to the apartment in St Pancras, I was earlier than I needed to be. My first meeting wasn't until 7 p.m. that night and it was only just ticking past midday. I needed Dutch courage in the meantime.

'Something to eat, love?'

'Whiskey, neat,' I told the barman. 'Don't care which.'

'Ah, an American,' he remarked. 'Reckon it's about bloody time your lot got involved, don't ya think?'

I downed the first, ordered another, then downed the second before I let out a shaky exhale.

'Indeed, I do.'

I had to resist the compulsion to skip from the pub, maintaining a slow and measured pace as I walked around a mound of rubble that had last week been a post office. I pushed through the iron gate of the apartment complex and into the stairwell of the building, my security escort lingering out on the street. I gave up all sense of decorum as I raced up the stairs, taking them two at a time – and in heels, no less! I arrived at the door breathless as I pushed the key into the lock and burst inside.

Harvey was shaving in the kitchen where the natural light was brightest. He had been hunched down in front of a portable mirror when I made my entrance, shirtless, razor in hand, and shaving cream smeared all over his face. I'd surprised him enough that he'd cut himself just a little, the smallest droplet of blood beginning to form on the real estate of his jaw that he'd actually managed to clear.

'Christ!' he cried, before dropping the razor on the ground and embracing me.

I flung myself at him, wiping the shaving cream away with my hand so I could kiss him properly. I ended up relocating most of it on to my coat instead, but I didn't care. As his lips touched mine, his tongue, his taste, his bite, nothing mattered except the fact we were touching each other. It wasn't just one of the scenarios I'd conjured up in my head at night to coax myself to sleep. It was real.

It was a truly bizarre thing, to have so much happiness in a time that was full of so much misery for everyone else. Yet love was not known for its convenience or punctuality. It didn't know right from wrong: it just saw a thing and pointed you in the direction of it. Or at least that's how I tried to rationalise it, because I had never intended to fall in love with Harvey. Once I had, I never intended to act on it. Not even when he said he loved me.

I knew Harvey was still a married man on paper, I knew he had two children – a boy and a girl – and if we lived through this war, I knew the idea of him officially leaving his family and giving up the ruse to run away with me was a fanciful one no matter how much he said it wasn't.

I knew all that and loved him anyway, wrapped up under the covers as he cradled me from behind. Loving Harvey Schwartz was the most selfish, reckless thing I'd ever done. It was lightning in a bottle, this pure happiness we had both been able to capture among one of the worst times in human history. In part, the war had made it easier for us. Any hard conversations we'd eventually need to have relied on both of us surviving, and the long periods without each other, the waiting and worrying, just intensified everything we already felt.

Yet it worked, somehow, his fingertips running through my hair as he caught me up on everything that had been happening in France over the last few months. That's where he was stationed as the handler for various Allied spies and as a gatherer of intelligence himself. It was an extremely risky job and one where there was no glory to be had. If he, Mildred and Lionel were successful at it, no one other than a group of two dozen people would ever know. But I knew. And so did he.

This was our routine, meeting in the apartment and – after confronting our base passions – curling up in bed like the rest of the war wasn't happening just outside the window. We couldn't risk communication through letters and the rare coded message when we were apart was kept strictly to business matters. Sometimes I'd get a late night or early morning call from Harvey, but they were rare and I always chastised him for it.

'No more flirting with the undertaker,' I had snapped down the line at him once. 'It's too great a risk and it's not worth dying so you can make a phone call to your sweetheart.'

'Ah, well, sweetheart: if you'd had the week I've had over here, you'd understand why this was the only thing worthwhile in the moment.'

I'd immediately felt bad, of course, telling him I loved him as he said it back but in a much more verbose and romantic way. I wasn't a wordsmith like he seemed to be. Every time we parted, he left me with a love letter that I would read and reread until I saw him again.

'Do you notice that when we have sex, there's always a massive gust of wind?' he said, the question surprising me as I twisted around to look at him. 'Something is knocked over or a window is blown open. Even when we had a tryst in Lionel's office in Birmingham that one time – remember?'

'Of course I remember.' I smirked, unsure how I was going to be able to explain away that every time he gave me an orgasm, I lost control. It was like a wild, elemental part of me was released and there was no stopping it.

'It's just weird, is all. Whenever I feel a breeze now I think of you, even if it's bloody freezing.'

I distracted him with a kiss, just gentle and just rough enough that his questions stopped. He'd shaved now, his jawline smooth as I ran my fingers along it. I didn't care either way, but Harvey always had a hang-up about me seeing him when he 'didn't look like a gentleman'.

'What time is?' I asked, my rose-coloured slip clinging to my body as I sat up and checked the gold pocket watch I had once stolen from that Spanish ship as a girl. 'It's ten to six.'

'Your meeting's at seven, isn't it, love?'

'Yes. And it's just the one, so I shouldn't be long.'

'Everything's jake then.'

He kissed the bare skin of my shoulder, pulling me back down on to the mattress with him. I sighed with contentment, nestling into his protective hold and resting my head on his chest.

'Did you have to grease Lionel to get away so early?' Harvey asked.

'Hmmm? Oh, no. He made me, actually. Said there wasn't anything else pending and I should get into the city sooner rather than later. He sends his regards, by the way.'

'That sly dog.'

'What do you mean?'

'He knows, honey. He has known about us for a while.'

'What? Harvey! Did you tell him?'

'Of course not, I would never do that to you. He just . . . subtly mentioned it when we were briefing after Dunkirk.'

'Good grief, what did he say?'

'That if I got you pregnant, he'd shoot me himself.'

I let out a sound that was a combination of a laugh and a cry of horror, biting my lip to stop anything else escaping.

'I . . . wow, actually that's not as bad as it could have been.'

'He said he'd murder me.'

'Yes, but he didn't say "stop thinking with your heart and start thinking with your head" or something dry.'

'He also said he'd never seen me happier, which was a strange thing to say to someone during a war.'

'I feel that way too,' I muttered, squeezing his hand. 'I'm constantly feeling guilty about how happy I am and feeling like I need to present sadder or something.'

'I know all about guilt,' he replied, a sad smile twitching over his face.

Involuntarily I glanced at his left hand, where his wedding ring should have been. It wasn't there. It hadn't been there for a while.

'I should get dressed,' I whispered, liberating myself from the bed. He let me go, watching as I opened my suitcase and retrieved the small bag of toiletries I kept there. My clothes were scattered all over the apartment and it was like a shameful treasure hunt before I retreated to the bathroom. I heard Harvey start the record player, an early hit from the Andrews Sisters coming through the speakers. They were his favourite musical act and it had been such a surprise to me when I'd learned that information. I couldn't help but smile as I fixed my make-up, Harvey's voice gently singing along to the lyrics of 'Tu-Li-Tulip Time'.

'Tu-li-tu-li-tu-li-tulip time,' he crooned.

There was clanging and banging, which meant he was cooking me something. When I slipped back out into the kitchen, he had a cigarette dangling from his lips as he flipped pancakes with a spatula.

'You gotta eat something,' he said, pre-empting my protests. 'You got here at lunch and the only thing you've eaten is my face off. You'll get illuminated if they offer you a single glass of wine at your meeting.'

'Pancakes are not a dinner food,' I rebutted, the smell drawing me closer.

'No, but they are both delicious and your favourite.'

'Make it quick then,' I huffed, not wanting to admit that he had me. 'And I've got your paperwork.'

I opened my suitcase wide, running my fingers carefully along the inner lining of the bag. There was an entire section hidden behind it, in case I was abducted and inspected for any reason. Inside were the six packages I'd made up and I placed them on the coffee table. I wrote colours on the top of each envelope, never names, but Harvey knew which shade belonged to which asset.

He set down two plates of pancakes, butter and maple syrup sliding over their smooth surface. Given wartime rations, this was a meal of significant luxury and I was starving.

'Here's the rainbow,' I said, gesturing to the assignment I was handing off to him. I hesitated, before placing a much larger, much heavier package down on the table right in front of him. 'And here's the other thing you asked for.'

He looked at me excitedly, snatching it up immediately and ripping it open as he inspected the contents.

'Honey, these are great. These are wonderful!'

I made an unhappy noise through a mouthful of pancakes, swallowing quickly so I could reply. 'They're the best I could do. You didn't have photos of everyone, just written descriptions of half the people you're trying to smuggle out of there so if the images I've doctored are a little off, they'll need to tweak their appearance to match them.'

'Of course, they know that already. How many are here?'

'The seventy identities you wanted, plus ten blanks.'

He paused flicking through the pages of a Spanish passport I had manufactured, mouth popping open with surprise.

'You . . . you made me blanks?'

I nodded. 'I'm scared for you, but I agree with what you're doing. I've seen the intel too, Harvey. I've heard the whispers. Those that aren't being murdered outright are being disappeared; they're being sent somewhere.'

'They're being eradicated,' he said. 'They're massacring Jews; they're massacring my people. America aren't getting involved yet, but I can't just sit idly by when I can do something now.'

'I know. Anything you need, you just tell me.'

'I need you to accept a gift.'

I blinked, dizzy at the change in direction. 'Now's not really . . .'

He slid a box across the table. I had to make the crucial decision to lower my latest bite of pancakes as the fork was dangerously close to my mouth. My fingernails ran over the leather of the packaging, clicking open the metallic latch and inspecting the contents.

'A gun?'

'You remember what I taught you? How to use it?'

'Of course, y—'

'Lionel might think keeping you close to him is the best way to keep you safe, but I would sleep easier knowing you can protect yourself with this if you need to.'

'I . . . I don't know, Harvey.'

He got to his feet, tilting my head upwards with a finger under the chin. 'Please, I love you. I can't lose you. Take this with you, everywhere.'

'All right,' I said, closing my eyes as I leaned my head against his stomach. His hands ran through my hair again, stroking it as he held me in place. 'I'll take the gun.'

Chapter 16

Dreckly Jones was waiting in line for an autograph. That was not a thing that made sense to her, but as she was jostled by the crowd lining up for their two seconds with the biggest stars of the Energen X Ironman Series, she was resigned to the fact that this was just something she *had* to do. And in her hand, a glossy photograph of the woman she was waiting to see: Kaia Craig.

Wearing a lavender full piece with the Energen X logo splashed down the side of her torso in the picture, the woman struck a pose as she stood there holding a fibreglass paddle. There was a half-smile on her face as she looked off in the distance, the sunset giving Kaia's skin a bronze glow. Her white-blonde hair was frozen in place, captured right at the moment the wind had whipped it up. Underneath the image was a list of her title wins, all of the words gibberish to Dreckly as she scanned them.

There were just two kids in front of her now as she inched further up the line, both of them in their early tweens, and Kaia posed for a photo with the first of them. Huge smile plastered on her face, Dreckly thought she kind of looked like a supermodel who had seen some shit. She was barely out of her teens herself, but there was something that eluded to what she'd been through besides the scar that ran from her lip and down her chin. Maybe she was just reading too much into it, her opinion informed by everything Amos had told her about this girl.

'Facts,' Dreckly had urged him. 'Stick to the facts and what is useful to us, not your feelings.'

It had been two weeks since they'd fled Sydney, with Dreckly choosing to head north towards Queensland. South was a bad idea: the seas got rougher the closer you got to Tasmania and Amos had barely escaped Tasmanian devil shifters once. The water got colder there too and the selkie needed warmth: he was still healing. He took moments off the boat to swim along-side it at intervals, but he would always return weak and tired. What they'd done to him could not be fixed overnight.

Thankfully she kept the *Titanic II* fully stocked and fully fuelled just for moments like the one she was currently living in. Yet the plan had never been to escape with a passenger, so she was moving through supplies quicker than she anticipated – specifically food. By the time they passed Byron Bay off the coast, Amos was needing to catch fish for their meals. Dreckly couldn't eat it the way he desired: raw. But she prepared and cook what he brought, which was doubly handy because the sheer act of hunting and catching live fish was the perfect way to rebuild his strength and sharpen his reflexes.

Airlie Beach had been her original destination, but when she took stock of the boat, she realised she'd have to make land a lot sooner. The Gold Coast was the only other reasonable option. It was a bustling, aquatic metropolis and blending there would be easier than anywhere else. It was also where Kaia lived, Amos had excitedly informed her. She wanted to roll her eyes and sarcastically tell him 'great', but her heart wasn't that cold yet. Nothing could heal you faster than love and she agreed to organise for the two of them to meet with the hope it would help him.

In return, he had to help her. Lorcan had been on her boat for one purpose – to detain her – along with those freaky twins. He clearly hadn't dug into much of what was physically on board, as all of her forgery materials remained intact and untouched. The locked drawers hadn't been broken. Her computer hadn't been accessed. If the situation was reversed, she would have gone through *all* of his shit. Perhaps he hadn't had enough time; getting her out of there the priority. Or perhaps his heart wasn't really in it. Yet soon as dawn broke on that first day, she searched the boat top to bottom looking for any kind of tracker he may have planted.

There was nothing in the interior, but there were a thousand places to hide things on a vessel. She'd powered down the engine when she felt confident the waters were calm enough and had Amos meticulously inspect the underside of the hull. She'd dived in herself, donning a wetsuit and examining every nook and cranny: from running her fingers along the Plimsoll line to even the hawse pipe where the anchor slid through. They didn't find anything. She prayed that it meant Lorcan hadn't placed a tracker and not that she and Amos had done a haphazard job of searching.

So they took it slow and they took it careful, a full week passing before Dreckly found a marina that met her needs in terms of providing them with enough security and enough clientele to make sure the *Titanic II* was just one of dozens of boats docked there. Then it had just been a matter of using one of the many disguises she kept for clients, scan through Kaia Craig's official website for an opportunity, and refuel.

Dreckly had never been to the Gold Coast before and it wasn't exactly her destination of choice. It reminded her a lot of Florida, a place she hadn't lingered. They did have the same benefit, however, and that was a lot of loudness and colour and distraction. In terms of places to hide, she wasn't sure why she hadn't considered it sooner.

'Excuse me, you're next.'

The man behind Dreckly in the line nudged her forward and she jumped, startled back to the present.

'Oh, ah, thank you,' she told him, before meeting the expectant expression of Kaia Craig as she waited for her at the signing table.

'Hi there.' The girl beamed, taking the picture of herself that Dreckly offered. There were several different types of metallic markers in a container near her hand and she had a silver one wedged between her fingertips and ready to go like a seasoned pro. 'What's your name?'

'I'm getting this signed for a friend,' she said.

'Great! That's so nice of you. What's their name?'

'Amos.'

If Dreckly hadn't been expecting it, she might have missed the way the woman's face changed for just a moment. The picture-perfect smile faltered ever-so-slightly and the tip of the pen paused on its way to make contact with the photograph.

'W-what's his last name?' Kaia asked.

'Waldman,' she supplied. 'Amos Waldman, but just Amos is fine.'

Kaia met her gaze and Dreckly held it, trying to shoot meaning out of her eyeballs like lasers. She was essentially using the same method her clients did when courting her: a public setting, a few choice keywords, and a minimal amount of risk.

'To Amos,' Kaia wrote. 'Just keep swimming.'

Her signature swished across the photograph dramatically.

'It's a shame your friend can't make it.'

'Believe me, he wanted to be here a lot more than I do. But he's under the weather.'

'Oh? Is it . . . serious?'

'We hope not. A visit from family and friends tonight might help. We'll see.'

Kaia's brow creased with understanding as she handed the photo back, Dreckly placing a note into the woman's hands underneath in a seamless gesture. She was good, this ironwoman. She didn't react, just smiled as she tucked her hands into the pockets of her denim cut-off shorts and safely deposited the piece of paper. All it said was the name of the marina in Coomera and a number that correlated to where they were docked on the jetty.

'Well—' Kaia beamed '— hopefully a Storm might come tonight, break this heatwave.'

'A Storm would be welcome.' Dreckly nodded; speaking in code was her forte. She knew neither of them were talking about the weather event, but rather Kaia's older brother who was pivotal in initially helping to secure Amos's freedom. The selkie had warned her that Kaia would likely be nervous about coming alone: she'd want company in the form of either her sibling or best friend, Cabby.

The former was actually just behind her, rocking back and forth on a chair as he engaged in conversation with one of the ironmen who didn't have anywhere near as big of a fan line as Kaia did. You didn't need to do a DNA test to work out they were related, both gangly and sporting mops of noodlelike hair that only looked that way if you practically lived amongst sun and sea salt. He must have felt her eyes on him, as he looked up. Storm Craig gave her a lazy smirk, clearly indicating that if she was checking him out, then he was willing to be checked.

'Thanks again,' Dreckly said, returning her focus to Kaia. 'Best of luck in the race.'

'Thank you,' she murmured.

The Energen X Ironman series ran from November to April, with just three of the eight events remaining for the year as they approached the end of January. This was just one of several massive press days they ran all across the country leading up to the next race, which was taking place at Kurrawa Beach on the weekend. It was a Wednesday, so this tent had been erected with brands hosting giveaways outside, local radio stations broadcasting from the lawns of the surf club, kids taking part in surf sports workshops, and fans lining up for a few moments with their favourite athletes.

Dreckly felt exposed in this setting and she didn't like it, eager to leave as quickly as she could and get back to the boat. Amos was there when she returned, which was a surprise because they'd decided during the day it was best to stay submerged and out of sight: at least until the sun set. Yet a rain and lightning storm had descended on the Gold Coast by mid-afternoon, meaning those who were usually out and about on the decks of their boats or happily trotting up and down the lengths of the jetty, weren't there. Their eyes weren't there. So Amos was hidden from sight, happily getting splattered with fresh raindrops from above when Dreckly – drenched – stepped on board. He sprung upright like a jack-in-the-box at her arrival.

'Did you see her? How was she? Do you think she understood?'

'Yes, good, and yes,' she answered, leaning against the bench in the kitchen as she dried herself off with a towel.

'So you think she'll come?'

'I don't know.' Dreckly sighed, falling quiet as she watched him where he sat at the stern.

'What is it?' he asked.

She gently shook her head. 'Nothing.'

'You look sad.'

'I'm always sad.'

'Sad*der*.'

'I . . . it's just you're sitting in Wyck's spot. That's where he'd always keep watch, Betty at his side.'

'Betty?'

'His gun.'

'Oh. Do you miss your friends?'

'I don't want to talk about that,' she told him, spinning on her heels as she headed for the bathroom.

It was rude, sure, but he was on *her* boat and she'd risked *her* life for him, so Dreckly guessed that bought her some leeway. She also didn't want to get into this again, Amos pressing her for all the details about the night they'd escaped. At first, the way he'd looked at her – like she was some kind of saviour – made Dreckly feel good. She'd watched as that was replaced with disappointment as she'd told him the truth: that she'd abandoned them, left all the others behind to fend for themselves. This selkie had endured but he was still just a child in her eyes. How could he ever understand the thing she valued most – freedom – came at a high cost?

She tried to wash away her guilt with a long shower and then a long nap. With just her to man the boat, there hadn't been much time for sleep in regular stretches and she felt like she was still catching up.

When she stirred, it was late: a lot later than she'd intended. Reaching over, she ran her fingernails across the name engraved on her pocket watch, this object one of the few things she'd been able to hold on to and treasure in her lifetime as it passed from one owner to another. It had required a few mechanical makeovers under the hood to ensure it remained in working order, Dreckly clicking it open to watch the second hand tick just past ten. The marina was quiet and the storm had eased for now, but the sky still sparked with white activity as lightning ran across it every few minutes. Thunder rumbled in the distance as she stumbled up the stairs from her bedroom, the growl matching one in her stomach.

'Why didn't you wake me?' she groaned to Amos, splashing water on her face.

'You needed the rest,' he replied, still sitting in the same spot he'd been when she first went below deck. 'You've been trying to make sure I didn't notice, but I did.'

She smirked. 'I did need it. Any sign of them?'

'No,' Amos answered, disappointment in his tone. 'Kaia would often come later, so I'm not worried.'

Dreckly joined him, sitting down on the edge of the boat and slipping her legs into the cool depths as his tail trailed in the water. She ran a hand through the substance, noting that her nails were getting to the point of shameful as the liquid moved away from her fingers in ripples. Katya would want to murder Dreckly if she saw the state of them, but on the list of priorities she had, that was *extremely* low. Barely a blip.

'Dreckly,' Amos whispered, grabbing her bare thigh and gripping it as if in a state of panic. She swallowed her sip, tracking his stare to the source of alarm. Walking along the jetty, quite far off in the distance, was Kaia Craig, her brother Storm, and the woman she had to assume was Cabby. *They brought the whole gang*, she thought, knowing how delighted this would make Amos. They were inspecting the numbers at each branch, looking for the one she had given them. Dreckly got to her feet, knowing they would need guidance as well as someone to unlock the security gate.

'No, I saw the woman you were talking about,' Storm was saying as she walked towards them, bare feet brushing over the synthetic material of the jetty surface. 'She was a babe.'

'You didn't say that,' Cabby snapped, seemingly much more interested in the story now.

'Because you're not single, are you? Let's stay focused on my interests for once.'

'Let's stay focused on finding this damn jetty,' Kaia countered.

'I'm just saying, yes, so she hit all the right buzzwords – but how do we know for certain this isn't a trap?'

'You don't,' Dreckly answered, causing all three of them to jump. 'Sometimes you've gotta go with your gut.'

Cabby leaned across, whispering to Storm, 'Total. Babe.'

'Right?'

'Where is he?' Kaia asked, marching quickly towards her. Dreckly held open the gate, pointing towards the *Titanic II* where it was docked two boats from the end. Any doubts she might have had about whether this human woman's feelings towards Amos were reciprocated were blown away in an instant as her face transformed. Dreckly couldn't be sure if she'd ever looked that way, but she'd certainly felt it as Kaia took off at a sprint. She ran past Amos, diving off the edge of the jetty and into the water. He disappeared from the back of the boat, the two of them re-emerging in each other's arms albeit only briefly. They dived under the surface, the pair completely vanishing again.

'Uh . . .'

'This usually takes a while,' Cabby said, patting Dreckly on the shoulder as she walked past. 'They dive under, swim away, pop up somewhere more discreet so Kaia can breathe—'

'And make out,' Storm muttered, winking at Dreckly as he followed after his friend. 'Nice to see ya again. Cabby, you got her phone?'

'She didn't bring it with her in case we were being followed.'

'Good. Was gonna say we can't lose another phone this way.'

Dreckly shut the gate after them, ushering the party on to her boat as they slumped around one of the padded benches inside. The silence was super uncomfortable. And awkward. Thankfully she didn't have to fill it.

'She does this a lot,' Storm said, jerking his head behind him.

'Does . . . what?'

'Takes weird swims at unusual hours,' Cabby supplied. 'Kaia makes a routine of it, picking all different kinds of bodies of water across the country when she travels. Always at an ungodly hour.'

'In case they're still tracking her,' Dreckly said, finally understanding.

'Yup,' the brother confirmed. 'It was bait at first, to see if they were still monitoring her. Still tracking all of us, really. It has the benefit of throwing them off too, because *if* they are, then they never know which swim is the one that *he* might be at. Been, what? Just over a year since she last saw him though. I knew she was getting worried, but also . . . hopeful, maybe, that he was happy with his people.'

'No aquatic humanoid left behind!' Cabby said, Storm and her laughing at a joke Dreckly didn't get. The phrase was close enough to 'no man left behind' that she felt a stirring of guilt in her stomach again. She had walked away from plenty of heroic situations in her life, but for whatever reason this one was sticking with her, niggling at her conscience, telling her she'd fucked up. *How would you feel, if you had been left behind?* That's what the little voice in her head asked as she waited to go to sleep at night, Dreckly promptly telling it to *fuck right off.*

A few nights ago, on one of those quiet, moonless nights out there on the open ocean, when it had been safest for Amos to swim, he had returned to the boat with two selkies in tow. He didn't know them, they weren't from his pondant, but they had puzzled at his injuries and questioned who he was with and why. He'd brought them to Dreckly and the *Titanic II*; she was the best person to converse with them because she knew the most about the situation.

Selkies weren't like humans. They weren't even like the rest of the supernaturals out there. Maybe it was because she was made up of half of them, but Dreckly trusted selkies implicitly. So they'd spoken. Amos had listened. Then she had sent one north, to find his people and alert them to where they'd be on the Gold Coast.

She'd sent the other one south, back towards Sydney and deep to where the local pondants lived. That one was to pass on all she knew about the abductions and the Treize seeking members of their own kind to experiment on, kill, and then eventually dissect. It was likely there were members of their families missing and these beings deserved to know why. More importantly, if their experiments continued to be unsuccessful like she suspected, the Treize would need more and everyone who could be warned, should be warned.

When the two selkies had dived under water and on to their respective tasks, she'd known she couldn't put off the moment any longer. She had to tell Amos the truth. With a deep breath, she'd exhaled the facts before waiting for his response.

'We have to go back,' he had said, matter-of-factly.

'We can't go back,' she'd scoffed.

'We can and we will. We shouldn't have run in the first place.'

'Okay, firstly there was no "we". You were unconscious, so I made the choice to leave the others behind. I made the choice to break out of there with just the two of us. I made the choice to run. You were not in the condition to stay and fight *an entire city's army of Treize*. Think about what you're saying! You're still recovering, you can't even shift properly.'

'I'm working on that!' he'd snapped. 'And . . . I don't know, I don't know what the right course of action was, but running wasn't it.'

'It's very easy to think in moral absolutes, Amos. But it's likely if I hadn't run, you'd be dead. I probably would be too.'

'Instead, others are.'

'Yes.'

'And you can live with that?'

'I live with it every day.'

They'd engaged in an intense stare-off then, each one convinced their position was the right one.

'We have to go back and help them,' he'd said.

'No,' Dreckly had replied, firm.

'We—'

'What would you do? Huh? How would you contribute?'

'I know I'm not like the other selkies you've met; clearly I can't do as much. But I know what's right and I think you do too; that's why you're fighting this. That's why you were so desperate to pass that information on to Ben and the other supernaturals you know. You wanted to help them, you wanted to stay; you were just scared. And that's okay, Dreckly.'

'Don't psychoanalyse me,' she'd snapped, getting to her feet and storming from the boat's deck as she'd gone to start the engine. She'd barked that she was continuing to the Gold Coast whether he was coming or not.

He was right, of course, but she wasn't going to admit that. She was right too: he wasn't well enough to survive without her. So he had stayed with her, journeying to the coastal city with Dreckly as they'd tried to maintain an uneasy peace. He'd kept trying to bring it up. She'd kept trying to avoid it. Part of finding Kaia was to help him heal, bring him happiness, but also get him off her back.

Kaia clearly had a time limit, some kind of threshold that she kept her diversion swims under. Dreckly had to guess she pushed it that night, with almost a full hour and a half passing before she reappeared on the jetty, dripping wet while Amos smiled nearby. Her friend was prepared, with Cabby having brought a towel *and* a change of clothes with her in a surprisingly deep straw bag that hung diagonally across her body.

She was glad to see them leave in truth, walking the trio out of the marina just so she would have the relief of knowing they weren't coming back. Storm offered his services as tour guide around the city if she ever needed them, which Dreckly gently declined, while Cabby just gave her a wave before she jumped into their waiting car. Kaia lingered, clearly wanting a moment alone with her.

'Amos told me what you did for him, what you risked,' she said, towel hung around her shoulders like she'd just finished a fight. 'I don't know how we can ever repay you. I mean, he has had time to recover since you both escaped but he's . . .'

'Still got a ways to go,' Dreckly finished, earning a nod from the young woman.

'Yeah.'

There was a beat before Kaia spoke again, Dreckly already feeling uncomfortable the longer she was away from the boat.

'You're not exactly . . . like him, are you?'

'No,' she replied. 'Not really.'

'Not really,' Kaia recited, looking thoughtful. 'If you're not one of them but you're not really one of us, then what are you?'

'I'm what the rest of the world is populated with,' she answered, voice low. 'What was here before you, what will likely be here long after you.'

Her response must have confirmed something for the young woman, something she had perhaps always wondered about since meeting Amos. *What else is out there?* In Dreckly's experience, humans were either driven mad with wondering or desperately in denial as they went back to pretending the world was the same way it had always been.

'You don't seem like the kind of chick who would exchange numbers or anything—'

'I don't have a phone.'

'Right, well, if you ever need a place to crash on the Gold Coast or any kind of help, the Craigs are always here.'

'I'll keep that in mind.'

'Do. You're a hero to me.'

Kaia had been reaching for the car door when she paused, the word 'hero' causing a reaction on Dreckly's face that she'd noted.

'What? You are, Amos thinks so too.'

'That's not what he said to me. And he's right.'

'Right about what?'

She rolled her eyes, turning her back to walk away when she stopped. The car was still there, engine running, but Kaia hadn't got inside. Dreckly inhaled deeply, the humid Queensland air feeling like it was sticking to her lungs as she breathed it in.

'We left people behind,' she said, barely louder than a whisper. '*I* left people behind.'

'I . . . I'm sure you did all you could.'

'I didn't. I actively chose not to help when I had the capability to do so. I valued my own escape – and his – more than their lives.'

The silence was heavy as she waited for the woman to reply. She thought she wasn't going to and Dreckly went to leave, taking barely more than two steps before Kaia spoke up.

'We can't be judged by our worst mistakes. Or even our last.'

Dreckly half-pivoted to look over her shoulder at her.

'I've made mistakes too, but . . . it's about what you do to correct them.'

'And if I choose not to?'

'Then you learn to live with it.'

Or you don't, Dreckly said to herself. She walked away completely this time, hearing the slam of the door and gravel beneath tyres as the car pulled away. There was the soft sound of water sloshing, the gentle hollow of dinking of boats as they bumped against the jetty, and her silent footsteps as she walked slowly back to the *Titanic II*. All the while, she was deep in thought. Amos was sitting where he'd been before their visitors had arrived and looked like a lovestruck idiot as he stared up at the stormy night sky. She dropped down next to him, resting her chin on her legs as she tucked them to her chest.

'Makes you appreciate it more, doesn't it?' he said, neck still craned upwards.

'What does?'

'Not being able to see the sky.'

Dreckly arched her head upwards as well, the clouds suddenly illuminated and then plunged back into darkness by a fork of blue lightning. Even with her father's beautiful words and beautiful hands and beautiful mind, he wouldn't have been able to capture the magnificent, ferocious beauty of what she was looking at right then. The rumble of thunder that preceded the second strike of lightning sealed it for her.

'Amos,' Dreckly whispered, 'we're going back for the others.'

Chapter 17

Past

I was desperately looking for honey, my face smeared with dirt as I tore through a cottage just outside of Béziers in the South of France. Placing a small flashlight between my teeth so I could see in the darkness, I used both hands to throw open kitchen cupboards and sort through storerooms as quickly as I could. The scenario wasn't all that different to my first night out in the real world once I had escaped Vankila. Back then I had been terrified and powered by sheer adrenaline as I'd fumbled through a very different cottage in Scotland. This time, however, I wasn't alone.

'We need to hurry, darling,' Harvey was saying, his back to me as his eyes searched outside for any sign of the German patrol we were trying to avoid. 'I can hear dogs barking and if they get close enough, they'll pick up our scent and never let go.'

'They won't,' I told him, my love completely unaware that the only reason we'd managed to elude our pursuers this long was because I'd been blowing our scents in the complete opposite direction. It was sending the dogs mad, confusing them and their owners to the point several had been shot because their handlers thought they'd caught some kind of rabies that was making them unreliable.

'You're the luckiest woman I know, but eventually that luck is going to run out,' he murmured.

With a triumphant grin, I spun around to face Harvey with two full jars of honey in each hand. 'You were saying?'

He rolled his eyes at me, shaking his head in disbelief. 'Let's ankle, we've got a lot of ground to cover before daylight and this whole area is teeming with Germans.'

'Calmness and clarity,' I said, throwing his favourite catch-phrase back at him. He looked annoyed for barely a moment, smiling as he listened to me say his own mantra.

'Calmness and clarity,' Harvey repeated. 'Now move.'

We were dressed as civilians, our weapons hidden so that, if we were stopped, we might slip by initial scrutiny if we weren't searched properly. If we were, well, there would be little to explain the six different knives I carried in a holster that wrapped around my torso like a handbag strap. I wore a blouse with loose buttons that could be popped quickly if I needed to get to a weapon *fast*.

Harvey had just the one knife, but two pistols, and he checked they had sufficient ammunition before stashing them back under his coat. He reached into my own jacket, hands brushing my hip as he pulled the pistol he had given me free. He reloaded it, tucking it back where it belonged while planting a rushed kiss on my lips.

Slipping outside, I waited behind him as he scanned the rear of the property. I did the same, reaching out and extending my senses through the particles of the air like invisible tendrils.

'Nothing,' he said. I agreed.

We walked speedily towards a thick section of forest that bordered this collection of homes, all of them empty with their occupants having wisely abandoned them long ago. That's what I told myself, at least. From what I'd seen after parachuting into France two years ago, I knew that it was more likely the families who had once lived here were dead. Or imprisoned.

I handed Harvey the flashlight as he searched for the section of undergrowth we were looking for, reaching down and pulling several leaves and branches off an uneven mound. There were two bikes hidden there and he tugged them loose. Wasting no time, I got on mine and began pedalling. Harvey was right behind me, catching up in a matter of minutes as we followed a dirt road out of town.

Bicycles were the quickest and quietest way to get anywhere, with our route leaving us exposed for the next hour and a half as we rode to nearby Narbonne. Yet we had no other choice. Moving at night gave us a little protection, but I was giving myself a migraine as I strained to locate any foot patrols that might be nearby. The only benefit we had was this road had been subject to heavy attack over the last six months, meaning the surface was too uneven for most forms of military trucks and cars.

'Long way from the Paramount lot,' Harvey said, puffing alongside me as we cycled.

We were forced to stop twice, dismounting and diving into the bushes at the side of the road when we spotted headlights up ahead. Harvey held me tight as we both ceased to breathe, listening as the motorbikes zoomed by on the first occasion and a foot patrol stomped past on the second. We got lucky, making it to Narbonne just on the other side of midnight and into the protection of the woods that provided not just cover for us, but cover for dozens of French resistance fighters who were using the natural landscape to their advantage.

Although not for much longer, if the Germans had their way. Troops were sent in intermittently but they were never that successful in an environment that benefited guerrilla tactics rather than sheer numbers. There were immense forests that led right up to the Spanish border and that's where most of the Jewish and French people desperate to escape the country had been successfully smuggled through. There were some two hundred refugees currently crouched and hiding in a section of bush, waiting for Harvey's return so he could guide them to safety.

He'd done it on more than a hundred occasions at this point, been captured four times and escaped three. On the other occasion, the train he was being transported on had been raided by American troops based on intel provided by Mildred and he had been freed. Harvey was one of the Gestapo's most wanted targets and, for the past twenty-four months, I had been helping him in the field. I was his secret weapon, he said.

He hadn't wanted me there, preferring that I was safe from harm at Lionel's base of operations in Barcelona. Yet once the lines of distribution became comprised and we couldn't physically get forged documents to Harvey in whatever part of France he was hiding at the time, the whole endeavour had been pretty useless. In the field, however, I had use. I'd reteamed with some of the armed forces training pals from the US for a specialist camp in the Scottish isles, with Mildred being the unexpected guest of honour. Somehow, despite the war, the demon still managed to look like a glamourous movie star with her perfectly lined red lips. Her presence had helped ease my fear of returning to that country, a fear which felt dull in comparison to all the other fears that had replaced it in the meantime. The skills Mildred taught me and the others over the course of three months helped somewhat: skills of sabotage and espionage. I was a good shot, but my years in floristry had made me more gifted with a blade than any of my comrades.

'That's better anyway,' Mildred had told me. 'You can kill a man more quietly with a knife.'

Suddenly Harvey's hold on my shoulder stopped me in my tracks, both of us freezing in place as we listened to the crack of a tree branch nearby. *It could just be a deer*, I thought. But deer didn't take deliberate, slow steps that stopped when ours did.

'I think we're being followed,' he whispered.

Harvey was, like most things, right. I watched him stiffen as the tip of a rifle was pressed to the back of his head. I felt the same pressure as one was pressed to mine as well and we were forced apart.

'Get up,' one of the soldiers said, a flashlight suddenly blinking on and shining right in my eyes.

I squinted them shut, unable to see who our assailants were with the brightness blinding us completely.

'Please,' Harvey said, speaking in English with a thick, performative French accent, 'we're just looking for food.'

'Is this them?' one of the officers asked in German.

'I think so, but they're on foot. We were expecting them on bikes.'

'Does it matter if they're riding a fucking elephant? We're after the American, not a bicycle.'

'He sounds French. And his hair is black: the description said red.'

That had been my doing: it was harder for a man to slip by unnoticed than a woman, so I was always dyeing and redyeing Harvey's hair, applying the same practices I had learnt in forgery. If he had ginger hair and a beard while visiting Marseille, you could be damn sure it was greying mutton chops by the time he passed through Nantes.

'What about the woman? I don't like the look of her.'

'I do,' another replied, ripping the woollen hat from my head so my hair tumbled down around my face. From a distance I could pass as a man, my clothing adding to that illusion, but as they stripped the jacket from my body there was no further way to disguise what I was. I put on a show of resisting, but in reality it was so I could shake the pistol at my hip loose along with the holster. Both fell to the ground in the scuffle and I kicked dried leaves over the top, none of the soldiers noticing as they kept the light and attention on my face.

I copped a backhand from the one in charge, which sent my flying and I heard an angry shout from Harvey. I fell on my stomach, momentarily dazed by the impact, but it gave me the opportunity to slip a hand inside my blouse and extract the knife of choice. It was curved, stainless steel, and with more blade than handle. That also made it very easy to hide.

'Get away from her!' Harvey shouted, in pretty much perfect French. I was proud that despite our dire situation, he was still maintaining his cover convincingly.

'Search her! If he's hiding something, he'll be hiding it on her.'

Take me away, I thought, willing the soldiers to drag me from Harvey. *Take me somewhere out of sight.*

They didn't, choosing to search me right there in front of him and leaving me no other choice as they pinned my hands behind my back. I went for the one in charge, who was laying into Harvey with his colleague while the other two searched me. My eyes widened as I imagined myself as the air, the breeze, moving in and around him as it was inhaled and taken into his lungs. Then I took it out, willing all the air in his body to leave as I squinted and sucked him dry. It took a few seconds to take effect, which I had learned was the case from other soldiers I had killed doing exactly this.

I was a killer now and much as I liked to think that's what the war had made me, I knew the instinct was always there, just below the surface. From the moment I'd threatened to set an alchemist on fire during the Vankila breakout as a child, I *knew* I could do it and I knew likely one day I would have to in order to survive. I didn't have the luxury of time to examine that more closely, but one day I was sure I would have to.

I'd never stolen the air from someone's lungs in front of anyone before, only tackling the feat in one-on-one situations. This wasn't ideal, but they'd also left me no other choice. The guard stopped, releasing Harvey as he stepped back and clutched at his throat. His eyes were blinking rapidly, and his cheeks were puffing up and down, like he was attempting to blow up an invisible balloon. He dropped to his knees, his associate looking shocked as he held Harvey in both hands but diverted his focus to the man in charge.

'Wilhelm?' the man said, voice uncertain. '*Wilhelm?*!'

That was all the diversion Harvey needed, launching himself forward and headbutting his captor. The man grunted and stumbled back, while Harvey dropped to the ground and pulled the knife from his boot. He stabbed the man right in the centre of his chest before the two soldiers searching me even realised what had happened.

Harvey threw a handmade garrotte he always carried with him around the throat of one man, while I let the blade slide down my sleeve and into my fingers as I calmly stepped forward and slit the throat of the other soldier from ear to ear. He dropped to his knees, clutching at his severed artery as hot blood spilled over his fingers. When I turned around to check on Harvey, he had just finished strangling the third assailant. We had a 'no guns' rule when we could manage it, the sound and even the smell having the potential to attract more heat than we could handle. Using our hands was messier, but it could potentially save our lives.

In unison, we turned to inspect the one who had been in charge. He was lying face down and Harvey rolled him over, examining the blueish grey complexion and feeling for a pulse.

'He's dead,' he said, panting from the exertion of the fight. 'I don't know what happened.'

'Looks like a heart attack,' I offered as Harvey looked up at me, the light from the discarded torches casting strange shadows over his face.

'Yeah.' He frowned. 'You're probably rig—'

There was a gunshot off in the distance and we both jumped, Harvey reaching across as he clicked off all the flashlights except for one. He searched the four soldiers' corpses quickly, while I grabbed my pistol, holster and jacket from the dirt. I wiped my blade clean on the trousers of a dead man, Harvey's chuckle drawing my attention.

'Doesn't even look like me,' he said, holding up an alert that had a very crude representation of him drawn on it. 'The chin is all wrong. This person does *not* have your skill set.'

Springing to his feet, he cupped my face in his hands as he examined the welt that was forming on my cheekbone. I flinched as he touched it, Harvey pulling me close.

'You all right?'

'Everything's jake,' I replied, relieved that he'd moved on from the soldier's heart attack so quickly. '*Et toi?*'

'Jake. We need to move, get closer to the rendezvous point before dawn.'

He took my hand in his, bags over both of our shoulders as we ran. We couldn't worry about the noise now; the sun was rising too quickly, and we needed to get as far from the bodies and as close to the safehouse as we could. By the time we arrived to find our French contact pacing nervously out the front of a hut hidden deep within the woods, we were drenched with sweat.

'Has it been raining?' he asked, lowering his weapon as he assessed our appearance. 'Mademoiselle, you have blood on you!'

'I'm fine, Benoît,' I puffed, although it had been so long since I had last eaten anything. I hunched over and gagged.

'Get in,' he ordered. 'Sleep, bathe, there's bread in there and I can keep watch. We can't move again until nightfall anyway.'

I stumbled inside, hearing Harvey quiz the resistance soldier about the status of the others. 'Marie just left, she said everyone is holding firm and resting up before the crossing on foot.

I have bikes here for the two of us, but, *monsieur*, it's going to be of very little use with the tanks—'

'Don't you worry about the tanks; I'll take care of that.'

I already had a mouthful of bread and several bites of cheese down my throat by the time Harvey stepped inside, closing the door behind him. The space was fairly barren, it being one of thousands of temporary structures that had been erected all over France and stocked with essential supplies for those who desperately needed them. This one had a cot, blankets, firewood, spare ammunition, a large bucket filled with water and radio equipment set up on a small table along with the food.

Harvey didn't much care about that as I recognised the look in his eyes and swallowed. He stormed towards me, taking my face in his hands as he pushed me up against the rough wood of the hut. I let out a soft moan of surprise as he kissed me, both our bodies wet with perspiration as he stripped us free of our clothes in a matter of seconds. He had it down to a fine art by this point, both of our built-up fear channelled into the physical act.

I spun around, Harvey's fingers slipping between my legs while his other hand ran over the curve of my waist, the mound of my breast, and finally to the dip of my throat.

'I love you,' he whispered, nipping at my e arlobe as his breath tickled the back of my neck. 'I love you so much, I would die if they hurt you. I love you. *I love you.*'

I bent over, pulling him inside of me and wanting to cry with relief as he began those familiar motions. I held on to the edge of the table as Harvey thrust from behind, his hands gripping my buttocks as I closed my eyes and gave myself over to the sensation completely. This was not healthy, this compulsion we had for each other, but it very much felt like the only thing keeping us alive as he covered my mouth to muffle the cries of pleasure and came inside me.

I bit his finger, unable to help myself as he leaned against me with exhaustion. He chuckled, pulling us back off the table and into the bed.

I was curled up in his arms, the two of us wrapped in the prickly blankets inside the hut as we chose to forgo sleep for other pleasures. It had been worth it; it always was.

'Harvey?' I said. He wasn't asleep, but he had his eyes closed as he lay there with a lazy smile on face.

'Mmm?'

'There's something I need to tell you.'

He opened one eye, examining my serious expression.

'My real name . . . it's not Tulip Han.'

He knew that, Lionel had mentioned it in front of Harvey many years ago that he was aware my name was a fake one. Yet he had never pushed me about it since, never prodded me to divulge details of a past I didn't want to give up. His fingers had been idly tracing shapes on my bare shoulder and he paused, letting me take the time I needed to get this out.

'It's Dreckly. Dreckly Jones.'

'Sweetheart,' he breathed, touching the crease between my eyebrows as I frowned. 'That's . . .'

He stopped trying with words, lifting his neck instead as he rolled me over and kissed me, slow but deep. Pulling back, his nose brushed mine as he scrutinised my face.

'Dreckly Jones, it's such a privilege to make your acquaintance.'

There was a sharp knock on the door, Harvey telling Benoît to 'come in' as I wiggled down deeper under the covers. He and Harvey had worked together since before the German invasion, so the status of our relationship came as no surprise. I felt Harvey tuck another corner of the blanket more carefully over an exposed shoulder, protecting my modesty.

'I'm sorry to interrupt, but I think we should go soon,' the Frenchman said.

I felt Harvey glance at the pocket watch I had gifted him, his name engraved in the gold and a small tulip drawn underneath.

'It's only just past two,' he said. 'Sunset isn't for another three hours at least.'

'*Oui*, but it has started to rain. There's a big storm coming; I can smell it.'

'You can smell it?'

'He's right,' I said, popping my head up. It was a thunderstorm, a big one, and the air far above us was crackling with activity. Harvey opened his mouth as if he was about to question me, but he must have seen something in my eyes. *Trust me.*

'All right, lucky one,' he replied, clearly annoyed at having to move ahead of schedule. 'We can't waste the head start if it's going to get dark earlier than usual.'

Benoît left us to get changed and we washed down as much as we could with the limited basin of water and soap at our disposal. We were putting dirty clothes back on again, neither of us having had the foresight to wash them and leave them out to dry post-coitus.

'There's something else,' Benoît said, as we emerged from the hut packed and ready to go just fifteen minutes later. 'Ramón never arrived.'

Harvey was sliding into his coat when he paused, casting a serious glance my way.

'What time was he supposed to be here?' I asked, trying to remain level-headed.

'Midday.'

He was two and half hours late, which was alarming. Ramón was a Spanish ally and one of the best shooters we had. He was also punctual, often leaving way ahead of schedule in case he needed to stop, hide, or take an alternate route due to unexpected German obstacles.

'You shouldn't have waited two and half hours to tell us!' Harvey snapped. 'Fuck.'

'I didn't want to panic!'

'It's okay, Benoît,' I said, running my hand down Harvey's arm in an attempt to soothe him. 'He might be okay, he might be on his way or just delayed, he might be injured, and we find him on the path. If he's none of those things, then we adapt.'

'Ramón was supposed to go with you to the tanks,' Harvey sighed.

'I'll go by myself.'

'No.'

'Yes.'

'No, Benoît will go with you instead.'

'*No*, we stick to the plan. You need someone to watch your back more than I do: your mission is more important. I can do this alone; you know I'm capable.'

His face was strained and it looked like he wanted to argue with me, but we'd had this conversation a long time ago. We would never let our love get in the way of a mission, especially when there were hundreds of human lives on the line. That situation hadn't arisen yet; we had always been able to make both things work. This time it was different.

He used the material of my jacket to yank me towards him, tugging my body against his as he stared into my eyes. Benoît turned away to give us some privacy.

He kissed my forehead, he kissed my nose, he kissed my lips. I never wanted him to stop kissing my lips, but he did.

'I love you, Dreckly Jones,' he whispered. I felt my face twitch with surprise at those words.

'I love you too, Harvey Schwartz.'

'You're the love of my life.'

Squeezing his face as I kissed him once more, my fingertips pressed hard into his cheeks before I pulled away. I took several steps back, feeling like I needed to force space between us.

'Mine too.'

He smiled a grim smile, patting Benoît on the back to let the man know our emotional display was over.

'We go,' Harvey said. 'You and I, as planned. We meet everyone at camp and then begin the final trek over the border. It will take us four hours with all the bodies, but Tulip here is going to be giving us the advantage.'

'Don't wait for me,' I warned him. 'It will be easier if I cross further down the border and alone after the havoc I'm about to cause.'

'Yes, my love.'

Without a pause, I set off, not able to look back and not wanting to as I feared that if I turned around, I would sprint to Harvey. And then everything would be lost. I had a job to do and it involved two extremely hostile jars of honey. There was a small German outpost that had been set up directly in the path of where the refugees needed to cross to reach the Spanish border and safety on the other side. It hadn't been there a week ago. Now there were three tanks and an increasing number of foot soldiers being moved in over the past five days.

That wasn't an enormous expenditure of resources; after all, the tanks were Panzer I. There were three other updated models deadlier, faster, more state of the art, and also more common across most of France. The Panzer I's were actually a blessing because it implied the enemy were stretched. The curse was that it meant they were also preparing to raid the forest, find and kill whoever they suspected of hiding there, and torture the traitors for information. The current path to Spain had been recalculated to skirt around this obstacle, but if they could be taken out of the picture altogether that was even better. The rain was bucketing down by the time I arrived at the perimeter, carefully sidestepping the dozens of tripwires and landmines they had used to secure their position.

They thought it brought them safety, so much so they had grown complacent in their security. The soldier that should have been watching the forest was inside the structure they had thrown up and – from the sound of it – enjoying a rowdy game of poker. This was good for me.

What wasn't good was the fact three transport vehicles were missing. There had been ten, with seven left, but I didn't like the idea of a handful returning at any time. Or where they might be presently. *Don't worry about what you can't control*, I thought to myself, watching as I gently blew the door shut on their poker game.

I couldn't sense the air movement of any other living human besides the soldiers inside, so I sprinted forward and crouched next to the first of three tanks. I already had the jar of honey in my hand and ready to go as I shuffled to the rear, locating the entry to the fuel tank from memory. I climbed up slowly and quietly, away from the direction of the two machine guns mounted at the front.

Pulling a Swiss Army knife free from my holster, I flipped the blade and slid it under the seal of the nozzle in a circular fashion. I had to go around the circumference twice, the rain making it difficult as my grip slipped. Finally, I got it open and poured the thick, sticky honey inside.

Molasses would have done the job just as well, but honey is what I had found and honey was what I used to render the tanks immobile once it mixed with the gasoline. They could fire into the woods all they wanted, but the object of their aggression should be well and truly out of range by now.

Retightening the lid, I moved on to the next one using the remainder of the jar that I had and a third of the second jar. Everything that was left went into the third tank, with the beauty of this sabotage being that they likely wouldn't even know an enemy had been there until hours later.

I checked the surrounds before sprinting over to the carport. Wiggling underneath each vehicle, caked in mud, I used cable cutters to disable the engines of the remaining seven vehicles. I rolled from one to the next, until I was at the transport furthest away from all the soldiers.

Crouching, I sprinted off into the forest and maintained a steady jogging pace as I headed in the opposite direction of the people I cared about. The final part of the plan was to let off a grenade somewhere in the woods, somewhere far away and remote enough that it would draw the soldiers there on foot. Yet when I encountered an unexpected foot patrol, it was an opportunity too good to miss. I made sure everyone was accounted for, all sixteen soldiers, and that there weren't any stragglers following behind.

Then I stalked them towards what I had to guess was the town of Prats-de-Mollo-la-Preste. When they passed the rubble of a bombed church, I knew they must be close to the outskirts of town and I ripped the pins free from the three grenades I was carrying. Like a World Series pitcher, I hurled them one after the other and when they were all gone, I let the air carry them to just in front of the patrol, a point in the centre, and a final one at the rear.

I was already sprinting by the time they exploded, not bothering to look as I heard the cries of surprise behind me and the ground trembling beneath my feet. I started running and I didn't stop, not as night fell and not as my calf muscles screamed at me to slow down as I trekked up a slippery ascent in the forest. I nearly didn't hear the soldiers until I was on top of them. In fact, I didn't hear them at all: that's how quiet they were. That's how *good* they were.

It was their heavy breathing that brought me to a stop, the six men deathly still in every capacity *except* how they were inhaling and exhaling heavily on their climb. I would have collided with the direct centre of them – three in front, three behind – but my most reliable strength kicked in and I was able to stop before they heard or saw. So I froze, slapping a hand over my mouth to quiet my own puffing as I watching them carefully pick through the forest in low light.

I knew where they were heading, because they weren't trekking into Spain or back into France. They were moving directly along the border, and, if they kept going, right towards where Harvey and the refugees would be. I had to guess that's what they were up, as they weren't talking to each other and they were dressed in dark brown, so I couldn't tell from their accents or discern from their clothing where their allegiances lay.

Instead, I had a choice. I was exhausted, absolutely spent, and I still had a night's worth of running to go because of what I had done both at the outpost and the massive manhunt that was likely to follow after the bombing of the foot patrol. These men were too deep to have been sent after me, so they were probably looking for Harvey. I had no grenades and my pistol carried four shots, which would mean even if I hit every target with perfect, deadly aim, I'd have to use just my knives and my powers on the other two in a physical fight. I wasn't sure if I could take them.

If I was careful, perhaps I could follow after the men and steal the air from their lungs, one by one, and hope the others in front didn't notice as their comrades fell. Yet that would take time and energy I didn't have.

Harvey had fourteen other soldiers with him. I had just me. I had to pray that would be enough for him to take on these six guys *if* he and the others weren't already across the border. In the moment, I made the snap decision to think about myself. I let the men pass; then – as soon as it was feasible – I crept forward and continued on my own route as quietly and quickly as I could.

I had to keep moving, slightly delirious as I refused to risk stopping for another break and instead ate the handful of sultanas I had with me, hydrating from a flask of water on the go, heels bleeding and back aching as I stumbled through the darkness.

I knew I'd arrived in Spain when the ground started to slope downwards, exhausted as I let gravity do most of the work on my descent. I still had to have my wits about me though, a broken ankle all it would take to see me stranded and dead out here. I made it to Figueres by the next night, weeping when I saw the glow of the town up ahead.

Yet I wasn't safe. Spain was full of just as many enemies, even if you didn't know they were watching you. I had to continue to be careful, given the way I looked would signpost everything I had been up to. There was a farmhouse on the path into town and I watched it for an hour, studying the occupants inside and waiting until they went to bed. They had a phone, which was the important thing, and I dialled the emergency number I needed. Someone picked up on the first ring, as if they were expecting me.

'Post Office,' the caller said.

'Incoming delivery,' I replied.

'Order number?'

I gave the code, which was the coordinates of the farmhouse when translated from the cipher that had been chosen.

'Thank you for being such a loyal customer. The earliest pick up for one of our post officers is tomorrow evening.'

I knew it wouldn't have been in the next few hours, but I felt my heart sink anyway.

'*Merci*,' I whispered, hanging up. I assessed the surrounds of the house, how quiet it was and how deep the breathing of the couple upstairs. Their teenage son was asleep down the hall.

Fuck it, I thought. Locating several tea towels, I filled the kitchen sink with hot water as quietly as I could, lathering myself in soap and spending a solid half an hour washing the dirt and blood and grime from my body.

Naked and shivering in the kitchen, I mopped up the mess and let the filthy water drain away. I carried a small first aid kit at all times and bit my tongue as I wrapped my feet, first applying healing salve and then thick bandages. I paused my activities just once, waiting for five minutes until the son resettled in bed. There was a half-folded pile of clean laundry in the hallway and I sent a mental thank you to my father, who could be the only angel watching over me with the foresight to provide fresh clothes.

Sure, they were that of a burly six foot one farmer, but they were warm and thick and I layered them heavily. I filled an empty milk jug with water, taking a few small items of food from the house so they wouldn't be noticed. Then I left, bringing all evidence of my presence with me save for the missing clothes. I burned my possessions, setting a small fire in the woods nearby and igniting anything that wasn't essential: my ruined garments, my documents, whatever could give me away.

Once I was done and had warmed my hands by the flames, I put out the blaze and covered it up with shrubbery as the smell of smoke filled my nostrils. I returned to the farmhouse, using a flashlight to carefully navigate into the highest point of the barn, which was a small, wooden ledge used to store hay. I hid myself behind a massive brick of it, there being a small broken slate that allowed for a view of the house outside and the road that approached in the distance.

This place spelled like pig shit and horses, but I was dry. And warm, *finally*. And as I ate slowly, saving rations for tomorrow, I managed to close my eyes and fall asleep.

Stirring the next day, I was grateful for the heavy rain having followed me from France as it meant my tracks would be hard if not impossible to follow. It also meant the farm was inactive, with the family who lived there coming into the barn only once to feed the livestock before remaining inside the rest of the day. My transport didn't arrive until dusk, a Spanish postal delivery van rumbling down the road with its lights off.

My body was stiff as I sprung from the hiding place, bandaged feet aching as I limped into the woods across from the farmhouse. I watched from a close distance for several minutes, until the headlights were turned on and then off again. I jogged forward, pulling open the doors to the back of the van and hiding myself beneath the loads of real mail that had been distributed and picked up that day.

'Two hours and we'll be in Barcelona,' the driver said, reversing slowing before turning back on to the main road. 'Maybe two and a half in this weather.'

'Any news about the others?' I asked, heart pounding in my throat. Harvey and I had done this dance enough times by now, but that didn't stop me being any less worried about him. No doubt he was sick with concern for me too.

'They made it,' he answered. 'Arrived early this morning.'

'Thank you, Father,' I whispered, knowing it would likely sound as if I was thanking God. Rather, I meant my *actual* father. I wasn't someone with a lot of faith, religious or otherwise, but there was just something about the past forty-eight hours that made me feel like a being that loved me deeply was watching over.

I fell asleep again, only waking as the postal van came to a complete stop and I reached for my pistol. Propping it up on my thigh, finger on the trigger, I listened as hard as I could to the sounds outside.

'Yes, I know. Tulip's *my* agent. Now get out of the way.'

I sighed with relief, slipping the gun back into the holster and climbing forward as Lionel yanked open the doors of the van. I practically threw myself out of the vehicle, Mr Fix-It himself catching me in an exhausted hug.

'Never thought I'd say this,' I puffed, 'But I'm glad to see your ugly face.'

I grinned up at him, only the smallest of smiles twitching over his expression as he helped me stand straight.

'I heard they made it back before me,' I said, spinning around as I examined the familiar sight of the courtyard at their Barcelona base. 'I need to see Harvey.'

I was already limping towards the main building when Lionel called out, something in his tone freezing me in my tracks.

'Tulip, wait. He's not here.'

I pivoted slowly, fear gripping my torso once again as the temporary elation gave way.

'W-what do you mean? They made it back, that's what th—'

'They made it back, some two hundred and eighty-six refugees. Plus a few extras Benoît picked up along the way.'

'But Harvey, what about Harvey? Lionel, why won't you look at me?!'

I didn't realise I was shouting, however the reactions from people around us made it clear that I was. The old spy master was crying, I realised. Gentle tears streaming down his face and he sniffed, as if deciding in that moment to pull himself together.

'He was killed, Tulip.'

'No.'

'He was shot in the stomach and they tried to save him, they did. They brought his body over the border—'

'*No!*'

'—but he died en route. They did everything they could.'

I screamed, dropping to my knees on the cold, stony ground as I tried to cover my mouth and stop from screaming again. My whole body spasmed with the shock of it, the immediate grief, as I fought to breathe.

That night in Barcelona, there was a windstorm more powerful than anything the city had experienced before, boats wrecked in the harbour, waves crashing over the shore, and the roofs of houses blown right off.

Some said the gale was so loud, it sounded like a woman's scream.

Chapter 18

Present

Dreckly could tell Katya was surprised to see her as she walked into the salon, her turquoise eyebrows rising high enough that they disappeared under her turquoise fringe. The counter girl didn't recognise her, which was good, because it meant her disguise was working enough to be effective. She gave her name, Tulip, and said that she had called ahead to book an appointment for a full acrylic set with nail art. Taking a seat opposite the salon's namesake, Katya's shock was replaced with disdain as she examined Dreckly's nails. She made a tut-tutting sound, shaking her head from side to side.

'I've had a lot going on,' Dreckly said, before her friend had a chance to chastise her.

'You don't say,' Katya replied through pursed lips. 'Didn't even think to bother hiding your appearance for me, hmm?'

'I got bangs,' she protested. 'And dyed my hair reddish brown.'

'*Please*. Dye it pastel purple and then we'll talk, amateur.'

'Melody didn't recognise me.'

'Have you ever watched the *Josie and the Pussycats* cartoon?'

'From the seventies?' Katya nodded. 'No.'

'Read the comic?'

'Nope.'

'Watched *Riverdale*?'

Dreckly gave the goblin a look.

Katya shrugged. 'Well, Melody is not the smart one.'

She felt a smile tug at the edge of her lips. 'Everyone has their talents.'

'Sure, Jan.'

'So . . . what's been happening lately?' Dreckly questioned.

'Oh, you know, the uzh,' the goblin said with a chuckle.

'It's going to take the full slot to do my claws – with nail art – so I guess we've got some time to talk about it.'

'Very sly,' Katya muttered, as she started pushing down Dreckly's cuticles with a curved implement. 'Where to begin? Thirteen ripping up the city, looking for any number of prominent folks who seem to have gone AWOL in the last three weeks. And I don't just mean those screechy ladies.'

Each one of her employees was engaged in loud chatter with their clients, wrapped up in their own solo worlds. Dreckly and Katya seemed just like them, even though the lingo of their conversation took a little internal translation. Thirteen meant Treize, which was the French word for the number. The screechy ladies were obviously banshees. And prominent folks meant supernaturals they both likely new.

'Any family members among that lot?' she queried.

'Seen and heard,' Katya replied. 'Unlike some.'

'Who?'

'Clash At Demonhead. Marsupials.'

Ruken was safe and accounted for. Those that weren't, however, included demons. Wombat shifters and probably any others that fit within the marsupial family.

'What about the Big Bad Wolf?'

She couldn't help the little flicker of hope she felt in her chest.

'Still asking what's the time.'

Dreckly let out the smallest sigh of relief, which she knew didn't go unnoticed by the goblin's keen eyes.

'I hope you weren't dumb enough to sail into town. I hear there are a lot of onlookers at the harbour this time of year.'

'It's the season for it,' Dreckly replied. 'And I drove.'

Her suspicions had been right. Enough time had passed that they had tracked her escape route to the fish market, to the boat and then . . . away. She always preferred the *Titanic II* as her transportation of choice, but that seemed like an unnecessary risk if they were watching the waterways. This was confirmed by the selkie contacts she'd made, who gave Dreckly the heads up that aquatic methods of transport should be avoided. The airports too were closely monitored and therefore out of the equation. There were really only a few options left and she'd chosen a twelve-hour drive as her means to return to Sydney, which she didn't enjoy. She would have enjoyed being caught less though, so a small sacrifice.

'Say I wanted to catch up with some *friends* while I was in town,' Dreckly said, watching as Katya carefully applied the first acrylic nail before she began shaping it. 'Where should I go?'

'I'll tell you on one condition.'

'What's that?'

'You let me paint Gudetama on your nails.'

Dreckly frowned as she searched for the meaning.

'The lazy egg thing? *With the butt?*'

'Fat asses are in, let me be trendy for once.'

'You're not painting Gudetama on my nails.'

'Guess you won't be having that reunion, then.'

Two and a half hours later as Dreckly walked under the flashing bulbs that announced she was at the State Theatre, she was less concerned about being followed by the Treize than she was about someone recognising she had a lazy egg *with a fat ass* painted on each of her ten fingers. Painted beautifully, mind you, with a few crystals and yellow glitter for garnish. But it was still a lazy egg *with a fat ass* and she was a grown woman. *Fuck it*, she thought. It had been worth it to get what she needed: a location.

Her footsteps echoed as she walked through the abandoned opulence of the Grand Assembly hall, with the entire theatre supposed to be closed for historic renovations. The perfect hiding place, really: they were right under the Treize's nose. Built in the late nineteen twenties, the State Theatre was a relic of an era long gone, when cinema was glamorous and over the top and going to the pictures was an *event*. It was an era Dreckly had lived through, right in the beating heart of it. It made her feel nostalgic.

Most cities had a few places like this, but Sydney really just had one. It was neoclassical with a gaudy edge: from the frames of the mirrored walls to the warm shade of the mosaic tiles beneath her feet. Gothic statues in dominant poses looked down on a room decked in gold and where there would usually be an usher in a bow tie beginning to herald guests into the main part of the theatre there was a wombat shifter instead: legs planted wide apart, arms crossed, face bemused.

'If there's anyone I've ever wanted to flap slap in my life, it's you, Dreckly Jones.'

'Shazza,' she said, by way of greeting.

'How'd you get in?'

Dreckly wiggled her fingers subtly, swirling an abandoned bucket towards the woman and using the air around her to send it floating into space. Shazza jumped, alarmed, but within a few seconds she was able to compose her features.

She grunted with approval. 'No more hiding then, I take it?'

Dreckly knew the woman was referring to her powers, yet the comment was layered with meaning.

'No more. I came back to help, however I can.'

Two thick strands of silver hair had escaped the shifter's ponytail, hanging in front of her face and making her look like a greying Lara Croft. She was even dressed in a pair of cargo pants and a tight, teal singlet that showed off her immense bosom. She was assessing Dreckly's value. She was assessing whether the offer of help was worth the trouble it might bring. She was assessing whether they needed her. Evidently, they did.

'Strewth,' she snorted. 'I'm not in a position to turn away an offer of assistance when it's readily made. Come on then, your courage has manifested at the right moment. Everyone's in the orchestra pit.'

When she said *everyone*, she really meant it: demons; goblins, including Katya's cousin(s); werewolves; shifters; and some women Dreckly couldn't immediately identify that could have been witches, banshees, or just human allies. There were nearly forty of them all tucked into the orchestra pit, clustered around a table that was covered in loose papers and – surprisingly – a platter of sliced fruit, vegetables, and cold slices. Sitting at the far end of the crowd was Ben, whose mouth popped open with surprise when he spotted her. He got to his feet, as if he wanted to move towards her immediately.

'Ross, for fuck's sake, weren't you on perimeter? What are you doing in here eating *snacks*?' Shazza barked at one of the shifters under her command. The man had a celery stick dangling between his lips like a cigarette and he froze.

'I went to pee.'

'Are you peeing right now?'

'No, but—'

'Then get the hell back out there! No one should be able to float their way past our defences; it's fucking embarrassing.'

Head down, shoulders slumped, he slinked out of the theatre, grumbling all the while.

'The witch cast protection spells; she wouldn't have been able to cross the threshold if she wasn't an ally.'

'Float?' Ben asked. He'd been inching his way towards her, through the crowd of people.

'You can *float*?' Ruken questioned.

'No,' Dreckly replied.

'She made a bucket float.'

'*A bucket*?' Ruken again, but her eyes were on Ben.

'You have telekinesis?' he asked.

'No!'

'You floated the bucket like someone with telekinesis,' Shazza murmured.

Ruken looked thoughtful. 'What kind of creature has telekinesis?'

'Wind elemental, may—'

'I DO NOT HAVE TELEKINESIS!' Dreckly shouted, the loose paper and maps that were on the table blowing off in a gust charged by her anger.

Everyone in the space fell silent, pointedly watching the display of power as the plate of fruit rattled on the spot. Taking a deep breath, she closed her eyes and steadied the storm inside herself.

'*Telekinesis.*'

'Shut up, Ruken,' Ben snapped. 'Let her fucking talk.'

The goblin had his hands up in surrender when Dreckly reopened her eyes, Ben towering over him as he stood beside her. She'd almost forgotten in the moment, her own problems seeming so immense, that Ben was an alpha werewolf. He was *the* alpha werewolf in this city, his pack's leader, and someone to be feared. When he turned to her, patience on his expression as he silently willed her to go on, his eyes were not the dark, inky black they usually were. They were illuminated now, glowing, yellow: the wolf.

'I'm a sprite,' she said, the group quiet for a moment before Shazza punctured the silence.

'Bullshit. I've seen sprites, knew one once. They can't do what you did with that bucket.'

'I can do a lot more than *float* a bucket by manipulating the air particles in the room,' she said, eyes glinting with danger. 'And you've never seen one like me. I'd wager maybe only a few of you have, since the Treize made breeding between earth elementals and selkies illegal in the eighteen hundreds.'

'Then what—'

'Versions of what I am, at best, the offspring of people like me and regular humans or supernaturals.'

'They're not real sprites?' Shazza asked.

'I mean, they are,' Dreckly backtracked. 'They're just not . . . you can only make the colour green with blue and yellow, right? But you add other colours to that mixture – white and red – and come up with something just as beautiful, but not the same.'

Ben was frowning, his brow furrowed as he looked at her. 'If the union between earth elementals and selkies was banned in the eighteen hundreds then . . .'

He trailed off, his eyes widening slightly as if he finally understood all her comments about their age gap.

'I'm over one hundred and thirty years old,' Dreckly said, 'which I just learned recently when I was "detained" by the same person who imprisoned my father and my mother when she was pregnant with me.'

'So you're immortal?' he asked, as if the conversation was only happening between the two of them.

'I'm not immortal,' she corrected. 'I just age differently to your kind, about three of your years equal one of mine.'

'Forty-four,' he whispered.

'You can breathe underwater, right?' Shazza pushed. 'Like, you don't have a tail b—'

'I can do lots of things that are helpful to the cause and to what you're trying to do,' Dreckly answered, the idea of exposing *all* of her secrets in one go hard for her to stomach. 'Yet I was under the impression time may be of the essence.'

Someone snorted. 'So *now* you want to help?'

'That's right.' Dreckly didn't recognise the face of the young female shifter who spoke.

'Why not back then, huh? Or does it only matter to you once it becomes personal, once *you* got captured and *you* had to break out?'

'It was always personal,' she answered, her voice sounding as deadly as she felt. If only this little bitch knew—

The warmth of Ben's hand touched her own, just a stroke of skin against skin as he ran a finger softly across the back of her hand. It calmed her, just a portion, but that was enough.

'When you all asked me for help weeks ago, to join you, I said no. I haven't survived as long as I have by getting involved in other people's causes.'

'It didn't bring you safety though, did it?' Shazza said quietly. 'They took you anyway.'

'They did. And I broke myself out along with one other. Someone else who's keen to help.'

Ruken and Shazza shared a look. 'We didn't hear of anyone else escaping. We thought the rest were left behind.'

'He wouldn't be on anyone's books except theirs and I deleted those files. Point is, you all asking me to stand along-side you and *fight* was asking me to give up the freedom I've spent over a century doing everything I can to protect. As for the others that I left behind in that place … I regret it, of course, but trying to save them would have meant risking my own freedom and making that decision for another being as well. I should have stayed. I didn't. I just want you to know why.'

The young shifter looked like she was about to roll her eyes. 'Is that why you're here, then? Ben got your message, no need to come back.'

'I'm not a hero like any of you. I don't have those instincts, I wasn't raised with them, just coming back here goes against every judgement I have.'

Ben cocked his head, asking without saying it out loud: why come then?

'Staying out of *it* is no longer an option,' Dreckly said, answering the unspoken question of the room. 'Neutrality doesn't guarantee safety in this climate. So I'm relying on the courage of all of you to provide me with some of my own.'

Glances were exchanged between the varying supernaturals, visually weighing her words and deciding whether she was worthy. It seemed leadership sat somewhere between Ben Kapoor and Sharon 'Shazza' Petersham, which made sense, as werewolves and shifters always had an affinity with each other. Shazza was at least twenty years older than Ben, in her mid-fifties, if Dreckly had to guess, and just as physically intimidating although in a totally opposite fashion.

'Strewth,' Shazza said, looking down at her hands as she chose her words carefully. 'I know what my gut is telling me to do.'

'What's that?' Ben questioned.

Shazza looked up at Dreckly as she spoke: 'Attack.'

There was dissent in the room, many voices feeling like this was a 'terrible' idea as they made their opposition known.

'They have to know we're coming!' someone was saying.

'Half the city has gone underground; they *know* that we *know*.'

'Anyone who didn't hide has been taken, and, after the breakout, they will have reinforced all of their security measures. There's the element of surprise, then there's the element of idiocy, Shaz.'

'How would we even get in? Just waltz up, knock on the door and be like "Oy, Beryl, sorry about it, love – we left some stuff behind."'

'They wouldn't be expecting it, I agree. But that's because they don't expect that we're *stupid*.'

'There are good people in there! Our people! If this is the end for us, let it be worth something – yeah? Think of all those others inside, how long they've probably been there.'

'There's no way in!'

Dreckly listened to their objections, watching the heated debate with interest. It was impassioned, but it wasn't nasty: everyone got their say, one way or the other. Ben leaned back and listened to their suggestions, only murmuring the occasional response as he weighed the options. It reminded her of the way Harvey led, working within an intimate circle but trying to make sure everyone felt like they had a chance to contribute.

'There *is* no! Way! In!'

'We flood it,' Dreckly said. It took a moment for the room to register her words so she repeated them. 'We flood it.'

'*What?!*' Ruken practically choked, but Shazza held up a hand to let Dreckly speak.

'Go on,' the wombat shifter said. 'What do you mean?'

'The facility is underground, all except the top floor, which is just the security entrance and loading bays. Everything that's important is below the water line and *right* on Cockle Bay.'

'And what?' Ruken questioned. 'We just drown all of our kind? Are you insane?'

'Not our kind, just theirs,' Dreckly responded. 'Every supernatural on our side is being held in one of those tubes, which are completely airtight. The entire facility could be underwater and if you were inside one of those, you would be fine. The air is piped in directly from above. Obviously there's a risk that one, maybe two, of ours could be on an operating table at that exact moment and if they're not a selkie, an elemental, or me, then they'll drown. Yet speaking from the perspective of someone who has been in that exact position, most would welcome it.'

'Only the Treize would drown,' Shazza muttered. 'They've restaffed, restrengthened: it's fifty people now at least. That's a lot of causalities.'

'Fifty people we weren't exactly going to be disarming with a tickle fight though,' Ben remarked, finally weighing in. 'We were going to kill them one way or the other. Drowning's a kinder end than the one I was planning for the staff members of a facility whose sole purpose is to cut us open and look at our insides.'

Shazza looked thoughtful, nodding her head at his comments for a moment. 'Okay, Dreckly. Explain to us how this could work.'

Dreckly sketched the fire evacuation map from memory, her recall as perfect as usual. It was one of the things that made grieving so hard for her: she remembered *everything*. In almost every other instance, including this one, it was endlessly useful. She used one of the errant pencils on the table to draw on the back of a massive sheet of butcher's paper, which had timetables written on one side. Once she was done with that, she added the details: the pipes that weren't on the map, the vents, any place air could pass through she had been able to sense and see during her brief time there.

'Level two is the first that dips below sea level,' she said, pointing. 'If you flooded that first, if there were any of our people on the slab and they were in the condition to escape, they could do so upwards.'

'Three is the floor they take you to for "operations"?' Ben asked.

'Yes.' She nodded. 'Everything else would flow down.'

'What about the structural integrity of the building?' Shazza asked.

Dreckly shrugged. 'I couldn't say, I'm not an engineer. Regardless, the rescue operation would need to be quick.'

'It will hold,' Ben said and she cast a sideways look at him.

'You're an engineer?' she questioned.

'What did you think I did for a day job?' he replied with a small shrug.

'Like . . . crime? Werewolf crime?'

He chuckled in that deep, dirty way she'd only heard during their candlelight dinner and in her bedroom. It made her think impure things, things she shouldn't be thinking of in the moment.

'The bigger question,' he said, smirking as if he knew where her mind had gone, 'is how we get our people out. Who among us is a proficient enough diver? I'm assuming you'd want to use these same tunnels that will flood the place as our entry and exit.'

'You would be correct.' Dreckly nodded.

'Then how . . .'

'I have a plan for that,' she said. 'What I'm going to need to know is how many of you can drive a boat?'

Several people raised their hands.

'Legally.'

Three lowered them.

'Okay, five. That helps.'

'Helps what?' Shazza asked.

'Get the survivors out of there. And when we do, you know the Treize is going to stop at nothing to find and kill *all of you*. Protection spells or not, you can't stay here. You can't stay in Sydney.'

The wombat shifter sighed heavily, like the weight of the world was on her muscular shoulders. In a way, it was: her world at least.

'I have a contingency plan for situations just like this: we go inland. There's people waiting for us and we'll be safe once we're there, I just . . . didn't anticipate taking so many people.'

'If you're willing to accept help, I know some Ravens who are up to the task.'

Shazza arched one eyebrow as she looked at Dreckly with curiosity. She didn't do much work with the motorcycle club; that was more Ben and the Kapoor pack's territory. But she knew them: any human affiliate who operated in and around the supernatural world was known.

'They'll . . . they'll help us?' she questioned.

'Mmm hmmm.' Dreckly nodded. 'If there's one thing they're good at, it's smuggling things across land.'

'So we're doing this?' Ben asked, grinning. 'We're actually doing this?'

'When?' Ruken pressed.

Dreckly defaulted to Shazza and Ben: they were the leaders here; they were the ones who commanded this merry band of rebels. The wombat shifter seemed to scrutinise each of them, narrowing her eyes as she examined their faces and assessed how ready they were.

'Tonight,' she said. 'We can't risk the fates of those inside by waiting longer.'

There was an echo through the group as they repeated the command, Dreckly feeling her own blood thicken at the very thought of it. *Tonight.* Tonight she would break the first rule her father ever taught her.

It was a calm evening, the sky clear with the exception of planes as they rushed to fly overhead before the Sydney Airport curfew meant the air would be entirely empty of mechanical birds. There was barely any breeze to break the stifling hot temperature, which was well above thirty-five even after the sun had dipped. All of this mattered, because it would make their task just slightly easier than it would have been on a freezing, rough night with the waters of the harbour churning in anger.

Their exit from the State Theatre was spread out, everyone leaving in small groups at different times and taking different routes so as to better mix among the everyday civilians. It was Ruken's idea for them to begin leaving in the late afternoon, just as peak hour was about to hit, and continue travelling right through it so they had the maximum amount of coverage. She doubted it was a coincidence that she and Ben were the last two left behind, the werewolf having been busy making final preparations the entire afternoon as everyone began rushing to complete their various tasks.

Every job was dangerous, but as he let out a deep sigh and slinked over to sit next to her, Dreckly was hyperaware that his was among the most dangerous. He – along with the young, angry shifter and a legion of others – was to create a diversion at the entry to the Treize's laboratory. They were to draw their eye to the calamity on land, so they wouldn't be paying attention to what was happening at sea.

'I want you to know,' he started, 'that I looked for you. I don't know what Wyck told you, but I knew something—'

'He told me,' Dreckly answered, cutting him off. She reached out and grasped his hand in hers, fingers intertwining as they sat there in the old yet surprisingly comfortable seats of the State Theatre. 'He told me that you came by, kept coming by after I went missing.'

'I know it was only a few days, but I didn't like the scent on the boat. Wyck said everything looked right and that's what was wrong, in a way. And something about the record player.'

'That fucking asshole,' she murmured. His eyebrows shot up in surprise. 'No, not Wyck.'

'Uh, the one who took you. The one who took your parents. He must be old too . . . Praetorian Guard?'

She nodded. 'Says he's a Custodian now, that he was here tracking the banshees and it's pure coincidence we crossed paths but . . . I don't know.'

'What's his name?'

Dreckly shook her head. 'Uh uh, no. I recognise that tone. You've gotta do something that's dangerous enough, Ben Kapoor. No vendetta settling, please. Besides, I want him.'

The werewolf chuckled, heat radiating from him as he watched the killer in her surface. He didn't shy away from it and she didn't have to keep it hidden at the risk of scaring him away like she had Harvey. She couldn't help but constantly do the back and forth comparing of the two, Ben the closest she'd ever come to feeling anything stir inside her the way it had for the dead soldier.

She'd been so quick to see their similarities that she'd never taken a moment to acknowledge their many and significant differences. Ben was seeing a version of her Harvey never had, a version she'd purposefully kept just beneath the surface because he was human and she was most definitely not. The double life and the energy it required to keep the two things separate wasn't there with him. She could use that energy for other things. Dreckly shoved his chest so his back was firmly pressed into the cushioned chair as she climbed over the top of him, her legs straddling either side of his hips.

'This is not where I saw this going,' Ben breathed, his words unsteady as Dreckly reached down beneath them and stroked the bulging hardness she felt there.

'Really?'

'I'm not saying you can't set me on fire, I just didn't realise we were playing with matches today.'

She bit his lip with the urgency of her kiss, Ben groaning loudly as she sunk into him. They would have to talk after this, about all of it: her history, her powers, her lives, Vankila, all of it. Yet they both needed to survive first and if there was one thing Dreckly understood after decades of walking this earth, tomorrow was never guaranteed. So when Ben pushed the hem of her skirt higher, up to her hips, and tore her underwear free, she didn't think about the implications as he kissed her like his life depended on it. Dreckly gripped his skin like it would keep her afloat, taking him deep inside of her as they both yelled out, the echoes bouncing around the historic building like a dirty memory. She rode him like there was no tomorrow, the pair finding the rhythm of each other's body so easily it scared her. When he came with a bark, face pressed against her sweaty chest, she held him tightly and he held her back. For all Dreckly knew, neither of them had a tomorrow.

By the time it ticked past sunset on the other side of 8 p.m., everyone except for ten supernaturals in their troupe had arrived at the Sydney Fish Markets. Those left behind were to be led by Ben on the streets outside of the Treize outpost in Barangaroo. They couldn't risk those that did make it to level one paying any further attention to what was happening down below, which is where the werewolf and his merry band of troublemakers would come in.

The entire Ravens M.C. was waiting at the jetty for them, bikes safely stored out of sight in the fish market's loading bay. There were some forty members preparing their transport, which was the most mishmashed fleet Dreckly had ever seen. Two small fishing trawlers would lead the pack, with three recreational vessels following that could each fit about twenty people – thirty if they stretched it – and bringing up the rear were five dinghies, which didn't look like much in comparison but they were quicker and more manoeuvrable in a pinch than any of the other boats.

'Not bad,' Shazza remarked, as Dreckly used her keys to open the gate to each jetty as their party filed down the long catwalk.

Zhang and his mum Jia were among the bikies, the pair having supplied some of the boats that would take them up into Cockle Bay. Wyck was watching on as Chino revved an outboard motor on one of the dinghies, making sure it would operate exactly as it needed to. She was always glad to see him, but in this instance more than ever. Dreckly placed a hand on his shoulder, not needing to say much else for her gratitude to be felt. She hadn't warned them she was coming back, even though she knew it was likely the motorcycle club would have offered her some kind of protection on her drive down. She didn't want to waste their resources and put them at extra risk, especially when she had a big favour to ask anyway.

So she had pulled up at the fish market the night before, unannounced, with a plan to get everyone in a whole heap of trouble. Chino and the boys were up for it, the motorcycle club having paid close attention to the situation in the city during Dreckly's absence. Whatever they had seen, whatever they had observed, they weren't a fan of. Most members of the Ravens M.C. were not white: they were multi-ethnic and a melting pot of the thousand different races that made up the tapestry of Australia. A huge part of their attitude about the police was informed by that, or – as Wyck had summarised for her once –'fuck cops, defund the police'. The Treize too closely resembled a police state and they understood the impact of that as it would roll on to affect them and their operations more completely in the coming years. They were helping them with more than just the aquatic transportation: it was the Ravens who were getting everyone out of town.

There was an arrangement made between Ben, Shazza and Chino, she wasn't sure specifically what it was. Yet Dreckly had cast a glance over her shoulder at one point to see the shifter's head dipped in conversation with the M.C.'s president just before they set sail. Those who knew what they were doing followed her steady path away from the jetty, each boat's wash trailing behind like a veil on a bride's wedding day, their procession moving slowly through Johnstons Bay, then wrapping around the curve of Jones Bay Wharf until Barangaroo was in sight.

It was well past peak hour, but they still needed to pass through a ferry route without clearance to do so before the assault began in earnest. Dreckly's boat was the only one that dropped anchor on the outskirts of Nawi Cove as she told the others to remain idling just in case. With her wetsuit rolled down to her hips and sports bikini exposed to the elements, she sighed and turned off the engine as she headed to the stern. Shazza was on board with her, following Dreckly and helping as she squirmed her way into the full-length sleeves of the foamy material.

'You sure this is far enough away?' the wombat shifter asked, zipping Dreckly up from tailbone to neck. She handed her the long cord that extended from the zipper.

'Yes,' she replied, taking it from her and tucking it under the Velcro pocket designed exactly for that purpose. 'There shouldn't be much pull from this distance, and after ten minutes, hopefully none.'

'Hopefully?'

'Have you done this before?' Dreckly countered.

The deep lines around Shazza's eyes wrinkled as she smiled, the marks running down her face like worn grooves. 'No, I see your point. We stay adaptable.'

'That's right. After ten minutes regardless, you're going to need to get closer and lead the others, because the further everyone has to travel out of the flooded labs the harder it's going to be.'

Shazza nodded, watching as Dreckly tied her hair up in a bun on top of her head and exhaled deeply. Closing her eyes, her toes curled over the edge of the boat as she took a step off and plunged underwater. The outside air might have been swelteringly warm, but Dreckly had anticipated how cold the water would be and she was grateful for the added protection of the wetsuit as gravity carried her deeper still. She could taste the salt on her lips, but it didn't sting her eyes as she opened them and felt her body's desire to float upwards for the first time. She might have lacked Amos or her mother's distinct tail, but there was still enough selkie traits in her DNA to make her thrive in this environment. It's why she always stayed close to the water: if nowhere else was safe, at least she knew here always would be. She was greeted by an example of that, expressions staring back at her through the darkness.

A smile spread over her face like warm butter on bread as she kicked to the surface, her head popping up almost sound-lessly. Dozens of other heads joined hers like moles emerging from underground, Dreckly hearing the surprised murmurs of the other supernaturals on the boats around them echo like a chorus. Selkies kept to themselves, mostly. They didn't engage in the petty political concerns of the land dwellers *usually*. They were rarely seen unless they wanted to be. She had to guess that the majority of the buoyant party had probably never seen one, let alone this many.

Seventy per cent of the Sydney pondant, one of the biggest in the country, was among them, including the two visitors they had met en route to the Gold Coast: Avary and Leviathan. Swelling the ranks were those from North Queensland, many either direct relatives of Amos himself or at the very least distantly connected. Other selkies had joined, the odd one or two from pondants all down the Australian east coast when they had learned what was happening. Amos, of course, was one of them.

Dreckly swam over to the edge of her boat, Shazza leaning down and passing her what looked like a utility belt ripped right from the torso of Batman himself. In reality, it was something she had asked Wyck to get for her. Dreckly had given him the exact specifications of what she was after, no doubt in her mind that he could source the materials in under five hours. He'd come through, of course, his contacts as sharp as ever. It was a grenade belt, two of them, each stocked with eight of the compact explosives.

'Cheers,' she said, taking them from her. The wombat shifter met her gaze, nodding. Now was the time for step one. Shazza grabbed the throwaway Nokia from her bra strap, texting quickly before dog-whistling loudly so all the other boats knew what was happening. In the distance, they heard an explosion followed by gunfire. Ben and his team had begun their assault. It was time. Paddling back towards the group, she carefully unclipped the grenades one by one and handed them to the sixteen individuals who were the fastest swimmers.

'Remember,' Dreckly began, 'Once you pull the pin, you have four seconds to be out of range. Place them where we discussed and the tunnels will be compromised, they'll flood. Then we move.'

She felt a hand on her shoulder, turning around to see Amos behind staring at her with resolve.

'What are we waiting for?' he asked.

There was a collective wave of splashes as the chosen sixteen ducked away, planting the explosives at the back door while the Treize's eye was fixated on the bang bang at their front. It would take less than a minute, with Dreckly counting in her head as Amos steadied her, bracing for impact. There was nothing heard above the surface of the water, but it was felt below. The newly created current tugged at her as a massive volume of water rushed to fill a void that hadn't been open before. The boats rocked behind her, bobbing from side to side.

Amos released her, Dreckly feeling her body float towards the underwater entrance that was being made through sheer force of pressure alone. She could see perfectly well underwater, but she couldn't breathe underwater the way her enemies thought. Wrapping the night sky around her, creating an invisible bubble, Dreckly slipped her hand around the shoulders of Amos. She tapped his neck to let him know she was ready and he dived.

Few things in the undersea realm were faster than a selkie and they sped through the water at a rapid pace, Dreckly looking on either side of her at more than fifty beings that had joined their descent. It was hard not to feel empowered, excited, and ecstatic about what they were doing.

Refocusing on their route, she tucked her head into the curve of the selkie's neck as brightness bloomed among the dark water ahead of them.

This was either the start of something or the end of it.

And Dreckly couldn't think of anywhere she'd rather be.

Chapter 19

Past

When the war was over, I could barely feel the victory. This was what Harvey had been fighting for and it was what he had died for. Without him there to see what his sacrifice had won, it felt hollow. It felt even worse knowing that my decision to let those soldiers pass in the forest, my own inaction and fear, had led to his death.

I'd seen where they were going and I'd guessed who they were hunting. And I'd still chosen to do nothing, hoping that Harvey and the others would have been long out of the line of fire by the time that posse of six arrived. They should have been, but they weren't, the extra people they'd picked up on the way meaning they were delayed. I'd inadvertently murdered the man I loved and it haunted me.

My misery was suffocating and Lionel forced me to see one of the psychologists on staff at the time, worried that I was going to kill myself. I hadn't made any attempts to determine if that was even possible, still unsure of so much about myself. Either way, my work was top secret and my clearance was classified, so the therapy was pointless. I couldn't say anything and I wouldn't have, even if I could.

I slept with a soldier during my last night in England, just to see if I could feel anything. I wanted the physical sensations to wake me up, the touch of another human to make me feel alive. Instead, I ran to bathroom afterwards and threw up. I felt sick with myself, like I had betrayed Harvey's memory just by having another soul see me naked.

The first thing I did when I returned to the United States was visit his grave. I'd missed the funeral – so had Lionel, Mildred, and all the others who had been stuck overseas continuing to fight the war in the twelve months following his death. But I wanted to do it, I didn't know why. When I'd inspected his body that night in Barcelona, it had nearly killed me. I'd had to be sedated, only to wake hours later and realise the horrible dream I'd had was actually reality. They insisted on sedating me again when I demanded to visit him a second time, so I was much calmer as I stroked the smooth skin of his face. His fist was still clenched shut and I prised his fingers open to find the pocket watch I had given him. He'd been holding it in his final minutes and I liked to imagine that he'd been thinking of me.

I inspected the wound entry point, right above his liver. I had seen that kind of injury before, red blood almost black as the foreign object nestled in a human being's liver. The longest I'd ever seen a soldier survive with that type of wound was twenty minutes, with medics having applied intense pressure to prolong his life so he could continue shooting at the same soldiers who had taken him down.

That man had died in immense pain, drenched in sweat but refusing to let them release even a morsel of pressure. He had wanted to fight right up until the end. That's exactly what

Harvey had done, killing three of the six soldiers who had surprised them in the night. Benoît had managed to fatally wound another two, their bodies found in the woods by the enemy later. Harvey had fought right up until the end, even though he knew there was no way to save himself. His grave didn't tell any of that story though. I wanted it to.

'Here lies Harvey Schwartz, loving father and husband.'

There was something in Hebrew written underneath that I couldn't read. Crouched down in front of his headstone, I touched the writing of his name and then jerked my hand away. It felt cold, dead. Like there was no part of him there at all. I knew it was a mistake, going there. If I had just acted, if I had just . . .

It was pointless, going over this again and again. Lionel had told me as much, saying that it was just as likely I would have died too if I had revealed myself and tried to combat the men single-handedly.

'We would have lost you *and* Harvey,' he had said back then, gently gripping my shoulder as he tried to console me. 'What good would that have done?'

He didn't know about my abilities. He didn't know that I stood a better chance than most. Would I have been killed as well? Likely. And they still would have had time to catch up to the others. Yet at least I wouldn't have had to live with the pain of visiting his grave while he was gone and I was left behind. I knew it would wreck me, coming here, but I did it anyway. I had to see.

'Excuse me.'

I spun around, freezing in place as I faced a woman dressed in all black. There were two kids at her side, barely teens: a boy and a girl.

'Sorry,' I muttered, quickly wiping away a tear as it streaked down my cheek. I marched away from them as fast as I could, resisting the urge to sprint like a coward. *I should have never come here; what was I thinking! This was such a mistake.*

I thought I was in the clear as my feet hit the footpath back to the main entrance, but an accompanying set of heel clacks told me I was wrong.

'Excuse me, excuse me, miss!'

I paused, closing my eyes before I turned around to face Mrs Schwartz.

'Did you know my husband? Did you know Harvey?'

I nodded. 'Yes, ma'am. We worked together during the war.'

'Oh . . . that's why you weren't at his funeral, I suppose. What kind of work did you two do together?'

'I'm afraid I can't answer that.'

'Right, yes, government *secrets* and all that. They can't tell me much of anything. What's your name?'

'Tulip Han,' I replied. 'I'm very sorry for your loss.'

I turned around and continued towards the car I had borrowed from Delun, desperate to be away from this woman and away from this place.

'Harvey had a tattoo,' the woman called, causing me to pause. 'You probably wouldn't understand, but in the Jewish faith we don't believe in marking our skin permanently like that. The Torah forbids it, but every burial society can make their own exceptions and . . . well, he was a war hero. He saved so many lives.'

I sniffed, dabbing my nose with a handkerchief. I knew where this was going.

'We hadn't seen each other much over the past few years, but it was the darnedest thing because . . . he was my husband. I would know if he had a tattoo, but I'd never seen it before. He must have gotten it during the war.'

She was searching my face for something, I could feel it like a flashlight skimming the surface of the water, trying to perceive what was below.

'It was a flower,' the woman said. 'A tulip, right here, just above his heart.'

I held Mrs Schwartz's gaze, certain the truth was plastered all over my expression but unwilling to say it out loud. The woman stared back, curious.

'I can tell you one thing,' I said, voice low. 'There were six men who shot at Harvey.'

'Yes, they sent some details to the family. They said he died a hero, saving as many people as he could and taking out all but one member of the attacking party who got away.'

'He didn't get away,' I replied.

'Oh? That wasn't mentioned in the report they gave us—'

'It won't be in any report. It won't be anywhere. Just you and I know it.'

My voice was steady as I held her gaze, watching as understanding swept her features.

'I must be getting back to our children,' she whispered, turning on her heels and walking towards Harvey's grave.

I nodded, watching her leave.

When news of Harvey's death began to spread far and wide, Mildred showed up without any announcement or fanfare. She knew what I needed and she'd arrived with intel on the escaped soldier. A name. A file. A last known sighting.

I never bothered to find out what she told Lionel or how she arranged it, I just knew that if I was to pursue this the Allies would disavow any connection to me as I would them if I was caught. We left together, crossing back behind enemy lines as we hunted the final survivor of the squadron that killed Harvey.

Mildred took me as far as the village where he had last been spotted, before embracing me in a tight hug and telling me that she would find me after the war, wherever we were and wherever that was. I couldn't thank her enough for the gift she'd given me and when I tried to say as much, she shushed me like she was embarrassed.

Finding the abandoned barracks the man had been living in, I hired a rogue werewolf to track him off the scent left behind on a few possessions. He'd been on the outskirts of Paris, holed up in a brothel with two other soldiers who I'd had to kill just to make sure they didn't leave the building knowing my face. Quick bullets to the skull for them, with time being something I intended to spend on the sole survivor. But the screams of the women present meant I had barely a few minutes to get done what I needed to, yet it was enough. Enough to tell him who I was, why I was there, and to make certain that he knew he was never making it out of there alive. I hadn't used a bullet on him, suffocating him instead and watching as the life drained from his eyes.

They said vengeance wasn't meant to make you feel better, that it would plague you. Yet it made me feel better, at least in the moment. I didn't want to have to kill again if I could avoid it, not for a long time, but if I was cornered I knew I would fight to come out on top. In a way, that's the security my father had wanted for me.

Leaving the cemetery and returning home, I was shattered. I couldn't even trade the usual barbs with Delun who was waiting for me, just thanking him for letting me borrow the car instead as I tossed him the keys.

'I filled up the tank,' I muttered, shutting Meili and Li Jun's front door behind me. They were out at the pictures, so I was home alone. It was how I preferred it, flopping down on the bed in the room that was once mine and curling up in a ball.

When I stirred many hours later, it was to the sound of voices coming from the kitchen. Sitting up with a wince, the light outside my window was dark, telling me that I had slept through the rest of the day. *Good*, I thought. Being unconscious hurt less than being conscious. Carefully opening the door just a crack, I eavesdropped on the Hans.

'She's different,' Delun was telling his parents. 'She has come back different.'

'She went to war, son,' Li Jun reasoned. 'People don't just come back from that the same.'

'They don't come back like this. Tulip's a ghost version of herself. My colleague Jefferson fought in the Great War and he was able to come back, get a teaching job, build a life for himself.'

I heard Meili sigh. 'What do you think she did over there, hmm? She wasn't some soldier who had one or two battles and then she's out. She was gone for *ten* years, Delun. Before war was even declared.'

'What does that mean?'

'You remember that man she came here with, the nice man?'

'Harvey,' Li Jun added. 'Nice man.'

'He recruited her. She was a spy. What do you think a decade of that work does to someone?'

'It kept us safe,' Li Jun muttered. 'When things got bad during the war, they never came for us, did they?'

'We aren't Japanese, Dad.'

He dispelled him with a click of his tongue and I could almost visualise the old man waving his hand in the air as he did a circle on the spot, feet shuffling around until he was back facing the same direction where he started.

Gently, I closed the door. I didn't want to hear any more. It hurt to know I was hurting them and I promised myself that I would do better, be less obviously miserable. The moment I pledged that, I was transported to a painful memory.

Before I went off for initial training, Lionel and Harvey had come to the house to speak to the Hans. It was partially out of respect and partially out of a need to reassure them they would be taking good care of me. It had only been a few months after the party in the Hollywood Hills and I had been doubting everything I had felt for Harvey in the lead-up to their visit. *It's all in your head*, I'd told myself every time I'd hung up the phone after one of our late-night conversations. I was completely over my infatuation, I'd sworn it, with my racing heartbeat nothing to do with him and everything to do with the new job I had signed up for.

Yet from the moment he'd showed up early to dinner, a bouquet of tulips in hand, I'd known I was a lost cause. Lionel had been carrying a bottle of Li Jun's favourite whiskey, like

I'd told him to, and as the five of us had sat down at the table and chatted over a meal, I couldn't stop staring at Harvey's right hand. He hadn't been wearing his wedding ring.

It means nothing. It's probably nothing.

Yet as Lionel had begun getting to the reason for their visit, the conversation serious, I'd felt Harvey's hand brush against mine under the table. I must have looked nervous or worried about how the Hans would take it, but the second his skin touched mine, I'd gripped for dear life. He'd squeezed back, giving me a sweet smile.

Lionel had left shortly after, unable to stay for dessert with 'so much to organise'. Harvey had stayed for hours more. Meili's attempts to teach him mah-jong had had her crying with laughter at the dining table: Harvey so determined to master the game on his first few attempts but frustrated by how absolutely terrible he was at it. Li Jun and Meili had retreated to bed after I'd practically had to shoo her out of the kitchen so the woman wouldn't stay and attempt to do the dishes.

'It's too much work for you, Tulip. Let me help, it will be quicker.'

'Mrs Han,' Harvey had interjected, 'you have my word that I'll stay here and assist with the matter of the dishes. She won't be up all night.'

He'd thrown her one of those disgustingly manipulative grins and I'd watched Meili melt, much the way I had. She'd relented, retreating to bed, and within a matter of minutes I felt the air from their bedroom change with the heavy breathing of sleep.

'You sap,' I'd said, whipping him with one of the tea towels I was using to dry while he washed.

'What?' Harvey had laughed, feigning innocence. 'I'm just here to help, in a strictly professional dishwashing sense.'

'Oh, *okay*. I see you putting the moves on Meili.'

He'd smiled, the two of us silent for a moment as we'd washed, just the sounds of the water splashing and dishes clinking over the soft music playing from the radio.

'Why don't you call her mum?'

I stiffened, getting nervous any time the questions veered towards the personal.

'Don't do that,' he'd murmured.

'Do what?' I'd asked innocently.

'Shut down the second I ask you something personal.'

Shit. 'If we're going to be spies, isn't keeping secrets part of the job? Ask no questions, tell no lies, Mr Schwartz?'

His sleeves were rolled up to his elbows, wrists wet as he'd pulled them from the sink and rested them on his hips.

'I don't want to keep secrets from you, Tulip.' He'd been seemingly oblivious to the water dripping down his trouser legs. My silence was testing him, I could see it.

'Okay, how about I tell you something first?' he'd begun. 'I started talking with a lawyer. A divorce lawyer. I know that you know my marriage is just to save face at this point. And not even my face at that.'

Good God, that was personal. Too personal! I'd been about to say as much when I'd paused.

'When?'

'When what?'

'When did you start talking to a divorce lawyer?'

'Oh, uh, actually it has been an ongoing conversation really. Started just over a year ago now.'

'A year ago . . .' I'd murmured, my mind whirring as I'd done the calculations.

'Yes, the week we met.'

'Harvey,' I'd whispered, a hand covering my mouth.

'I'm sorry, I know it's improper and if you feel nothing for me then I won't speak another word of it. All is fair in love and war. But that night at the party, I could have sworn the same thing driving me towards you was driving you right back.'

'I . . .?'

'You're trembling.'

'No, I'm not.'

He'd cackled. 'You don't have to fight me on everything, I swear to God.'

He'd stepped forward, taking my hands in his. I'd watched him do it, unable to pull away and not wanting to. He'd kissed my fingertips gently, not seeming to mind all the scars that marked them from years of floristry. His sweet lips had touched my knuckles, his eyes watching me as he did, then the palm of my hand, and the inside of my wrist, right where my radial artery was. He'd frowned, inspecting it more closely.

'Tulip, your pulse is racing.'

I'd spread my fingers wide, hand running over the material of his shirt and the small mounds created by buttons. I'd paused above his heart, feeling the heavy thud through his skin and right down into my own bones.

'I'm not the only one,' I'd whispered.

'I always thought love should be like the *Titanic II.*'

'What?' I'd chuckled, confused.

'It should take us both down with it.'

I'd moved towards him, slowly so as not to startle a cornered beast. His hands had slid around my waist and right there in that Burbank kitchen, we'd shared our first kiss.

Delun was wrong: I wasn't a ghost version of myself. I'd returned to America with a ghost following my every waking moment.

Hours later, when I thought everyone was asleep, I drank a cup of green tea and stood in that exact same spot in the kitchen. When the light switched on behind me, chasing away the darkness, I instinctively reached for the pistol in the holster at my hip. I wasn't wearing it, of course. My fingers just made contact with the silk of my pyjamas instead.

'Sit down,' Meili ordered, shuffling around the kitchen with purpose as she started brewing a new pot.

'I—'

'That cup is ice cold, Tulip.'

She emptied it into the sink, pulling out a chair at the dining table and pointing at it with a non-verbal direction to sit that was a thousand times louder. I did as ordered, running my hands over my face and through my hair as it had started to grow out again. It was like I blinked and then all of a sudden there was a bowl of steaming hot soup in front of me, along with a plate of dumplings.

'How . . . what happened to my tea?'

'Your appetite replaced it. Now eat.'

The old woman sat down across from me, giving the clear impression that she wouldn't move until every morsel of the meal was gone. She was even drinking her own cup of green tea, taunting me.

'I've killed people, you know,' I grumbled.

'Not when you were this skinny you didn't.'

I sighed, picking up the chopsticks as I fished a mouthful of noodles out of the bottom of the bowl. It was the best thing I had ever eaten and, somehow, I didn't know exactly how, I found myself crying as I ate the most delicious meal of my life.

'Oh,' Meili purred, reaching a hand across the table to touch my forearm. 'I'm sorry, you're not that skinny. You're very fat.'

I coughed and laughed at the same time, shaking my head.

'No, it's not you, it's . . . I haven't had soup in years, Meili. I haven't had *your* soup in years. Zowie, I can't even remember the last time I had anything with proper spice.'

'It tastes like home, yes?'

I nodded, slurping loudly. It was testament to my vulnerable state that Meili didn't chastise my poor table manners.

'I know your soul aches, child. It ached from the moment I met you, nearly thirty years ago. I look like a completely different woman and you . . . you've barely aged on the outside, but I fear you're old on the inside.'

'Meili—'

'People will notice eventually, that you're not like others. I always suspected it, but now . . .'

'I have good genes?' I offered feebly.

'No one has genes *that* good, ha!'

She was quiet as I continued to eat, watching me carefully.

'I don't want to leave you,' I whispered. 'I don't want you and Li Jun to be alone as you get old.'

'Get old? We're already old! I'm sixty-two, he's sixty-four, but we'll live forever the two of us. You know that, no God would dare.'

I chuckled.

'Plus, Delun has never heard of contraception and that wife of his is about to have their fifth child. *Fifth!* We'll never be alone hard as we try.'

'So that's it? You're telling me to just leave? Never come back?'

'No, I hope you will. I'll understand if you don't. But you need to go away for a while, let people forget your face and forget your name. Have some adventures, fall in love, make mistakes. We'll always be here, or there. You can find us.'

It was simultaneously the saddest and most beautiful thing anyone had ever said to me.

I listened to Meili. In fact, I wondered how many years she and Li Jun had been discussing my future, because although both of them cried and held me close as I boarded a plane to Hawaii, they seemed emotionally prepared for my departure. It was the shove I needed, both for my own safety and theirs.

Not that Hawaii was an island haven unmarked by the war. It was almost defined by it at this point, yet I found there to be something grounding about that. So much of the world seemed determined to forget the horror of the past few years, rather than acknowledge it and learn from it and grow from it.

I settled in the coastal town of Hilo, Hawaii, which was still rebuilding itself after a tsunami had swept through a few months earlier, killing some one hundred and sixty people. Honolulu had been my first choice, but the supernatural presence on the island of Oahu was too active, too constant. I sought out somewhere quieter instead, with mountains that I could hike and beaches that I could submerge myself into whenever I wanted.

I changed my name, changed my hair, changed my whole fucking life as I tried not to focus on my grief. Yet it was near impossible: Harvey's memory could be everywhere and anywhere when you were the one generating it.

I moved into a low-rise apartment complex that was owned by a man named Jimmy Alualu who was short in stature, but tall in spirit. I don't think I ever saw him without a huge smile on his face, always asking about how my day was or what I thought the weather would be like tomorrow when he saw me on the street.

He was never nosy, though. He never pried into my business or asked questions about why the woman in apartment three didn't seem to have many friends and always walked the island alone. The only time he became curious was when he saw me drawing in a sketchpad on the back balcony. He asked to see my handiwork when I dropped off the rent days later and I showed him, Jimmy offering me a job on the spot.

'I guessed you worked for yourself, but if you need a few days a week, I'm looking for an apprentice at the shop.'

'What kind of shop?'

'Alualu Tattoo! Best on the island! Probably third best in all of Hawaii.'

I enjoyed his honesty. 'I don't know anything about tattoos. I don't even have one.'

'Firstly, you understand line and depth and composition and shade. That's crucial right there! Secondly, they're contagious: just being this close to me and *wham*! You'll have your own art.'

He ran the shop with his older sister, Haukea, who was the gifted artist in the family. Her speciality was florals, with people travelling from all over to have her needle ink frangipanis or native Hawaiian flowers on their flesh. Jimmy was good at the business side of things, sticking mainly to traditional tattoos and managing the myriad of things you needed to manage when a tattoo parlour was just one of five operations you had functioning.

It turned out to be a job I was well suited for, as I was someone who always needed to be learning something new so I could keep my mind active and off the darker thoughts. I liked the sketching, I liked the designing when I was able to move off the catalogue and away from the more popular choices, I liked the methodical cleaning of tools and I liked the challenge of working with a difficult canvas: skin. I liked the smell of disinfectant, I liked the soundtrack of constant buzzing, and eventually I liked the way it felt when the needle made contact with my skin.

It satisfied like an itch that was both pleasurable and painful to scratch, with Haukea starting work on an enormous back piece that took years to complete with the time factored in for healing. I wrote postcards to Meili and Li Jun, receiving the occasional one back from Delun too, and made phone calls to them twice weekly.

They told me that Lionel had come by, asking after me. That he had done so several times before he stopped coming. The deposits into my bank account were still being made, so in my mind we were very much done. He left a letter that was forwarded on to me and I read it, writing a thoughtful response that was more sentimental than I had intended it to be. I left no return address.

For ten years I had peace, waking every day and looking up at the two volcanoes that bookended Hilo from my bedroom window. I swam in the morning, baptising myself as I plunged below the waves and resisted Jimmy's push to teach me how to surf 'like every other normal human being on the island'. I worked in the day, took college classes at night, and before the sunset I returned to the beach where I swam again.

Sitting on the sand, skin damp and towel wrapped around my waist, I wiggled my toes through the sand and thought of Harvey. His son would be grown and I wondered if he looked like his father. I wondered if it would hurt me to find out. On me always was a letter Harvey had written, back during the first year of the war, Lionel said.

He'd given it to his friend with the instruction that if he was to be killed, it must go to me and no one else. If he hadn't died, if things hadn't gone the way they did, if the war had ended and he'd rethought that talk of divorce and left me to go back to his wife, I wondered if I would still have loved him as much. Happy endings were a con and, in lieu of that, I had to settle for the fact I'd known my soulmate for nine years – been with him for eight – and that was longer than many people would ever know.

The words in that letter said as much. And more. He told me he didn't believe in 'that love at first sight crap', but how he felt like he'd bloomed in the months since he'd met me, and how, in the years since, he'd fallen deeply, madly, in love.

I would never burn that letter, never willingly destroy it. Time would, I knew. So I had the sentiment inked on my body forever, where Harvey's fingertips had often trailed over my skin and up my spine. I wore his blooms on my back, and those of my father as well. Orchids for Meili and roses for Li Jun, all of the people I had loved.

Inevitably, the time came for me to move on from Hilo. I couldn't stay there – or anywhere – forever. The clock was always ticking on my freedom.

Chapter 20

The selkies slowed their descent, the massive current ripping water into the building enough to tug them where they needed to go. Besides the occasional pivot or redirection here and there, they could conserve energy this way. They would need it to push against this same flow to get out of the building, with the additional strain of a passenger on their back. Dreckly was the one non-selkie among them, but she was essential as no one knew the layout of the complex better than she did.

She couldn't swim like they could or navigate half as well, but, so long as she could hitch a ride, Dreckly could survive at this depth. There were four tunnels open to them, the grenades having more than done the job as they swam through the gaping holes and into the building. Visibility was poor here, debris and dirt and dust particles swirling around them in a brown haze. Dreckly used bubbles of air to separate the smog like a curtain, showing the selkies in her tunnel a clear path forward. Those in the other three would have to figure it out on their own.

The pressure of the water had done the job for them, the fifth level entirely flooded by the time they reached it. Half the tubes were full, Dreckly not liking the implication. It meant sometime in the last three weeks, the Treize had cleared out a number of beings that had been there previously. Where they had gone and what had been done to them was the biggest worry. She unlinked herself from Amos's shoulders, letting her body be pulled slowly around the room with the current as she inspected each tube. Some of the creatures she recognised and they clearly recognised her, most safely encased in the glass prisms as the exterior around them disappeared underwater.

Spinning around, a jet of bubbles escaped her mouth as she screamed and collided with the flesh of another creature. It was a corpse, dead and stiff as it floated in front of her. An older man – probably in his fifties, she guessed – as she tried to scramble away from the body and the unseeing eyes that were fixed on her. He'd been in a plain, white shirt that was dotted with blood from an impact wound at his forehead. His wrist displayed the tattoo that marked him as Askari, fingers clenched as he'd tried to hold on to something.

Dreckly reached down, grabbing one of the metal stands that showed digital label information on the prisoner like they had been curated in a horrible museum. It kept her in place and she watched as the dead man bobbed away with the current. *Calmness and clarity*, she said to herself, urging her heartbeat to return to normal levels. Waving her hands in front of her face, she got the attention of Amos and the selkies around her who had been doing a sweep of the room. Dreckly held up her fingers, counting out the number seven on her digits.

'Get the selkies first,' she mouthed, conscious of the others joining their ranks as they emerged from the tunnels. 'They can help free the others.'

The selkie prisoners were partially an experiment: it didn't matter if water flooded their tubes as they were already full. Yet it would help everyone else figure out the quickest way to get the tubes open so that when they moved on to those who were still being supplied with fresh air, they didn't have to waste valuable breathing time. Dreckly swam towards the first group, who were using a tool pack they had brought with them to prise the prison open.

One was giving the other instructions, both working from the top and bottom simultaneously to provide leverage. It was taking too long. Dreckly had an idea, and, kicking away from them, she swam in the direction of the corpse. Any dead Treize worker would do, really, and she felt the eyes of the fire elemental she recognised monitoring her closely as she neared the spot where the dead man had been lodged. She tried not to look at his face as she searched the pockets of his pants, finally finding the swipe pass clipped to the back of his belt. She ripped it loose, swimming back to the fire elemental.

'I know you,' they said, examining her through one eye. The other had been swollen shut.

'The others?' Dreckly mouthed, hoping the being would understand her. They didn't, so she repeated the message until the elemental nodded.

'Not here,' they replied. 'Some are dead. The rest were taken upstairs.'

Dreckly swore, lurching out and grabbing the tail of a selkie that swam by her. They stopped, floating closer. She pointed at the elemental, mouthing the word 'explain', as the selkie nodded and turned to the being.

'You're going to need to take a big breath,' the selkie told them. 'We'll release you from the tube and swim you out as quickly as we can. Can you do that?'

'You're getting us out of here?'

'That's right.'

'Shit, then I'll clench my butthole if that's what it takes.'

The selkie laughed, looking around for a moment as they assessed the current and repositioned themselves behind the tube. Dreckly waved the swipe pass in front of their face so they could see it, making a 'boom' gesture with her fingers so they would understand how quickly this would happen. They nodded, the fire elemental puffing out their cheeks as they gulped a mouthful of air. Dreckly ran the card across the reader and tapped the 'purge' button. They were blown backwards, with a small rush of water obscuring her view for a moment.

When Dreckly batted several strands of floating hair out of her face, the selkie already had their hands firmly clasped around the waist of the elemental and were swimming away towards the exit. *Good*, she thought. *This would be quicker than the tools*. A few of the readers had been destroyed so they would still need to physically prise some of them open, but as she took Amos through the process she felt relief knowing how much quicker this would be.

'Take it,' she mouthed, forcing it into his hands. The selkie examined it for just a beat before ordering another being to look for more Treize corpses and locate swipe passes so they could accelerate the process.

'Where are you going?' he asked.

She pointed. 'Up.'

He was one of the few people who would understand what she meant and why that was important to her. She'd left others behind once, to be experimented on and extracted and poked and prodded and killed. She wouldn't do it again. If everyone upstairs was already dead, then there's nothing they could do. If they weren't, then she couldn't leave them to that fate. Amos couldn't either.

He immediately handed the swipe card off to Leviathan, grabbing Dreckly by the elbow and swimming them both forward.

'Then I'll come with you. You shouldn't go alone.'

He pursed his lips into a strange shape, something like a high-pitched whistle coming from them. Dreckly flinched as it cut through the water. It was a call to arms in a way, with Avary and two others joining their party as they moved towards where the elevator should have been. The doors were open, as if someone had tried to get inside, but the shaft was entirely empty. Dreckly hung back as the selkies checked, their usually long hair pulled back in tight braids and buns. Amos turned around, ushering her forwards.

'We go up,' he said, Dreckly not needing his assistance as her legs built up a rhythm and she used her eight-beat kick to flow up the elevator shaft with the rush of water.

She broke through the surface, froth bubbling around her as the selkies' heads popped up too. They were riding the increasing water level, bobbing there as they neared the next floor.

'The fourth level is below us,' Avary said.

Their voices weren't quite as steady once they were above

water. Selkies spoke with what sounded like lisps, the words clicking and slippery in places they shouldn't be, full sentences testament to how rarely they emerged from the depths. Amos, however, was different.

'Were the doors open?' Amos questioned.

'No.'

'Open them up. Look how quickly we're rising. What floor are we going to?'

'Third,' Dreckly answered.

'It's flooding too fast if we want to get to anyone up there. Open the fourth level doors so the water has somewhere to go.'

'Wait,' Dreckly said, grabbing Avary's shoulder before she ducked down. 'We need to get to level three first. I'm not exactly keen to climb my way up the cables, are you?'

Avary barked a laugh, nodding as the four of them looked upwards as the water rose closer and closer to the doors. They waited for the water level to make it past at least the halfway point before they prised the doors open, Amos and Dreckly being swept inside with a wave of water. They slid unceremoniously down the hallway, Avary and the other selkie disappearing back down the elevator shaft where they opened up the fourth level.

'Brace,' Amos ordered, both of them gripping the frames of doorways as the water withdrew in a gush and found a new avenue to occupy. Breathing normally, Dreckly stumbled to her feet as she got her bearings and looked around. The fluorescent lights fixed into the ceiling finally blinked off for good, a red glow replacing them as the building switched over to backup power.

'It's too quiet,' Dreckly said, feeling *more* nervous if possible. 'We should be hearing the ruckus above. Gunfire. Shouting. Anything.'

'They soundproof each level,' Amos replied. 'So you can't hear the screams.'

The look on the selkie's face must have been similar to the one sailors saw before they were dragged to their deaths in the stories. It was *murderous*.

'What are you doing?' she asked, watching as her friend crouched over. He let out a grunt like he was in pain and she stepped forward, reaching a shaking hand out to touch his shoulder. She gasped, watching in amazement as his tail split into two, Amos panting with effort as he attempted to speed up the transformation. Wading forward, she helped him up as he stumbled into a standing position.

'I thought you—'

'I couldn't.' He smiled, the determined focus on his face being replaced with relief. 'I never could before, but I've been practising with Avary and, well . . . if you were willing to risk it all to come back, I wanted to make sure I was actually useful.'

'Amos,' she whispered, truly touched. She hesitated before embracing him in a hug, so relieved that *whatever* was coming, at least she had this most unlikely friend by her side. 'Legs or no legs, I'd take you over an entire pondant any day.'

He chuckled. 'Good, because I don't know how long I can maintain this.'

His human legs didn't look very human at all: even in the low light it was clear they were not anatomically correct. It wasn't just the lubricated, scaly texture but the shape that was all wrong. They did the job though, meaning that he was able to push forward as Dreckly threw an arm around him for extra balance.

'Let's motor, then, while the others are checking the fourth floor to see if anyone can be saved.'

Dreckly was doubtful, pausing their progress for a moment as she crouched down to inspect the body of a woman floating face down in the hall. The terrible angle her neck was resting at told her the lady was dead even before she rolled her over, so she tried to concentrate on finding what she needed first. Whoever she was, she was significant enough to have three swipe passes on her person and a physical set of keys, all which Dreckly grabbed.

'Check every room as fast as you can,' she said, handing one of the cards to Amos.

'Okay.' He nodded. 'I'll start at the opposite end. This level wraps around like a U-shape, so we'll meet in the middle.'

'Gotcha.'

It was smarter to stay together, but it was faster if they worked separately. Throwing her knees up high as she waded, Dreckly fell into a rhythm as she armed herself with one of the blades from the holster at her thigh and pushed into the first room, then the second, then the third. Those were mostly labs used for examining test results and all of them were empty, the occupants having cleared out as soon as things went to shit. The fourth room made her pause; it was essentially a morgue with the chest of four supernatural beings clasped open and their insides exposed mid-autopsy.

She had to look, she had to check that each was definitely dead. One of them was a demon that looked familiar to her,

Dreckly's mind flipping like the pages of a book until they fell open on the memory of this creature slumped unconscious in one of the tubes when she had first woken up imprisoned in this very same building. They had been thick, stocky, and horned just like Yixin. She'd wondered at the time if they were a distant relation and as her shaking hand hovered over their face, gently shutting their eyelids, she prayed that they weren't. She felt her stomach heave with repulsion and she threw up, her vomit floating around her knees as she let herself be sick.

Be disgusted later, she told herself. *Be active now.*

She moved to the next room, number five, which was an empty biopsy suite, before she paused at the front of number six. Dreckly had passed through the swinging doors of this spot once and she looked down at the darker water that was leaking out of them now. Blood. The inside was bright, some kind of self-powered lamp still working as she rushed forward into the tight space. Strapped to the stretcher was Ben Kapoor, completely naked and half sitting up as he paused in the middle of freeing himself. Suddenly the quieted commotion upstairs made a lot more sense. He blinked, as if not really seeing her properly and he shook his head slightly.

'Dreckly, I can't tell if it's you or whatever they've pumped me with,' he said, chest heaving.

'It's me,' she said, noting how he had morphed his human arm into a werewolf claw to partially tear himself free. There was a gargling sound from the corner and she registered the huddled figure of a scientist, clutching at their throat as they attempted to stop the blood that was pumping from their neck in rhythmic squirts. Ben's claws were wet with human fluid, the werewolf shrugging as he continued to slash himself free.

'What happened?!' she said, cutting his legs loose as he climbed off the stretcher. 'Are the others—'

'No,' Ben replied. 'I'm the only one they got; I made sure of it.'

'The rest of the troupe?'

'Dead or fled. I wasn't about to let them take any of my people alive.'

'Except for yourself, you fucking heroic dumbass! Ever stop to think that your escape was more important?'

'Everyone's important,' he answered, deathly serious. 'If this is what it took to create a successful diversion, then I was willing to do it.'

'How lucky for you then that I'm here to counteract your heroism.' She ducked under his shoulders, offering him support as he got his bearings. 'You right?'

'Yeah, just . . .' He laughed, shocking her completely. 'The irony of this situation, huh? I tried to recruit *you* to the cause or whatever you call it and—'

'I get it, I get it, mock me in motion though. We need to check the other rooms and then get out of here. Do you know if there was anyone else on this floor? And can you find pants? Jocks, even?'

'Why? You've seen me naked before. *Multiple* times.'

'I have, yes, but there are fifty odd selkies and who knows how many other escapees that don't need the added trauma of looking at your huge, swinging dick right now.'

He blinked again, mouth trying to say something but no words coming out. Ben shrugged, admitting defeat as he grabbed a pair of jocks from the side bench, Dreckly helping him into them as the effects of the drugs still had him moving slowly. He went to grab a shirt and she stopped him.

'You'll move quicker without it,' she said.

'Quicker? What, are we swimming out of here?'

She stared at him. He stared back.

'Fuck,' he swore. 'I thought we might go up.'

'Down, baby. Down and out.'

They limped out of the room and back into the hallway. The next two rooms had three survivors from the tubes below, all in worse states than Ben but two able to move on their own. The third was unconscious, Dreckly looking at the emaciated form of the goblin Ben lifted into his arms. She had sent the other two ahead to keep checking the rooms so they could make it to Amos as quickly as possible. The water level was rising again and she was conscious of the fact they were losing time. Carrying her out into the hallway, she knew the were-wolf was hurting as she heard the sound of his laboured breaths with the additional weight.

'You think we should leave her,' he said, not in an accusatory tone but just matter of fact.

Dreckly cast the goblin a sideways look, the creature not looking much older than fifteen but probably three times that.

'Is she breathing?' she asked, watching as he went to check her pulse. 'Her breath, Ben. Not her pulse. Is there any air going in and out of her lungs?'

He held a hand in front of her nostrils and mouth, frowning.

'A little.'

Dreckly leaned forwards, covering her mouth like she was about to whisper a secret as she breathed *life* into the girl. That's what it would have looked like, but really it was just a force of oxygen. The goblin's lips trembled, but she didn't wake. Her breathing increased after that, steadying somewhat.

'I'll figure it out,' Dreckly said. 'If I take her with me, she'll have the best shot. I can't guarantee she'll make it though.'

'That's okay.' He nodded, seemingly pleased with that response. 'At least we'll have the body for her people.'

They neared the final bend of the U-shape, Amos now up ahead and the two additional escapees with their backs to them. There was enough water flooding the passage now that Avary and the other selkie could swim into the hallway, neither of them choosing to exert energy on creating legs as they stayed horizontal. Ben looked down at his crotch self-consciously as they were joined by the selkies, leaning over and whispering to Dreckly when they weren't looking.

'Where are selkie dicks?' he asked.

'What?'

'You're half selkie, right? You should know.'

'Now? You want to know about merman dick *now*?'

'I might die on the way outta here! Let me die with that knowledge.'

She laughed, half in disbelief. 'Have you ever seen whales have sex?'

'*What?!* No! Why, have you?'

'Well, there's your motivation for living: stay alive so you can Google whale dicks when we're out of here. Then you'll have your answer.'

He looked thoughtful, that expression disappearing in an instant as one of the survivors shouted out a warning.

'NOT THAT DOOR!' they cried, as an escapee from a different room lifted up the swipe pass.

It was too late, the reader beeping and the creature looking back with surprise as it opened. An enormous bladed tentacle shot out almost immediately, wrapping around their torso and sinking into their flesh in one move. They screamed, yanked sideways through the opening and into the room.

'SHUT IT!' Ben screamed. 'SHUT IT! SHUT IT!'

Dreckly was the fastest wader, making it to the door before the others and noticing for the first time that it was steel plated. It opened inwards, not outwards, and she had to step through the threshold to get the handle.

'Holy fuck,' she breathed, not pausing for a second as she began backing out as quickly as she could.

There had been other creatures in that room, clearly, yet they had been entirely consumed by what was at the centre of it. It looked like – there was no other way to put it – a giant asshole, with thousands of teeth pulsing at different layers to the entrance. There were tentacles extending outwards in every direction, thick and thin.

There were eyes, massive black, glossy eyes and as she stared into them she could see intelligence there. And pain, *so much* pain. Dreckly was a natural thing, she was the product of two of the most natural things in the world, and she could see the truth just by looking at what was staring at her with lidless orbs for eyes. This was *no* natural thing. This was some unearthly mutation the Treize had cooked up in their labs, desperately searching for a cure to whatever ailed the Three. No cure was worth this, however.

'Please,' she shouted at it, believing as much as hoping it could understand her. 'Please let them go.'

The tentacles slowed, the beastie showing some cognitive recognition. Dreckly was begging for the life of a supernatural she didn't know, but she was urging whatever creature or creatures that had made up the beast she was looking at to remember, to recognise friend from foe, to show mercy. She was pleading her case to the morsel of a soul that might have been left. Her attempt bought the escapee additional seconds, seconds she should have used to shoot them instead of trying to reason with what was in front of her. As it was, her begging was useless and she watched in abject horror as tentacles ripped their bottom half clean from their top. It silenced their screams and their suffering at least.

'NO!' she screamed, using one of her knives to slash at another tentacle as it attempted to wrap around her ankle.

Dreckly struggled with the weight of the door and the flow of the water pushing against it despite how hard she was tugging. She cried out as a tentacle wrapped around her knee, the blades cutting into her skin like a squid that had spent too much time in metal shop. She held on to the door handle as her feet were ripped out from under her, the monster attempting to pull her back towards where it was digesting its earlier victim. Victims.

'STAY BACK!' she cried as the selkies tried to rush to her aid. They couldn't pass through the doorway or they too would be prey, the tentacles seemingly not able to reach much further than that. Dreckly had no choice but to hold on with one hand as she used her other to stab blindly through the water. There was bringing a knife to a gunfight, then there was bringing a knife to a mutant sphincter fight. Both were essentially useless.

'ARGH!' she screamed, as the tentacle tightened and a second looped around her knee. She felt the handle weaken in her wet, slippery grip.

'Dreckly!' Ben exclaimed, appearing in the doorway as he tossed the unconscious goblin to one of the selkies. 'Give me your hand!'

'I can't,' she panted, still stabbing through the water. She was hurting the creature, she could feel the tentacles loosen each time, and that was the only thing keeping her out of its teeth. 'Grenade!'

He looked confused, but she gestured with her chin to her hip where there was one she had kept for an emergency strapped to the outer belt. Ben's eyes widened when he saw it, lunging into the creature's tentacle range and then back out again with that unrivalled werewolf speed. He didn't hesitate, pulling the pin and hurling it right into gaping mouth of the monster. He shifted his hands back to werewolf claws, plunging them into the water and ripping at the tentacles. The creature had swallowed the explosive and released her with the added assault from Ben, Dreckly pushing herself upwards as the werewolf grabbed her and ran from the room.

'RUN!' he screamed, but the selkies had already heard her call for the bomb in the first place. She saw a tail disappear down the elevator shaft with a splash, the red lights above them flashing on and off as they ran. It was only four seconds until the explosion, but it felt like four hours as Ben dragged her. Someone had obviously already taken the unconscious goblin and remaining survivor, Dreckly unsure if the former would make it without the forced air bubble she had intended to place around her. Avary was risking it regardless, with just Amos's head bobbing above the water as he yelled at them to move faster.

The ground shuddered beneath them as they dived, Dreckly pulling the stale air towards her as she envisioned it wrapping around Ben's face like a bandage. Amos had them both gripped by their forearms, one in each hand as he yanked them after him. Dreckly tried not to notice the fissures she saw appearing in the concrete, the selkie trying to outrun them before bursting out on to the final level. Two selkies had been waiting for them at the elevator shaft and she heard Ben cry out as she let go of Amos, swimming immediately for one of the two others.

'She'll be fine,' she heard Amos say. 'She knows what she's doing and knows I'll be faster with just one of you. And yes, you have her to thank for the breathing.'

The selkie Dreckly had been swimming towards was hit from above, a massive chunk of the ceiling colliding with their body and pinning them to the ground in a swirl of blood and fluids. She shrieked, paddling backwards just in the nick of time as the other selkie zipped into his friend's place and looped their hands around her torso. The water was blurring past her eyes so fast, Dreckly could barely see anything except for flashes of grey that she hoped were the surviving selkies rushing for the tunnels and not more debris as the entire structure seemed to cave in around them.

There wasn't much she could do besides wiggle so her face was pressed against their chest and legs wrapped around their silky tail as it whipped backwards and forwards as quickly as possible. She clenched her eyes shut, trying to ignore the pain in her lacerated legs, and gripped as tightly as she could. She prayed they would make it to the surface and not be buried in a watery graveyard. There was a blast of pressure behind them, pushing the pair quicker than she thought possible as they jetted out of the tunnel and into the expanse of cold harbour water.

The selkie kept swimming though, sensing something she couldn't as the blast pushing them forward began to suck them back. But the laws of physics had met their match, the rest of the selkies waiting for them as they dragged the duo forward, towards the boats, despite the tug urging them the other way. They broke the surface victoriously, like a cork shot from a champagne bottle. Hands were on her but she relaxed as she felt the humid night air on her face, not caring how hot it was as she was lifted on to the back of one of the boats.

Dreckly felt slightly drunk as she looked around, realising Amos was talking to her as she was slid backwards. Her legs were worse than she thought, she noted with some surprise as blood gushed across the deck. She must have asked after him, as Ben was suddenly beside her and shouting something at *someone*.

Cuts always look worse with water, she thought. These weren't gonna be as bad as they looked. There was smoke bellowing from the city skyline and she registered the shouts of the selkies, pointing, directing everyone to move *now* as the boat engines began. She felt the vibrations through her spine as she was laid on to her back, someone cutting her legs free of the wetsuit and applying a tourniquet.

Dreckly smiled, the hardness of the deck nice and firm beneath her head. She didn't have anything left to do; she could rest now. Turning her head to the side, she stared at the angelic face of the goblin girl they'd rescued. She thought she was asleep, just like Dreckly wanted to be. Yet there was no air escaping her lips, no oxygen from her nostrils as she lay there, body rocking slightly with the motion. The goblin was dead. With a sigh, Dreckly closed her own eyes, hoping their victories had outweighed the losses that night.

Chapter 21

Past

Sharm El-Sheikh off the coast of Egypt was essentially a resort town, reminding me so much of the hundreds of other resort towns I had visited just like it over the years. I didn't intend to stay long, just a month, before making my way south to the mouth of the Nile. Because it was a resort town, it was easy to blend: mostly Russian tourists swarming the hotels and night-clubs and restaurants almost year-round. It was always winter somewhere and it was always warm in Sharm El-Sheikh.

I wasn't on vacation, however; I had a purpose. There was something about growing older that made you examine who you were at your very core, what made up the essence of you. It was the same compulsion that drove old ladies to create family trees and old men to start investigating the meaning behind family crests. According to my paperwork, I had just turned forty. I wasn't sure what the supernatural equivalent of a midlife crisis was, but I was quite certain I was in the throes of one.

I'd returned to America in an attempt to re-centre myself, but Los Angeles in the eighties just made me feel a sense of displacement more than anything. I baulked standing in front of the massive mall structures that people flocked to like it was the location of a new church. I felt very far removed from the energy of those who passed through the doors with big hair and even bigger debts. I stayed with Mildred for several months, who – despite all that she had seen and all that she had experienced – had found herself drawn back to Los Angeles.

She was a literal relic from another time, but somehow she managed to move through the decades like she belonged there, swapping her satin and fitted gowns for denim and smeared blue eye shadow that was befitting of the era. I couldn't help but think it looked ridiculous on everyone else *except* Mildred.

'We've earned this break, don't you think?' my old friend had asked, practically shouting over the New Order track that was pulsing through the nightclub we had found ourselves in.

I'd thought about her question as I'd sipped my overpriced martini, watching as the bodies danced and laughed and snorted and shrieked around us.

'I . . . just don't know where I fit in anymore.'

Mildred had nodded, as if she had been exactly where I was. For all I knew, she had.

'So find out.'

I'd nearly choked on the olive I was biting into. Her answer had been so simple, yet so surprising. I'd gawked at her as she took a swig from the bottle of cheap beer she adored despite everything about her indicating the contrary.

'Find out,' she'd repeated. 'I know you can. You don't need my help to do it. Dare say, you don't need anyone's.'

'Not true.' I had smirked. 'But sweet of you to say. What will you do without me?'

'Exactly what I did in the sixties. And the seventies. Chill out.'

Mildred had done anything but 'chill out' in the years since the war had attended, becoming incensed as she watched the humans start yet *another* war with Vietnam. She'd joined the Black Panthers instead, then the Weather Underground, then . . . this break she was talking about now. Maybe Mildred was tired now, I'd thought; I certainly was.

'How about one more dance?' the demon had asked, eyes illuminated as she'd watched the mass of people. 'The dancing is horrible, but if it's going to be a while between catch-ups then we may as well . . .'

I'd laughed, downing the rest of my drink as I'd got to my feet, toes aching in the neon pumps Mildred had demanded I wear.

'Let's dance, bitch.'

And we had. I'd danced until my toes bled, danced until my stomach hurt from laughing, danced until Mildred pulled me close and told me she'd see me at 'the next war'. I didn't know if I had the strength to survive another and I hoped she was wrong.

Instead, I'd looked for remnants of the old Hollywood, the Hollywood I knew, yet it wasn't there: even if the president was a former failed star. His acting was about as good as his leadership and when Reagan was succeeded by a Bush, I stopped paying attention to politics altogether. It was dangerous to live in the past, but it was the only place that felt familiar to me as I brought fresh flowers to the graves of Meili and Li Jun.

They had passed fifteen years earlier, damn near living up to their prediction that they were immortal. Li Jun had died in his sleep, Meili following only a week later, and I had been lucky enough to be there for them both. I'd held the hand of the woman who had been more of a mother to me than anyone I had ever known; Meili Han passing with a vice-like grip. Delun's death in a car accident had come before both of them, with his children and their grandchildren now adults with families of their own.

I visited Clara's grave too, bringing her three over-the-top bouquets that would have delighted her in life. 'Hollywood's "It" Girl', it read on the plaque, as I sat on the grass and looked out over the rolling green hills of Forest Lawn Memorial Park. It was in Glendale, not far from the former home of the Hans, and deer dotted the landscape as they casually sauntered over to eat the flowers left at various grave sites. There was a rustling in a bush nearby and a doe stuck her head out, black eyes blinking as she eyed the bouquets at my feet.

'Not a chance,' I told it, shaking my head.

At least not until I'm gone, I thought.

Egypt had been a whole new venture in every possible way. I'd had the benefit of it being much easier to blend, hiding my appearance under a niqab so that only my veiled eyes were visible. It wasn't necessary, I could have gotten around just as easily in a hijab or long-sleeves and shorts like many of the tourists, but my choice gave me more freedom.

I was taking risks now. Egypt was a hotbed of supernatural activity, and Cairo in particular, where I had based myself initially. It was a city full of alchemists, most of them running apothecaries and perfumeries just outside of the central tourist district in Giza. It was easier to watch and remain unwatched there.

The Treize's largest supernatural library was in Cairo and used mainly by Askari. I didn't risk going inside, instead finding an alchemist I could bribe to do my bidding instead. They loved money and they loved information, so I felt fairly certain I could exploit both of their loves safely and get what I wanted. It was very Mr Fix-It of me and I couldn't help but think Lionel would be proud of my cunning.

My own research had shown that the oldest selkie stories in the world tracked back to Africa, so it had made sense to visit the continent and dig up what I could find. That – and the bribes – had led me in turn to Sharm El-Sheikh and from there to the Nile, where it was rumoured the selkies had existed in harmony with the humans who lived on those banks for thousands of years.

The manuscripts the alchemist had transcribed confirmed what I had already determined based on tales from my father and other accounts from sailors over the years. A selkie could present in many forms, depending on where they came from and the gifts of their specific pondant. They were true shapeshifters, although they were never given proper credit for it. A dolphin or dugong might be more useful in one chosen scenario, a shark or a humanoid in another, meaning the Treize had always struggled to track and identify the species broadly if the members of that species didn't want them to. Which they didn't.

Off the island of Philae, I let my gut guide me towards the person I was looking for. Time had given me a radar for other supernaturals, my perception able to pick up on things everyday humans failed to see. And there they were, adjusting several flags as they fluttered in the wind on the deck of a felucca. The new term was transgender, but there was no shortage of older definitions: *fa'afafine, hijra, nadleeh*. This person was that, looking like an extension of the boat itself as they dressed head-to-toe in white garments that glimmered ever so slightly.

'You looking for something?' they asked, not bothering to turn around but knowing I was there.

'Someone to sail me up the Nile,' I called from the riverbank. 'I can pay well.'

'Just you?'

'Just me.'

They turned around, examining me with X-ray-like scrutiny. I was dressed in loose, khaki clothing with a wide-brimmed hat gifted from Mildred fastened on my head.

'It will take three days, maybe less if the weather holds.'

I tilted my head. 'It's Egypt, the weather always holds.'

They gave me a price. I bartered. Li Jun would have smiled with satisfaction if he was there.

'Better jump on then. We can leave at dusk.'

I only had the one backpack, purposefully choosing to travel light, and I climbed on board. They introduced themselves as Tan, just Tan, and they barked a series of commands at me so that soon I was running around the felucca and making preparations for them to set sail immediately. In fact, the orders didn't stop. Tie that here, loosen that there, move starboard, that's port, and so on. I was flustered, completely out of my depth and not accustomed to the specifics of sailing.

By the time we sat down for a meal of falafel and pitta bread hours later, I was exhausted. And starving. Tan offered me wine and I shook my head, choosing to stick to the bottled water I'd brought. They shrugged, nonchalant.

'How long have you been here?' they asked, shaking their hair loose from a bun. It was black and beautiful and glossy, so much so it took me a few seconds to catch up to the fact I hadn't replied yet.

'Eight months,' I answered.

'Where?'

'Cairo.'

'What did you think of our fair city?'

I gave them a sideways look at the description, to see if they were joking. There was a smirk playing on their face as well.

'I thought there were a lot of cars,' I said carefully. 'A lot of motorcycles. A lot of noise. A lot of people.'

They nodded. 'The quiet life is not what you go to Cairo to seek. So tell me, what did you go there to seek?'

'Answers.'

They nodded again, as if that was the response they'd been expecting. 'And they led you here.'

'They did.'

They sighed, looking up at the clear night above them. It was quiet on the water, just a gentle lapping against the side of the felucca, but the sky was loud and exploding with activity. A never-ending sea of what you thought was just blackness at first, but the longer you looked you saw shades of blue and purple and sometimes even light pink swirled in. Then there were stars; tiny white specks that exist in numbers you can't even begin to count. They glitter and burn, even when you're not looking at them. Even in death.

'That's what stars look like,' my father's voice said, swimming back to me. 'Just on a very different canvas.'

'It has been a while,' Tan murmured, watching me as I gawked at the night. 'Since one like you came by.'

'A sprite?'

'A true sprite. There are sprites everywhere, but true sprites? What Askari have on their census data is generations later, diluted versions of abominations like you.'

'Abominations,' I repeated, the word poisonous on the tongue.

'Wherever you came from, you've heard that term levelled at you, I bet. Why else the secrecy, hmm?'

They had a point.

'I'm a guardian. Do you know what that is?'

I nodded. 'You vet us,' I said, reciting what I had paid good money to learn from the transcriptions of an alchemist. 'You were banished from below and your penance is to guide home those of us who come looking for it.'

'Bully for you. But I was not banished, I chose this: it is an honourable service and after I die, someone else will take over the honour for me. Also, I do more than that: I teach you how to live, how to survive, so sprites don't just cease to exist altogether.'

And that's what Tan taught me to do, our duo sailing up and down the Nile over the next month as they showed me how to run a boat of my own and why it was important. They explained things about myself I had always known but hadn't understood until then, like the need to be close to water and the anxiety I felt when I wasn't. The air too, why I had power over it and could bend it to my will. I was the result of the union of two elements: earth and water. My birth provided unity with a third: air.

They asked what I knew of my origins. The East China Sea was all I could say and my mother's name: Tiānshǐ. I told Tan that I wasn't even sure if that was correct or just what my father had called her.

'It means "angel",' I said. 'She was an angel to him.'

'You chose.'

'Excuse me?'

'Selkies are not born he or she,' Tan said. 'They're born like me, like any of the hundreds of fish species who don't have a "gender". Sometimes nature or necessity might dictate, like clownfish, sometimes selkies choose, sometimes they remain how they are.'

They gestured to themselves for emphasis, before taking my arm and leaning overboard until we hovered just above the surface of the Nile. Tan splashed water over our skin and I watched with fascination as I saw the smallest of shapes arise.

'Feel,' they instructed. I traced the shapes on their skin, noting the swirls and lines and dots like it was a whole other language. In a way, it was. 'Now feel yours.'

My markings were completely different, I could feel it immediately. It was as clear to me as the difference between yellow and blue.

'This is how you will know your people, names or not. They will know you. They have always known you.'

Tan wasn't surprised I had managed as well as I had for as long as I had on my own. Some things could be learned, they said. Others were instinct, with both selkies and elementals working better when they relied on the latter. It made sense their offspring would be much the same way. Time was my curse, Tan told me. Selkies had regular, human lifespans. Elementals did not, with the years of a sprite falling somewhere in between.

'When you know and properly understand who you are, be careful,' Tan murmured, as they instructed me on how to read tidal charts. 'That information is your greatest power and your biggest weakness. Let the diluted loudly proclaim their spriteness and the werewolves flash their might, but be careful when showing yours and with whom you show it to. The Treize will do anything to lock you back up in that cage and gawk at you for eternity.'

'I'd gladly welcome death before I'd welcome their cage.'

'When cornered, you may have to. And when you need to run, always run to the sea. It's where you were birthed from and where you'll be safest.'

Each day, I had woken to the sound of morning prayer echoing across the water. Tan would often be emerging from the depths of the Nile, tail all but gone by the time they gripped their hand to the railing and climbed back on board the felucca. When I left Tan, it was with reluctance. Forward momentum was all I had, however, and the selkie was a bridge not a destination.

That was Zhoushan, a multilevel city in the eastern Chinese province of Zhejiang. I'd gone to Shanghai first, visiting so many of the places Meili and Li Jun had told me about in my youth. It felt like a pilgrimage in the most authentic sense, yet I wasn't looking for expanded meaning. I was clear on all that they had meant to me and I marvelled at the sheer menace of that bustling city as the early nineties took hold. What the Hans would think of this place in a whole different century, I could only guess.

I sourced a boat when I got to Zhoushan, island hopping as I followed the myths and stories that were scattered along the coast right to their centre. Calculation and planning could only take you so far. Some things required a leap of faith and, in this case, mine was massive.

I analysed the weather, waiting until it was the calmest evening. I left the port at sunset, travelling outwards until my digital wristwatch started beeping, the screen flashing with green light as it told me it was midnight.

Far enough, I thought, switching off the engine of the old trawler I had hired. It was much too big for one person, the owner had said. I had paid him in cash and he had stopped saying things.

Closing my eyes, I took a steadying breath. And then another. *Another*. I had to get my ass in gear, otherwise I would stay on this boat all night fucking *breathing* rather than doing what I had come to do. I peeled off my clothing, stripping down to a blue full-piece swimsuit that was cut high over my hips.

Climbing up on to the starboard side, I gripped the railing as I crouched down and peered over the edge. The water sparkled below, a full moon reflecting perfectly on the surface of the water like a glowing buoy. *Dive in and swim to it*, I said to myself. *Just dive in and swim.*

I leapt, feeling like I was moving in slow motion as my fingertips touched the ocean and gravity slid me deeper, inch-by-inch, until the water ran over my forearms, my shoulders, my back, my butt, my legs, and finally my toes. Diving into the unknown was more than just some motivational mantra slapped up on a poster to me. I was living it.

My hair was at my tailbone and it pulled behind me like a black flag trailing in the wind. The momentum from the dive brought me to stop, my eyes not stinging as I opened them and squinted around. It was just black, endless. I couldn't see anything.

Feeling my chest begin to strain as I ran out of air, it was a reminder that I was my mother's daughter but also my father's. I let myself float to the surface, taking a measured breath as I treaded water.

The horizon was out there, somewhere. The dark water and the dark sky bled together so it was impossible to tell where one ended and the other began. Swimming around, I couldn't even see land or any of the lights dotting the shoreline from this far out. There was only the boat for company, bobbing on the water.

'This is some brave shit I'm doing right now, Harvey,' I whispered, trying not to let my teeth chatter as I was hit by a cool current. 'Okay, *sure*, not Harvey Schwartz levels of brave, but if I get eaten by a tiger shark at least I'll get to see you soon.'

It was a horrible thought, but I was resigned to my fate at this point. I wasn't suicidal – I would have handed myself over to the Treize if that was the case – yet I had chosen to put myself in this situation in the hope it would mean something.

There was a splash behind me, and I froze, too afraid to look and see what it was. There was another, my heartbeat thudding faster as I watched a small wave wash past me and fade out. Ripples hit the back of my body and I closed my eyes, sensing their presence as clearly as I could sense a pending sunrise.

'Do you not want to greet us, daughter?' a voice said, speaking a version of Mandarin that sounded almost slurred to my ears.

'After you've come all this way?' another spoke.

My eyes flung open and I paddled my body around, air ricocheting from my lungs as I processed the sight. Blue eyes were staring back at me, not just one set, but *dozens*. More were appearing, heads popping up from under the surface one at a time, like word was spreading below about their long-lost visitor.

I tried counting, but every time a new selkie would burst above the surface it would throw me off and I would have to reset back to zero.

I didn't react as a hand touched my skin, gentle webbed fingers running over my extended arms while I felt more movement at my legs, twisting up my limbs like an explorative eel. They were reading me, I knew. They were reading my markings and learning that I belonged to them in part.

They had obviously been expecting me. Despite all of Tan's vehement proclamations that I needed to push past fear and make the journey on my own, give myself over to the unexpected, they had clearly helped out. The selkies weren't blindsided by my appearance. They welcomed it.

I felt a smile twitching on to my face as the selkies swam forward, touching me, stroking my hair, whispering their greetings to me. The selkie right in front of me grinned back with the same serrated smile I imagined my mother might have had.

'I've been waiting so long to meet you,' I whispered, feeling tears drip down my cheeks and into the not-so-empty waters.

Chapter 22

Present

Silk sheets. Dreckly usually hated the idea of them, especially in Australia when they started sticking to you the instant your skin got too hot. Ironically, despite being on the outskirts of the desert, it was freezing at night so she moved through the sheets like water. Her head was resting on Ben's bare torso, arms reached back above her so she could trace the groove of his abdominal muscles without looking. Her hair was draped over his body like a scarf, the two of them comfortable in the small but cosy darkness of the caravan.

It frightened her – just a little bit – how easy it was to be with him, the werewolf sticking close to her in the fortnight since an entire fleet of supernaturals had fled Sydney. Their mission had casualties: five selkies were dead, not every survivor had made it, and half of Ben's team had been obliterated.

'It doesn't feel like we won,' Shazza had said one night, head hung in grief.

'That's war,' Dreckly replied. 'You never really win.'

It was one of the first morsels of truth she began to divulge about herself. After all, there was little point in keeping secrets now. Her actions had committed Dreckly to being all in: she had the scars to prove it. Her lacerations had required fifty stitches, which she'd been unconscious for the application of. She felt the pain when she woke up, however, sharp and burning, as she tried to remind herself it could have been so much worse. An artery and she would have been dead, just like nearly a dozen others who had been crushed, shot, drowned, or blown apart.

Still, the majority of them were well enough and the next step of the plan was activated quickly. The Ravens M.C. had transport waiting at the White Bay Cruise Terminal, the supernaturals clearing off the boats as others swept in to eradicate them of any physical evidence. She would have been sad about missing an opportunity to say goodbye to the selkies as they were driven away from the water and inland, but it was only a brief intermission. They'd headed to Western Australia, the exact opposite end of the country to where they had caused the most amount of trouble. There was a powerful coven of witches who had created something of a sanctuary there, with Kala Tully having organised passage. That's where she had woken, in something of an immaculate caravan city built under the shelter of enormous gumtrees. The Great Australian Bight was on one side of them, the Great Victoria Desert on the other, with their Great Potential Exit any which way they chose.

'The Treize don't step foot into the Nullarbor Plain,' Ben had told her one night, as he'd lain next to her in a bed big enough to fit them both. He'd needed to heal too, rest, and he'd been insistent about doing it by her side. Truthfully, it was nice to wake up next to somebody again. She'd forgotten what that felt like, how comforting it could be to hear someone else's quiet breathing in the middle of the night.

The thing she didn't say, which relieved her more than anything, was that his desire to be close to her meant that he had forgiven Dreckly for abandoning them first time round. When she'd woken one early morning to find Ben alert and playing with her hair, she'd given in to her desire and kissed him. It had been nice, not set the world on fire *nice*, but definitely enough to kickstart a smoulder. They hadn't slept together then, Dreckly aware that if they did when impending death wasn't on the horizon she'd likely have to confront the ramifications of her actions. Instead, they'd talked.

'This land is beyond their control,' he'd explained. 'Always was, always will be. Not just because of the witches, but the wolf pack here is the oldest in the world.'

Beneath the Nullarbor there was a spiderweb of underwater cave systems, deep and impenetrable to most. To the selkies, it was their way to stay in touch. They'd had to abandon the coast off Sydney too, knowing the Treize would destroy anyone they found underwater as soon as they worked out that the selkies had helped. So everyone who was threatened had scrambled just like their land-walking counterparts. When she was strong enough, Ben had taken her to see Amos. Dreckly had to resist the order not to dive in the water and risk infection, but she lunged forward instead, embracing her new friend in a hug.

'I'm so proud of you for doing the right thing,' he said, as Ben helped her back upright.

'You bullied me into it,' Dreckly said, laughing softly. 'You and your human girlfriend.'

She knew he'd feel a pang of sadness at being apart from Kaia: that sensation was one she recognised intimately as she thought about Harvey. Yet Amos was surrounded by his own kind, Avary visible floating among the mass of selkies and giving her a subtle nod of recognition. That was more important right then, Dreckly hoping the woman would continue to impart some of her knowledge to the young selkie.

On the drive back, Dreckly had Ben stop at a farmer's market that was being held in the sports field of a high school. It was a risk. It was also essential. She used all of the cash she had on her to prepare a massive feast of dumplings that night when they returned. He was mostly terrible at it, unable to follow the instructions Dreckly gave him that had been passed on from Meili and her mother before that. She lost count of how many she made, the task deeply soothing to her as it merged Dreckly's past with her present.

She would have stayed there among their party all night, the company of new and old allies like a drug to her. Eventually Ben pulled her away, so she could eat a portion of what she'd prepared, and then they'd retreated back to the caravan.

The sex was slow, careful, and powerful as their bodies negotiated around their many injuries. He held her tightly to him, her legs wrapped around his torso as he built up a knee-quaking rhythm. Dreckly had needed the release so badly and she could feel the surprise in Ben as she let her hunger for him take over.

Then they'd talked, which was more dangerous than the sex in her mind. She could separate the latter and protect her heart. The former made it all the trickier as Ben caught her up on everything that had been happening since the Ravens M.C.

had left them there and scattered to the wind as well. She brought him up to speed too, except on a very different subject: her life. Just small fragments of it at first. They'd spoken about the war, which was hard for all that represented and even harder because it was something she discussed with almost no one. They had talked and talked, until it felt like they had talked themselves out, lying there in quiet bliss instead.

'I can't love you,' she murmured, breaking the easy silence he so often made for her. She twisted her head just enough so that he could see she was serious. 'I need you to know that.'

Ben's mouth was amused, but his eyebrows held a frown as he scrutinised her expression.

'Okay . . .'

'My soulmate died, Ben. I'm broken and I've lived with that for a long time. I'm used to the fracture. I've learned how to like the pieces that are left but . . . I'm not whole like that. I don't have it left in me and I need to be honest about that to you, before anything further.'

He didn't say a word for a heavy minute, yet his silence said quite a lot. Ben had glanced at her stitches, which were due out any day now, as if to say *wounds heal.* Some did. She had lived with hers long enough to know they were part of her.

'You think people have only one soulmate?' he questioned. 'Like, there's *only* one right ying to someone else's yang?'

'I—'

'Only one yuck to your yum?'

She snorted, arching her neck up at him. 'Yuck to your yum?'

'You know what I'm saying. And I don't believe that, by the way. I don't believe there's only *one* soulmate for every person. That doesn't even logistically make sense.'

'Love doesn't make sense,' she countered. 'And, well, you're young.'

'Ha, oh my Goooood, I *get* it. You're older than me and I'm younger, fark. Dock that baggage already.'

They were both laughing loud enough that she didn't hear the knock on the caravan door, but he did with his werewolf hearing.

'One minute, Shazza,' he called, sitting up. 'Come on, we're needed.'

'Needed?' she asked. It was well past two in the morning. Only supernaturals were 'needed' at this hour.

'It's a summit, if you will. Figure out what's next. There were visitors travelling in for it, foreigners I don't know.'

'Most of us are foreign here,' she replied, beginning to get dressed alongside him.

'How long did you have with him?' Ben asked, shrugging into his singlet. 'This soulmate of yours.'

'We knew each other for almost a decade. Together for eight.'

'Years?'

She nodded.

'Fuck,' he sighed. 'It would take me a while to get over that too.'

Dreckly didn't reply. She wasn't certain there was a 'getting over it' portion to the grief she'd grown familiar living with. She didn't miss her father any less. Or Meili or Li Jun. Even Delun, if she was feeling particularly sensitive. She thought of Yixin, Clara, Dorothy, Mildred, Lionel, Jimmy and Haukea, Tan, Chino, Wyck, Amos, the dozens of others as time weighed down on her. It was a curse, living on while others came and went. Yet it felt like for the first time in nearly eighty years, Dreckly wasn't stagnant anymore. She was in motion again.

There were nearly one hundred parties assembled for the summit, it really living up to its name as it took place in an outdoor amphitheatre illuminated by glowing lanterns. The distinct musk of mosquito spray was their signature scent while they were out here and Dreckly took a seat beside Ben, who was the representative of not just his pack but *all* east-coast Australian packs.

Glancing around at her positioning, she noted that Shazza was joined by other types of shifters and Avary was present too, her legs obscured beneath a flowing skirt. There were even banshees there, dozens showing up in the past few days and among them one of Sadie Burke's many sisters, Shannon. Dreckly felt a jolt of electricity run down her spine as her eyes ran over the demons, a familiar face stepping out from behind Fairuza and her father. Mildred looked like she had glided off the set of *The English Patient*, khaki trousers belted at her waist and a fine, white blouse that matched the scarf stylishly framing her face.

Dreckly went to get to her feet and march across the space between them, but her friend shook her head subtly. *Soon*, Mildred's devilish smile said. *First, revolution.* Her eyes darted to the centre of the massive group, directing Dreckly's attention to where proceedings had already officially begun. The witch Kala Tully was speaking, a statuesque white-haired woman watching her closely while the glowing ghost of a man stood by her side.

Behind them was one of the largest men she'd ever seen, not just in height but in girth. He was even taller than the poltergeist and his female counterpart. There was a comically small woman with olive skin and jet-black hair leaning against him. She probably would have been regular human lady height, but next to the giant she seemed *tiny*. She must have sensed Dreckly staring at her and she glanced over, one white eye and one brown looking at her with curiosity. There was a green-stone necklace hanging around her throat, glinting under the illumination of a lantern.

Dreckly was about to slink back into the mass of other creatures, this positioning too prominent for someone of her status when she paused. It wasn't just Ben who had cleared a spot for her, but the goblins Katya and Ruken too. Each of the folks she recognised were either the strongest of their species or the designated leaders chosen to represent them. She was meant to represent her people, the sprites, or what-ever was left of them. That revelation was *a lot* and she had to catch up to what Kala was saying as she pushed her thoughts aside.

What they had done in Sydney was important and they'd been under-planned and under-resourced when they'd accomplished it. Going forward, they would be more careful. There would still be risks and causalities, but the coordinated take-down of the Treize was beginning now, in this exact moment, as meetings just like theirs took place among supernaturals spread around the world.

Kala handed over to the blond giant, who spoke with a Scottish accent so thick Dreckly wasn't the only one who leaned forward as if a closer proximity would suddenly make him clearer. His name was Heath, he said. He had been Praetorian Guard for over a thousand years and more recently, he'd been a spy for their side. He assured them that things might seem overwhelming right now, but the Treize had never faced a united force before. Species-specific rebellions? Yes. A democratic uprising? No. They were that. In a matter of months, maybe weeks, there would be a seminal event that he couldn't reveal at the moment. Yet it would change their world and change their future. It was happening somewhere close, however, and they needed to make sure their next mission was big enough to concentrate the Treize's forces across the opposite side of the globe. It also needed to be something important.

'Since this first jail break has been so successful, why not another aye?' he suggested.

'Where?' Ruken questioned.

'There are four strategic targets we can hit simultaneously, but nothing would hurt the Treize more than one in particular.'

She knew the answer before he said it out loud.

'Vankila.'

There was an impenetrable wall of silence following his statement, every being understanding the significance. It was Shazza who first sliced the party with a response.

'It's impossible!' she began. 'We barely accomplished what we did and we still had losses. Without Dreckly, we would probably be on some cold slab getting cut open right now. Vankila is a *whole* other scale.'

'That's why we use a *whole* other crew,' Heath countered. 'Those who survived Sydney don't have to partake, but they'll be needed elsewhere, and I can't guarantee the safety of a task from here on out. In fact, I can guarantee their *un*safety.'

The white-haired woman introduced herself as Casper – the ghost being named Creeper and her twin brother – while she tried to back Heath up.

'We know the top level of Vankila is for temporary prisoners: those like Jonah Ihi, who were locked up as punishment for perceived crimes and released after several years. That's just the foam on top; beneath there's thousands who could help us and who deserve their freedom.'

'And monsters!' Ruken said, speaking up with assured nods from the goblins in his corner. 'We all heard about the creature blown up in the Sydney lab. That wasn't born, that was *made* by the Treize in their quest to . . . what, extract vital genes from other supernaturals to keep the Three alive, yeah?'

'Yes.' Heath nodded. 'The Three have always helped keep the Treize one step ahead but with them slowly dying and refusing to help any longer, they'll lose that advantage. The experiments were designed to help them extend it, albeit unsuccessfully.'

'Right,' Ruken pressed, 'say we break in, who knows what we could be breaking out. We don't know what's in there and, even from an odds perspective, we're screwed! It's too well manned.'

Those gathered erupted in discussion, people talking over the top of each other and protesting suggestions while throwing others forward. It was just like the orchestra pit in the State Theatre, she thought, but on a much bigger and pricklier scale. With the Three dying, the supernatural government knew their power to rule was dangling by a thread, and, if they didn't find a way to strengthen it, everything would snap.

'This isn't the time to have doubts,' the woman who was with Heath said. She was also Scottish, her accent surprising Dreckly but her words full of authority. She couldn't have been more than twenty-five, she guessed, yet when she spoke it was a command. People shut up. Ben whispered her name in Dreckly's ear: Tommi Grayson. Rogue werewolf. Ihi affiliate. Illegitimate daughter of Jonah Ihi.

Of course, she thought, understanding why the woman had seemed familiar to her. She'd known Jonah in life, made identity documents for him just like she now did for his nephew Simon Tianne and widow Tiaki Ihi. He was years dead, but whatever it was about Tommi Grayson, she carried that same almost indiscernible energy.

Dreckly had expected other members of the Ihi pack to be there and when she'd questioned Ben about when that arrival was expected, he'd told her quietly in the privacy of their caravan that they weren't coming. They had stayed behind in New Zealand, protecting something important, something vital to that event Heath had eluded to changing the supernatural world as they knew it. They had sent an emissary instead: this female werewolf who both felt and didn't feel like them.

'We're convinced that what we're doing is the right thing, aye?' Tommi Grayson asked of the group. 'That it's the only way forward?'

There were murmurs of agreement through those assembled as her voice carried, people added 'fuck yeah' and 'definitely' to the chorus. She gave one stiff, sharp nod as if that was the only answer she expected.

'We all want freedom from the dictatorship that is the Treize,' she continued, 'but that's going to come at a cost.

Most of us have already spilled blood just to be here, but I can see it in your eyes that every single one of you believes it was worth it.'

'Fine,' Ben said, getting up. 'I'm keen as anyone else here to blow the place apart. My sister is imprisoned in Vankila.'

'My half-brother too.' Tommi nodded. There was a pause of mutual understanding for a moment, Dreckly unable to avoid the pang as she watched these werewolves circle each other. Brown skin, muscled bodies, impassioned causes: she knew just by looking at them that Ben and Tommi made more sense than she and Ben did. The way the hulking Scot hovered nearby, however, told her the she-wolf was well and truly spoken for.

'I'd do anything for a chance to get Sushmita out,' Ben continued, '*but* it's the oldest prison of our kind. There's a Cold War bunker built on top that's a tourist attraction for people visiting that area of Scotland or whatever. The prison itself is miles below ground. We'd need more than just blueprints and we couldn't guarantee the ones we had were even accurate. We'd need to interview someone who worked there, probably several current and past staff members. Prison guards. Cleaners. Alchemists. Then what? How do we get in? What's the layout? How do we get away? Is that even the purpose?'

Shazza patted him on the back as she joined him.

'No one has *ever* escaped from Vankila and lived to talk about it,' the wombat shifter agreed.

Dreckly felt her skin itch and her left foot was tapping a rhythm no one else could hear. Mildred's gaze felt like a laser across the group as the two women stared at each other, the demon the only other being who suspected her truth.

Maria Lewis

Dreckly got to her feet, her movement stopping Shazza's impassioned pleas and Ben's calls for sanity. He would feel betrayed by this, she guessed, learning about the knowledge Dreckly had kept to herself when Sushmita had been locked up there for years.

'Actually, that's not entirely true,' she announced. 'One person has escaped Vankila and survived.'

She paused before she looked at Ben, meeting his gaze. 'Me.'

Glossary

Alchemist Those who have the ability to infuse and convert materials with magical properties through a combination of symbols, science and ceremony. Alchemists were instrumental in the founding of the Treize, particularly the Askari themselves. Obsessed with immortality, it's rumoured their formula is responsible for the prolonged lives of Praetorian Guard soldiers and Custodians.

Arachnia Traditionally considered a nightmarish vision from Japanese folklore, arachnia emerged from the shadows relatively late compared to other supernatural species and were discovered to have existed worldwide. Their natural state is comparable to a large, spider-like creature, with traits similar to the arthropod.

Askari Foot soldiers and collectors of ground truth. The first point of call in the supernatural community, they simultaneously liaise and gather information. Mortal, yet members often work their way up into the Custodian ranks. Identified by a wrist tattoo, which is the alchemist symbol for wood to signify a strong foundation.

The Aunties A pack within the Ihi pack, this fearsome all-women group are responsible for voting on and enforcing pack law.

Banshee Thought to be extinct by the wider supernatural community before remerging in Australia, a banshee is a supernatural being cursed with the ability to sense death or impending doom in its various forms. Exclusively female.

Bierpinsel A large, colourful tower in the centre of Berlin: the Bierpinsel is the base of Treize operations for Germany and much of Europe.

Blood pack The family unit a werewolf is born into by direct descent, usually operating on a specific piece of geographical territory.

Coming of age A ritual all werewolves must complete before they're considered mature members of their blood pack. A wolf can only choose to go 'rogue' once they have survived the coming of age.

Coven A grouping of witches within a particular area, covens can include members of the same biological family as well as women of no biological relation. No two members of a coven have the same magical ability, with similar powers spread out over other covens as an evolutionary defence mechanism. Members of a coven can draw on each other's powers, giving them strength and safety in their sisterhood.

The Covenant The series of rules established for banshees to follow once they were deported en masse from Ireland, Scotland and Wales in the seventeen hundreds. If The Covenant is broken, the penalty can range from imprisonment in Vankila to death.

Custodians The counsellors or emotional guardians of beings without other help, assistance or species grouping. Immortality is a choice made by individual Custodians, with those choosing it identified by a necklace with an Egyptian ankh.

Demon One of the oldest forms of supernatural beings, pure-blood demons are known for being reclusive and rarely interact with those outside of the paranormal world. Certain species of demon have a fondness for the flesh, leading to half-blood demon hybrids usually identifiable via physical traits like horns or tusks (often filed down so it's easier to blend in to society).

Elemental Originally thought to be those who could control the elements – earth, air, fire and water – elementals are paranormal beings descended directly from nature. Able to physically become the elements if they so desire, they share a strong allegiance with shifters, werewolves and selkies.

Ghost Translucent and bluish grey in colour, ghosts are the physical manifestation of one's soul after death. Their presence in the realm of the living can be for several reasons, ranging from an unjust demise to a connection with a person or place. The strength of any particular ghost varies case-to-case.

Ghoul Usually found in underground sewer systems and living in nest formations, ghouls are considered a lower class of paranormal creature due to their lack of intelligence or individual personality traits. With razor sharp claws and serrated teeth, they can be deadly in numbers.

Goblin Highly intelligent and supernaturally agile, goblins are known for their speed and lethal nature if provoked. Although not immortal, they have exceedingly long lives and prefer living in urban environments such as cities or large towns. They are one of several paranormal species impacted by the lunar cycle.

Medium A being that can communicate with and control the dead, including spirits and ghosts. Extremely rare, the full range of their abilities is unknown and largely undocumented.

Outskirt Packs The collective description for werewolf packs from the Asia-Pacific region who fought against the Treize – unsuccessfully – for the right to self-govern and expose their true nature to the human world. Formed in 1993 and disbanded upon defeat in 1998, key leaders included Jonah Ihi, Sushmita Kapoor and John Tianne. This conflict was known as the Outskirt Wars.

Paranormal Practitioner The healers and medical experts of the unnatural world. Usually gifted individuals themselves, they wield methods outside of conventional medicine.

Praetorian Guard A squadron of elite warriors that quell violence and evil within the supernatural community. They're gifted with immortality for their service. Founded by a member of the original Roman Praetorian Guard.

Rogue A werewolf who chooses to live and operate outside of their blood pack.

The Rogues Comprised of rogue werewolves who have decided to leave their blood packs, this group functions from within the nightclub Phases in Berlin and includes global members who have come of age.

Selkie The source of mermaid and merman folklore, selkies are aquatic humanoids that inhabit any large body of water. Despite some human features, pondants of selkie from certain parts of the world have been known to take the form of marine animals like seals, dolphins and sharks.

Shifter Found globally, shifters have the ability to transform into one specific creature depending on their lineage. Often confused with werewolves due to their capacity to take animal shape, shifters can transform outside of the full moon both fully and in-part.

Spirit Incorrectly compared to ghosts, spirits are their more powerful counterparts. A term used to describe the dead who can travel between pre-existing plains and occasionally take some physical form, they usually preoccupy themselves with the business of their direct ancestors.

Sprite Said to be the result of a union between selkies and earth elementals, sprites are highly secretive and rarely identify themselves to other supernatural creatures. They struggle being around members of their own kind and prefer to live close to nature.

The Three A trio of semi-psychic women who guide the Treize in regards to past, present and future events. The subject of the phrase 'hear no evil, see no evil, speak no evil'. Origin and age unknown.

Treize The governing body of the supernatural world comprising of thirteen members of different ages, races, nationalities, abilities, species and genders. Given their namesake by four French founders, they oversee the Praetorian Guard, Custodians, Askari and Paranormal Practitioners.

Vampire Rodent-like creature who lives off the blood of animals or people (whatever they can get). Endangered in the supernatural community due to widespread disease.

Vankila The Treize's supernatural prison, located in St Andrews, Scotland, and built hundreds of metres below a Cold War bunker.

Werewolf Considered one of the most volatile and ferocious paranormal species, werewolves are humans that shift into enormous wolf-hybrids during the nights of the full moon. Outside of the lunar cycle they retain heightened abilities, such as strength and healing, with the most powerful of their kind able to transform at will and retain human consciousness. Often found living in blood packs, they are resistant towards most forms of paranormal government.

Witch A woman naturally gifted with paranormal abilities that can be heightened with study and practice. Although the witch gene is passed down through the female line, skills vary from woman to woman regardless of blood. Witches believe their power is loaned to them temporarily by a higher being, who redistributes it to another witch after their death. Highly suspicious and distrustful of the Treize due to centuries of persecution, they are closed off from the rest of the supernatural community.

Acknowledgments

This was the most ambitious book I've undertaken in terms of scope and scale, so there are a great many people to thank for helping me not fuck it up entirely (I take full responsibility for any fuck-ups you do note, they are the result of my inability rather than that of my sources).

The team at Little, Brown, obviously: spearheaded by Anna Boatman but also including Sarah Murphy and Donna Hillyer whose keen eyes and keen fandom have made this story so much better. My agent, Ed Wilson, for arking up on my behalf and passionately fighting for the things I believe in without any qualifiers.

Sophie Ly, long-time friend and fan of this series whose contributions, suggestions and perspectives helped make Dreckly Jones who she is. Kimie Tsukakoshi, the only person allowed to play Dreckly on screen. The real Klaws By Katya, hopefully this is satisfyingly kawaii for you. The forgers, who shall remain nameless cos I'm not a cop. Peter Fitzsimons, for his insights into the bad-assery of female spies during World War II like Nancy Wake.

The Town's *true* Florist in Roisin McGown, for her green thumbery. All of the amazing folks at the Australian Centre

For Moving Image (ACMI), namely Chelsey O'Brien for an education on amazing women like Clara Bow and Dorothy Arzner and Matt Millikan for letting me go off on research tangents (wtf happened to Louis Le Prince, Edison? HUH?!). Forrest Satchell, for the insider info on secret Hollywood and road trip singalongs to Josie and the Pussycats. Dionne Gipson, Holly Logan and David Ramsey: the Holy Trinity of Tim Tam lovers and who have all shown me sides of Los Angeles I would have never seen, high as a kite or otherwise. Lexi Alexander, always, for being 'the most stubborn Arab' and refusing to ever let me pay (fucko).

The Howard conglomerate: Blake, Sam (that ass that ass she bad), Hazel and Keaton: forever feeling undeserving of your love, support, friendship and groupchat. My girls for bringing the Black Up: Ramona, Jean-Anne, Rae and Anna. Keegan Buzza and James Stein for being my favourite husbands. Authorly supporterlies in Keri Arthur, Angela Slatter, Alison Goodman, Jodi McAlister, Nicola Scott, Alan Baxter, and so many others. Just generally great creative women who have helped guide me and give me advice at vital moments: Kodie Bedford, Rarriwuy Hick, Gen Fricker, and Tracey Vieira. Hau Latukefu for providing the soundtrack I write every book to and whose enabling and mentorship of storytellers inspires me endlessly.

Gonna end on the bibliophiles: thank you to those who love books, champion them, buy them, talk about them, sell them. Whether they're mine or someone else's, you keep us afloat. Thank you.

Praise for Maria Lewis

'Journalist Maria Lewis grabs the paranormal fiction genre by the scruff of its neck to give it a shake' *The West Australian*

'Author Maria Lewis has created her own pop culture universe' *Daily Telegraph*

'[Maria Lewis] easily weaves the magic into each page of this spin-off to her already successful Who's Afraid series with another strong female lead' *The Nerd Daily*

'Gripping, fast-paced and completely unexpected . . . Maria Lewis is definitely one to watch' *New York Times* best-selling author Darynda Jones

'If you love a strong female lead, then *Who's Afraid?* by Maria Lewis is a must-read' Buzzfeed

'If you want a fresh, funny, sexy & downright sassy take on the werewolf genre then this series is for you' Geek Bomb

'She writes kick-ass monsters and things that go bump in the night with a flair for the awesome' Reviewers of Oz

'Truly one of the best in the genre I have ever read' Oscar nominated film-maker Lexi Alexander (*Green Street Hooligans, Punisher: War Zone, Arrow, Supergirl*)

'It's about time we had another kick-arse werewolf heroine – can't wait to find out what happens next!' *New York Times* best-selling author Keri Arthur

'*The Witch Who Courted Death* is an unashamedly feminist story about a woman out for revenge' *Readings*

'A feminist take on two well-known classic ghosts and witches – giving them the Lewis makeover and throwing them into her renowned supernatural world' *Aurealis*

'It's Underworld meets Animal Kingdom' ALPHA Reader

'The next *True Blood*' *NW Magazine*

'Lewis creates an intriguing world that's just begging to be fleshed out in further books' *APN*

'Definitely worth reading over and over again, as well as buying multiple copies. Great stocking stuffers, those werewolf books' Maria Lewis' mum